Dear Reader,

My daughter was recently lamenting the fact that a lot of movies don't empower the heroine—something her four-year-old daughter has noticed. It is one reason why I like to write about strong heroines.

But even a strong heroine can use a little help. That is why I love that these two books, with their also strong heroes, are being sold together.

In *Premeditated Marriage*, Charlotte "Charlie" Larkin is cursed when it comes to the men she dates. They all meet untimely deaths. Then Gus Riley, a true-crime writer, shows up to research her for his next book. It's only when they pretend to be a couple do they draw out the killer—and discover their feelings for each other.

Cowboy's Redemption's Lola Dayton is an independent, strong woman—until her parents die after joining a cult in the mountains of Montana. Little does she know that she is walking into a trap. After escaping, she is saved by cowboy Colt McCloud for one magical night where the two find solace in each other.

The next morning Lola is gone. Colt has no idea that she has been taken prisoner or that she is running from a crazed cult leader who wants her for his own—until she shows up on his ranch to tell him that not only has she been kept a prisoner on the cult's complex for the past year, but the cult leader has taken the daughter she gave birth to from that one night with the cowboy.

Happy reading!

B.J.

B.J. Daniels is a *New York Times* and *USA TODAY* bestselling author. She wrote her first book after a career as an award-winning newspaper journalist and author of thirty-seven published short stories. She lives in Montana with her husband, Parker, and three springer spaniels. When not writing, she quilts, boats and plays tennis. Contact her at bjdaniels.com, on Facebook or on Twitter, @bjdanielsauthor.

Books by B.J. Daniels

Harlequin Intrigue

The Montana Cahills

Cowboy's Redemption

Whitehorse, Montana: The McGraw Kidnapping

Dark Horse
Dead Ringer
Rough Rider

HQN Books

The Montana Cahills

Renegade's Pride
Outlaw's Honor
Hero's Return

Visit the Author Profile page
at Harlequin.com for more titles.

B.J. DANIELS

NEW YORK TIMES AND USA TODAY
BESTSELLING AUTHOR

COWBOY'S REDEMPTION
&
PREMEDITATED
MARRIAGE

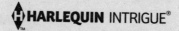

ISBN-13: 978-1-335-95234-9

Cowboy's Redemption & Premeditated Marriage

Copyright © 2018 by Harlequin Books S.A.

Recycling programs for this product may not exist in your area.

The publisher acknowledges the copyright holder of the individual works as follows:

Cowboy's Redemption
Copyright © 2018 by Barbara Heinlein

Premeditated Marriage
Copyright © 2002 by Barbara Heinlein

This edition published by arrangement with Harlequin Books S.A.

For questions and comments about the quality of this book, please contact us at CustomerService@Harlequin.com.

® and TM are trademarks of Harlequin Enterprises Limited or its corporate affiliates. Trademarks indicated with ® are registered in the United States Patent and Trademark Office, the Canadian Intellectual Property Office and in other countries.

Printed in U.S.A.

™ www.Harlequin.com

CONTENTS

COWBOY'S REDEMPTION   7

PREMEDITATED MARRIAGE   203

This one is for Stelly, who even at four loves stories where the heroine gets to help save herself.

COWBOY'S REDEMPTION

Chapter One

Running blindly through the darkness, Lola didn't see the tree limb until it struck her in the face. It clawed at her cheek, digging into a spot under her right eye as she flung it away with her arm. She had to stifle the cry of pain that rose in her throat for fear she would be heard. As she ran, she felt warm blood run down to the corner of her lips. The taste of it mingled with the salt of her tears, but she didn't slow, couldn't. She could hear them behind her.

She pushed harder, knowing that, being men, they had the advantage, especially the way she was dressed. Her long skirt caught on something. She heard the fabric rend, not for the first time. She felt as if it was her heart being ripped out with it.

Her only choice was to escape. But at what price? She'd been forced to leave behind the one person who mattered most. Her thundering heart ached at the thought, but she knew that this was the only way. If she could get help...

"She's over here!" came a cry from behind her. "This way!"

She wiped away the warm blood as she crashed through the brush and trees. Her legs ached and she didn't know how much longer she could keep going. Fatigue was draining her. If they caught her this time...

She tripped on a tree root, stumbled and almost plunged headlong down the mountainside. Her shoulder slammed into a tree trunk. She veered off it like a pinball, but she kept pushing herself forward because the alternative was worse than death.

They were closer now. She could feel one of them breathing down her neck. She didn't dare look back. To look back would be to admit defeat. If she could just reach the road before they caught up to her...

Suddenly the trees opened up. She burst out of the darkness of the pines onto the blacktop of a narrow two-lane highway. The glare of headlights blinded her an instant before the shriek of rubber on the dark pavement filled the night air.

Chapter Two

Major Colt McCloud felt the big bird shake as he brought the helicopter low over the bleak landscape. He was back in Afghanistan behind the controls of a UH-60 Black Hawk. The throb of the rotating blades was drowned out by the sound of mortar fire. It grew louder and louder, taking on a consistent pounding that warned him something was very wrong.

He dragged himself awake, but the dream followed him. Blinking in the darkness, he didn't know where he was for a moment. Everything looked alien and surreal. As the dream began to fade, he recognized his bedroom at the ranch.

He'd left behind the sound of the chopper and the mortar fire, but the pounding had intensified. With a start, he realized what he was hearing.

Someone was at the door.

He glanced at the clock on his bedside table. It was after three in the morning. Throwing his legs over the side of the bed, he grabbed his jeans, pulling them on as he fought to put the dream behind him and hurry to the door.

A half dozen possibilities flashed in his mind as he moved quickly through the house. It still felt strange to be back here after years of traveling the world as an Army helicopter pilot. After his fiancée dumped him, he'd planned to make a career out of the military, but then his father had died, leaving him a working ranch that either had to be run or sold.

He'd taken a hundred-and-twenty-day leave in between assignments so he could come home to take care of the ranch. His father had been the one who'd loved ranching, not Colt. That's why there was a for-sale sign out on the road into the ranch.

Colt reached the front door and, frowning at the incessant knocking at this hour of the morning, threw it open.

He blinked at the disheveled woman standing there before she turned to motion to the driver of the car idling nearby. The engine roared and a car full of what appeared to be partying teenagers took off in a cloud of dust.

Colt flipped on the porch light as the woman turned back to him and he got his first good look at her and her scratched, blood-streaked face. For a moment he didn't recognize her, and then it all came back in a rush. Standing there was a woman he'd never thought he'd see again.

"Lola?" He couldn't even be sure that was her real name. But somehow it fit her, so maybe at least that part of her story had been true. "What happened to you?"

"I had nowhere else to go." Her words came out in a rush. "I was so worried that you wouldn't be here." She burst into tears and slumped as if physically exhausted.

He caught her, swung her up into his arms and carried her into the house, kicking the door closed behind him. His mind raced as he tried to imagine what could have happened to bring her to his door in Gilt Edge, Montana, in the middle of the night and in this condition.

"Sit here," he said as he carried her in and set her

down in a kitchen chair before going for the first-aid kit. When he returned, he was momentarily taken aback by the memory of this woman the first time he'd met her. She wasn't beautiful in the classic sense. But she was striking, from her wide violet eyes fringed with pale lashes to the silk of her long blond hair. She had looked like an angel, especially in the long white dress she'd been wearing that night.

That was over a year ago and he hadn't seen her since. Nor had he expected to since they'd met initially several hundred miles from the ranch. But whatever had struck him about her hadn't faded. There was something flawless about her—even as scraped up and bruised as she was. It made him furious at whoever was responsible for this.

"Can you tell me what happened?" he asked as he began to clean the cuts.

"I... I..." Her throat seemed to close on a sob.

"It's okay, don't try to talk." He felt her trembling and could see that she was fighting tears. "This cut under your eye is deep."

She said nothing, looking as if it was all she could do to keep her eyes open. He took in her torn and filthy dress. It was long, like the white one he'd first seen her in, but faded. It reminded him of something his grandmother might have worn to do housework in. She was also thinner than he remembered.

As he gently cleaned her wounds, he could see dark circles under her eyes, and her long braided hair was in disarray with bits of twigs and leaves stuck in it.

The night he'd met her, her plaited hair had been pinned up at the nape of her neck—until he'd released it, the blond silk dropping to the center of her back.

He finished his doctoring, put away the first-aid kit,

and wondered how far she'd come to find him and what she had been through to get here. When he returned to the kitchen, he found her standing at the back window, staring out. As she turned, he saw the fear in her eyes—and the exhaustion.

Colt desperately wanted to know what had happened to her and how she'd ended up on his doorstep. He hadn't even thought that she'd known his name. "Have you had anything to eat?"

"Not in the past forty-eight hours or so," she said, squinting at the clock on the wall as if not sure what day it was. "And not all that much before that."

He'd been meaning to get into Gilt Edge and buy some groceries. "Sit and I'll see what I can scare up," he said as he opened the refrigerator. Seeing only one egg left, he said, "How do you feel about pancakes? I have chokecherry syrup."

She nodded and attempted a smile. She looked skittish as a newborn calf. Worse, he sensed that she was having second thoughts about coming here.

She licked her cracked lips. "I have to tell you. I have to explain—"

"It's okay. You're safe here." But safe from what, he wondered? "There's no hurry. Let's get you taken care of first." He'd feed her and get her settled down.

He motioned her into a chair at the kitchen table. He could tell that she must hurt all over by the way she moved. As much as he wanted to know what had happened, he thought she needed food more than anything else at this moment.

"While I make the pancakes, would you like a hot shower? The guest room is down the hall to the left. I can find you some clothes. They'll be too large for you, but maybe they will be more comfortable."

Tears welled in her eyes. He saw her swallow before she nodded. As she started to get to her feet, he noticed her grimace in pain.

"Wait."

She froze.

"I don't know how to say this delicately, but if someone assaulted you—"

"I wasn't raped."

He nodded, hoping that was true, because a shower would destroy important evidence. "Okay, so the injuries were…"

"From running for my life." With that she limped out of the kitchen.

He had the pancake batter made and the griddle heating when he heard the shower come on. He stopped to listen to the running water, remembering this woman in a hotel shower with him months ago.

That night he'd bumped into her coming out of the hotel bar. He'd seen that she was upset. She'd told him that she needed his help, that there was someone after her. She'd given him the impression she was running from an old boyfriend. He'd been happy to help. Now he wondered if that was still the case. She said she was running for her life—just as she had the first time they'd met.

But that had been in Billings. This was Gilt Edge, Montana, hundreds of miles away. Didn't seem likely she would still be running from the same boyfriend. But whoever was chasing her, she'd come to him for help.

He couldn't turn her away any more than he'd been able to in that hotel hallway in Billings last year.

LOLA PULLED OUT her braid, discarding the debris stuck in it, then climbed into the steaming shower. She stood under the hot spray, leaned against the smooth, cool tile wall of the shower and closed her eyes. She felt weak from hunger, lack of sleep and constant fear. She couldn't remember the last time she'd slept through the night.

Exhaustion pulled at her. It took all of her energy to wash herself. Her body felt alien to her, her skin chafed from the rough fabric of the long dresses she'd been wearing for months. Stumbling from the shower, she wrapped her hair in one of the guest towels. It felt good to free her hair from the braid that had been wound at the nape of her neck.

As she pulled down another clean towel from the bathroom rack, she put it to her face and sniffed its freshness. Tears burned her eyes. It had been so long since she'd had even the smallest creature comforts like good soap, shampoo and clean towels that smelled like this, let alone unlimited hot water.

When she opened the bathroom door, she saw that Colt had left her a sweatshirt and sweatpants on the guest-room bed. She dried and tugged them on, pulling the drawstring tight around her waist. He was right, the clothes were too big, but they felt heavenly.

She took the towels back to the bathroom to hang them and considered her dirty clothing on the floor. The hem of the worn ankle-length coarse cotton dress was torn and filthy with dirt and grime. The long sleeves were just as bad except they were soiled with her blood. The black utilitarian shoes were scuffed, the heels worn unevenly since she'd inherited them well used.

She wadded up the dress and shoved it into the bathroom wastebasket before putting the shoes on top of it, all the time feeling as if she was committing a sin. Then again, she'd already done that, hadn't she.

Downstairs, she stepped into the kitchen to see Colt

slip three more pancakes onto the stack he already had on the plate.

He turned as if sensing her in the doorway and she was reminded of the first time she'd seen him. All she'd noticed that night was his Army uniform—before he'd turned and she'd seen his face.

That he was handsome hadn't even registered. What she'd seen was a kind face. She'd been desperate and Colt McCloud had suddenly appeared as if it had been meant to be. Just as he'd been here tonight, she thought.

"Last time I saw you, you were on leave and talking about staying in the military," she said as he pulled out a kitchen chair for her and she sat down. "I was afraid that you had and that—" her voice broke as she met his gaze "—you wouldn't be here."

"I'm on leave now. My father died."

"I'm sorry."

He set down the plate of pancakes. "Dig in."

Always the gentleman, she thought as he joined her at the table. "I made a bunch. There's fresh sweet butter. If you don't like chokecherry syrup—"

"I love it." She slid several of the lightly browned cakes onto her plate. The aroma that rose from them made her stomach growl loudly. She slathered them with butter and covered them with syrup. The first bite was so delicious that she actually moaned, making him smile.

"I was going to ask how they are," he said with a laugh, "but I guess I don't have to."

She devoured the pancakes before helping herself to more. They ate in a companionable silence that didn't surprise her any more than Colt making her pancakes in the middle of the night or opening his door to her, no questions asked. It was as if it was something he did all the time. Maybe it was, she thought, remembering the first night they'd met.

He hadn't hesitated when she'd told him she needed his help. She'd looked into his blue eyes and known she could trust him. He'd been so sweet and caring that she'd almost told him the truth. But she'd stopped herself. Because she didn't think he would believe her? Or because she didn't want to involve him? Or because, at that point, she thought she could still handle things on her own?

Unfortunately, she no longer had the option of keeping the truth from him.

"I'm sure you have a lot of questions," she said, after swallowing her last bite of pancake and wiping her mouth with her napkin. The food had helped, but her body ached all over and fatigue had weakened her. "You had to be surprised to see me again, especially with me showing up at your door in the middle of the night looking like I do."

"I didn't even know you knew my last name."

"After that night in Billings… Before I left your hotel room, while you were still sleeping, I looked in your wallet."

"You planned to take my money?" He'd had over four hundred dollars in there. He'd been headed home to his fiancée, he'd told her. But the fiancée, who was supposed to pick him up at the airport, had called instead with crushing news. Not only was she not picking him up, she was in love with one of his best friends, someone he'd known since grade school.

He'd been thinking he just might rent a car and drive home to confront the two of them, he'd told Lola later. But, ultimately, he'd booked a flight for the next morning to where he was stationed and, with time to kill, had taken a taxi to a hotel, paid for a room and headed for the hotel bar. Two drinks later, he'd run into Lola as he'd headed from the bar to the men's room. Lola had saved him from getting stinking drunk that night. Also from driving to Gilt Edge to confront his ex-fiancée and his ex-friend.

"I hate to admit that I thought about taking your money," she said. "I could have used it."

"You should have taken it then."

She smiled at him and shook her head. "You were so kind to me, so tender..." Her cheeks heated as she held his gaze and remembered being naked in his arms. "I'm sure I gave you the wrong impression of me that night. It wasn't like me to...with a complete stranger." She bit her lower lip and felt tears well in her eyes again.

"There is nothing wrong with the impression you left with me. As a matter of fact, I've thought of you often." He smiled. It was a great smile. "Every time I heard one of those songs that we'd danced to in my hotel room that night—" his gaze warmed to a Caribbean blue "—I thought of you."

She looked away to swallow the lump that had formed in her throat before she could speak again. "It wasn't an old boyfriend I was running from that night. I let you believe that because I doubted you'd have believed the truth. I did need your help, though, because right before I collided with you in that hallway, I'd seen one of them in the hotel. I knew it was just a matter of time before they found me and took me back."

"Took you back?"

"I wasn't a fugitive from the law or some mental institution," she said quickly. "It's worse than that."

He narrowed his gaze with concern. "What could be worse than that?"

"The Society of Lasting Serenity."

Chapter Three

"The fringe religious cult that relocated to the mountains about five years ago?" Colt asked, unable to keep the shock from his voice.

She nodded.

He couldn't have been more stunned if she'd said she had escaped from prison. "When did you join that?"

"I didn't. My parents were some of the founding members when the group began in California. I was in Europe at university when they joined. I'd heard from my father that SLS had relocated to Montana. A few years after that, I received word that the leader, Jonas Emanuel, needed to see me. My mother was ill." Her voice broke. "Before I could get back here, my mother and father both died, within hours of each other, and had been buried on the compound. According to Jonas, they had one dying wish." Her laugh could have cut glass. "They wanted to see me married. Once I was on the SLS compound, I learned that, according to Jonas, they had promised me to him."

"That's crazy." He still couldn't get his head around this.

"Jonas is delusional but also dangerous."

"So you were running from him that night I met you?"

She nodded. "But, unfortunately, when I left the hotel the next morning, two of the 'sisters' were waiting for me and forced me to go back to the compound."

"And tonight?" he asked as he pushed his plate away.

Lola met his gaze. "I escaped. I'd been locked up there since I last saw you within miles of here at the Montana SLS compound."

Colt let out a curse. "You've been held there all this time against your will? Why didn't you—"

"Escape sooner?" She sounded near tears as she held his gaze.

He saw something in those beautiful eyes that made his stomach drop.

Her voice caught as she said, "I had originally gone there to get my parents' remains because I don't believe they died of natural causes. I'd gotten a letter from my father right before I heard from Jonas. He wanted out of SLS, but my mother refused. My father said he feared the hold Jonas had on her and needed my help because she wasn't well."

"What are you saying?"

"I think they were murdered, but I can't prove it without their bodies, and Jonas has refused to release them. Legally, there isn't much I can do since my parents had signed over everything to him—even their daughter."

Murder? He'd heard about the fifty-two-year-old charismatic leader of the cult living in the mountains outside of town, but he couldn't imagine the things Lola was telling him. "He can't expect you to marry him."

"Jonas was convinced that I would fall for him if I spent enough time at the compound, so he kept me there. At first, he told me it would take time to have my parents' remains exhumed and moved. Later I realized there was no way he was letting their remains go anywhere even if he could convince me to marry him, which was never going to happen."

Maybe it was the late hour, but he was having trouble making sense of this. "So after you met me…"

"I was more determined to free both my parents and myself from Jonas forever. I wasn't back at the compound long though, when I realized I was pregnant. Jonas realized it, too. I became a prisoner of SLS until the birth. Then Jonas had the baby taken away and had me locked up. I had to escape to get help for my daughter."

"Your daughter?"

She met his gaze. "That's why I'm here… She's *our* daughter," she said, her voice suddenly choked with tears. "Jonas took the baby girl that you and I made the first night we met."

COLT STARED AT HER, too shocked to speak for a moment. *What the hell?* "Are you trying to tell me—"

"I had your child but I couldn't contact you. Jonas kept me under guard, locked away. I had no way to get a message out. If any of the sisters tried to help me, they were severely punished."

He couldn't believe what he was hearing. "Wait. You had the baby at the compound?"

She nodded. "One of the members is a midwife. She delivered a healthy girl, but then Jonas had the child taken away almost at once. I got to hold her only for a few moments and only because Sister Amelia let me. She was harshly reprimanded for it. I got to look into her precious face. She has this adorable tiny heart-shaped birthmark on her left thigh and my blond hair. Just fuzz really." Tears filled her eyes again.

Colt ran a hand over his face before he looked at her again. "I'm having a hard time believing any of this."

"I know. If Jonas had let me leave with my daughter, I wouldn't have ever troubled you with any of this," she said.

"You would never have told me about the baby?" He hadn't meant to make it sound like an accusation. He'd expected her to be offended.

Instead, when she spoke, he saw only sympathy in her gaze. "When I met you, you were on leave and going back the next day. You were talking about staying in the Army. Your fiancée had just broken up with you."

"You don't have to remind me."

"What you and I shared that night…" She met his gaze. "I'll never forget it, but I wasn't fool enough to think that it might lead to anything. The only reason I'm here now is that I need help to get our daughter away from that…man."

"Don't I have a right to know if I have a child?"

"Of course. But I wouldn't be asking anything of you—if Jonas hadn't taken our daughter. I'm more than capable of taking care of her and myself."

"What I don't understand is why Jonas wants to keep a baby that isn't his."

She didn't seem surprised by his skepticism, but when he looked into her eyes, he saw pain darken all that beautiful blue. "I can understand why you wouldn't believe she's yours."

"I didn't say that."

"You didn't have to." She got to her feet, grabbing the table to steady herself. "I shouldn't have come here, but I didn't know where else to go."

"Hold on," he said, pushing back his chair and coming around the table to take her shoulders in his hands.

She felt small, fragile, and yet he saw a strength in her that belied her slim frame. "You have to admit this is quite the story."

"That's why I didn't tell you the night we met about the cult or the problems I was having getting my parents' remains out. I still thought I could handle it myself. Also I doubt you would have believed it." Her smile hurt him soul deep. "I wouldn't have believed it and I've lived through all of this."

He was doing his best to keep an open mind. He wasn't a man who jumped to quick conclusions. He took his time to make decisions based on the knowledge he was able to acquire. It had kept him alive all these years as an Army helicopter pilot.

"So what you're telling me is that the leader of SLS has taken your baby to force you to marry him? If he's so dangerous, why wouldn't he have just—"

"Forced me? He tried to…join with me, as he put it. He's still limping from the attempt. And equally determined that I will come to him. Now that I've shamed him…he will never let me have my baby unless I completely surrender to him in front of the whole congregation."

"Don't you mean *our* baby?"

Lola gave him an impatient look. Tears filled her eyes as she swayed a little as if having trouble staying upright after everything she'd been through.

He felt a stab of guilt. He'd been putting her through an interrogation when clearly she was exhausted. It was bad enough that she was scraped, cut and bruised, but he could see that her real injuries were more than skin deep.

"You're dead on your feet," he said. "There isn't anything we can do tonight. Get some rest. Tomorrow…"

A tear broke loose and cascaded down her cheek. He caught it with his thumb and gently wiped it away before she let him lead her to the guest bedroom where she'd showered earlier. His mind was racing. If any of this was true…

"Don't worry. We'll figure this out," Colt said as he pulled back the covers. "Just get some sleep." He knew he wouldn't be able to sleep a wink.

Could he really have a daughter? A daughter now being held by a crackpot cult leader? A man who, according to Lola, was much more dangerous than anyone knew?

Lola climbed into the bed, still wearing his too-large sweats. He tucked her in, seeing that she could barely keep her eyes open.

"Dayton." At his puzzled look, she added, "That's my last name." They'd shared only first names the night they met. But that night neither of them had been themselves. She'd been running scared, and he'd been wallowing in self-pity over losing the woman he'd thought he was going to marry and live with the rest of his life.

"Lola Dayton," he repeated, and smiled down at her. "Pretty name."

He moved to the door and switched off the light.

"I named our daughter Grace," she said from out of the darkness. "Do you remember telling me that you always loved that name?"

He turned in the doorway to look back at her, too choked up to speak for a moment. "It was my grandmother's name."

LOLA THOUGHT SHE wouldn't be able to sleep. Her body felt leaden as she'd sunk under the covers. She could still feel the rough skin of Colt's thumb pad against her cheek and reached up to touch the spot. She hadn't been wrong about him. Not that first night. Not tonight.

She closed her eyes and felt herself careening off that mountain, running for her life, running for Grace's life. She was safe, she reminded herself. But Grace...

The sisters were taking good care of Grace, she told herself. Jonas wouldn't let anything happen to the baby. At least she prayed that he wouldn't hurt Grace to punish her even more.

The thought had her heart pounding until she realized the only power Jonas had over her was the baby. He wouldn't hurt Grace. He needed that child if he ever hoped to get what he wanted. And what he wanted was Lola. She'd seen it in his eyes. A voracious need that he thought only she could fill.

If he ever got his hands on her again... Well, she knew there would be no saving herself from him.

COLT KICKED OFF his boots and lay down on the bed fully dressed. Sleep was out of the question. If half of what Lola had told him was true... Was it possible they'd made a baby that night? They hadn't used protection. He hadn't had anything. Nor had she. It wasn't like him to take a chance like that.

But there was something so wholesome, so innocent, so guileless...

Rolling to his side, he closed his eyes. The memory was almost painful. The sweet scent of her body as she lay with her back to him naked on the bed. The warmth of his palm as he slowly ran it from her side down into the saddle of her slim waist to the rise of her hip and her perfectly rounded buttocks. The catch of her breath as he pulled her into him and cupped one full breast.

The tender moan from her lips as he rolled her over to look into those violet eyes.

Groaning, Colt shifted to his back again to stare up at the dark ceiling. That night he'd lost himself in that delectable woman. He'd buried all feelings for his former fiancée into her. He'd found salvation in her body, in her arms, in her tentative touch, in her soft, sweet kisses.

He closed his eyes, again remembering the feel of her in his arms as they'd danced in his hotel room. The slow sway, their bodies joined, their movements more sensuous than even the act of love. He'd given her a little piece of his heart that night and had not even realized it.

Swinging his legs over the bed, he knew he'd never get any rest until he checked on her. Earlier, he'd gotten the feeling that she wanted to run—rather than tell him what had brought her to his door. She hadn't wanted to involve him, wouldn't have if Jonas didn't have her baby.

That much he believed. But why hadn't she told him what she was running from the night they'd first met? Maybe he could have helped her.

He moved quietly down the hallway, half-afraid he would open the bedroom door only to find her gone and all of this like his dream about being back in Afghanistan.

After easing open the door, he waited for his eyes to adjust to the blackness in the room. Her blond hair lay like a fan across her pillow. Her peaceful face made her appear angelic. He found himself smiling as he stared down at the sleeping Lola. He couldn't help wondering about their daughter. She would be three months old now. Did she resemble her mother? He hoped so.

The thought shook him because he realized how much he wanted to believe her. A daughter. He really could have a daughter? A baby with Lola? He shook his head. What were the chances that their union would bring a child into this world? And yet he and Lola had done more than make love that night. They'd connected in a way he and Julia never had.

The thought of Julia, though, made him recoil. Look how wrong he'd been about her. How wrong he'd been about his own mother. Could he trust his judgment when it came to women? Doubtful.

He stepped out of the room, closing the door softly behind him. Tomorrow, he told himself, he would know the truth. He'd get the sheriff to go with them up to the compound and settle this once and for all.

Colt walked out onto the porch to stare up at the starry sky. The air was crisp and cold, snow still capping the highest peaks around town. He knew this all could be true. Normally, he would never have had intercourse with a woman he didn't know without protection. But that night, he and Lola hadn't just had sex. They'd made love, two lost souls who'd given each other comfort in a world that had hurt them.

He'd been heartbroken over Julia and his friend Wyatt. Being in Lola's arms had saved him. If their lovemaking had resulted in a baby...a little girl...

Yes, what was he going to do? Besides go up to that compound and get the baby for Lola? He tried to imagine himself as a father to an infant. What a joke. He couldn't have been in a worse place in his life to take on a wife and a child.

He looked across the ranch. All his life he'd felt tied down to this land. That his father had tried to chain him to it still infuriated him—and at the same time made him feel guilty. His father had had such a connection to the land, one that Colt had never felt. He'd loved being a cowboy, but ranching was more about trying to make a living off the land. He'd watched his father struggle for years. Why would the old man think he would want this? Why hadn't his father sold the place, done something fun with the money before he'd died?

Instead, he'd left it all to Colt—lock, stock and barrel, making the place feel like a noose around his neck.

"It's yours," the probate attorney had said. "Do whatever you want with the ranch."

"You mean I can sell it?"

"After three months. That's all your father stipulated. That you live on the ranch for three months full-time, and then if you still don't want to ranch, you can liquidate all of your father's holdings."

Colt took a deep breath and let it out. "Sorry, Dad. If you think even three *years* on this land is going to change anything, you are dead wrong." He'd put in his three months and more waiting for an offer on the place.

When his leave was up, he was heading back to the Army and his real job. At least that had been the plan before he'd found Lola standing on his doorstep. Now he didn't know what to think. All he knew was that he had to fly. He didn't want to ranch. Once the place sold, there would be nothing holding him here.

He thought about Lola asleep back in the house. If this baby was his, he'd take responsibility, but he couldn't make any promises—not when he didn't even know where he would be living when he came home on leave.

Up by the road, he could see the for-sale sign by the gate into the ranch. With luck, the ranch would sell soon. In the meantime, he had to get Lola's baby back for her. His baby.

He pushed open the door and headed for his bedroom. Everything was going to work out. Once Lola understood what he needed to do, what he had to do...

He lay down on the bed fully clothed again and closed his eyes, knowing there was no chance of sleep. But hours later, he woke with a start, surprised to find sunlight streaming in through the window. As he rose, still dressed, he worried that he would find Lola gone, just as she had been that morning in Billings.

The thought had his heart pounding as he padded down to the guest room. The door was partially ajar. What if none of it had been true? What if she'd realized he would see through all of it and had taken off?

He pressed his fingertips against the warm wood and pushed gently until he could see into the dim light of the room. She lay wrapped in one of his mother's quilts, her long blond hair splayed across the pillow. He eased the door closed, surprised how relieved he was. Maybe he wasn't a good judge of character when it came in women—Julia a case in point—but he wanted to believe Lola was different. It surprised him how *much* he wanted to believe it.

LOLA WOKE TO the smell of frying bacon. Her stomach growled. She sat up with a start, momentarily confused as to where she was. Not on the hard cot at the compound. Not locked in the claustrophobia-inducing tiny cabin with little heat. And certainly not waking to the wonderful scent of frying bacon at that awful prison.

Her memory of the events came back to her in a rush. What surprised her the most was that she'd slept. It had been so long that she hadn't been allowed to sleep through the night without being awakened as part of the brainwashing treatment. Or when the sisters had come to take her breast milk for the baby. She knew the only reason, other than exhaustion, she'd slept last night was knowing that she was safe. If Colt hadn't been there, though…

She refused to think about that as she got up. Her escape had cost her. She hurt all over. The scratches on her face and the sore muscles were painful. But far worse was the ache in her heart. She'd had to leave Grace behind.

Still dressed in the sweatshirt and sweatpants and barefoot, she followed the smell of frying bacon to the kitchen. Colt had music playing and was singing softly to a country music song. She had to smile, remembering how much he'd liked to dance.

That memory brought a rush of heat to her cheeks. She'd told herself that she hadn't been in her right mind that night, but seeing Colt again, she knew that was a lie. He'd liberated that woman from the darkness she'd been living in. He'd brought out a part of her she hadn't known existed.

He seemed to sense her in the doorway and turned, instantly smiling. "I hope you don't mind pancakes again. There was batter left over. I haven't been to the store. But I did find some bacon in the freezer."

"It's making my stomach growl. Is there anything I can do to help?"

"Nope, just bring your appetite." He motioned for her to take a seat. "I made a lot. I don't know about you, but I'm hungry."

She sat down at the table and watched him expertly flip pancakes and load up a plate with bacon.

As he set everything on the table and took a chair, he met her gaze. "How are you feeling?"

"Better. I slept well." For that he couldn't imagine

how thankful she was. "On the compound, they would wake me every few hours to chant over me."

"Sounds like brainwashing," Colt said, his jaw tightening.

"Jonas calls it rehabilitation."

He pushed the bacon and pancakes toward her. "Eat while it's hot. We'll deal with everything else once we've eaten."

She looked into his handsome face, remembered being in his arms and felt a flood of guilt. If there was any other way of saving Grace, she wouldn't have involved him in this. But he had been involved since that night in Billings when she'd asked for his help and he hadn't hesitated. He just hadn't known then that what he was getting involved in was more than dangerous.

Once Jonas knew that Colt was the father of her baby... She shuddered at the thought of what she was about to do to this wonderful man.

Chapter Four

Colt picked at his food. He'd lied about being hungry. Just the smell of it turned his stomach. But he watched Lola wolf down hers as if she hadn't eaten in months. He suspected she hadn't eaten much. She was definitely thinner than she'd been that night in Billings a year ago.

But if anything, she was even more striking, with her pale skin and those incredible eyes. He was glad to see her hair down. It fell in a waterfall of gold down her back. He was reminded again how she'd looked the first time he'd seen her—and when he'd opened the door last night.

"I've been thinking about what we should do first," Colt said as he moved his food around the plate. "We need to start by getting you some clothing that fits," he said as if all they had to worry about was a shopping trip. "Then I think we should go by the sheriff's office."

"There is somewhere we have to go first," she said, looking up from cutting off a bite of pancake dripping with the red syrup. "I know you don't trust me. It's all right. I wouldn't trust me, either. But don't worry, you will." She smiled. She had a slight gap between her two front teeth that made her smile adorable. That and the innocence in her lightly freckled face had sucked him in from the first.

He'd been vulnerable that night. He'd been a broken man and Lola had been more than a temptation. The fact that she'd sworn he was saving her that night hadn't hurt, either.

He thought about the way she'd looked last night when he'd found her on his doorstep. She still had a scratch across one cheek and a cut under her right eye. It made her look like a tomboy.

"You have to admit, the story you told me last night was a little hard to believe."

"I know. That's why you have to let me prove it to you."

He eyed her suspiciously. "And how do you plan to do that?"

"Do you know a doctor in town who can examine me?"

His pulse jumped. "I thought you said—"

"Not for that. Or for my mental proficiency." Her gaze locked with his. "I need you to know that I had a baby three months ago. A doctor should be able to tell." He started to argue, but she stopped him. "This is where we need to start before we go to the sheriff."

He wanted to argue that this wasn't necessary, but they both knew it was. If a doctor said she'd never given birth and none of this was real, then it would be over. No harm done. Except the idea of him and Lola having a baby together would always linger, he realized.

"I used to go to a family doctor here in town. If he's still practicing…"

DR. HUBERT GRAY was a large man with a drooping gray mustache and matching bushy eyebrows over piercing blue eyes.

Colt explained what they wanted.

Dr. Gray narrowed his gaze for a moment, taking

them both in. "Well, then, why don't you step into the examination room with my nurse, Sara. She'll get you ready while I visit with Colt here."

The moment Lola and Sara left the room, the doctor leaned back in his office chair. "Let me get this straight. You aren't even sure there is a child?"

"Lola says there is. Unfortunately, the baby isn't here."

The doctor nodded. "You realize this won't prove that the child is yours—just that she has given birth before."

Colt nodded. "I know this is unusual."

"Nothing surprises me. By the way, I was sorry to hear about your father. Damn cancer. Only thing that could stop him from ranching."

"Yes, he loved it."

"Tell me about flying helicopters. You know I have my pilot's license, but I've never flown a chopper."

Colt told him what he loved about it. "There is nothing like being able to hover in the air, being able to put it down in places—" he shook his head "—that seem impossible."

"I can tell that you love what you do, but did I hear you're ranching again?"

"Temporarily."

A buzz sounded and Dr. Gray rose. "This shouldn't take long. Sit tight."

True to his word, the doctor returned minutes later. Colt looked up expectantly. "Well?" he asked as Dr. Gray took his seat again behind his desk. Colt realized that his emotions were all over the place. He didn't know what he was hoping to hear.

Did he really want to believe that Lola had given birth to their child to have it stolen by some crazy cult leader? Wouldn't it be better if Lola had lied for whatever reason after becoming obsessed with him following their one-night stand?

"You wanted to know if she has recently given birth?" the doctor asked.

"Has she?" He held his breath, telling himself even if she had, it didn't mean that any of the rest of it was true.

"Since she gave me permission to provide you with this information, I'd say she gave birth in the past three months."

Just as she'd said. He glanced at the floor, not sure if he was relieved or not. He felt like a heel for having even a glimmer of doubt. But Lola was right. He'd had to know before he went any further with this. It wasn't like he really knew this woman. He'd simply shared one night of intimacy all those months ago.

There was a tap at the door. The nurse stuck her head in to say that the doctor had another patient waiting. Behind the nurse, he saw Lola in the hallway. She looked as if she'd been crying. He quickly rose. "Thank you, Doc," he said over his shoulder as he hurried to Lola, taking both of her hands in his. "I'm sorry. I'm so sorry. You didn't have to do this."

Her smile was sad but sweet as she shook her head. "I just got upset because Dr. Gray is so kind. I wish he'd delivered Grace instead of..." She shook her head. "Not that any of that matters now."

"It's time we went to the sheriff," he said as he led her out of the building. She seemed to hesitate, though, as they reached his pickup. "What?"

"Just that the sheriff isn't going to be able to do anything—and that's if he believes you."

"He'll believe me. I know him," he said as he opened the pickup door for her. "I went to school with his sister Lillie and her twin brother, Darby. Darby's a good friend. Both Lillie and Darby are new parents. As for the sheriff—Flint Cahill is as down-to-earth as anyone I know and I'm sure he's familiar with The Society of Lasting Serenity. Sheriff Cahill is also the only way we can get on church property—and off—without any trouble."

She still looked worried. "You don't know Jonas. He'll be furious that I went to the law. He'll also deny everything."

"We'll see about that." He went around the truck and slid behind the wheel. As he started the engine, he looked over at her and saw how anxious she was. "Lola, the man has taken our daughter, right?" She nodded. "Then I don't give a damn how furious he is, okay?"

"You don't know how he is."

"No, but I'm going to find out. Don't worry. I'm going to get to the bottom of this, one way or the other."

She looked scared, but said, "I trust you with my life. And Grace's."

Grace. Their child. He still couldn't imagine them having a baby together—let alone that some cult leader had her and refused to give her up to her own mother.

Common sense told him there had to be more to the story—and that's what worried him as he drove to the sheriff's department. Sheriff Cahill would sort it out, he told himself. As he'd said, he liked and trusted Flint. Going up to the compound with the levelheaded sheriff made the most sense.

Because if what Lola was telling him was true, they weren't leaving there without Grace.

SHERIFF FLINT CAHILL was a nice-looking man with thick dark hair and gray eyes. He ushered them right into his office, offered them a chair and something to drink. They took chairs, but declined a beverage.

"So what is this about?" the sheriff asked after they were all seated, the office door closed behind them.

Colt could see that Lola liked the sheriff from the moment she met him. There was something about him that exuded confidence, as well as honesty and integrity. She told him everything she had Colt. When she finished, though, Colt couldn't tell from Flint's expression what he was thinking.

The sheriff looked at him, his gray eyes narrowing. "I'm assuming you wouldn't have brought Ms. Dayton here if you didn't believe her story."

"I know this is unusual." He glanced over at her. Her scrapes and scratches were healing, and she looked good in the clothes they'd bought her. Still, he saw that she kept rubbing her hand on her thighs as if not believing she was back in denim.

At the store, he'd wanted to buy her more clothing, but she'd insisted she didn't need more than a couple pairs of jeans, two shirts, several undergarments and hiking shoes and socks. She'd promised to pay him back once she could get to her own money. Jonas had taken her purse with her cash and credit cards. Her money was in a California bank account. Once she had Grace, she said she would see about getting money wired up to her so she could pay him back.

Colt wasn't about to take her money, but he hadn't argued. The one thing he'd learned quickly about Lola was that she didn't expect or want anything from him— except help getting her baby from Jonas. That, she'd said, would be more than enough since it could get them both killed.

At the time, he'd thought she was exaggerating. Now he wasn't so sure.

"I believe her," Colt told the sheriff. "What do you know about The Society of Lasting Serenity?"

"Just that they were California based but moved up here about five years ago. They keep to themselves. I believe their numbers have dropped some. Probably our Montana winters."

"You're having trouble believing that Jonas Emanuel would steal Lola's child," Colt said.

Flint sighed. "No offense but, yes, I am." He turned to Lola. "You say your only connection to the group was through your parents before their deaths and your return to the States?"

"Yes, they became involved after I left for college. I thought it was a passing phase, a sign of them not being able to accept their only child had left the nest."

"You never visited them at the California compound?" the sheriff asked.

"No, I got a teaching job right out of college in the Virgin Islands."

Flint frowned. "You didn't visit your parents before you left?"

Lola looked away. "By then we were…estranged. I didn't agree with some of the things they were being taught in what I felt was a fringe cult."

"So why would your parents promise you to Jonas Emanuel?" the sheriff asked.

She let out a bitter laugh. "To *save* me. My mother believed that I needed Jonas's teaching. Otherwise, I was doomed to live a wasted life chasing foolish dreams and, of course, ending up with the wrong man."

"They wanted you to marry Jonas." Flint frowned. "Isn't he a little old for you?"

"He's fifty-two. I'm thirty-two. So it's not unheard-of."

The sheriff looked over at Colt, who was going to be thirty-three soon. Young for a major in the Army, he knew.

"I doubt my parents took age into consideration," Lola said. "One of the teachings at the SLS is that everyone is ageless. My parents, like the other members, were brainwashed."

"So you went to the compound after you were notified that your parents had died," the sheriff said.

"I questioned them both dying especially since earlier I'd received a letter from my father saying he wanted out but was having a hard time convincing my mother to leave SLS," she said. "Also I wanted to have them buried together in California, next to my older sister, who was stillborn. My parents were both in their forties when they had me. By then, they didn't believe they would ever conceive again."

"So you had their bodies—"

"Jonas refused to release them. He said they would be buried as they had wished—on the side of the mountain at the compound. I went up there determined to find out how it was that they had died within hours of each other. I also wanted to make him understand that I would get a lawyer if I had to—or go to the authorities."

"That's when you learned that you'd been promised to him?" the sheriff asked.

"Yes, as ridiculous as it sounds. When I refused, I was held there against my will until I managed to get away. I'd stolen aboard a van driven by two of the sisters, as they call them. That's when I met Colt."

"Why didn't you go to the police then?" Flint asked.

"I planned to the next morning. I'd gone into the back of the hotel when I saw one of the sisters coming in the front. I ducked down a hallway and literally collided with Colt. I asked for his help and he sneaked me up to his room."

The sheriff looked at Colt. "And the two of you hit it off. She didn't tell you what she was running from?"

"No, but it was clear she was scared. I thought it was an old boyfriend."

Flint nodded and looked to Lola again. "You didn't trust him enough to ask for his help the next morning?"

"I didn't want to involve him. By then I knew what Jonas was capable of. This flock does whatever he tells them. The few who disobey are punished. One woman brought me extra food. I heard her being beaten the next morning by her own so-called sisters. When I had my daughter, they took her away almost at once. I could hear her crying, but I didn't get to see her again. The women would come in and take my breast milk, but they said she was now Jonas's child. He called her his angel. I knew I had only one choice. Escape and try to find Colt. I couldn't fight Jonas and his followers alone. And Jonas made it clear. The only way I could see my baby and be with her was if I married him and gave my life to The Society of Lasting Serenity."

Flint pushed back his chair and rose to his feet. "I think it's time I visited the compound and met this Jonas Emanuel."

Chapter Five

Colt followed the sheriff's SUV out of town toward the Judith Mountains. The mountains began just east of town and rose to the northeast for twenty miles. In most places they were only about ten miles wide with low peaks broken by stream drainages. But there were a number of peaks including the highest one, Judith Peak, at more than six thousand feet.

It was rugged country. Back in the 1950s the US Air Force had operated a radar station on top of the peak. The SLS had bought state land on an adjacent mountaintop in an isolated area with few roads in or out. Because it was considered a church, the SLS had rights that even the sheriff couldn't do anything about.

So Colt was nervous enough, but nothing compared to Lola. In the pickup seat next to him, he could feel her getting more agitated the closer they got to the SLS compound. He reached over to take her hand. It was ice-cold.

"It's going to be all right," he tried to assure her—and himself. If what she'd told him was true, then Jonas would have to hand over the baby. "Jonas will cooperate with a lawman."

She didn't look any more convinced than he felt. He'd dealt with religious fanatics for a while now and knew that nothing could stop them if they thought they were in the right.

"Jonas seems so nice, so truthful, so caring," she said. "He's fooled so many people. My parents weren't stupid. He caught them in his web with his talk of a better world." She shook her head. "But he is pure evil. I hate to even think what he might have done to my parents."

"You really think he killed them."

"Or convinced my mother to kill herself and my father."

Colt knew that wouldn't be a first when it came to cult mania.

"Clearly the sheriff wasn't called when they died. Jonas runs SLS like it's his own private country. He told me that his religious philosophy requires the bodies to be untouched and put into the ground quickly. Apparently in Montana, a religious group can bury a body on their property without embalming if it is done within so many hours."

The road climbed higher up the mountain. Ahead, the sheriff slowed. Colt could see that an iron gate blocked them from going any farther. Flint stopped, put down his window and pushed a button on what appeared to be an intercom next to the gate. Colt whirred down his window. He heard a tinny-sounding voice tell him that someone would be right down to let them in.

A few minutes later, an older man drove up in a Jeep. He spoke for a few moments with the sheriff before opening the gate. As Colt drove through, he felt the man's steely gaze on him. Clearly the SLS didn't like visitors. The man who'd opened the gate was wearing a gun under his jacket. Colt had caught sight of the butt end of it when the man got out of his rig to open the gate.

As they passed, he noticed something else interesting. The man recognized Lola. Just the sight of her made the man nervous.

LOLA FELT HER BODY begin to vibrate inside. She thought she might throw up. The memories of being imprisoned here for so long made her itch. She fought the need to claw her skin, remembering the horrible feel of the cheap cloth dresses she was forced to wear, the taste of the tea the sisters forced down her throat, the horrible chanting that nearly drove her insane. That wasn't all they'd forced on her once they'd quit coming for her breast milk. There'd been the pills that Sister Rebecca had forced down her throat.

She felt a shiver and hugged herself against the memories, telling herself she was safe with Colt and the sheriff. But the closer they got to the compound, the more plagued she was with fear. She doubted either Colt or the sheriff knew who they were dealing with. Jonas had gotten this far in life by fooling people. He was an expert at it. At the thought of what lies he would tell, her blood ran cold even though the pickup cab felt unbearably hot.

"Are you all right?" Colt asked, sounding worried as he glanced over at her.

She nodded and felt a bead of perspiration run down between her shoulder blades. She wanted to scratch her arm, feeling as if something was crawling across it, but feared once she started she wouldn't be able to stop.

Just driving up here brought everything back, as if all the crazy they'd been feeding her might finally sink in and she'd be a zombie like the other "sisters." Isn't that what Jonas had hoped? Wasn't that why he was just waiting for her return? He knew she'd be back for

Grace. She couldn't bear to think what he had planned for her.

By the time they reached the headquarters and main building of the SLS, there was a welcome group waiting for them. Lola recognized Sister Rebecca, the woman Jonas got to do most of his dirty work. Sister Amelia was there, as well, but she kept her head down as if unable to look at her.

Lola felt bad that she'd gotten the woman in trouble. She could still hear Amelia's cries from the beating she'd received for giving her extra food. She could well imagine what had happened to the guards after she'd escaped. Jonas would know that she hadn't been taking her pills with the tea. Sister Amelia would be blamed, but there had been nothing Lola could do about that.

Flint parked his patrol SUV in front of the main building. Colt parked next to him. Lola felt her body refuse to move as Colt opened his door. She stared at the two women standing like sentinels in front of them and fought to take her next breath.

"Would you feel better staying out here in the truck?" Colt asked.

She wiped perspiration from her lip with the back of her hand. How could she possibly explain what it was like being back here, knowing what they had done to her, what they might do again if Colt didn't believe her and help her?

Terrified of facing Jonas again, she thought of her baby girl and reached for her door handle.

COLT WONDERED IF bringing Lola back here wasn't a mistake. She looked terrified one moment and like a sleepwalker the next. What had they done to her? He couldn't even imagine, given what she'd told him about her treatment. They'd taken her baby, kept her locked up, hadn't let her sleep. He worried that was just the tip of the iceberg, though.

One of the two women, who were dressed in long simple white sheaths with their hair in braided buns, stepped forward to greet them.

"I'm Sister Rebecca. How may we help you?" Appearing to be the older of the two, the woman's face had a blankness to it that some might have taken for serenity. But there was something else in the eyes. A wariness. A hardness.

"We're here to see Jonas Emanuel," the sheriff said.

"Let me see if he's available," she said, and turned to go back inside.

Colt started to say something about Jonas making himself available, but Flint stopped him. "Let's keep this as civilized as we can—at least to start."

The second woman stood at the foot of the porch steps, her fingers entwined and her face down, clearly standing guard.

A few moments later, Sister Rebecca came out again. "Brother Emanuel will see you now." She motioned them up the porch steps as the other woman drifted off toward a building in the pines where some women were washing clothes and hanging them on a string of clotheslines.

"Seems awfully cold to be hanging wash outside this time of year," Colt commented. Spring in Montana often meant the temperature never rose over forty in the mountains.

Sister Rebecca smiled as if amused. "We believe in hard work. It toughens a person up so a little cold weather doesn't bother us."

He thought about saying something about how she

wasn't the one hanging clothes today in the cool weather on the mountaintop, but he followed the sheriff's lead and kept his mouth shut.

As Sister Rebecca led them toward the back of the huge building, Colt noticed the layout. In this communal living part of the structure, straight-backed wooden chairs were lined up like soldiers at long wooden tables. Behind the dining area, he could hear kitchen workers and the banging of pots and pans. An aroma arose that reminded him of school cafeterias.

What struck him was the lack of conversation coming from the kitchen, let alone any music. There was a utilitarian feeling about the building and everything in it—the workers included. They could have been robots for the lack of liveliness in the place.

Sister Rebecca tapped at a large wooden door. A cheerful voice on the other side said, "Come in." She opened the door and stood back to let them enter a room that was warm and cozy compared to the other part of the building.

A sandy-haired man, who Colt knew was fifty-two, had been sitting behind a large oak desk. But now he pushed back his office chair and rose, surprising Colt by not just his size, but how fit he was. He had boyish good looks, lively pale blue eyes and a wide, straight-toothed smile. He looked much younger than his age.

The leader came around his desk to shake hands with the sheriff and Colt. "Jonas Emanuel," he said. "Welcome." His gaze slid to Lola. When he spoke her name it was with obvious affection. "Lola," Jonas said, looking pained to see her scratched face before returning his gaze to Colt and the sheriff.

"We need to ask you a few questions," Sheriff Cahill said, introducing himself and Colt. "You already know Ms. Dayton."

"Please have a seat," Jonas said graciously, offering them one of the chairs circled around the warm blaze going in the rock fireplace to one side of the office area. Colt thought again of the women hanging wet clothes outside. "Can I get you anything to drink?"

They all declined. Jonas took a chair so he was facing them and crossed his legs to hold one knee in his hands. Colt noticed that he was limping before he sat down.

"How long have you known Ms. Dayton?" Flint asked.

"Her parents were founding members. Lola's been a member for the past couple of years," Jonas said.

"That's not true," she cried. "You know I'm not a member, would never be a member."

Colt could see that she was even more agitated than she'd been in the truck on the way up. She sat on the edge of her chair and looked ready to run again. "Just give me my baby," she said, her voice breaking. "I want to see my baby." She turned in her chair. Sister Rebecca stood at the door, fingers entwined, head down, standing sentry. "My baby. Tell her to get my baby."

Colt reached over and took her hand. Jonas noticed but said nothing.

"As you can see, Ms. Dayton is quite upset. She claims that you are holding her child here on the property," the sheriff said.

Jonas nodded without looking at Lola. "Perhaps we should speak in private. Lola? Why don't you go with Sister Rebecca? She can make you some tea."

"I don't want any of your so-called tea," Lola snapped. "I want my child."

"It's all right," Flint said. "Go ahead and leave with her. We need to talk to Jonas. We won't be long."

Lola looked as if she might argue, but when her gaze fell on Colt, he nodded, indicating that she should leave. "I'll be right here if you need me." Again he could feel Jonas's gaze on him.

After Sister Rebecca left with Lola, the leader sighed deeply. "I'm afraid Lola is a very troubled woman. I'm not sure what she's told you—"

"That you're keeping her baby from her," Colt said.

He nodded sadly. "Lola came to us after her parents died. She'd lost her teaching job, been fired. That loss and the loss of her parents... We tried to help her since she had no one else. I'm sure she's told you that her parents were important members of our community here. On her mother's death bed, she made me promise that I would look after Lola."

"She didn't promise Lola to you as your wife?" Colt asked, and got a disapproving look from the sheriff.

"Of course not." Jonas looked shocked by the accusation. "I had hoped Lola would stay with us. Her parents took so much peace in living among us, but Lola left."

"I understand she ran away some months ago," Flint said.

"A year ago," Colt added.

Again Jonas looked surprised. "Is that what she told you?" He shook his head. "I foolishly suggested that maybe time away from the compound would be good for her. Several of the sisters were making a trip to Billings for supplies. I talked Lola into going along. Once there, though, she apparently became turned around while shopping and got lost. In her state of mind, that was very traumatic. Fortunately, the sisters found her, but not until the next morning. She was confused and hysterical. They brought her back here where we nursed her back to health and discovered that while she'd been lost in Billings, she'd been assaulted."

Colt started to object, but the sheriff cut him off. "She was pregnant? Did she say who the father was?"

Jonas shook his head. "She didn't seem to know." The man looked right at Colt, his blue eyes giving nothing away.

"Where is the baby now?" Flint asked.

"I'm afraid the infant was stillborn. A little boy. Which made it all the more traumatic and heartbreaking for her since we all knew that she had her heart set on having a baby girl. I'm not sure if you know this, but her mother had a daughter before Lola who was stillborn. I'm sure that could have played a part in what happened. When Lola was told that her own child had been stillborn, she had a complete breakdown and became convinced that we had stolen her daughter."

"Then you won't mind if we have a look around," the sheriff said.

"Not at all." He rose to his feet, and the sheriff and Colt followed. "I'm so glad Lola's been found. We've been taking care of her since her breakdown. Unfortunately, the other night she overpowered one of her sisters and, hysterical again, took off running into the woods. We looked for her for hours. I was going to call your office if we didn't hear from her by this afternoon. When she left, she forgot her pills. I was afraid she'd have another psychotic event with no one there to help her."

"Don't you mean when Lola *escaped* here?" Colt asked.

Jonas shook his head as if trying to be patient. "Escaped?" He chuckled. "Do you see razor wire fences around the compound? Why would she need to escape?

We believe in free will here at Serenity. Lola can come and go as she pleases. She knows that. But when she's in one of her states..."

"What kind of medication is she on?" the sheriff asked.

"I have it right here," Jonas reached into his pocket. "I had Sister Rebecca bring it to me when I heard that you were at the gate. I was so glad that she had come back for it. I believe Dr. Reese said it's what they give patients with schizophrenia. I suppose she didn't mention to you that she'd been taking the medication. It helps with the anxiety attacks, as well as the hallucinations."

"Dr. Reese?" Flint asked.

"Ben Reese. He's our local physician, one of the best in the country and one of our members," Jonas said.

"I'd like to see where the baby was buried," Colt said.

"Of course. But let's start with the tour the sheriff requested."

Colt memorized the layout of the buildings as Jonas led them from building to building. Everywhere they went, there were people working, both men and women, but definitely there were more women on the compound than men. He saw no women with babies as most of the women were older.

"Our cemetery is just down here," Jonas said. Colt followed Jonas and the sheriff down a narrow dirt path that wound through the trees to open in a meadow. Wooden crosses marked the few graves, the names of the deceased printed on metal plaques.

He spotted a relatively fresh grave and felt his heart drop. It was a small plot of dark earth. What if Jonas was telling the truth? What if Lola had had a son? *His* son? And the infant was buried under that cold ground?

"It is always so difficult to lose a child," Jonas was

saying. "We buried him next to Lola's parents. We thought that would give her comfort. If not now, later when she's…better. We're waiting for her to name him before we put up the cross."

"I think I've seen enough," Sheriff Cahill said, and looked at Colt.

Colt didn't know what to think. On the surface, it all seemed so…reasonable.

"Sister Rebecca took Lola to the kitchen," Jonas said. "Lunch will be ready soon. I believe we're having a nice vegetable soup today. You're welcome to join us. Some of the sisters are better cooks than others. I can attest that the ones cooking today are our best."

"Thank you, but I need to get back to Gilt Edge," Flint said. "What about you, Colt?"

He knew the sheriff wasn't asking just about lunch or returning to town. "I'll see what Lola wants to do," he said, after taking a last look at the small unmarked grave before heading back toward the main building.

"If Lola is determined not to stay with us, I just hope she'll get the help she needs," Colt heard Jonas tell the sheriff. "I'm worried about her, especially after your visit. Clearly she isn't herself."

LOLA SHOVED AWAY the cup of tea Sister Rebecca had tried to get her to drink. She'd seen Colt and the sheriff go out to search the complex with Jonas. "I know you hid her the moment the sheriff punched the intercom at the gate. Please…" Her voice broke. "I just want to see her so I know she's all right."

Sister Rebecca reached over to pat her hand—and shove the tea closer with her other hand.

Lola jerked her hand back. "You can't keep her. She's

mine." Tears burned her eyes. "Keeping a baby from her mother…"

"You aren't taking your medication, are you? It makes you like this. You really should take it so you're more calm."

"Brain-dead, you mean. Half-comatose, so I'm easy to manipulate. If you keep me drugged up, I won't cause any trouble, right?"

"You wouldn't have left here if you'd been taking your medication." Sister Rebecca shook her head. "You know we were only trying to help you. I should have been the one giving you your medication instead of Sister Amelia. She let you get away with not taking it and look what's happened to you, you poor dear."

Lola scoffed. "As if you care. And Sister Amelia didn't know anything about what I was doing," she said quickly, fearing that the next beating Amelia got could kill her. "I was hiding them under my tongue until she turned away."

The woman nodded. "Well, should you end up staying here, we won't let that happen again, will we."

"I'm not staying here."

Sister Rebecca said nothing as the front door opened and Colt came in. Through the open doorway, Lola could see Jonas and the sheriff standing out by the patrol SUV. She could tell that Jonas had convinced the sheriff that she was crazy.

Standing up too quickly, Lola knocked over her chair. It clattered to the floor. Dizzy, she had to hang on to the table for a moment. When the light-headedness passed and she could let go, she started for the door. But not before she realized Colt had seen her having trouble standing.

She swept past him, determined not to let the sheriff

leave. Her baby was hidden somewhere in the complex. Jonas had had one of his followers hide her. The sheriff had to find her. Lola had to convince him—

At the sound of a baby crying, she stumbled to an abrupt stop. "Do you hear that?" she called down to the sheriff from the top of the porch steps. "It's my baby crying." He looked up in surprise. So did Jonas. Both seemed to stop to listen.

For a moment, Lola thought that she had imagined it. Fear curdled her stomach. She felt Colt's hand on her shoulder as he reached for her. She could see that they believed Jonas. Her eyes filled with tears of frustration and pain.

And then she heard it again. A baby began to squall loudly. The sound was coming from the laundry. She shrugged off Colt's hand and ran down the steps. Jonas reached for her, but she managed to sweep past him. Grace. It was her baby crying for her. She knew that cry. She'd heard it in the middle of the night when the sisters had come for her breast milk. Somehow Grace had known she was here.

"Lola, don't," Jonas called after her. "Sister Rebecca, help Lola. She's going to hurt herself."

She could hear running footsteps behind her, but she was almost to the laundry-room door. Sister Rebecca had set off an alarm. As Lola burst into the room, a half dozen women were already looking in her direction. Lola paid them no mind. She ran toward the woman holding the baby.

Inside this room with the washers and dryers going, though she could barely hear the baby crying, all Lola could think about was getting to the woman before they hid Grace away again. Reaching the woman, she heard the infant let out a fresh squall as if the mother had pinched the poor thing.

Lola grabbed for the baby, but the woman swung around so all she got was a handful of dress cloth from the woman's shoulder.

"Lola, stop." It was the sheriff's voice as he stepped between her and the woman with the child. "May I see your baby," he said to the woman.

Chapter Six

Colt watched the woman with the infant look at Jonas standing in the doorway. The leader nodded that she should let the sheriff look. Colt held his breath as the woman turned so they could see the baby she held. The infant had stopped crying and now looked at them with big blue eyes fringed with tear-jeweled lashes.

"Grace?" Lola whispered as she tried to see the baby.

"May I?" the sheriff asked, and held out his arms.

After getting Jonas's permission, the woman released the baby to Flint. He carefully pulled back the knitted blanket the infant was wrapped in. Colt found himself holding his breath.

The sheriff peeked under the gown the baby wore. Colt knew he was looking for the small heart-shaped birthmark that Lola had told him about. He checked under the baby's diaper. His shoulders fell a little as he looked up at Lola and shook his head. "It's a little boy."

"No," Lola cried. "I heard my baby. This isn't the baby I heard crying. It can't be. Sister Rebecca pulled the alarm. She warned them to hide my baby." She looked from the sheriff to Colt and back again before bursting into tears.

Colt stepped to her and pulled her into his arms. She cried against his chest as he looked past her to the sheriff. He'd watched the whole thing play out, holding his breath. The baby the sheriff had taken from the woman was adorable and about the right age. Was it possible Lola was wrong about the sex of the infant she'd given birth to? Maybe the baby hadn't died.

But Lola had been so sure it was a little girl. She'd convinced him. And there was the tiny heart birthmark that Lola had seen on their daughter. But what if she was wrong and Jonas was telling the truth about all of it?

Now he felt sick. He thought of the small grave next to Lola's parents'. He felt such a sense of loss that it made him ache inside. He pulled Lola tighter to him, feeling her heart breaking along with his own.

As the sheriff spoke again with Jonas, Colt led Lola out of the laundry and down the path toward his pickup.

"I heard her," she said between sobs. "The first baby I heard. It was Grace. I know her cry. A mother knows her baby's cry. Sister Rebecca pulled the alarm to warn them so they could hide her again." She began to cry again as he led her to the truck and opened the passenger-side door for her. "Please, Colt, we can't leave without our baby."

He tried to think of what to say, but his throat had closed with all the emotions he was feeling, an incredible sense of loss and regret. It broke his heart to see Lola like this.

Lola met his gaze with a look that felt like an arrow to his chest before she climbed into the pickup. As he closed the passenger-side door, the sheriff walked over. "You all right?" Flint asked.

All Colt could do was nod. He wasn't sure he would ever be all right.

"I think we're done here," the sheriff said. "If you want to take it further…"

He shook his head. "Thanks for your help," he managed to get out before walking around to the driver's side of his pickup. As he slid behind the wheel, he saw that Lola had dried her tears and was now sitting ramrod straight in her seat with that same look of surrender that tore at him.

He started the engine, unable to look at her.

"You don't believe me. You believe…" She stopped and he looked over at her. She was staring straight ahead. He followed her gaze to where Jonas was standing on the porch of the main building. There was both sympathy and pity in the man's gaze. "He's lying." But Lola said it with little conviction as Colt started the pickup and headed off the compound.

LOLA CLOSED HER EYES and leaned back against the pickup as they headed down the mountain road. What had she expected? That Jonas would just hand over Grace? She'd been such a fool. Worse, she feared that they'd made things worse for Grace—not to mention the way Colt had looked at her. Leaving them alone with Jonas had been the wrong thing to do. She knew what that man was like. Of course the sheriff would believe anything the leader told him. But Colt?

"What did Jonas tell you?" She had to ask as she squeezed her eyes shut tighter, unable to look at him. "That I'm crazy?"

"He said your baby died. That it was a little boy. He showed me the grave."

She let out a muffled cry and opened her eyes. Staring straight ahead at the narrow dirt road that wound down the mountain, she said, "Is that what convinced you I was lying?"

"Why didn't you tell me you were on prescription medication?" Colt asked.

She let out a bark of a laugh. "Of course, my *medication*. What did he tell you it was for?"

"He hinted it was for schizophrenia and that after your breakdown—"

"Right—my breakdown. What else?"

He glanced over at her. "He said you were fired from your teaching job."

Tears blurred her eyes. She bit her lower lip and drew blood. "That at least is true. I resisted the advances of the school principal. When some materials in my classroom went missing, I was fired. Three days later, I heard that my parents had died. Perfect timing," she said sarcastically. "I'm not a thief. I wouldn't give in, so she did what she said she would, she fired me, claiming I stole the materials. It was my word against hers—even though it wasn't the first time something like that had happened involving her. I had planned to fight it once I took care of getting my parents remains returned to the California cemetery. So what else did Jonas tell you about me?"

"That you're a troubled young woman."

"I am that," she agreed. "Given everything that has been done to me, I think that is understandable." Ahead she could see Brother Elmer waiting at the gate for them. Elmer was her father's age. When she'd first arrived at the compound, she'd asked him what had happened to her parents and Elmer had been too terrified to talk to her. She'd only had that one opportunity. Since then Elmer had kept his distance—just like the rest of them.

"Stop up here, please," Lola said, even though the gate was standing open.

Colt said nothing and did as she asked.

She put down the truck window as Colt pulled along-side the man. Elmer met her gaze for a moment before he dropped his head and stared at his feet. "Elmer, you know I'm not crazy. Help me, please," she pleaded. "You were my father's friend. Tell this man the truth about what really goes on back there in the compound."

Elmer continued to focus on the ground.

"Okay, just tell me this," she said, her voice crack-ing with emotion. "Is Grace all right? Are they taking good care of her?" She didn't expect an answer. She knew the cost of going against Jonas. Everyone did. If she was right and Jonas had had her parents killed...

Elmer raised his head slowly. As he did, he grabbed hold of the side of the truck, curling his fingers over the open window frame. His fingers brushed her arm. His gaze rose to meet hers. He gave one quick nod and removed his hands.

"You should move on now so I can close this gate, Sister Lola."

COLT BLINKED, TELLING HIMSELF he hadn't just seen that. His heart beat like a war drum. He swore under his breath. He'd seen the man's short, quick nod. He'd seen the compassion in Elmer's eyes.

Jonas Emanuel was a liar.

Colt wasn't sure who he was more angry with, Jonas or himself. He'd bought into the man's bull. He'd *be-lieved* him. But the man had been damned convincing. The grave. The pills. The crying baby that wasn't Grace.

Shifting the pickup into gear, he felt as if he'd been punched in the gut numerous times. He kept seeing that tiny grave, kept imagining his son, their son, lying in a homemade coffin under it—just as he kept seeing Lola sobbing hysterically in his arms after hearing what she thought was her baby crying.

"Lola."

"Please, just leave me alone," she said as she closed her window and tucked herself into the corner of the pickup seat as he pulled away, the gate closing behind him. When he looked over at her a few miles down the road, he saw that anger and frustration had given way to emotional exhaustion. With the sun streaming in the window, she'd fallen asleep.

Colt was thankful for the time alone. He replayed everything Lola had said, along with what Jonas had told him. He hadn't known what to believe because the man was that persuasive. Jonas had convinced the sheriff— and Flint Cahill was a shrewd lawman.

But as he looked over at the woman sleeping in his pickup, he felt his heart ache in ways he'd never experienced before. He would slay dragons for this woman. He wanted to turn around and go back and...

He couldn't let his emotions get the best of him. He never had before. But this woman had drawn him from the moment he'd met her. He thought about the fear he'd seen in her eyes that first night. There'd been no confusion, though. If anything, they'd both wanted to escape from the world that night and lose themselves in each other. And they had. He remembered her naked in his arms and felt a pull stronger than gravity.

Would he have believed her if she'd told him on that first night what was going on? Probably not. Look how easily he'd let Jonas fool him. Colt was still furious with himself. He would never again question anything she told him.

Glancing in the rearview mirror, he wasn't surprised

to see that they were being followed. Everything she'd told him had been true.

So where was the child he and Lola had conceived? He couldn't bear the thought of Grace being in Jonas's hands. But he also knew that they couldn't go back there until they had a plan.

As he slowed on the outskirts of Gilt Edge, Lola stirred. She shot him a glance as she sat up.

"Before we go back to the ranch, I thought we'd get something to eat," he said, keeping his eye on the large dark SUV a couple of car lengths behind them.

"There is no reason to take me back to the ranch. You can just pull over anywhere and let me out."

"I'm not going to do that."

"I can understand why you don't want to help me, but I'm not leaving town until—"

"You get Grace back."

She stared at him. "Are you mocking me?"

"Not at all," he said, and looked over at her. "I'm sorry. I should have believed you. But I do now."

Tears welled in her eyes and spilled down her cheeks. "You believe me about Grace?"

"I do. I saw that armed guard who let us through the gate. I saw him nod when you asked him about Grace."

She wiped at her tears. "Is that what changed your mind?"

"That and a lot of other things, once I had time to think about it. That first night, you were scared and running from something, but you weren't confused. Nor do I think you were confused the next morning. You checked my wallet to see who I was. You considered taking the four hundred dollars in it, but decided not to. Those were not the actions of a troubled, mentally unstable woman. Also, we're being followed."

Lola glanced in her side mirror. "How long has that vehicle been back there?"

"Since we left the compound."

She seemed to consider that. "Why follow us? If they wanted to know where you lived..."

"I think they are more interested in you than me, but I guess we'll find out soon enough. That's the other thing that made me believe you once I was away from Jonas's hocus-pocus disappearing-baby act. I saw guards armed with concealed weapons around the perimeter of the compound. While there might not be any razor wire and a high fence, that place is secure as Fort Knox."

"So how are we going to find Grace and get her out of there?"

"I don't know. I haven't worked that out yet."

She looked at him as if afraid of this change in his attitude. "The sheriff believes Jonas."

"I don't blame Flint. Jonas is quite convincing. He certainly had me going."

Lola let out a bitter laugh. "How do you think he got so many people to follow him to Montana? To give him all their money, to convince them that to find peace, they needed to give up everything—especially their minds and free will."

"Why wasn't he able to brainwash you?" he asked as he glanced in the rearview mirror. Their tail was still back there.

"I don't know. The meditation, the chanting, the affirmations on the path to peace and happiness? I blocked them out, thinking about anything else. Also, I didn't buy into any of it. I was surprised my father did. It's one reason I didn't see them for so many years. My father wrote me and I spoke with my mother some on the phone, but there was no way I was going to visit them on the compound and they never left except to move to Montana with SLS."

"How was it your father was one of the founding members if it wasn't like him to buy into Jonas's propaganda?"

"My father would have done anything to make my mother happy. That's why he didn't leave after he quit believing in Jonas. He wouldn't have left her there alone. I'm sure he finally saw what my mother couldn't. That Jonas was a fraud. I feel terrible for those lost years."

"The man at the gate…"

"Elmer? He and my father were friends. It's possible that, like my father, he has doubts about SLS and Jonas. Also, not everyone is easily brainwashed into believing everything Jonas says. They might believe he has a right to my child because he says so. But that doesn't mean some aren't sympathetic to a mother losing her baby, our baby, to Jonas."

"I still don't understand how Jonas thinks he can get away with this."

"Because he has."

He glanced over at her, seeing that she was right. Jonas did rule that compound like it was his own country, and because his society was considered a church, he was protected.

"He has Grace," she said. "He knows I can't live without her. Except he's wrong if he thinks I'll let him keep my child, let alone that I would ever be his wife."

Colt glanced over at her. "So he knows we'll be back."

Chapter Seven

Lola looked out the side window as the road skirted Gilt Edge. Her heart beat so loudly that she thought for sure Colt would be able to hear it. Tears stung her eyes, but this time they were tears of relief.

Colt believed her.

The liberation made her weak. She'd seen his face earlier in the laundry when the baby had turned out not to be hers. She'd seen the heart-wrenching sympathy in his gaze, as well as the pain. He'd been so sure at the moment that she was everything Jonas had told him. A mentally unstable woman who couldn't accept the death of the baby she'd carried for nine months. *His* baby.

But Colt had seen the truth. He'd seen Elmer's slight nod, and when he looked at everything, he knew she was telling the truth.

She wiped at her tears, determined not to give in to the need to cry her heart out. They still didn't have Grace. Her stomach ached with a need to hold her baby. Jonas had Grace and that alone terrified her. Would he hurt the baby to get back at her?

No. He'd fooled the sheriff. He would feel safe and superior. He would simply wait, knowing, as Colt said, that they'd be back. Or at least she would. Jonas thought he'd fooled Colt, too.

She tried to assure herself that Jonas wouldn't hurt Grace just to spite her. The baby was his only hope of getting Lola back to the compound. She'd looked into Jonas's eyes as they'd left. He hadn't given up on her being his wife. He would need Grace if he had any hope of making that happen.

At least that must be his thinking, she told herself. It would be a cold day in hell before she would ever succumb to the man. And only then so she could get close enough to kill him.

"Do you think Jonas knows I'm Grace's father?" Colt asked, dragging her out of her dark thoughts. "He looked me right in the eye and told me that you swore you didn't know who the father was."

"I did. I was afraid he'd come after you. Or send some of his men to hurt you—if not kill you. He was quite upset to realize I was pregnant. I told him I didn't know your name. You were just someone who'd helped me."

"Helped himself to you. Isn't that what Jonas thought?"

She shrugged. "He was so angry with me. I'm not sure when he decided he wanted my baby. Our baby."

"Well, he can't have her."

"We will get her back, won't we?"

He reached over and took her hand.

"I mean, if you dig up the grave and prove that—"

"Lola, that would take time and be very iffy. First off, that is probably what Jonas is expecting us to do. Second, even if we had proof that your baby didn't die, I'm not sure we could get a judge to send up an army to search the place for Grace."

"Then what do we do?" She felt close to tears again.

"The problem is that it is hard for the authorities to get involved in these types of pseudo-religious groups, especially when, according to Jonas, you're a member—and so were your parents. It's your word against Jonas's. So I'm afraid we're on our own. But that's not a bad thing." He smiled at her. "I'll do everything in my power and then some to bring Grace home to you."

She smiled and squeezed his hand, knowing that she could depend on Colt.

COLT PULLED UP in front of the Stagecoach Saloon on the outskirts of Gilt Edge. The large dark SUV that had been following them drove on past. He tried to see the driver, but the windows were tinted too dark. The license plate was covered with mud, no accident either, he figured.

But it didn't matter. He knew exactly where it had come from.

"The sheriff's brother and sister own this place," Colt said as he parked and turned off the engine. "They serve some of the best food in the area. I thought we'd have something to eat and talk. It shouldn't be that busy this time of the day."

Lola's stomach growled in answer, making him smile. "I thought I would never eat after Grace was taken from me. But soon I realized that I needed my strength if I had any hope of getting her back. Not that I was given much food on the compound."

They got out, Lola slowing to admire the place. "I love this stone building."

"It was one of the original stagecoach stops along here. Lillie Cahill bought it with her brother Darby, to preserve it." He pushed open the door and Lola stepped in.

"Something smells wonderful," she whispered to Colt as they made their way to an out-of-the way table by the window. All this time eating nothing but the swill that had come out of the compound kitchen had left her ravenous.

There were a few regulars at the bar but other than that, the place was empty. A man who resembled the sheriff came over to take their orders. He had Flint's dark hair and gray eyes and was equally good-looking. "Major McCloud," the young man said, grinning at Colt.

"Just Colt, thank you."

"I heard you were back. Welcome home. Again, so sorry about your father."

"Thanks, Darby." All of the Cahills had been at the funeral. Colt's father would have liked that. He'd always respected their father, Ely Cahill, even though a lot of people in this town considered him a nut. "This is my friend Lola."

Darby turned to Lola and said, "Nice to meet you."

"Congrats on the marriage and fatherhood. How's your family?" Colt asked, since that's what small-town people did. Everyone knew everyone else. He was sure Darby had heard about Julia and Wyatt since they'd all gone to school together.

"Fine. Lillie's married and now has a son, TC. She married Trask Beaumont. If you're sticking around for a while, you'll have to meet Mariah and my son, Daniel. Don't know if Flint mentioned it, but his wife, Maggie... Yep. Expecting."

Colt laughed. "Must be somethin' in the water. Which reminds me. Ely still kickin'?"

Darby laughed. "Hasn't changed a bit. Still spends most of his time up in the mountains when he's not hanging around the missile silo." He sighed. "So what can I get you?"

"What's cooking today? Something smells delicious."

"Our cook, Billie Dee, whipped up one of her down-home Texas recipes. Today it's shrimp gumbo. Gotta warn ya, she's determined to add some spice in our lives and convert us Montanans."

"I'll have that," Lola and Colt said in unison, making Darby chuckle.

"Two coming up. What can I get you to drink?"

Colt looked at Lola. "Two colas?" She nodded and Darby went off to place their order.

"What was that about… Ely?"

"The Cahill patriarch. Famous in these parts because back in 1967, he swore he was abducted by aliens next to the missile silo on their ranch." Colt explained how the government had asked for two-acre plots around the area for defense back in the 1950s. "You might have seen that metal fence out in one of my pastures? There might be a live missile in it. No one but the government knows for sure."

"The missile silos on your property would be scary enough, but aliens?"

He laughed and nodded. "What makes Ely's story interesting to me is that night in 1967 the Air Force detected a flying-saucer type aircraft in the area. Lots of people saw it, including my father."

"So it's possible Ely is telling he truth as he knows it," she said, wide-eyed.

He shrugged. "I guess we'll never know for certain, but Ely swears it's true."

Darby brought their colas, and they sat in companionable silence for a few minutes.

"It feels so strange to be in a place like this," Lola

said. "It's so…normal. I haven't had normal in way too long."

"How long had you been held at the compound before I met you in Billings?"

"Almost a month. The first week or so I was trying to get my parents' remains released to a mortuary in Gilt Edge. Jonas had been kind enough to offer me a place to stay until I could make arrangements. I didn't realize that he was lying to me until I tried to leave and realized there were armed guards keeping me there. At least I wasn't locked up in a cabin that time. I had the run of the place, or I would never have gotten away in the back of the van when the sisters drove to Billings."

And Colt would never have met her. They would never have made love and conceived Grace, Colt thought. Funny how things worked out.

Darby put some background music on the jukebox. The sun coming in the window gave the place a golden glow. Colt had been here a few times when he was home on leave. He was happy for Lillie and Darby for making a go of the place.

"How did you manage to get away this last time?" he asked.

"I'd been hiding my pills under my tongue until Sister Amelia left my cabin. I would spit them out and poke them into a hole I'd found in the cabin wall. The night I escaped, I pretended to be sick and managed to distract Sister Rebecca. When she wasn't looking, I hid the fork that was on my tray. She didn't notice that it was missing when she took my tray and left. I used the fork to pick the lock on the window and went out that way."

Darby returned a few moments later, accompanied by a large woman with a Southern accent carrying two steaming bowls of shrimp gumbo.

"Billie Dee, meet Colt McCloud," Darby said as he joined them. "Colt and I go way back. He's an Army helicopter pilot who's finally returned home—at least for a while, and this is his friend Lola."

"Pleased to meet you," the woman with the Texas accent said. "Hope you like my gumbo."

"I know we will," Colt said, and took a bite.

"Not too spicy for you?" the cook asked with a laugh.

"As long as it doesn't melt the spoon, it's not too spicy for me," Colt said, and looked to Lola.

She had tasted the gumbo and was smiling. "It's perfect."

Billie Dee looked pleased. "Enjoy."

Darby refilled their colas and gave them pieces of Billie Dee's Texas chocolate sheet cake to convey both "welcome home" and "glad to meet you."

Left alone again, Colt asked, "How are you doing?"

Lola realized that she felt better than she had in a long time. Just having food in her stomach made her feel stronger and more able to hold off the fear and frustration. She needed her baby.

But Colt believed her, and that made all the difference in the world. That felt like a huge hurdle given how convincing Jonas could be. Even more so, she was glad that she hadn't been wrong about Colt. They'd only been together that one night, but she hadn't forgotten his kindness, his tenderness, his protectiveness. Just having someone she could depend on… Her heart swelled as she looked over at him. "We're going to get Grace back, aren't we?"

JONAS STOOD AT the window of his cabin. He'd had his cabin built on the side of the mountain so he could look down on the compound. For a man who'd started with nothing, he'd done all right. He often wished his father was still alive to see it.

"Look, you sanctimonious old son of a bitch. You, who so lacked faith that I would accomplish anything in my life. You, who died so poor that your congregation had to scrape up money to have you buried behind the church you'd served all those years. You, who always managed to cut me down as if you couldn't stand it that I might do better than you. Well, I did!"

Thinking about his father made his pulse rise dangerously. He had to be careful not to get upset. Stress made his condition worse. So much worse that some of his followers had started to notice.

He stepped over to the small table where he kept his medication. He swallowed a pill and waited for it to work. He tried not to think about the father who had kicked him out at sixteen. But it wasn't his old man who was causing the problem this time. It was Lola.

"Lola." Just saying her name churned up a warring mix of emotions that had been raging inside him for some time. Over the years, a variety of willing women had come to his bed in the night. He'd turned none of them away, but nor had he wanted any of them to keep for himself. Until Lola.

Her mother had shown him a photograph of her daughter back when Maxine and her husband, Ted, had joined SLS. The Society was just getting on its feet in those days. The Daytons' money had gone a long way to start things rolling.

Jonas had especially liked Maxine, since he knew she was the one calling the shots. Ted would do anything for his wife. And had. All Jonas had to do was steer Maxine in whatever direction he wanted her to go and Ted would come along as a willing participant.

If only they were all that easy to manage, he thought now with a sigh.

The photo of Lola had caught him off guard. There was a sweetness, a purity in that young face, but it was what he saw in her eyes. A fire. A passion banked in those mesmerizing violet eyes that had made him want to be the one to release it.

He'd done everything he could to get the Daytons to bring Lola to the California ranch. But the foolish girl had taken off right after high school to attend a college abroad. She'd wanted to become a teacher. Jonas had groaned when Maxine told him, and he'd conveyed his thoughts.

I think she could be anything she wants to be with my help. I really want to help her meet her potential. Lola is destined to do so much more than teach. She and I could lead the world to a better place. She might be the one person who could bring peace to the world.

Maxine had loved it, but Lola hadn't been having any of it. Right after college she'd headed for the Virgin Islands to teach sixth-grade geography at a private school down there. What a waste, he'd thought, not just for Lola but for himself. He had imagined what he could do with a woman like that warming his bed at night. They could run SLS together. Lola would bring in the men. He'd bring in the women. They could build an empire and live like royalty.

He'd known that Ted wasn't happy after the move to Montana. Jonas had heard him trying to get Maxine to leave. That was the first time that Jonas had realized that Ted had held out on him. Ted hadn't bought into SLS either mentally or financially. He hadn't turned over all his money. He'd set some aside for Lola, and no small amount, either.

Ted's dissatisfaction and attempts to get Maxine to leave hadn't fitted into Jonas's plan. He suddenly realized there was only one way to get Lola to come to him. Maxine and Ted would have to die—and soon.

Getting Maxine to sign a paper of her intentions to persuade Lola to marry him had taken only one private session with her. Maxine had bought into SLS hook, line and sinker. If she wanted to save her daughter... He'd promised to give Lola the kind of life her mother had only dreamed of. Then he'd had Ted and Maxine disposed of and, just as he'd planned, Lola flew to Montana, bringing all that fire inside her.

But he'd underestimated her. She was nothing like her mother. He'd thought that his charm, his wit, his sincerity would work on the daughter the way it had on her mother. That was where he'd made his first mistake, he thought now as he watched dusk settle over the compound.

There'd been a series of other mistakes that had led to her getting pregnant by another man. That was a blow he still reeled from. But it hadn't changed his determination to have Lola, one way or another. Not even some Army pilot/rancher could stop him. No, he had the one thing that Lola wanted more than life.

She would be back. And this time, she wouldn't be leaving here again.

Chapter Eight

After shrimp gumbo at the Stagecoach Saloon, Colt took them to the grocery store. He and Lola grabbed a cart and began to fill it with food. He loved her enthusiasm. After being locked up and nearly starved for so long, she was like a kid in a candy store.

"Do you like this?" she would ask as she picked up one item after another.

"Get whatever sounds good to you."

She scampered around, quickly filling the cart with food she obviously hadn't had for a while as he grabbed the basics: milk, bread, eggs, butter, bacon and syrup.

"I suspect you can live on pancakes," she said, eyeing what he'd added to the cart.

He'd only grinned, realizing that he'd never enjoyed grocery shopping as much as he had with her today. They felt almost like an old married couple as they left the store. He found himself smiling at Lola as she tore into a bag of potato chips before they even reached the pickup. He unloaded their haul and had started to replace the cart in the rack when he heard someone call his name.

"Colt?"

He froze at the sound of Julia's voice. Somehow he'd managed not to cross paths with her since he'd been back in town, but only because he'd shopped either very early or very late. He'd picked a bad day to run out of groceries, he thought now with a grimace.

"Colt?"

Lola set her potato chip bag in the back of the pickup bed and walked over to join him. He could feel her looking from him to Julia, wondering why he wasn't responding. With a silent curse, he turned to face the woman he'd been ready to marry a year ago.

Julia looked exactly the same. Her dark hair was shorter, making her brown eyes seem even darker. She looked good, slim and perfect in a dress and heels. Julia always liked to dress up—even to go to the grocery store. Gold glittered at her ears, her neck and, of course, on her ring finger, along with the sizable diamond resting there. The one he'd bought hadn't been nearly as large.

He swore under his breath. As many times as he'd imagined what it would be like running into her again, he'd never imaged this. Lola was watching the two of them as if enjoying a tennis match.

Colt had hoped that he wouldn't feel anything, given what Julia had done to him. But he'd believed in this woman, believed they would share the rest of their lives; otherwise, he would never have asked her to marry him. It had taken him almost three years to pop the question. He'd wanted to be sure. What a fool he'd been.

"I heard you were back," Julia said, and glanced from him to Lola beside him. "I was so sorry to hear about your father. I was at the funeral…"

He'd seen her and managed to avoid her.

"How are you?" she asked, sounding as if she cared. As if sensing who this woman was and what she'd meant to him, Lola reached over and took his hand, squeezing it gently.

"I'm good," he said, squeezing back. "And you?"

"Fine." She looked again at his companion, her gaze going to their clasped hands.

"I heard you've put the ranch up for sale." Julia hesitated. She brushed a lock of her hair back from her forehead, looking not quite as confident. "Does this mean you're going back into the military?" His joining the Army's flight program had been a bone of contention between them.

He shook his head, as if what he planned to do was any of her business.

"I was just wondering," she said, no doubt seeing him clenching his teeth. "I was hoping that if you were staying around Gilt Edge we could…" Again she hesitated. "Maybe we could have a cup of coffee sometime and just talk."

Just talk the way they had before she'd had an affair with Wyatt? Or talk the way they had when she hadn't shown up at the airport to give him a ride home?

"Our last conversation…" Julia looked again at Lola for a moment. "It went so badly. I'd left you messages. I had no way of knowing you hadn't gotten them or the letter I sent."

"You were clear enough on the phone the last time we talked," he said, wishing she would just say whatever it was she needed to say so he didn't have to keep standing there. He could tell that she was waiting for him to introduce her to Lola, but his heart was beating too hard. Julia and Wyatt had hurt him badly. Her and one of his friends? Equal amounts of anger and regret had him shaking inside.

But he didn't want to get into an argument here in

the grocery store parking lot in front of Lola. He didn't want Julia to know just how much she and Wyatt had hurt him. And he feared that if he started in on her, he wouldn't be able to stop until all of his grief and rage and hurt came pouring out.

"I'm glad you're home." Julia looked from him to Lola again and forced a weak smile. "It was good to see you. If you change your mind about that cup of coffee…" She stood for a moment, looking awkward and unsure, something new for Julia, he thought. And he realized that she needed him to tell her it was okay, what she'd done. That he forgave her. That he wanted her and Wyatt to be happy. Julia was struggling with the guilt.

That alone should have made him feel better, he thought as she turned and left them standing there. Instead, he felt as if he'd been ambushed by a speeding freight train.

"I'm sorry," Lola said as she let go of his hand.

He couldn't speak so merely nodded as he took the cart to the rack and quickly returned to the pickup. Lola grabbed her potato chips out of the back and joined him in the cab. He'd expected her to be full of questions.

Instead, she buckled up, holding the bag of potato chips as if she'd lost her appetite, and quietly let him process what had just happened. He was thankful to her for that. And for taking his hand back there.

"Thanks," he said, after he got the truck going and drove out of the parking lot.

"It was the first time you've seen her since…since the breakup." It wasn't a question, but he answered it anyway.

"I've managed to avoid her. Just my luck…" He shook his head.

"I can see how painful it is."

"I'm more angry than hurt."

Lola looked out the side window. "Betrayal is always painful." She hugged herself.

He glanced over at her, thinking what a strong, determined woman she was. Not the kind who would give up when things got a little tough.

"Julia turned out not to be the woman I thought she was," he said. "I'm better off without her."

Lola said nothing, no doubt sensing that no matter what he said, he wasn't completely over his former fiancée or what she had put him through.

It made him angry that his heart hadn't let go of the hurt. The anger he didn't mind living with for a while.

WHAT WOULD LOLA do now? That was the question Jonas knew he should be asking himself as he stepped back inside his warm, elegantly furnished cabin.

She must think him a complete fool. Her great escape. He let out a bark of a laugh. Did she really think she could have gotten away unless he'd let her? Sure, he'd had his men chase her with instructions to make sure that she got away.

He'd known she would run straight to the father of her baby. As if he hadn't known she was lying about not knowing who she'd lain with. He scoffed at the idea. Sister Rebecca had seen her with a man near the hotel bar that night. Unfortunately, Lola and the man had disappeared on the elevator too quickly.

But Rebecca had managed to get the information. Major Colt McCloud. An Army helicopter pilot. Jonas would ask what she could see in a man like that, but he wasn't that stupid. The man was good-looking, part cowboy, part flight jockey. He had just inherited a large ranch.

Not that Jonas had been certain Colt McCloud was the man who'd knocked Lola up. No, he hadn't known that until today when the man had shown up with Lola and the sheriff.

Lola was too bound up from her conservative upbringing to go to bed with just anyone. So she'd seen something beyond Colt McCloud's good looks. Jonas swore under his breath as he moved to the fireplace to throw on another log. Just the thought of the cowboy pilot made his blood boil. How dare the man come up here making demands.

Jonas thought he might have convinced Colt that Lola was unstable and not to be believed. She'd certainly played into his plan perfectly when she'd lost it in the laundry room. But he couldn't be sure about Colt. The man was probably smitten with Lola and would want to believe her.

At least the sheriff wouldn't be returning. He'd been sufficiently convinced. Law enforcement always backed off when it came to churches. Just like the government did. He smiled at the thought of how he'd been able to build The Society of Lasting Serenity without anyone looking over his shoulder.

Until now.

"You could return the baby," Sister Rebecca had dared to say to him before the dust had even settled earlier today. "You know she'll be back if you don't."

"Mind your place," he'd snapped. He'd seen how jealous the older woman was of Lola. He suspected she'd been mean to her, cutting her rations, possibly even being physically abusive to her. He hadn't stopped it, wanting Sister Rebecca's loyalty.

But now he wondered how much longer he might be able to count on Rebecca. Once Lola was back—and she would be back—Sister Rebecca might have to be taken down a notch or two. Then again, maybe it was time to retire her. Not that she would ever be allowed to leave. She knew too much.

Strange how a valuable asset could so quickly become a liability.

As soon as he had Lola… Yes, he would dispose of Sister Rebecca. It would be almost like a wedding gift for his new wife. Not that he would tell Lola what had really happened to the older woman. Let her believe he'd given Rebecca a golden parachute and sent her off to some island to bask in the sun for the rest of her days.

He stared into the flames as the log he'd added began to crackle and spark. If he was Colt McCloud, what would he do? Jonas smiled to himself, then picked up the phone. "We're going to need more guards tonight, especially around the cemetery."

AFTER RUNNING INTO JULIA, Colt had known it was just a matter of time before he and Wyatt crossed paths. He'd promised himself that when it happened, when he finally did see his traitorous, former good friend, he would keep his cool. He wasn't going to lose his temper. If Wyatt wanted Julia, a woman who would betray her fiancé while he was fighting a war oceans away, then she was all his.

He'd visualized seeing both of them, but even in his imagination, he hadn't known what he would do. He'd told himself that he would tell them both off, make them feel even more guilty, if possible, hurt them the way they had hurt him.

But look what had happened when he'd seen Julia. He'd been boiling inside, his heart pounding, anger and hurt a potent mixture. And he'd said none of what he'd planned. Instead, he hadn't wanted them to know how much they'd hurt him. Or even how angry he still was.

After seeing Julia, it made him wonder when it could happen with Wyatt. How would Wyatt react? He just hoped Lola wouldn't have to witness it again. Colt thought that Wyatt must be dreading the day when they would come face-to-face again as much as he was. Colt hoped he'd given Wyatt a few sleepless nights worrying about it. Because, in a town the size of Gilt Edge, a meeting had to happen.

But Colt was sorry that it had to happen at this moment as he stopped to get gas on the way out of town. Lola had gone inside the convenience mart to use the ladies' room.

As he stood filling the pickup with gas, Wyatt drove up, pulling to a pump two away from him.

Colt froze, his heart in this throat, as he watched Wyatt get out of his pickup and step to the fuel pump. He thought about staying where he was, pretending he never saw him. But that was way too cowardly. Anyway, he wanted to get this over with.

He finished fueling his truck and walked down the line of gas pumps. Wyatt looked up and saw him and seemed to freeze. They'd grown up together, hung out with many of the same friends since grade school. It was only after college that Colt, needing to do something more with his life, had enlisted in the Army helicopter program.

Wyatt had tried to talk him out of it. "Why do you need to go so far away? You're going to get yourself killed and for what?"

Colt hadn't been able to explain it to him. So he'd left to fly and fight while Wyatt had stayed on his family ranch and stolen Julia.

He took a step toward the man he'd thought he'd known better than himself. As he did, he wondered what he would come out of his mouth or if he would be able to speak. His pulse thundered in his ears as he advanced on his former friend.

"Colt." Wyatt was a big, strong cowboy. He put up both hands in surrender but held his ground. "Colt, whatever you're thinking—"

Colt hit him hard enough to drive him back a couple of steps. Wyatt banged into the side of his pickup.

"I don't want to fight you," Wyatt said as one large hand went to his bleeding nose.

"That's good," Colt said. "Since you'd probably take me." He knew that might be true since Wyatt had a few inches on him and a good twenty pounds, but as angry as he was, he'd fight like hell.

His hands were balled into fists, but he didn't hit him again. Wyatt's bleeding nose looked broken. Colt was reminded of the time Wyatt had taken on the school bully, a kid twice his size back then. His former friend was tough and had never backed down from a fight in all the time Colt had known him.

He took a step back, hating that he was remembering the years of their friendship. His eyes burned with tears, but damned if he was going to cry. Looking at Wyatt, he realized that losing Julia had hurt; losing someone he'd considered a close friend, though, had ripped out his heart.

He turned on his heel and walked back to his pickup before he made a complete fool of himself. His knuckles hurt, but nothing like his heart as he listened to Wyatt get into his truck and drive away.

LOLA HAD SEEN everything from the front window of the convenience store when she'd come back from the restroom. The "fight" had ended quickly enough.

She didn't have to ask who the man had been.

Wyatt Enderlin. When she'd asked Colt about him, he'd said they'd been friends. "It's a small town. We make friends for life here." She could imagine how much Wyatt's betrayal hurt Colt.

She pushed open the door and walked out to Colt's truck, climbing in without a word. Out of the corner of her eye, Lola saw him rub his skinned and swollen knuckles before he climbed behind the wheel.

It wasn't until they were in the pickup headed toward the ranch that Colt said, "You saw?"

She hesitated, forcing him to look over at her. "I wanted you to hit him again."

He smiled sadly at that. "I hadn't planned to even hit him once."

"Do you feel better or worse?"

Chuckling, he said, "Better and worse."

"Well, you got that out of the way."

"Right, I got to see them both on the same day. Lucky me." He drove in silence for a few minutes. "Wyatt and I were like brothers at one point growing up. I'd always wanted a brother…" He shook his head.

"He was your friend."

"*Was* being the key word here. My other friends like Darby Cahill never would have done that."

"Which hurts worse?" she finally asked.

Colt shot her a glance before turning back to his driving. "Wyatt."

"Maybe one day—"

"I don't think so. Being in the military you learn which men you can trust in battle. Those are the men you want watching your back. Wyatt, as it turned out, isn't one of them."

"I'm sorry." She let the words hang in the air for a moment. "Do you believe in fate?"

They were almost at the turnoff to the ranch. Ahead she could see the for-sale sign. They hadn't talked about it. She doubted they would because she already knew from the first time they'd met how Colt felt about flying the big birds in the military.

"Fate?" he asked, glancing at her for a moment before he slowed for the turn.

"Maybe it was fate that has brought us all to this point in our lives."

FATE? LOLA COULDN'T be serious. If his fate was having his fiancée hook up with his good friend behind his back, then he'd say he was one unlucky bastard. He said as much to Lola.

"I was thinking more about the way we met."

Instantly he hated having rained on her parade like that.

"If Julia hadn't broken up with you and had met you at the airport like she was supposed to, then you wouldn't have been in that hotel that night and I wouldn't have…"

Would some other man have saved her? Or taken advantage of a young woman who was obviously inexperienced and desperate? The thought made him sick to his stomach, but he wouldn't have known because he would never have laid eyes on Lola Dayton.

Nor would he be worrying about how to get their baby away from a madman at an armed and dangerous cult compound at the top of a mountain, he thought as he parked in front of the house at the ranch and shut off the engine.

But as he looked over at Lola, the anger he'd been

feeling ebbed away. "You're right," he said, softening his tone as he reached over and squeezed her hand. "It definitely was fate that brought us together." Damn fickle fate, he thought, realizing with growing concern how much Lola was getting to him.

He put Julia, Wyatt and the past out of his mind and concentrated on what to do next. He knew what he was going to have to do. It went against his military training. A man didn't go in alone with no backup. Nor did he take matters into his own hands. He went through proper channels.

But there was no way the sheriff was going to be able to get a warrant to have whatever was buried on the church grounds exhumed—even if Colt could talk Flint into doing it. Jonas would fight it and drag out the process. Meanwhile, that madman had their baby. Baby Grace, the daughter he had yet to lay eyes on.

After helping put the groceries away, he went into the ranch office. The maps were in a file—right where his father had kept them. He found the one he needed and spread it out on the desk.

"We need proof that Jonas is lying," Lola said from the open doorway.

"Proof won't do us any good. We need to find Grace and get her out of there."

"But that grave. If you dig it up—"

Colt shuddered at the thought. "That's exactly what Jonas will expect me to do." He recalled a shortage of manpower on the compound. But a woman could be just as deadly with a gun, he reminded himself. "While they're busy guarding the cemetery, I'll find Grace."

"I'm going with you," she said, stepping into the small office.

He shook his head, hating how intimate it felt with

her in here. "It's going to be hard enough for me to get onto the grounds—and away again—without being caught."

"Exactly. They will expect you and will have doubled the guards. You're going to need me."

He started to argue, but she cut him off. "I have lived there all this time. I know the weakest spots along the perimeter. I also know the guards. And, maybe more important, I know where to look for Grace."

Admittedly, she made a good argument. "Lola, if we are both caught, no one will know we're up there. If Jonas is as dangerous as you think he is, we'll end up in the cemetery."

"If one of us is caught, then the other can distract them while whoever has Grace gets away."

He hated that her argument made sense, more sense than him trying to find Grace on his own. "Can you draw a map of the place?"

She nodded.

"Good. We leave at midnight."

LOLA HADN'T DARED HOPE, but as she watched Colt studying the web of old logging roads around the mountain compound on the map, she let herself believe they could succeed. They would get in, find Grace and slip back out with her. Once she had Grace in her arms, no way would she let anyone rip her out again. Especially Jonas.

"I'll need paper and a pen," she said as she leaned over the desk. Their gazes met for a moment, his gaze deepening. She felt goose bumps ripple over her skin. Heat rushed to her center. Then he quickly looked away and began searching for what she needed.

She drew a map of the compound buildings, marking those that were used for housing. "I know you got a tour, but I thought this would help. As you can see there are two women's dorms, one for the women with babies. There is only the one men's dorm on the opposite side the main building."

"What's this?" Colt asked as he moved to her side to point at a large cabin away from the others and at the top of her diagram.

"Jonas's. He likes to look down on his followers."

"And this one at the bottom right?" His fingers brushed hers.

A shiver ran the length of her spine. She felt her nipples harden to pebbles under her top. "That's the storage room, shop and health center." Her voice cracked with emotion.

"And this one bottom left?" There was no doubt. He'd purposely brushed against her as he pointed to the only other structure. The bare skin of his arm was warm. His touch sent more shivers rippling through her. Her nipples ached inside her bra.

"Laundry." She turned enough to meet his eyes. What she saw made her molten inside. His gaze was dark with desire as his fingers trailed up her arm to brush against the side of her breast.

WHAT THE HELL *are you doing?* As if he could stop himself. He looked into Lola's beautiful violet gaze and knew he was lost. He wanted her. Needed her. Thought he would die if he didn't have her right now. This had been building inside him all day, he realized. Maybe since the first time he'd met her.

"Colt?" she breathed, and shuddered as his fingers brushed over the hard tip of her nipple. She moaned softly, her head going back to expose her slim silken neck.

He bent to kiss her throat, nipping at the pale skin,

and felt her shiver before trailing kisses down into the hollow between her breasts. "Yes, Lola?" he asked, his muffled voice as filled with emotion as hers had been.

When she didn't answer, he raised his head to look into her eyes. He held her gaze, seeing the answer in all that lovely blue.

Cupping her other breast, he backed her up against the office wall and dropped his mouth to hers. Her lips parted and he took the invitation to let his tongue explore her as his free hand found the waistband of her jeans and slipped inside.

She let out a gasp as he found the sweet cleft between her legs. "Colt." This time it was a plea. She was wet. He began to stroke her, drawing back to look into her eyes. Her head was back and her mouth open. Tiny sounds escaped her lips as he slowly stroked, until he could feel her quiver against his fingers and finally cry out.

Withdrawing his hand, he swung her up into his arms and strode to his bedroom. He didn't want to think about later tonight when they would go up the mountain. Nor did he want to think about the future or even why he was doing this right now.

All he knew was that he wanted her more than his next breath. The only thing on his mind was making love to this woman who had captivated him from the first time he'd laid eyes on her.

Chapter Nine

Just before midnight, Lola and Colt loaded into his pickup and headed toward the SLS encampment. Colt had programmed his phone with the latest GPS information and had mapped out their best route up the mountain.

They'd both dressed in dark clothing. Lola had borrowed one of his black T-shirts. Her blond hair was pulled up under one of his black caps.

Earlier, after making love several times, they'd showered together, then sat down again with the map. His plan was to approach this like a battle.

Lola had showed him on her diagram what she thought was the best way in—and out again. The layout of the compound was star shaped, with the large main building at its center. It was where everyone ate, met for church and meetings, and where Jonas had his office.

From it, the other buildings formed the points of a star. At the top was Jonas's cabin, on the left center were the women's two dorms and on the right, the men's dorm. At the bottom was the laundry to the left and the health center, shop and storage building to the right.

"Once we grab Grace, someone will sound the alarm. Everyone will get a weapon and go to the edge of the property."

"The SLS is sounding less and less like a church by the moment," Colt had said.

"If the intruder or escapee is caught, a second signal will sound announcing the all clear," she'd said.

Colt had studied her for a moment. He couldn't help thinking of her earlier, naked in his arms. He wondered if he could ever get enough of this woman. "You're sure about this?"

She'd smiled, nodding. She really did have an amazing smile. "Whichever one of us has Grace gets out if the alarm goes off. Whoever doesn't have her distracts the guards to give them a chance to escape."

"Who will have Grace?" he'd asked.

"I guess it will depend on who finds her first. Once we approach the housing part, someone is bound to see us."

Colt would have preferred a more comprehensive plan. "You must have some idea where they are keeping Grace."

"Normally, she would be in the second women's dorm where the other babies are kept," she'd said. "But Jonas will know that I haven't given up. He might have ordered that Grace be kept in the other women's dorm."

"Where were they keeping you before you escaped?"

She'd drawn in a tiny box. "That's the cabin. It serves as the jail."

"And you could hear Grace crying when they came to pump your breast milk?" She'd nodded. "You're thinking they had our baby in this dorm, the farthest one to the west and closest to the cabin where you were being kept. I'll take that one, then head east to the second women's dorm if I don't see you. They won't expect us to come in from different directions."

"We'll meet up there. Or if the alarm goes off, just try to meet back at the pickup"

Now, as the road climbed up the mountain, he looked over at Lola. She appeared calm. Her expression was one of determination. She was going after her baby. *Their* baby. Her last thought was her own safety.

His heart ached at the thought of their lovemaking. He couldn't let anything happen to this woman. Grace needed her. He needed her, he thought and pushed the thought away. What he needed was to get himself, Lola and their baby out of that compound alive tonight. Later he'd think about what he needed, what he wanted, what the hell he was going to do once Lola and Grace were safe.

The night was thankfully dark. Low clouds hunkered just over the tops of the tall ebony pines. No stars, let alone the moon, shone through. Colt thought they couldn't have picked a better night.

Still, he was anxious. So much was riding on this and he felt they were going in blind. What he did know had him both worried and scared. If Jonas or any of his followers caught them…

He couldn't let himself go down that trail of thought. If they wanted to get Grace out of there, they had no choice but to sneak in like thieves, find her and take her. Isn't that what Jonas had done?

LOLA HAD BEEN lost in thought when Colt pulled the pickup over, cut the engine and doused the lights. She'd been thinking about the ocean and the time she'd almost drowned.

Her father had saved her, plucking her from the depths and carrying her to the beach. She remembered lying on the warm sand staring up at the sky and gasping for breath as her father wept in relief over her.

She had no idea why that particular memory had surfaced now. Anything to keep her mind off what was about to happen once they reached the compound. She'd learned to let her mind wander during Jonas's attempts to brainwash her. She would think of anything but what was happening—just like now.

With the headlights off, they were pitched into blackness. She listened to the tick, tick, tick of the cooling engine, her heart a hammer in her chest.

"You ready?" he asked, his voice low and soft.

She nodded and locked gazes with him. Colt looked as if there was something he wanted to say. She'd seen that same look earlier after they'd made love.

Earlier, she'd put a finger to his lips. She hadn't wanted him to say the words that he thought he needed to say. Colt was an honorable man, but she couldn't let him say things that he'd later regret. Nor had she been able to bear the thought of him pouring his soul out to her at that moment. Just as now.

There was too much riding on what they were about to do. Emotions were high and had been since she'd appeared at his door in the middle of the night. There was no need to say anything then or now, though she understood his need. She too wanted to open her heart to him because both of them knew how dangerous this mission was. Neither of them might get out of this alive.

Just as he started to speak, she opened her door and stepped into the darkness. She gulped the cold springnight air and fought her fear for Colt and their daughter, a gut-wrenching fear that made her eyes burn with tears.

COLT SAT FOR a moment alone in the cab of the dark

pickup. What had he been about to say? He shook his head. Lola had cut him off—just as she had earlier.

He sighed, wondering at this woman.

Then he got out, and the two of them headed through the dark pines for the hike to the compound.

They moved as silently as they could once their eyes adjusted to the darkness under the towering pines. A breeze stirred the boughs high above them, making the pines sigh.

Colt led the way until they were almost to the SLS property. The whole time, he'd been acutely aware of Lola behind him.

Now he stopped and motioned her forward. They stood inches apart for a long moment, listening.

Lola had suggested entering the property on the opposite side of the cemetery and the farthest away from any main road up to the mountaintop.

The main road was gated, so Jonas wouldn't be expecting them to come that way. That was also the most visible, so they'd opted for this approach.

But now it was time to separate. Colt could feel the tension in the air, as well as the tension between them. Lola had made it clear that she didn't want any words of undying love. But, after everything they'd shared, he felt the need to say something, do something.

He drew her close, looked into her violet eyes and kissed her.

"What was that?" she demanded in a whisper. "It felt like a goodbye kiss."

He shook his head and leaned close to whisper, "A promise to see you soon." As he drew back, he saw her smile. "Good luck," he whispered, and turned and headed in the opposite direction, his heart in his throat. If things didn't go well, he didn't want his last memory to be of her standing in the darkness, looking up at him with those big blue eyes and him not doing a damned thing.

Now he thought of her slightly gap-toothed smile and held it close to his heart for luck. Ahead he saw the no-trespassing sign and knew a guard wasn't far away.

LOLA TOUCHED HER TONGUE to her lower lip as she made her way through the pines. Just the thought of Colt's kiss made her heart beat a little faster. If she'd been falling for him before that moment, well, she'd just fallen a little further. She warned herself that this wasn't any way to go into a relationship.

Her mother would have called it "going in the back door." Maxine would not have approved of Lola having a baby out of wedlock when she could have married Jonas and given Grace a father.

But Grace did have a father. A fine father. Lola just didn't see them becoming a family. She shook the thought from her head and tried to concentrate. Getting Grace back, that was all that mattered.

She hadn't gone far when she saw a faint light bobbing through the trees ahead of her.

Ducking down, she watched as Elmer made his way along the edge of the property. She waited until he was well past her before she rose and sneaked onto the compound. The only lights were the ones outside the buildings that illuminated parts of the grounds.

Lola edged along the pines until she reached the edge of the men's dorm. Only one light shone at the front. She moved cautiously along the back, keeping to the dark shadows next to the building and being careful not to step on anything that might make a sound.

She had no desire to wake anyone, though she

thought the men's dorm was probably fairly empty. All of the men would be on guard duty tonight and maybe even some of the women.

Elmer would be turning back soon on his guard circuit. If she hurried, she should be able to reach the closest women's dorm and slip inside the nursery before he started back this way.

Before the first time she'd escaped, she'd had the run of the place, including the one women's dorm, where she'd stayed with the sisters. She'd even helped with the babies a few times. Because of that, she knew where to find the main nursery.

"If I find her first, how will I know her?" Colt had asked.

She'd smiled and said, "You'll know her and she'll know you."

"No, seriously."

"There were two babies born in the past six months that I know of. The boy we saw in the laundry and Grace."

At the end of the men's dorm, Lola stopped to listen. She heard nothing on the breeze. The distance between her and the women's dorms was a good dozen yards— all of them in the glow of the men's dorm light.

She looked for any movement in the darkness beyond. Seeing none, she sprinted the distance and dropped back into the shadows. Her heart pounded as she waited to see if she'd been spotted by one of the guards. The only one she'd seen was Elmer, but she knew there were others stationed around the compound, more than usual, just as she'd told Colt.

As she caught her breath, she thought of Colt and wondered where he was. Saying a silent prayer for his safety, she crept along the edge of the building to the door to the main nursery and grasping the knob, turned it.

COLT RECOGNIZED THE guard as one he'd seen here yesterday. The man looked tired and bored as he moved along the edge of the property and fiddled with the handgun holstered at his hip.

The guard had only gone a few feet when he stepped into the shadows and suddenly drew his weapon like an Old West gunfighter. He took the stance for a moment, pointing the gun into the darkness ahead of him and then holstered his weapon again as he moved on to practice his fast draw a few yards later.

Colt had been startled for a moment when the guard had suddenly drawn his weapon. He'd been more than a little relieved to see that the man's gun was pointing only at some imaginary person in the dark.

He slipped behind the man, closing the distance from the dense pines to the edge of the closest women's dorm. Stopping to listen, he heard a sound that froze him in place.

A low growl followed by another. This part of the country had its share of bear from black bear to grizzly. But the low growling sound he'd just heard wasn't coming from the darkness, he realized. Instead, it floated out of the open window on the back side of the women's dorm. Someone was snoring loudly.

It gave him good cover as he moved cautiously along the dark side of the building. Only a dim light shone inside. Staying as far back as possible, he peered in. The large room was filled with bunk beds like a military barrack. He recognized the woman in the closest lower bunk. Sister Alexa, a woman Colt had met in passing the day Jonas gave him the tour.

She let out a snort and stirred. He saw her eyes flicker and he froze. She blinked for a moment before her eyes fluttered shut and her snoring resumed.

Colt ducked away from the window and made his way down to the end that Lola said could house a second nursery. The outside light high over the front door of the main building cast a circle of golden light.

He watched from the dark shadows at the edge of the light. He'd only seen two guards so far, one on the way in and another crossing the complex, before he'd made his way to the far end of the building where he would find the nursery.

From where he stood, he could see toward the cemetery where Lola's parents were buried. He wondered about the small mound of fresh dirt next to them. Was something buried under there?

Jonas seemed like a man who didn't take chances. At the very least, he would have buried a small wooden casket. Colt remembered seeing the shop on his tour of the complex. Followers made wooden crosses in the shop that they sold when they went into town to raise money for the poor, Lola had told him. She said she doubted the poor ever saw a dime of it.

"I think it's Jonas's way of keeping them busy and making a little extra cash. The crosses are crude, but I think people feel sorry for the followers and give them money."

He thought now about the small casket he'd seen in one corner of the shop during his tour and swallowed hard. What if Jonas had filled the casket under that mound of dirt since their visit?

The thought made his stomach roil. He pressed his back against the side of the women's dorm and waited for the guard he'd seen earlier to cross again.

From inside the women's dorm, he heard a baby begin to cry. His heart lodged in his throat. Grace?

LOLA TURNED THE knob slowly. The door creaked open an inch, then another. A small night-light shone from one corner of the room, illuminating four small cribs. In one of the cribs, a baby whimpered.

She looked toward the doorway into the sleeping room with its bunk beds. She could hear someone snoring softly, heard the rustle of covers and then silence.

Her heart pounded as she slipped through the door and into the nursery. The first two cribs were empty. She moved to the third one. The baby in it was small. A newborn. Sister Caroline's baby, she realized. Caroline had been due when Lola had run away from the compound that night.

She stepped to the last crib, looked down at the sleeping baby and felt her heart begin to pound.

COLT STOOD AGAINST the wall in the darkness outside the nursery. Inside, he heard the sound of footfalls as someone awakened in the dorm and headed for the nursery.

A few moments later, he heard a woman talking soothingly. The baby quit crying. He could hear the woman humming a tune to the child, but he didn't recognize the song.

Then again, he knew no children's songs. He tried to imagine himself getting up in the middle of the night to calm his crying infant and couldn't. It was so far from what he'd been doing for the last eleven years.

What kind of father would he make when he didn't even know a song he could sing a child? Or could even imagine himself doing something like that? In all his years he'd never held a baby. He'd be afraid he would drop it with his big clumsy hands.

He could see the woman's shadow as she'd come into the room and now watched her swaying with the infant in her arms, singing softly, willing the baby back to sleep. Was the baby Grace?

He waited, staying to the dark shadow of the building as, in the distance, he saw the guard come back from making his rounds. The man was headed for the men's dorm. Change of shift? He hadn't anticipated that and realized he should have.

Where he was standing, the man would have to pass right by him. Colt had no chance of going undetected. Nor could he move away from the building without being seen.

Inside the nursery, he saw the shadow of the woman move. The singing continued as she seemed to lay the infant back into its crib. The man was getting closer now. His head was down. He looked tired, bored, ready to call it a night.

Where was his replacement? For all Colt knew, there could be another guard headed from the opposite direction.

He realized the music had stopped inside the nursery. Reaching over, he tried the door. The knob turned in his hand.

He had no choice. He could stay where he was and be seen by the guard, or he could chance slipping into the nursery and coming face-to-face with the woman tending the baby.

He slipped into the nursery to find it empty except for four cribs lined up against one wall. As the door closed behind him, he heard voices outside. Two men. And then silence.

Colt waited a few more seconds before he approached the cribs and saw that all but one of the cribs was empty.

He moved quietly to the crib being used and looked down at the sleeping baby. The infant lay on its back, eyes closed. He carefully reached in and pulled up the homemade shift the baby wore.

FOR A MOMENT, Lola couldn't move or breathe. Her heart swelled to bursting as she looked down at the precious sleeping baby. She would have recognized her baby anywhere, but still, with trembling fingers, she lifted the hem of the infant's gown.

There on Grace's chubby little left thigh was the tiny heart-shaped birthmark. A sob rose in her throat. She desperately wanted to lift her daughter from the crib. For so long she'd yearned to hold her baby in her arms.

She tried to get control of her emotions, knowing that once she picked up Grace, she would have to move fast. With luck, Grace wouldn't cry. But being startled out of sleep she might, and it would set off an alarm that would awaken the women in the dorm, if not the whole complex.

Lola wiped at the warm tears on her cheeks as she stared at her daughter. Grace was beautiful, from her tiny bow-shaped mouth to her chubby cheeks. As if sensing her standing over the crib, Grace's eyes fluttered and she kicked with both legs.

Lola grabbed two of the baby blankets stacked next to the cribs. Reaching down, she hurriedly lifted her daughter. Grace started, her eyes coming wide-open in alarm.

Quickly wrapping her infant in the blankets, Lola turned toward the door and felt a hand drop to her shoulder.

Chapter Ten

Lola had been in midstep when the hand dropped to her shoulder. The fingers tightened, forcing her to stop. She turned, terrified of who she would find standing behind her.

Sister Amelia put a finger to her lips before Lola could speak. Their gazes locked for what seemed an eternity. Neither looked away until Grace stirred in Lola's arms.

"Go," Amelia whispered, and pushed her toward the door. From back in the dorm came the sound of footfalls. "Go!"

Lola stumbled out the door, Grace wrapped in a blanket and clutched to her chest. Behind her, she heard Sister Amelia say something to the woman who'd awakened. Then the door closed behind her and she was standing out in the dark of the building.

Run! The thought rippled through her, igniting her fight-or-flight impulse. She had Grace. If she could get her off the compound…

From the dark, she heard a sound. A whisper of movement. A dark shadow emerged and she saw it was one of the guards. She recognized him by the arrogant way he moved. Brother Zack. She'd seen the way the former military man looked at her when he thought no one was watching. She'd heard that he'd been drummed out of the service but could only guess for what. He'd struck fear in her the nights when she knew he was the guard working outside the cabin where she was being held.

If Sister Rebecca hadn't been in charge of her "rehabilitation" and had sisters coming every hour or so to chant over her, Lola feared what Brother Zack might have done.

Now she watched him move through the darkness, her heart in her throat. Had he seen her? He appeared to be headed right for her. From inside the baby blankets, Grace whimpered.

COLT CHECKED THE BABY. No heart-shaped birthmark on either chubby leg. The moment he lifted the thin gown, the baby began to kick. Its eyes came open. Colt froze, afraid to breathe. The baby's gaze became more unfocused. Its eyes slowly closed.

He took a breath and let it out slowly. Grace wasn't here. He stepped toward the door. The floor creaked under his boot. He froze again, listening. With a glance over his shoulder, he stepped to the door, pushed it open a few inches and slipped outside.

The dark night felt like a shroud over the complex. Only circles of golden light from the outside lamps illuminated a few spots around the complex. He waited for his eyes to adjust, keeping himself tucked back against the shadow of the building. Nothing seemed to move but the pine boughs in the breeze.

Off in the distance, an owl hooted, then the night fell silent again. He had no idea how long he'd been inside the nursery or where the guards might be now.

On the way in, he'd thought they'd been changing shifts. That meant the new ones might be more alert, having just started. He thought of Lola. She'd gone to the other women's dorm. Had she found Grace?

His fear was that Jonas would want the baby closer to him, knowing Lola wouldn't give up. But wouldn't he want one of the sisters watching over her? Jonas didn't seem like a hands-on father figure. Colt wondered if he, himself, was. He could only hope that Lola had already found Grace.

He looked around, but saw no one. It appeared that most of the guards were out by the cemetery. Jonas had thought Lola would try to get evidence to take to the sheriff. He had thought no one believed her—not even Colt. Maybe especially Colt.

He spotted one of the guards moving slowly through the pines out on the perimeter. He wanted desperately to go look for Lola, but they'd agreed that the best plan would be for them to meet at the pickup. That way if one of them was caught, the other could go for help rather than walk into a trap that would snare them both.

As soon as the guard was out of sight, Colt crossed between the buildings and worked his way along the dark side of the second women's dorm.

He reached the end of the building and looked to the expanse of open land he would have to cross to reach the dark safety of the pines.

As he started to take a step, he heard a sound behind him and spun around to come face-to-face with Lola. One glance at her expression told him that the bundle in her arms was Grace.

She took a step toward him, smiling, tears in her eyes, and suddenly the night came alive with the shrill scream of an alarm.

LOLA FELT GRACE start at the horrible sound. From inside the blankets, the baby began to cry. Lola tore the blankets from the crying baby and thrust Grace's wriggling small body at Colt. "Take her and go!" she cried. "Go! I'll distract them." She could see that he wanted to argue. "Please."

He grabbed the now-screaming baby and, turning toward the pines, ran.

Lola felt a fist close on her heart as she looked down at the empty blanket in her hand. She didn't have time for regrets. She'd gotten to see her daughter, hold her for a few priceless minutes, but now she had to move, and she knew the best way to make the alarm stop.

Grabbing up several large stones lying along the side of the building's foundation, she quickly wrapped them in the baby blankets, then hugged the bundle against her chest. It wouldn't fool anyone who got too close, but it might work long enough to get her where she needed to go.

Turning, she hurried back toward the center of the compound. She desperately needed to distract the guards and give Colt a chance to escape with Grace.

SLS members poured out of the dorms in their night-wear. She half ran toward Jonas's cabin, screaming at the top of her lungs. Guards came running from all directions.

Zack saw her and charged her. He would have taken her down, but Jonas had come out of his cabin. Seeing what was happening, he shut off the alarm with his cell phone.

"Leave her alone, Brother Zack!" he yelled down. "Don't hurt the baby."

Zack stopped just inches from her. She could see his disappointment. He hadn't cared if he hurt the baby. He had been looking forward to getting his hands on her.

"Bring her to me," Jonas ordered.

Zack reached for her, but she jerked back her arm.

One of the rocks shifted and she had to grip her bundle harder.

"Never mind, Brother Zack," Jonas called down. "Lola, I know you don't want to hurt the baby. Come up to my cabin. I promise I won't hurt you or the child."

As if she believed a word out of his mouth. But she walked slowly up the hill, holding the bundle of rocks protectively against her breast.

She listened to make sure that none of the guards had stumbled across Colt and Grace. But there'd been no more activity at the edge of the complex, no shouts, no gunshots. Jonas had sounded the all clear siren. His followers were slowly wandering back to either their beds or their guard duty.

Before she reached the steps to the cabin, Jonas told Zack to leave only a few guards on duty. The rest, he said, could go to bed for what was left of the night.

Clearly he thought that the danger was over and that Lola had acted alone.

She stopped at the bottom of the porch steps and looked up at Jonas. He had a self-satisfied look on his face. He thought he'd won. He thought he had her and he had Grace.

"How did you get here?" Jonas asked suddenly, looking past her.

"I stole his pickup."

"Colt McCloud's? I thought he was your hero?" he mocked.

"Some hero," she said. "But that doesn't surprise you, does it? You knew he'd believe you and not me."

Jonas almost looked sorry for her. "The man's a fool."

She hugged the bundle tighter.

"You should come in. It's cold out here," he said. "Is the baby all right?"

She knew he had to be wondering how Grace had been able to sleep through all of the racket. He had to be getting suspicious.

"She is so sweet," Lola said, glancing down for a moment to peel back of the edge of the blanket so only she could see what was inside. She smiled down at the rock. "She really is an angel." She wanted to give Colt as much time as possible to get away with Grace, but she knew she couldn't keep standing out here or Jonas was going to become suspicious.

"As I've said all along," he agreed as she mounted the steps. He reached for the baby, but she turned to the side, holding the bundle away from him.

"Please, let me hold her just a little longer." Tears filled her eyes at just the thought of the few minutes she'd had Grace in her arms and the thought that they might be all she was going to get.

Jonas relented. "Of course, hold her all you want. There is no reason you should be separated from your child. If you stay here, you will have her all the time. Imagine what your life could be like here with me."

"I have." She hoped she kept the sarcasm out of the voice as she moved to the middle of the room, giving herself a little elbow room.

"We could travel. Europe, the Caribbean, anywhere your heart desired. We could take Angel with us."

"Her name is Grace."

He ignored that as he started to close the door. He froze and cocked his head, taking in the bundle in her arms again. "It really is amazing she slept through all of that noise," he said again.

"She knows she's with her mother now. She knows she's safe."

Jonas looked out the still-open doorway as if suddenly not so sure about being alone with her. She saw Zack watching them.

Lola knew she had no choice. Zack was watching, expecting trouble, and Jonas was getting suspicious. She had no choice.

"Europe? I love Europe," she said, and saw Jonas relax a little. He waved Zack away and closed the door. She looked around, remembering the last time she'd been brought here. Jonas had told her that he would make her his wife—one way or another. He'd tried to kiss her and she'd kicked him hard enough in the shin to get away and, apparently, given him a permanent limp.

Behind her, she heard him lock the door and limp toward her.

Chapter Eleven

Colt reached the pickup. All the way, he'd hoped that he would find Lola waiting for him even though he knew there was little chance of that.

Still, he was disappointed when he got there to find he was alone. Grace had quit crying not long after they'd left the compound. He was grateful for that since he was sure it had helped him get away.

He opened the passenger-side door, the dome light coming on as he laid the bundle Lola had given him on the seat to get his first look at his daughter.

A pair of big blue eyes stared up at him. He lost his heart in that moment. He touched the perfect little cheek, soft as downy feathers. She did resemble Lola, but he thought he could see himself a little in her, too.

"Hi, Grace," he whispered, his voice breaking. Tears welled in his eyes. He swallowed the lump in this throat. He had the baby, but what now?

He turned off the dome light, realizing that if someone had followed him, they would be able to see him through the pines. He stared into the darkness, willing Lola to appear.

He had to assume that Jonas had her by now. He'd heard the alarm go off and then another signal, which he'd assumed must be the all clear. Why would Jonas sound it unless he'd thought there was nothing more to fear?

Which meant he had Lola. She'd sacrificed herself to save her daughter. Their daughter.

He looked toward the dark trees, silently pleading for that not to be the case. He needed her. Grace needed her.

They had Lola. He couldn't leave without her. But he couldn't go back for her with the baby for fear of getting caught.

Nor could he stay there much longer. If Jonas suspected she hadn't come alone…

"What are we going to do, Grace?" he asked as he wrapped her in his coat and watched her fall back to sleep.

WITH HER BACK to Jonas, Lola reached into the baby blanket with her free hand and slowly turned to face him.

"What really happened to my parents?"

He had been moving toward her but stopped. "They were getting old, confused toward the end. Your mother came down with the flu. It turned into pneumonia. Your father stayed by her side. She was getting better and then she just…died."

She nodded, knowing that it happened at her mother's age, and not believing a word of it. "And my father?"

"I think he died of grief. You had to know how he was with your mother. I don't think he could live without her."

That too happened with people her parents' age who had been married as long as they had. "You didn't have them killed?" She said it softly so he wouldn't think it was an accusation. It wasn't like she expected the truth.

"Lola." There was that disappointing sound in his voice again. He took a step toward her. "Why must you always think the worst of me? Your parents believed in me."

Well, at least her mother had—until he'd had her killed, Lola thought. She wondered if he'd done it himself and realized how silly that was. Of course, he hadn't. Her heart went out to her parents. She couldn't bear thinking about their last moments.

"I took care of your baby for you. I wouldn't hurt a hair on that sweet thing's head. Or on yours. Let me see her." He was close now, and she feared he would make a grab for the baby.

She loosened her hold on the baby blanket bundle a little and faced him, her hand closing tightly around the rock inside.

"Thank you for taking care of her," she said, letting her voice fill with emotion.

"I will take care of you, too—if you give me a chance." He was getting too near—within reaching distance.

She took a step toward him, closing the distance between them as she pretended to hold out the baby for him to take. She had to be close. She had to make it count. It was her only hope of getting out of here and being with Grace.

As Jonas opened his arms for the baby, she pulled out the rock and swung it at his head. He managed to deflect the blow partially with his hand—just enough to knock the rock from her hold.

But she'd swung hard enough that the rock kept going. It caught him in the temple. He stumbled back. She pulled out the second rock, dropping the baby blankets, as she swung again.

This time, he didn't get a chance to raise an arm.

The rock connected with the side of his head. His blood splattered on the rock, on her hand. He stood for a moment, looking stunned, then he went down hard on the wood floor.

Lola didn't waste any time. For all she knew he could be out cold—or only momentarily stunned and soon sounding the alarm so the whole cult would be on her heels.

She ran just as she had before. Only this time, she wasn't leaving her baby behind.

COLT HAD NEVER had trouble making a decision under duress. He'd been forced to make quick ones flying a chopper in Afghanistan. But one thing he'd never done was leave a man behind.

He couldn't this time, either. He'd purposely not taken a weapon into the compound earlier. They'd needed to get Grace out clean, and that meant not killing anyone—even if it meant getting themselves killed.

Now he took the weapons he would need. He was changing the rules—just as he was sure Jonas was. Wrapped in his coat, he laid Grace down on the floorboard of the pickup. She would be plenty warm enough—as long as he came back in a reasonable amount of time.

Locking the pickup door, he turned back toward the woods and the SLS compound. He wasn't leaving without Lola. And this time, he was armed and ready to fight his way in and out of the place if he had to.

LOLA FELT A sense of déjà vu as she ran through the woods. Her pulse hammered in her ears, her breath coming out in gasps. And yet she listened for the sound of the alarm that would alert the SLS members to fill the woods. Jonas would not let her get away if he had to run her to ground himself.

If he was able.

She had no idea how badly he'd been hurt. Or if he was already hot on her heels.

She crashed through the darkness, shoving away pine boughs that whipped her face and body. Colt had said how important it was for them get in and out of the compound without causing any more harm than was necessary.

"We're the trespassers," he'd told her. "We're the ones who will get thrown in jail if we fail tonight. We need to get in there and out as clean as possible."

She thought about the blood on the rock and could see something staining her right hand as she ran. Jonas's blood. She hadn't gotten out clean. She might have killed him. A cry escaped her lips as her ankle turned under her and she fell hard.

She struggled to get up as she hurriedly wiped the blood on the dried pine needles she'd fallen into. But the moment she put pressure on her ankle, she knew she wasn't going far. She didn't think it was broken, but she also couldn't put any weight on it without excruciating pain.

Grace. Colt. She had to get to them. They would have left by now, but she couldn't stay here. She couldn't let Jonas or one of his sheep find her. If Jonas was still alive. The thought that she might have killed him made her shudder. It had been one thing to wish him dead, to think she could kill him to save her daughter, but to actually know that she might have killed the man…

She crawled over to a pine tree and used the trunk to get to her feet. As she started to take a step, she saw a figure suddenly appear out of the blackness of the trees.

Lola felt a sob rise in her throat. She'd never been so glad to see anyone in her life. Colt. He seemed just as overwhelmed with joy to see her. She'd thought he would have left—as per their plan. But he couldn't leave her.

Another sob rose as he ran to her, grabbed her and pulled her to him, holding her so tightly she could hardly breath. "Lola," he kept saying against her hair. "Lola."

She couldn't speak. Her throat had closed as she fought to hold back the tears of relief. As he let go, she stepped down on her bad ankle and let out a cry of pain.

"You're hurt. What is it?" he asked, his voice filled with concern.

"My ankle. I'm not sure I can walk."

He swung her up in his arms and carried her through the trees to the truck. She hadn't realized how close she was to where they'd parked it earlier.

She looked around, suddenly scared. "Grace? Where's Grace?"

He unlocked the passenger side of the pickup, opened the door and picked up a bundle wrapped in his coat. She heard a sound come from within the bundle as Colt helped her into the pickup and put Grace into her arms. The tears came now, a floodgate opening. No longer could she hold back.

Tears streaming down her face, she turned back the edge of Colt's coat, which was wrapped around the infant. "Grace," she said as Colt slid behind the wheel, started the truck and headed off the mountain.

Lola held her baby, watching her daughter's sweet face in the faint light as Grace fell back asleep. She thought she could stare into that face forever. For so long she'd feared she'd never see her again, never hold her. She wiped at her tears and looked over at Colt. He smiled and she could see the emotion in his face.

"Have you met your daughter?" she asked.

"I have," he said, his voice sounding rough. "We got acquainted while we were waiting for you, until I couldn't wait any longer and had to come looking for you."

"I'm so thankful you did."

"Let's go home," he said, his voice breaking.

Tears filled her eyes again as she looked from him to their daughter. She pulled Grace close as they left the mountain and headed toward the ranch. Home.

Chapter Twelve

Jonas came to, lying on his back in a pool of his own blood. His hand went to the side of his head and came away sticky. He stared for a few moments at his fingers, the tips bright red, before he tried to sit up.

His head swam, forcing him to remain where he was. He couldn't remember what had happened. Had he fallen? He'd been meaning to have one of the brothers fix that rug to keep the corner from turning up.

But from where he lay, he could see that the rug wasn't to blame. Not twelve inches from him sat a rock the size of a cantaloupe. A dark stain covered one side of it. Nearby was a baby blanket and another rock of similar size.

Memory flooded him along with a cold, deadly rage. The pain in his skull was nothing compared to the open wound of Lola's betrayal. His heart felt as if it had been ripped out of his chest.

He thought of those moments when she'd been holding what he thought was her infant in her arms. They'd been talking and she had made it sound as if she was weakening toward him. His heart had soared with hope that she was finally coming around. He had so much to offer her. Had she finally realized that she'd be a fool to turn him down?

He'd been so happy for those moments when he'd thought things were going to work out with her and even the baby. That other man's baby, but a baby Jonas was willing to raise as his own as long as Lola became his wife and submitted to him.

The shock when she'd pulled the rock from the baby blankets was still painfully fresh. It had taken him a moment, his arms outstretched as he'd reached to take her and the infant to his bosom. The shock, the disappointment, the disbelief had slowed his movements, letting the rock get past his defenses and stun him just long enough that she was able to pull out the second rock and hit him much harder.

He closed his eyes now. He was in so much pain, but a thought wriggled its way through. His eyelids flew open. His mind felt perfectly clear, making him aware of the quiet. He recalled the alert alarm going off. When Lola had come to him with the baby... Yes, he recalled. He'd sounded the all clear signal.

Why hadn't there been another alert? He had to assume that Lola had gotten away. Gotten away with the baby. If she'd been caught, she would have been brought to him by now. And if Sister Rebecca had checked the crib and found the baby missing...

For a moment, he thought the alarm must have sounded while he'd been unconscious. But if that was true, then Brother Zack would have come to check on him and found him lying here, bleeding to death.

Two things suddenly became crystal clear. Even through the excruciating pain, he saw now that Lola couldn't have acted alone. She would have had help to get the baby off the compound. And her showing up at his door with what he thought was the baby was only a diversion.

He let out a bitter laugh. As persuasive as he'd been, it was just as he'd feared. He hadn't convinced Colt Mc-Cloud that the woman was unbalanced, that their baby boy had died, that he should leave Lola while he could.

Apparently, she'd been more convincing than he had been. He grimaced at the thought. Admittedly, he had to give her credit—her plan had worked. Or had it been Colt McCloud's plan? He closed his eyes, cursing the man to hell. Colt was a dead man.

But so was he, he realized, if he didn't get help. He was still bleeding and even more light-headed. He felt around for his cell phone to activate the alarm.

He had to turn his head to find it. The pain was so intense that he almost passed out. He closed his hand around the phone and, leaving bloody fingerprints, hit the button to activate the alarm.

His hand holding the phone dropped to his side as the air filled with the shrill cry of the alert. Any moment Brother Zack would come bursting through the door. He could always depend on Zack.

Unlike someone else, he thought, remembering his second realization. If he was right, Colt had taken the baby while Lola had pretended to be acting alone. The alarm had sounded and she had known that she couldn't get away. So she'd come up to Jonas's cabin with the rocks in the baby blankets.

But wouldn't someone have checked the baby's crib? And then wouldn't Sister Rebecca, who was responsible for the infant, have realized the baby was gone and summoned help? Pulled the alarm again?

As Brother Zack burst through the front door and rushed to him, Jonas felt the steel blade of betrayal cut even deeper. One of his flock had betrayed him.

Chapter Thirteen

Colt woke to find Lola and the baby sleeping peacefully next to him. He felt his heart do a bump in his chest. The sight filled him with a sense of joy. A sense that all was right in the world.

Last night on the way down the mountain he'd felt like they were a family. It was a strange feeling for a man who'd been so independent for so long. They'd been exhausted, Lola barely able to walk on her ankle. He'd gotten them both inside the house and safe as quickly as he could.

With Grace sleeping in the middle of his big bed, he'd taken a look at Lola's ankle. Not broken, but definitely sprained badly. He'd wrapped it, both of them simply looking at each other and smiling. They'd done it. They'd gotten Grace back.

He had questions, but they could wait. Or maybe he never had to know what had happened back at the compound. He told himself it was over. They had Grace. That was all the proof they needed against Jonas should he try to take either the baby or Lola back.

They'd gone to bed, Grace curled between them, and fallen asleep instantly.

At the sound of a vehicle, Colt wondered who would

be coming by so early in the morning as he slipped out of bed and quickly dressed.

Someone was knocking at his front door by the time he reached it. He peered out, worried for a moment that he'd find Jonas Emanuel standing on his front step.

"Sheriff," Colt said as he opened the door.

"A moment of your time," Flint said.

Colt stepped back to let the sheriff enter the house. Flint glanced around, clearly looking for something.

He'd been wondering how Jonas was going to handle this. He'd thought Jonas wouldn't call in the sheriff about the events of last night. He still didn't think he would. But this was definitely not a social call.

"What can I help you with, Sheriff?"

Flint turned to give him his full attention. "Jonas reported a break-in at the SLS compound last night. I was wondering if you knew anything about that."

"Was anything taken?"

Flint smiled. "Apparently not. But Jonas was injured when he tried to apprehend one of the intruders."

That was news. Colt thought of Lola just down the hall still in bed with Grace. Last night when he was wrapping her ankle, he'd seen what looked like blood on her sleeve. But he hadn't want to ask what she'd had to go through to get away.

"He see who did it?" Colt asked.

"Apparently not," Flint said again.

Just then the sound of a baby crying could be heard down the hall toward the bedroom.

Flint froze.

"So nothing was taken," Colt said. "Jonas's injuries…"

"Aren't life-threatening at this point," Flint said as Lola limped down the hall from the bedroom, the baby in her arms.

Lola spotted the sheriff and stopped, her gaze flying to Colt. She looked worried until Colt said, "You remember Lola. And this is our daughter, Grace."

Colt moved to her to take the baby. He stepped to the sheriff, turning back the blanket his daughter was nestled in.

Every time he saw her sweet face his heart swelled to overflowing. She was so precious. Having never changed a diaper in his life, he'd learned quickly last night.

Now he lifted the cotton gown she'd been wearing when Lola had taken her from the crib last night at SLS to expose the tiny heart-shaped birthmark.

"Our baby girl," Colt said. "We'll be going to the doctor later today to have her checked over—and a DNA test done, in case you were wondering."

Flint nodded solemnly, and Colt handed Grace back to Lola. As she limped into the kitchen with the baby, the sheriff said, "I'm not going to ask, but I hope you know what you're doing."

"That little girl belongs with her mother."

The sheriff met his gaze. "And her father?"

"I'm her father."

Flint sighed. "I was at the hospital this morning taking Jonas's statement. He isn't filing assault charges because he says he doesn't know who attacked him. I see Lola is limping."

Colt said nothing.

"You sure this is over?" the sheriff asked.

"It is as far as I'm concerned."

Flint nodded. "Not sure Jonas feels that way. Got the impression he's a man who is used to getting what he wants."

Colt couldn't have agreed more. "He can't have Lola and Grace, but I don't want any trouble."

The sheriff shook his head at that. "I'm afraid it won't be your choice."

He knew a warning when he heard one. Not that he had to be told that Jonas was dangerous. "He's brainwashed those people, taken their money and keeps them up on that mountain like prisoners."

Flint nodded. "A choice each of them made."

"Except for the children up there."

"You think I like any of what I saw on that mountain?" Flint swore. "But you also know there is nothing I can do about it. That's private property up there. Jonas has every right to keep trespassers off. Not to mention it is church property, holy ground under the law."

"I have no intention of going up there."

"I wish I thought it was that simple." The sheriff had taken off his Stetson when he'd come into the house, and now he settled his hat back on his head. Turning, he started for the door. "You know my number," he said over his shoulder. "I'll come as quickly as I can. But I fear even that could be too late."

"Thanks for stopping by, Sheriff."

At the door, Flint turned to look back at him. Lola had come out of the kitchen carrying the baby. She was smiling down at Grace, cooing softly.

Flint's expression softened and Colt remembered that Darby had mentioned the sheriff's wife was pregnant. "Have a good day," Flint said, and left.

Jonas listened to the doctor tell him how lucky he was. He had a monster headache and hated being flat on his back in the hospital when he had things that needed to be done—and quickly.

"You lost a lot of blood," the doctor was saying. "If your...friend hadn't gotten you here when he did..."

"Yes, it is fortunate that Brother Zack found me when he did," Jonas said. He didn't need the doctor telling him how lucky he was. He was very aware. But a man made his own luck. He'd learned that when he'd left home to find his own way in life.

Not that he discounted what nature had given him—a handsome, honest-looking face, mesmerizing blue eyes and snake-oil-salesman charm. But he was the one who'd taken those gifts and used them to the best of his ability. Not that they always worked. Lola, a case in point. They'd worked enough, though, that he was a very rich man and, until recently, he would have said he had very loyal followers who saw to his every need. What more could a man ask for?

"You're going to have a headache for a while, but fortunately, you suffered only a minor concussion. A fall like that could have killed a man half your age. Like I said, lucky."

"Lucky," Jonas repeated. "Yes, Doctor, I was. So when can I be released?"

"Your laceration is healing quite nicely, but that bandage needs to be changed regularly so I'd prefer you stay in the hospital at least another day, maybe longer."

That was not what he wanted to hear. "One of the sisters could change my bandage for me. Really, I would be much more comfortable in my own home. I have plenty of people to look after me."

The doctor wavered. Jonas knew that the hospital staff would be much more comfortable with him gone, as well. A half dozen of the brothers and some of the SLS sisters had been coming and going since his "accident." He'd seen the way the hospital staff looked at them, the men in their black pants and white shirts, the woman in their long shapeless white dresses.

"I'd prefer you stay another day at least. I'll give instructions to one of your...sisters for after that. We'll see how you're doing tomorrow."

"I'm feeling so much better. I promise that when you release me, I will rest and take care of myself." His head ached more than he had let the doctor know. He didn't want any medication that would make his brain fuzzy. He needed his wits about him now more than ever.

"Like I said, we'll see how you are tomorrow," the doctor said, eyeing him suspiciously. The man knew Jonas couldn't be feeling that good, not with his head almost bashed in. He also knew the doctor had to be questioning how he could have hurt himself like this in a fall.

Jonas just wished he would go away and leave him alone.

"I need to ask you about these pills you've been taking," the doctor said, clearly not leaving yet. "One of your church members told me they were for a bad heart, but that's not the medication you're taking."

"No, it's not for a heart ailment," Jonas had to admit. "I'd prefer my flock not worry about my health, Doctor."

"If you're suffering from memory loss at your age, then we need to run some tests and see—"

"I have early-onset Alzheimer's," Jonas interrupted. The doctor blinked.

"It is in the beginning stages, thus the pills I'm taking. I can assure you that I'm being well taken care of."

The doctor seemed at a loss for words.

"I believe Brother Zack is waiting in the hall," Jonas said to the doctor. "Would you ask him to step in here? I need to talk to him."

Realizing he was excused, the doctor left. A few moments later, Zack stuck his head in the door.

Jonas motioned him in. "Close the door. Have you seen Sister Rebecca?"

"Not since last night."

"Who was on duty at the second nursery last night?" he asked.

Zack frowned. "Sister Alexa." His eyes widened as he realized what the leader was really asking. "Sister Rebecca was taking care of the...special baby."

The angel. That's what Jonas had told his flock. That he'd had a vision and Lola's baby was a chosen one.

"Sister Rebecca." Jonas nodded and closed his eyes for a moment. He'd known it, but had needed Zack to verify his suspicions. Rebecca had been with him since the beginning. If there was anyone he knew he could trust, could depend on, it was her. He slowly opened his eyes and stared up at the pale green ceiling.

Zack stood at the end of the bed, waiting. Rebecca and Zack had never gotten along. Jonas blamed it on simple jealousy. Both were in the top positions at SLS. He knew how much Zack was going to enjoy the task he was about to give him.

"Go back to the complex," Jonas told him. "I want Sister Rebecca—" if she was still there "—restrained. Use the cabin where Sister Lola stayed. Guard it yourself." He finally looked at Zack, who nodded, a malicious glint in his gaze even as he fought not to smile.

"I'll take care of it."

AFTER THE SHERIFF LEFT, Colt stepped to Lola and Grace and pulled them close. He knew the sheriff was worried and with good reason. Jonas was an egomaniac who enjoyed having power over other people. He ran his "church" like a fiefdom. He would be incensed to have lost Lola and the baby, but there was really nothing he could do. At least not legally. Once the DNA results came back, once they had proof that Grace was Colt's daughter...

He tried to put it out of his head. Jonas was in the hospital. He'd lied to the sheriff. It was over. Hopefully, the man would move on with some other obsession.

Colt cooked them breakfast while Lola fed Grace. He loved watching them together. It made his heart expand to near bursting.

Their day was quickly planned. First the DNA tests, then shopping for baby things. Never in his life had Colt thought about buying baby things, but now he realized he was excited. He wanted Grace to have whatever she needed.

At the doctor's office DNA samples were taken, then Colt took Lola and Grace to the small-box store on the edge of town. He was amazed at all the things a baby needed. Not just clothing and a car seat, but bottles and formula, baby food, diapers and wipes.

"How did babies survive before all of these things were on the market?" he joked, then insisted they get a changing table.

"It's too much," Lola said at one point.

"It's all good," he'd said, wanting only the best for his daughter. At the back of his mind, like a tiny devil perched on his shoulder, a voice was saying, "What are you doing? You are going back on assignment soon."

He shoved the thought aside, telling himself that he'd cross that bridge when he got there. He still had time. But time for what? There hadn't been any offers on the ranch. It was another thought that he pushed aside. Instead, he concentrated on Lola and Grace, enjoying being with them. Enjoying pretending at least for a while that they were a family.

He didn't even need the DNA test. That was all Lola. "We need it for Jonas should he ever try to take Grace again," she'd said. "Also, I don't want you to have doubts."

"I don't have any doubts."

She'd given him a dubious look. "I want it settled. Not that I will ever ask anything of you. And I will pay you back for all the baby things you bought. I called this morning and am having some money wired to me."

"That isn't necessary."

But she said nothing, a stubborn tilt to her chin. He hadn't argued.

Instead, he took them back to the Stagecoach Saloon where, the moment they walked in, he knew that Billie Dee was cooking up her famous Texas chili.

Lillie Cahill Beaumont just happened to be there visiting her brother, along with Darby and his wife, Mariah. They oohed and aahed over Grace and Lola did the same with their babies.

By the time they got home, Colt was ready for a nap, too. After Lola put Grace down, she came into the bedroom and curled up against him. He held her close, breathing in the scent of her. He'd never been more happy.

Chapter Fourteen

The next day, Jonas couldn't wait for the doctor to stop by so he could hopefully get out of the hospital. He knew that Zack was taking care of things on the complex, but he worried. He still couldn't believe that Rebecca would betray him. It shook the stable foundation that he'd built this life on. Never would he have suspected her of deceiving him.

When the doctor finally came by, he hadn't wanted to send Jonas home yet. It took a lot of lying to get the doctor to finally release him. It was late in the day before he finally got his discharge papers.

Elmer picked him up at the hospital and drove him to the compound. He liked Elmer, though he'd seen the man's faith in their work here fading. He and Lola's father had been friends. Jonas suspected Elmer only stayed because he had nowhere else to go. But that was all right. Jonas still thought that when the chips were down, he could depend on Elmer.

Once at the compound, Zack was waiting, Excusing Elmer, Jonas let Zack help him inside. He was weak and his head ached, but he was home. He had things that needed to be taken care of and had been going crazy in the hospital.

Three of the sisters entered his cabin, fussed over

him until he couldn't take it any longer and sent them scurrying. The pain in his head was better. It was another pain that was riding him like a dark cloak on his shoulders.

As soon as he was settled, Jonas asked Zack to bring him Sister Rebecca. "She's still detained in the small cabin, right?"

"She is," Zack said.

"How is her...attitude?"

"Subdued."

Jonas almost laughed since it didn't seem like a word Zack would ever have used. "Subdued? Is she on anything?"

"No, but I've had the sisters chanting over her every few hours. I thought it was something you would have done yourself had you been here."

He was both touched and annoyed by Zack taking this step without his permission. But he needed Zack more than ever now so he let it go. "You did well. Thank you."

Zack beamed and Jonas saw something in the man's eyes that gave him pause. Zack wanted to lead SLS. The man actually thought he had what it took to do it. The realization was almost laughable.

"Bring Sister Rebecca to me," he said, and closed his eyes, his head pounding like a bass drum. He wondered if he shouldn't have put this off until he was feeling better.

Zack hurried out, leaving him peacefully alone with his thoughts. Lola had made a fool out of him by sleeping with Colt McCloud. To add to his embarrassment, she'd gotten pregnant. That child should have been his.

Instead, he'd put aside his hurt, his fury, his embarrassment and offered to raise the baby as his own. Still, she'd turned him down. How could she have humiliated him even more?

He let out a bark of a laugh. What had she done? She'd almost killed him—after giving him hope that she was weakening. The latter hurt the most. Offering hope was a poisonous pill that he'd swallowed in one big gulp. And now even his flock was turning against him.

Was he losing his mind faster than he'd thought? Could he trust his judgment?

He started at the knock on the door, forgetting for a moment that he'd been expecting it. "Come in."

The moment Rebecca walked through the door, he could see the guilt written all over her face. Brother Zack stood directly behind her. He started to step into the cabin, and Jonas could tell Zack thought he was going to get to watch this.

"That will be all, Zack."

The man looked surprised and then disappointed. But it was the flicker of anger he saw in Zack's eyes that caused concern.

Jonas watched his right-hand man slowly close the door, but he could tell he'd be standing outside hoping to hear whatever was going on. Was Zack now becoming a problem, too?

He saw Sister Rebecca quickly take him in. In her gaze shone concern and something even more disturbing—sympathy, if not pity. His head was still bandaged, dark stitches under the dressing, but his headaches were getting better. Stuck in the hospital, he'd had plenty of time to think over the past two days.

It was bad enough to be betrayed by Lola, even worse by Sister Rebecca, because he'd come to depend on her. She had to have known that Lola's baby had gone missing. It would have been the first thing she would have checked. Seeing the baby missing, she should have come to him.

He was anxious to talk to her, but as he looked at her standing there, he felt a loss of words for a moment. He kept telling himself that he was wrong. Sister Rebecca had been with him for years. She wouldn't betray him. Couldn't. He'd always thought she was half in love with him.

Which was probably why she hadn't come to him to let him know the baby wasn't in her crib. Even if she'd seen Lola with that bundle in her arms entering his cabin, she should have come to him. If she had, his head wouldn't be killing him right now. But he suspected Rebecca had wanted to be shed of Lola and the baby he was so determined to make his.

Since Zack had locked up Rebecca, she would know she was in trouble. He wondered what story she would tell him and how much of it he could believe?

COLT ALMOST CHANGED his mind. Things had been going so well that he didn't want or need the interruption. He enjoyed being with Lola and Grace. If he said so himself, he'd become proficient at diaper changes and getting chubby little limbs into onesies. He liked the middle-of-the-night feedings, holding Grace and watching her take her bottle. Her bright blue eyes watched him equally.

"I'm your daddy," he'd whispered last night, and felt a lump rise in his throat.

So when Julia had called and said it was important that they meet and talk, he hadn't been interested.

"If this is about you needing me to forgive you—"

"No. It's not that," she'd said quickly. "I doubt you can ever forgive me. I know how badly I hurt you."

Did she? The news had blindsided him. Hell, he'd been expecting her to pick him up at the airport—not break up with him to be with one of his friends. He still couldn't get his head around how that had gone down. No warning at all. He'd thought Wyatt hadn't even liked Julia. He knew that Darby didn't think she was right for him. Not that Darby had ever said anything. But Colt had been able to tell.

He could laugh now. He used to think that Darby just had his expectations set too high. But then Colt had met Mariah and realized that his friend had just been holding out for the real thing. Darby had done well.

"Julia, I can't see what meeting you for coffee could possibly—" It had been Lola who'd insisted he meet with Julia. She'd walked in while he was on the phone. As if gifted with ESP, she'd motioned to him that he should go.

"Fine," he'd said into the phone. "When and where?" He had just wanted to get it over with.

Now he drove past the coffee shop, telling himself that there was nothing Julia could say that would change anything. But she'd sounded…strange on the phone. He suspected something was up. Did he care, though?

He circled the block, saw a parking space and pulled his pickup in to it. For a moment he sat behind the wheel debating what he was about to do. And why had Lola been all for him seeing his ex? Was she worried that he wasn't over Julia? Or was she hoping to hook the two of them up again?

He'd heard her on the phone calling a car dealership to order a vehicle. "You don't have to do that. You can use my pickup whenever you want."

"I need my own car, but thank you," she'd said.

He thought of the discussion they'd had after he'd hung up from Julia.

"I knew that was Julia on the phone," Lola had said. "I wasn't eavesdropping. You talk to her in a certain way." She'd shrugged.

"A certain way?"

"I can't describe it, but you owe her nothing."

"Then why should I meet with her?"

"Because it won't be over until you tell her how you feel," Lola had said.

He had laughed. She made life seem so simple, and yet could her life have been any more complicated when he'd met her? "Okay, I'll meet with her with your blessing."

"You don't need my blessing."

He stepped to her and, taking her shoulders in his hands, pulled her close. "All I care about is you and Grace. You have to know that."

"So you'll talk to her. You'll be honest. You'll see if there is anything there that you might have missed. Or that you want back."

He'd wanted to argue the point, but she'd put a finger to his lips.

"You should go. She'll be waiting."

Let her wait, he thought now as he glanced at his watch. Let her think he wasn't coming—look how she'd treated him at the Billings airport.

Then, just wanting to be done with this, he climbed out and walked down to the coffee shop. It was midafternoon. Only a few tables were taken. Julia had chosen one at the back. Where no one would see the two of them together and report back to Wyatt?

As he pushed open the door, he saw her frowning

down at her phone. Checking the time? Or reading a text from Wyatt?

She looked up as if sensing him and motioned him over. "I got you a coffee—just the way you like it."

Except he'd never liked his coffee that way. Julia had come out to the ranch when they'd first started dating with some caramel-mocha concoction. When he'd taken a sip, he'd had to force a smile and pretend he'd liked it. His mistake.

"It's good, huh. I thought you'd like it. You always have the same boring coffee. I thought we'd shake things up a bit," she'd said. And from then on, she'd decided that was the way he liked his coffee.

"Thanks," he said now, without sitting down, "But I never liked my coffee that way. I'll get my own." He moved to the counter and ordered a cup of black coffee before returning to the table.

She looked sullen, pouting like she used to when he'd displeased her—which was often enough that he knew this look too well.

"So what is it you want?" he asked as he sat down but didn't settle in. He didn't plan to stay long and was regretting coming here, no matter what Lola had said. He couldn't see how this could help anything.

Julia let out a nervous laugh. "This is not the way I saw this going."

"Oh?"

She seemed to regroup, drawing in a long breath, sitting up a little straighter. He was suddenly aware that she'd dressed up. He caught a hint of the perfume she used to wear when they were together because he'd commented one time that he liked it. He frowned as he realized she hadn't been wearing it the day they'd accidentally run into each other.

"What's going on, Julia?"

She looked away for a moment, biting down on the corner of her lower lip as if nervous. He used to think it was cute.

"I've made a terrible mistake. I didn't mean to blurt it out like that, but I can tell you're still angry and have no patience with me. Otherwise, you wouldn't have been so late, you would have drunk the coffee I ordered you and you wouldn't be looking at me as if you hated me."

He wasn't going to try to straighten her up on any of that. "Mistake?"

Julia looked at him as if she thought no one would be that daft. "Wyatt. I was just so lonely, and it looked as if you were never going to quit the military and come home…"

"How did you two get together? I always thought Wyatt didn't like you."

She mugged a face at him. "You don't need to be cruel."

"I'm serious. He never had a good word to say about you. Or was he just trying to keep his feelings for you from me?"

"I have no idea. And I don't care. He probably didn't like me. Maybe that's why we aren't together anymore."

Colt realized he wasn't surprised. Julia hadn't gotten him to the altar. He remembered that had been the case with an earlier boyfriend, too. Looked like there was a pattern there, he thought but kept it to himself.

"That's too bad."

"I can tell that you're really broken up over it."

After the initial shock had worn off, he'd actually thought Julia and Wyatt wouldn't last. Julia was beautiful in a classic way, but definitely high maintenance. He could see that clearly after being around Lola. As for Wyatt, well, he'd never had a serious girlfriend. He'd always preferred playing the field, as he called it.

"I'm sincerely sorry it didn't work out. Is that all?"

"Colt, stop being so mean." She sounded close to tears. She glanced around to make sure no one had heard her. "I feel so bad about what I did to you."

"You shouldn't." He realized he meant it. For a while, he'd hoped she choked on the guilt daily. Now he didn't feel vindictive. He realized he no longer cared.

"I know how hurt you must be."

"I was hurt, Julia. That was one crushing blow you delivered, but I've moved on."

"With that woman you were with the other day? Are you in love with her?"

Now there was the question, wasn't it? "It's complicated."

"It doesn't have to be." She reached across the table and covered his hand.

He pulled his free. "Are you suggesting what I think you are?"

She looked at him as if to say, *No one can be this dense.* "I want you back. I'll do anything." She definitely sounded desperate.

Colt had played with this exact scheme in his mind on those long nights in the desert after she'd dumped him. It had been like a salve that made him feel better. Julia begging to come back to him. Him loving every minute of it before he turned her down flat.

Now it made him feel uncomfortable because he no longer wanted to hurt her. If anything, he felt indifferent and wondered what he'd ever seen in this woman. He couldn't help comparing her to Lola. Julia came up way short.

"Julia, you and I are never getting back together. Truthfully, I doubt we would have made it to the altar."

"How can you say that?" she demanded. "You asked me to marry you."

"I did. But I didn't realize then how wrong we were for each other. I overlooked things, thinking they would change once we were married. Now I know better. I'm sure it was the same for you. Otherwise, how could you have fallen so quickly in love with another man?"

She seemed at a loss for words.

"So I imagine we both would have realized we weren't right for each other before we made a huge mistake."

Julia stared at him as if looking at a stranger. "I don't believe this."

Had she expected him to take her back at the snap of her fingers? The flutter of her eyelashes? She really hadn't known him. Even if he'd never met Lola, he wouldn't have taken Julia back. She'd proved the kind of woman she was—not the kind a man could ever trust.

Colt got to his feet. "You should try to work things out with Wyatt. Now that I think about it, you two belong together."

Her eyes widened, then narrowed dangerously. "Do you realize what you're throwing away? And for what? That…that…woman I saw you with the other day?" She made a distasteful face.

"Easy, Julia," he said, lowering his voice. "You really don't want to say anything about the mother of my child."

"What?" she sputtered.

"Lola and I have a beautiful daughter together."

Openmouthed, she stared at him. "Lola? That's not

possible. You can't have known her long enough to... Are you going to *marry* her?"

"I haven't asked her yet, but you know me. I like to take my time. Also, I'm a little gun-shy after my last engagement."

Julia pushed to her feet. He'd never seen her so angry. It made him want to laugh because he realized, with no small amount of relief, that had he married her, he would have seen her like this a lot.

The one thing he did know was that he was completely over her. No hard feelings. No need for retribution. No need to ever see this woman again.

"This never happened," she said with a flip of her head. "You hear me? You're right. Wyatt and I are perfect together. We're going to get married and be happy."

He smiled. "So you and Wyatt aren't broken up." He let out a bark of a laugh. "Good to see that you haven't changed. Give Wyatt my regards."

Julia stormed out. Colt finished his coffee and threw away the cups Julia had left behind. He smiled as he headed for the door. He couldn't wait to get home to Lola and Grace.

Chapter Fifteen

Lola saw the change in Colt the moment he walked in the door. It was as if a weight had been lifted off his shoulders. He was smiling and seemed…happy.

"I guess I don't need to ask how it went." Her heart had been pounding ever since Julia's phone call. A woman knows. Julia wanted more than Colt's forgiveness. A woman like that would try to hold on to him, to keep him in the wings—if she didn't already want him back.

Colt met her gaze. "She wants me back."

It felt as if a fist had closed around her heart, but she fought not to let him see her pain. "That must seem like a dream come true."

He laughed. "I'll admit at one time it would have been. But no," he said with a shake of his head as he stepped to her. "It would never have happened even if I hadn't met you. But now that I have…" He leaned down to kiss her softly on the mouth. As he drew back, he saw that she was frowning.

"I don't want you giving up the woman you love because of me and Grace," she said quickly. "I told you. We can take care of ourselves."

"That wasn't what I meant." His blue-eyed gaze locked with hers and she felt a bolt of heat shoot to her core. "Julia is the last person on earth that I want."

She swallowed. "But you asked her to marry you."

"I did." He chuckled. "And I have no idea why I did. Honestly, I feel as if I dodged a bullet. But I don't want to talk about her. I want you," he said as he drew her close again. "Is Grace sleeping?"

While he'd been gone, Lola had practiced what she was going to say to him. But when she looked up into his blue gaze and saw the desire burning there, it ignited the blaze inside her.

She told herself that they could have a serious talk later. There was time. Colt was in such a good mood, she didn't want to bring him down. She cared too much about him. But that was the problem, wasn't it? She was falling in love with him. And that was why she and Grace had to leave before Colt did something stupid like ask her to stay.

LATER, AFTER MAKING LOVE and falling into a sated sleep, Colt heard Grace wake up from her nap and slipped out of bed to go see to her. "Hi, sweetheart," he said as he picked her up and carried her over to the changing table. As he changed her, he talked to her, telling her how pretty and sweet she was.

She was Lola in miniature, from her pert nose to her bow-shaped mouth to her violet eyes. And yet, he saw some of himself in the baby—and knew it might be only because he wanted it to be true. They hadn't gotten the DNA results, not that he was worried.

What bothered him was how much he wanted to see himself in Grace. How much he wanted to tell her about all the things he'd teach her as she grew up. What he wanted to do was talk about the future with Grace— and Lola.

Getting Lola's baby back was one thing, but seeing

himself in this equation? He would have said the last thing he needed was a family. He was selling the ranch and going back into the service. That had been his plan and he'd always had a plan.

Now he felt rudderless and aloft, not knowing if he was up or down. What would he do if not go back to flying choppers for the Army? Ranch?

He stared into Grace's adorable face, feeling his heart ache at the thought of being away from her. He picked her up, holding her as he felt his heart pounding next to hears. Fatherhood had always been so far off in the future. But now here it was looking back at him with so much trust... He thought of his own father, his parents' disastrous marriage, how disconnected he'd felt from both of them.

He knew nothing about being a father or a husband. A part of him felt guilty for asking Julia to marry him. True, he'd put her off for years. It had come down to break up or marry her. He'd thought it was what he'd wanted.

Now, though, he knew his heart hadn't been in it. What he'd told Julia earlier had been true. He doubted they would have made it to the altar. After he'd put that diamond—she'd picked it out herself—on her finger, all she'd talked about was the big wedding they would have, the big house, the big life.

He'd let her talk, not really taking her seriously. He should have, though.

While Lola... Well, she was different. Her heart was so filled with love for their child that she'd risked her life numerous times. He'd never met anyone like her. And Grace... She smiled and cooed up at him, her gaze meeting his, and he felt her steal another piece of his heart if she hadn't already taken it all.

"Does she need changing?" Lola asked from the doorway.

"All taken care of. She just smiled at me."

Lola laughed. "I saw that." She'd been watching from the doorway, he realized. He wondered how long she'd been there. She was wearing one of his shirts and, he'd bet, nothing under it. She couldn't have looked sexier.

His cell phone rang. Lola moved to him to take the baby.

After pulling out his phone, Colt felt a start when he saw that it was Margaret Barnes, his Realtor, calling. He'd forgotten about her, about listing the ranch. All that seemed like ages ago.

"Hello?" he said as he headed out of the nursery.

"Colt, I have some good news for you. I have a buyer for your ranch."

For a moment he couldn't speak. He looked back at Lola and Grace from the doorway. Lola was rocking the baby in her arms, smiling down at her, and Grace was cooing and smiling up at her mother—just as she had done moments before with her father.

"Colt, are you there?"

"Yes." He saw Lola look up as if she heard something in his voice.

"You said to find a buyer as quickly as I could. If you have some time today, stop by my office. I can get the paperwork all ready. The buyer is fine with your asking price and would like to take possession as soon as possible."

He felt as if the earth was crumbling under his feet. Yes, he'd told her to find a buyer and as quickly as possible. But that had been before. Before Lola had shown up at his door in the middle of the night. Before he'd known about Grace.

"What is it?" Lola asked, seeing his distress as she joined him in the living room. "Bad news?"

He stood holding his phone after disconnecting. "That was the Realtor."

Lola hadn't asked about the for-sale sign on the road into the ranch and he hadn't brought it up. But Lola knew what his plans had been months ago. The night they'd met he'd told her he was going to accept another Army assignment rather than resign his commission, like he'd been planning before that night, to marry Julia.

"Does she have a buyer for the ranch?" Lola asked, giving nothing away.

He wasn't sure what kind of reaction he'd been expecting. His gaze went to Grace in her arms. He felt his heart breaking. Lately, his only concern had been protecting Lola, getting Grace back and making sure that horrible Jonas didn't have either of them.

He hadn't thought about the future. Hadn't let himself. "I think we should talk about—" His phone rang again. He checked it, hoping it was the Realtor calling again. He'd tell her he needed more time.

It was the doctor calling. He glanced at Lola and then picked up. "Doc?" he said into the phone.

"Your test results are back. You're welcome to come by and I would be happy to explain anything you didn't understand about DNA testing."

"Let's just cut to the chase, Doc."

Silence hung on the other end of the line for a long few moments. "The infant is a match for both Lola and you, Colt."

"Thanks, Doc." He looked to Lola, who didn't appear all that interested. Because she'd known all along.

"Are you all right?" she asked.

He nodded, but he wasn't. Grace had fallen back to

sleep in her arms. Had there ever been a more beautiful, ethereal-looking child? No wonder Jonas had wanted her. Wanted her and Lola.

If he looked like a man in pain, he was. Lola and the baby had taken his already topsy-turvy life and given it a tailspin. All he'd wanted just days ago was to get out of this town, out of this state, out from under the ranch his father had left him and the responsibility that came with it.

Now, though, he no longer wanted to run. He wanted to plant roots. He wanted to make them a family. "I think we should get married." The words were out and he wasn't sorry to hear them. But he should have done something romantic, not just blurted them out like that.

To his surprise, Lola smiled at him. "That's sweet, but…it's too early, isn't it?"

Too early? Like in the morning or—

"We hardly know each other."

"I'd say we know each other quite well," he said as he picked up the tail end of his shirt she was wearing.

She laughed and playfully slapped his hand away as she headed for the spare room that they'd made into a makeshift nursery. "You know what I mean."

He followed her and watched as she put Grace down in the crib. "We have a daughter."

"Yes, we do. But we can't get married just for Grace. You know that wouldn't work."

"But neither can I let the two of you walk out that door," he said.

"Colt, that door will soon be someone else's."

She had a point.

"I won't sell the ranch."

She gave him a pointed look. "I owe you my life and Grace's. But I also owe you something else. Freedom.

Grace and I can take care of ourselves now. Jonas is no longer a problem. He isn't going to bother us, not after the sheriff saw our daughter and knows that Jonas lied about keeping her from me. My parents set aside money for me should I ever need it and I saved the money I made teaching. Grace and I will be fine."

"But *I* won't be fine."

She looked at him, sympathy in her gaze.

"Lola, I need you. I need you and our daughter. I want us to be a family."

Tears welled in her eyes as she tried to pass him. "Colt."

He took her in his arms. "I know we haven't known each other long. But the night we met, we connected in a way that neither of us had before, right?" She nodded, though reluctantly it seemed. "And we've been through more than any couple can ever imagine, and yet we worked together and pulled it off against incredible odds. If any two people can make this work, it's you and me."

She smiled sweetly, but he could tell she wasn't convinced. "We're good together, I won't deny that. But, Colt, you don't want to ranch. You admitted that to me the first night we met. Now you're talking about keeping the ranch just to make a home for me and Grace? No, Colt. You would grow to resent us for tying you down. I see how your eyes light up when you talk about flying helicopters. That's what you love. That's where you need to be."

He wanted to argue, but he couldn't. She'd listened to him. She knew him better than even he knew himself. "Still—"

"No," she said as she moved down the hallway to the

room that they now shared. She began to pick up her clothing. "This is best and we both know it."

It didn't feel like the best thing to do. He'd come to look forward to seeing Lola's face each morning, hear her singing to the baby at night and spending his days with the two of them.

"Promise you won't leave just yet," he said, panicking at the sight of her getting her things ready.

She stopped and looked at him. "I'll stay until the ranch closes so you can spend as much time with Grace as possible. But then we have to go."

"It isn't just Grace I want to spend time with," he said as he drew her close. He kissed her and told himself he'd figure out something. He had to. Because he couldn't bear the thought of either of them walking out of his life.

JONAS STUDIED THE woman before him, letting her wait. Sister Rebecca was what was known as a handsome woman. She stood almost six feet tall with straight brown hair cut chin-length. Close to his own age, she wasn't pretty, never had been. If anything, she was nondescript. You could pass her on the street and not see her.

That was one reason she'd worked out so well all these years. She didn't look dangerous. A person hardly noticed her. Until it was too late.

Studying her, Jonas admitted that he'd come to care very deeply for her. He had depended on her. Her betrayal cut him deeper even than Lola's. Fury gripped him like fingers around his throat.

Along with guilt, he saw something else in her face now. She knew that he knew what she'd done.

"Rebecca?"

She raised her gaze slowly. The moment she met his eyes, her face seemed to crumble. She rushed to him to fall to her knees in front of his chair. "Forgive me, Father," she said, head bowed. "Please forgive me."

He didn't speak for a moment, couldn't. "For almost getting me killed or for letting Lola get away with the baby?"

She raised her head again. While pleas for forgiveness had streamed from her mouth, there was no sign of regret in her eyes.

"You stupid, foolish woman," he said with disgust, and pushed her away.

She fell back, landing hard. He watched as she slowly got to her feet. Her dark eyes were hard, her smile brittle. Defiance burned behind her gaze, a blaze that he saw had been burning for some time. Why hadn't he seen it? Because he'd been so consumed with Lola for so long.

"I have done whatever you've asked of me for years," she said, anger making her words sharp as knives hurled at him.

"As you should, as one of my followers," he snapped.

She let out a humorous laugh that sent a chill up his spine. "I wasn't just one of your followers."

He felt for his phone and realized he'd left it over on the table, out of his reach. Zack had said he would be right outside the door. But would he be able to get in quickly enough if Rebecca attacked? Jonas knew he wasn't strong enough to fight her off. Rebecca probably knew it, too.

"Many times you were wrong, but still I did what you asked without question," she continued as she moved closer and closer until she was standing over him. "All these years, I've followed you, looked up to you, trusted that you were doing what was best for our community, best for me."

He swallowed, afraid he'd created a monster. If he was being honest, and now seemed like a good time for it, he'd let her think that one day the two of them would run SLS. He'd trusted her above all others, even Zack.

"You didn't sound the alarm when you found the crib empty," he said, trying to regain control and get the conversation back on safer ground.

She shook her head. "No, when I found Sister Amelia standing next to the empty crib, I told her to go back to bed and let me handle it. I thought about sounding the alarm, but then I didn't. In truth? I was overjoyed to see the brat gone, along with her mother."

"That wasn't your decision to make."

She smiled at that. "You would destroy everything for that woman? You would take her bastard and raise it as your own? I thought of you as a god, but now I see that you are nothing but a man with a man's weaknesses."

The truth pierced his heart and he instantly recoiled. "You will not speak to me like this or there will be serious consequences."

A chuckle seemed to rise deep in her, coming out on a ragged breath. "Will you have the sisters chant more over me? You've already locked me up. Or..." Her gaze was hard as the stone Lola had used to try to bash his head in. "Will you have me killed? It wouldn't be the first time you've had a follower killed, would it?"

The threat was clear in her gaze, in her words. Rebecca knew too much. She could never leave this compound alive, and they both knew it.

He grabbed for his phone, but she reached it first.

She held the phone away from him, stepping back, daring him to try to take it from her.

"This is ridiculous, Sister Rebecca. You would throw away everything we have worked so hard for out of simple jealousy?"

She raised a brow, but when she spoke her voice betrayed how close she was to tears again. This was breaking her heart as much as his own. "I know you. After all these years, I know you better than you know yourself. You'll go after her and that baby. You'll have her one way or another even if it means destroying everything."

He stared at her, hearing the truth in her words and realizing that he'd let her get too close. She *did* know him.

She looked down at the phone in her hand, then up at him. She pushed the alarm. The air on the mountaintop filled with the scream of the siren.

When Zack burst through the door, she threw Jonas his phone and, with one final look, turned and let Zack take her roughly by the arm and lead her back to her prison.

She wouldn't be locked up there long, Jonas thought. He owed her that at least, he thought as he sounded the all clear signal. But things weren't all right at all and he feared they never would be again.

Chapter Sixteen

Colt had been worried that the sheriff was right, that Jonas wasn't going to take what had happened lying down. Hearing that Jonas had been released from the hospital, he'd almost been expecting a visit from the SLS leader.

He'd been ready, a shotgun beside the door. But the day had passed without incident and so had the next and the next.

The days seemed to fly by since he'd signed the ranch papers and deposited a partial down payment from the buyer. He'd kept busy selling off the cattle and planning the auction for the farm equipment. He tried not to think about the liquidation of his father's legacy, telling himself his old man knew how much he hated ranching. It was his own fault for leaving Colt the ranch.

He was in the barn when he heard footfalls behind him and turned to see Lola. "So the buyer doesn't want any of this?" she asked.

"No, I believe he plans to subdivide the property. It won't be a ranch at all anymore."

"And the house?"

"Demo it and put in a rental probably."

Lola said nothing, but when he saw her looking out the barn door toward the mountains, there was a wistfulness to her he couldn't ignore.

"I'm not leaving Montana. This will always be my home. I'm just not ranching. With what I got from the sale, I can do anything I want." But that was it. He didn't know what he wanted. His heart pulled him one way, then another.

"How long has your family owned this property?" she asked.

"My great-grandfather homesteaded it," he said. "I know it must sound disrespectful of me to sell it."

She shook her head. "It's yours to do with whatever you want, right?"

"Yes." He didn't bother to tell her that the three-month stipulation his father had put on it was over. "You were right. I'm not a rancher. I have no interest."

"But you're a cowboy."

He laughed. "That I will always be. I'm as at home on a horse as I am behind the controls of a helicopter. Ranching is a different animal altogether. Most ranchers now lease their land and let someone else worry about the critters, the drought, the price of hay. Few of them move cattle on horseback. They ride four-wheelers. Everyone seems to think ranching is romantic." He laughed at that. "It's the most boring job I've ever done in my life."

"That's why you're selling," she said with a smile. "It's the right thing."

He hadn't needed her permission, but he was thankful for it. As much as he denied it, there was guilt over selling something his father had fought for years to keep.

Nor had he contacted the Army about his next assignment, putting that off, as well. He still had plenty of leave, so there was time.

He'd also put off his Realtor about when the new

owners could take possession. It sounded as if they hoped to raze the house as soon as he moved out.

He knew he couldn't keep avoiding giving a firm date and time, but once that happened Lola and Grace would be gone.

"Where will you go?" he asked Lola.

"Probably back to California. At least for a while." The car she'd ordered had come, and she'd been able to get to her funds and make sure Jonas couldn't access them. She'd had to get a new driver's license since Jonas had taken her purse with hers inside, along with her passport and checkbook and credit cards.

Colt had heard her on the phone taking care of all that. No wonder he could feel the days slipping away until not only this ranch and the house he'd grown up in were gone, but also Lola and the baby. He worried that once he went back to the Army, this would feel like nothing more than a dream.

Yet, he knew that he would ache for Lola and Grace the rest of his life—if he let them get away. He'd always see their faces and yearn for them.

He'd never felt so confused in his life. What would he do if not go back to the Army? He was almost thirty-three. He couldn't retire even if he wanted to, which he didn't. He wanted to fly. But he couldn't ask Lola and Grace to wait for him for the next two to five years. He couldn't bear the thought of her worrying about him, or the worst happening and him never making it back.

His cell phone rang. Margaret again. "I'd better take this," he said to Lola. As she walked back toward the house, he picked up. "Margaret, I might have changed my mind."

Silence. "It's too late for that and you know it. Colt, what is this about?"

A woman and a child. The rest of my life. Regrets.

"If you're having second thoughts about selling the ranch—"

"I'm not. I just need a little more time to get off the property."

More silence. "I'll see what I can do but, Colt, they are getting very impatient. I need to tell these buyers something concrete. I can't keep putting them off or they are going to change their minds or fine you, which they can under the contract you signed." She sounded angry. He couldn't blame her.

As he looked out at the land, he had a thought. "I'll be in first thing in the morning."

"What does that mean?" she asked after a moment.

"I have an idea."

She groaned. "Could you be a touch more specific?"

"I'm selling the ranch, but there's something I need."

"Okay," she said slowly. "Why don't we sit down with them in the morning, if you're sure you won't change your mind."

He pocketed his phone and watched Lola as she slipped in the back door of the house. Taking off his Stetson, he wiped the sweat from his brow with his sleeve. "Do something," he said to himself. "Do something before it's too late."

"SHE'S STAYING ON the ranch with Colt McCloud," Zack told Jonas later that afternoon.

"Is the baby with them?"

"I've had the place watched as you ordered. They took the baby into town the next morning, bought baby clothes and supplies, and returned to the ranch."

So they were settling in. They thought it was over. "What kind of security?"

"No security system on the house. But I would imagine he has guns and knows how to use them since he's a major in the Army."

"I'm sure he does." That's why they would strike when the cowboy least expected it. He looked past Zack toward the main building below him on the hill. "You led church this morning?"

He nodded.

"What is the mood?"

Zack seemed to consider that. "Quite a few of them are upset over Sister Rebecca."

He'd suspected as much. "I'll lead the service tonight." Zack didn't appear to think that was going to make a difference. Jonas thought about the things that Rebecca had said and ground his teeth. He still had a headache, and while his wound was healing, it was a constant reminder of what Lola had done to him. Worse, she'd bewitched him, put a spell on him as if sent by the devil to bring him down.

Did he really want her back, or did he just want to retaliate? Did it matter in the long run? His memory was getting worse. The pills didn't seem to be working. He couldn't be sure how long he had until he was a blubbering old fool locked up in some rest home.

He shook his head. He wasn't going out that way. "I don't want Lola or the baby injured."

"What about McCloud?"

"Kill him and dispose of his body. I know the perfect place. If possible, leave no evidence that we were there."

COLT LEFT THE barn headed for the house, suddenly excited that his idea just might be the perfect plan. "Lola?" he cried as he burst through the back door.

"Colt?" She was standing in the kitchen wearing an

apron that had belonged to his mother. He hadn't seen it in years. She must have found it in a drawer he and his father had obviously never bothered to look in.

"What?" she asked, seeing the way he was looking at her.

"You look so cute in that apron, that's all." He stepped to her. "I'm selling the ranch."

"I know."

"You were right. I'd make a terrible rancher, always did. This was my father's dream, not mine. I'm a helicopter pilot."

She nodded. "I thought we already knew this. So you're going to take the commission the Army is offering you."

"No."

She tilted her head. "No?"

"No," he said, smiling. "For years, my friend Tommy and I have talked about starting our own helicopter service here in the state. We're good at what we do. With the money from the ranch, I can invest in the birds we'll need."

"That sounds right up your alley. But are you sure?"

He nodded. "Come here." He put his arm around her waist and ushered her over to the window. "Look out there. See that."

"Yes? That mountainside?"

"Imagine a house in that grove of aspens and pines. The view from there is incredible. Now imagine an office down by the road and a helipad. The office would be just a hop, skip and a jump from the house. We'd have everything we need for Grace and any other children we have."

LOLA SMILED AT HIM, caught up in his enthusiasm. "Isn't that land part of the ranch?"

He grinned. "I'm going to buy it back."

"Aren't you being a little impulsive?"

"Not at all. I've been thinking about this for years." He seemed to see what she meant and turned her to face him. "And I've been thinking about being with you since that first night. With you and Grace here... Lola, I've fallen for you and Grace..." He shook his head. "It was love at first sight even before I knew for certain that Grace was mine. I want you to stay. I want us to be a family."

"Colt, do you know what you're saying?" But it was what he wasn't saying that had her stomach in knots. She knew he wanted her and Grace, but she wouldn't let herself go into a loveless marriage just to give her daughter a home.

She said as much to him.

He stared at her. "Damn it, Lola, I love you."

She blinked in surprise. All their lovemaking, their quiet times together, those moments with Grace. She'd waited to hear those words. Well, maybe not the "damn it, Lola" part. But definitely the "I love you" part. Her heart had assured her that he loved her and Grace. And yet, she wouldn't let herself believe it was true until he finally told her.

"I love you," he repeated as if they were the most honest words he'd ever spoken. "I've only said those words twice to a woman. With Julia, it was over two years before I said them. I don't think it was a co-incidence that I held off. With you... I've been wanting to say them for days now."

"Oh, Colt, I've been waiting to hear them. I love you, too."

He reached into his pocket and pulled out a small velvet box.

Lola gave a small gasp.

"This ring was handed down from my great-great-grandmother to my great-grandmother to my grandmother. When my grandmother gave it to me, she made me promise only to give it to a woman who was my equal." He opened the box.

She looked down at a beautiful thick gold band circled in diamonds. "Oh, Colt." Her gaze went to his. "I don't understand. Julia—"

"I didn't give it to her."

"Why?"

He shrugged. "I don't know. It didn't seem…right for her. She picked out one she liked uptown."

Her heart went out to him. Julia had hurt him badly in so many ways, only proving how wrong she was for him almost from the start.

"Now I realize that I was saving this ring so I could live up to the promise I made my grandmother," he said. "I want you to wear it." He dropped to one knee. "Will you marry me, Lola Dayton, and be my wife and the mother to my children?"

She smiled through the burn of tears. "Yes."

He slipped the ring on her finger. It fit perfectly. "Now what is the chance of that?" he said to her, only making her cry and laugh at the same time.

Swinging her up into his arms, he spun her around and set her down gently. "For the first time in so long, I am excited about the future."

She could see that he'd been dragged down by the ranch, Julia and the past, as well as his need to do what he did so well—fly.

Colt kissed her softly on the mouth. She felt heat rush through her and, cupping his face in her hands, kissed him with the passion the man evoked in her.

He swung her up in his arms again, only this time he didn't put her down until they reached the bedroom.

THAT EVENING, JONAS held church in the main building. He'd gathered them all together to give them the news. He could feel the tension in the air. There'd been a time when he'd stood up here and felt as if he really was a god sent to this earth to lead desperate people looking for at least peace, if not salvation.

As he looked over his flock, though, all he felt was sad. His father used to say that all good things end. In this case, the preacher was right.

"Brothers and sisters. I have some sad news. As you know, Sister Rebecca has chosen to leave us. It is with a heavy heart that I had to let her go." He wondered how many of them knew the truth. Too many of them probably. He was glad he'd had Zack bury her far away from the compound.

"But that isn't the only news. I have decided that it is time to leave Montana." His words were followed by a murmur of concern that spread through his congregation. "As many of you know, I'm in poor health. My heart... I'm going to have to step down as your leader."

The murmurs rose. One woman called out, "What's to become of us?"

He'd bilked them out of all their money. A lot of them were old enough now that they would have a hard time getting a job. He didn't need this crowd turning on him as Sister Rebecca had.

"Brother Zack will be taking those who want to go to property I've purchased in Arizona. It's farmable land, so you can maintain a life there. Each of you will be given a check to help with your expenses."

The murmur in the main building grew louder. "If

you have any questions, please give those to Brother Zack. I trust him to make sure that each and every one of you will be taken care of." That quieted them down, either because they were assured or because they knew how Zack had taken care of other parishioners who'd became troublesome.

"It is with a heavy heart that I must step down, but I know that you all will be fine. You will leave tomorrow. Go with Godspeed." He turned and walked away, anxious to get back to his cabin and pack. The sale of his property would be enough to pay off his followers—not that he would be around to hear any complaints after tonight.

He rang for Zack. Since he'd told Zack of his plan, the man had been more than excited. Jonas had recognized that frenzied look in Zack's eyes. He'd seen it in his own. Zack would be Father Zack. God help his followers.

"I need you to pick about six brothers and a few sisters for a special mission," he told Zack. It would be one of their last missions under him.

Zack nodded, clearly understanding that he needed to pick those who would still kill for their leader.

"Make sure one of them is Brother Elmer."

"Are you sure? I mean—"

"Already questioning my authority?" he asked with a chuckle.

"No, of course not."

"Good. I have my reasons."

"I'll get right on it," Zack said, and left him alone.

Jonas looked around the cabin. He'd had such hopes when he'd moved his flock to Montana. He couldn't get maudlin now. He had to think about his future. He stepped to the safe he had hidden in the wall, opened it and took out the large case he kept there full of cash and his passport. Next to it was Lola's purse.

He took that out, as well, and thumbed through it even though he knew exactly what was in it since he'd often looked through it. He liked touching her things. He found her passport. Good, it was up-to-date. He'd deal with getting the baby out of the country when it came time.

After putting Lola's passport beside his own into his case, he closed the safe. There was nothing keeping him here after tonight. He would have everything he'd ever dreamed of, including a small fortune waiting in foreign banks across the world.

He thought of his father, wishing he could see him now. "Go ahead, say it. You were right about me, you arrogant old sanctimonious fool. I was your worst nightmare and so much more. But you haven't seen anything yet."

Chapter Seventeen

Colt woke to the sound of both outside doors bursting open. The sudden noise woke the baby. Grace began to cry in the room down the hall. Lola stirred next to him and Colt, realizing what was happening, grabbed for his gun in the nightstand next to him.

Moments before he had lain in bed, with Lola beside him.

They were on him before he could draw the gun. They swept into the room, both men and women. Colt fought off the first couple of men, but a blow to the back of his head sent him to the floor and then they were on him, binding his hands behind him, gagging him, trussing his ankles and dragging him out of the house.

He tried to see Lola, but there was a group of women around her, helping her dress. In the baby's room, he heard Grace quiet and knew they had her, as well.

The strike had been so swift, so organized, that Colt realized he'd underestimated Zack—the only ex-military man in SLS. Clearly he had more experience at these kinds of maneuvers than Colt had thought.

Still stunned from the blow to his head, he was half carried, half dragged to a waiting van.

"Take care of him, Brother Elmer," he heard Zack say, the threat clear in the man's tone. Zack must have known that Brother Elmer was a weak link. "Brother Carl will go with you to make sure the job is done properly."

The van door slammed. Elmer started the engine and pulled away. The whole operation had taken less than ten minutes.

"DON'T HURT HIM!" Lola had cried as Colt was being dragged from the bedroom. Three women blocked her way to keep her from going after the men.

"Dress!" Sister Caroline ordered.

"My baby?"

"Grace will be safe as long as you do what we ask," Sister Amelia said. But there was something in Amelia's tone, a sadness that said not even she believed it.

Lola had no choice. They had Colt. They had Grace. She dressed quickly in a blouse and jeans, pulled on her sneakers and let the women lead her outside to a waiting van.

Sister Shelly was already in the van and holding Grace.

"Let me hold her," Lola said, steel in her voice.

The women looked at one another.

"Give the baby to Lola," Sister Amelia said and Shelly complied.

She sat holding the now-fussing Grace as the van pulled away. "Where are they taking Colt?"

No one answered. Her heart fell. Hadn't she feared that Jonas would retaliate? He'd be humiliated and would have to strike back. Isn't that what the sheriff had warned them about?

But what could he hope to achieve by this? The sheriff would know who took them. The first place Flint Cahill would look was the compound.

She remembered something she'd overheard while a prisoner at SLS. Some of the women had been worried that Jonas wasn't himself, that his memory seemed to be failing him. He often called them by the wrong names, got lost in the middle of a sermon. They questioned in hushed voices if it was his heart or something else, since they'd seem him taking pills for it.

"What is going on?" Lola asked, sensing something different about the group of women.

"We're leaving Montana," Sister Amelia said, and the other sisters tried to hush her. "She'll know soon enough," Amelia argued. "Father Jonas announced it earlier. He's selling the land here. Some are going to a new home in Arizona. Others…" Her voice broke. "I don't know where they're going."

Lola realized that their leader wasn't here. "Where is Sister Rebecca?" The question was met with silence. "Amelia?"

"She's gone."

"Everyone is leaving," Sister Shelly said, sounding near tears. "Father Jonas… He's letting Brother Zack lead the group in Arizona. He will be Father Zack now."

Lola couldn't believe what she was hearing as the van reached the highway and headed toward the compound. "He's putting Zack in charge?" She knew that the women in this van must feel the same way she did about Zack. "Did Jonas say what he is planning to do?"

Silence. Lola hugged Grace to her, her fear mounting with each passing mile as the van turned onto the road up to the mountain. Lola saw no other taillights ahead. No headlights behind them. Where had they taken Colt?

COLT COULDN'T SEE OUT, but he could tell that Elmer and Carl weren't taking him to the compound. He had a pretty good idea what their orders had been when Zack had told Elmer to take care of him.

He was furious with himself. He'd thought Jonas would have no choice but to give up. He should have known better. He should have taken more precautions. Against so many, he knew he and Lola hadn't stood a chance.

When they'd gone to the compound and rescued Grace, he'd thought this could be settled without bloodshed. It was why he hadn't taken a gun to the compound the first time that night. He didn't want to kill one of Jonas's sheep. They were just following orders, though blindly, true enough. But he hadn't wanted trouble with the law.

Now, though, he saw there was no way out of this. Jonas had taken Lola and Grace. Nothing was going to stop him. He was going to end this once and for all no matter whom he had to kill.

Colt rolled to his side. They'd bound his wrists with plastic ties. He worked to slip his hands under him. If he could get a foot into the cuffs, he knew he could break free.

As he did, he watched the men in the front seat. Neither turned around to check on him. He got the feeling they didn't like being awakened in the middle of the night for this any more than Colt had. And now they had been ordered to kill someone. They had to be questioning Jonas and the SLS. He already knew that Brother Elmer had a weak spot for Lola and her baby.

He managed to get his hands past his butt. He lay on his back, catching his breath for a moment before he pushed himself up. Once he had his hands in front of him…

The van slowed. Elmer shifted down and turned onto a bumpy road that jarred every muscle in Colt's body. Colt caught a glimpse of something out the back window and realized where they were taking him. The old gravel pits outside of Gilt Edge. He caught the scent of the water through the partially opened windows up front. It was the perfect place to dump a body. Weighted down, there was a good chance the remains would never be found.

He felt his heart pound as he worked to free his wrists. The plastic restraints popped—but not louder than the rattle of the van on the rough road. Colt went to work on the ones binding his ankles.

As the van came to a stop, he resumed his original position, his hands behind him, feet together as he lay on his side facing the door.

Both men got out. He waited, wondering if either of them was armed or if the plan had been simply to drown him.

The van door opened noisily. "Can you get him out?" Elmer asked his companion.

Carl grunted but reached for him.

Colt swung his feet around and kicked the man in the chest, sending Carl sprawling in the dirt. He followed with a quick jab to Elmer's jaw. The older man stumbled and sat down hard on the ground.

So far, Colt hadn't seen a weapon, but as he jumped out, he saw Carl fumbling for something behind him. The man came up with a pistol. Right away, Colt saw that he wasn't comfortable using it. But that didn't mean that Carl wouldn't get lucky and blow Colt's head off.

He rushed around the back of the van to the driver's side. Grabbing open the door, he leaped in and started the van. As he threw the engine into Reverse, he saw Carl trying to get a clear shot. Elmer had stumbled to his feet and was blocking Carl's way—either accidentally or on purpose.

Colt didn't try to figure out which as he hit the gas. The van shot back. He cranked the wheel hard, swinging the back end toward the two men.

Carl got off two shots. One bullet shattered the back window of the van. The other took out Colt's side window, showering him with glass, and just missing his head before burying itself in the passenger-side door.

Elmer had parked the van close to the edge of the gravel pit, no doubt to make unloading his body easier.

As Colt swung the van at the two men, they tried to move out of the way. But Elmer was old and lost his footing. He was the first to go tumbling down the steep embankment and splash into the cold, clear water.

Carl had been busy trying to hit his target with the gun so he was caught unaware when the back of the van hit him and knocked him backward into the gravel pit. He let out a yell as he fell, the sound dying off in a loud splash.

Colt shifted into first gear and tore off down the bumpy road, thankful to be alive. He hoped both men could swim. If so, they had a long swim across the pit to where they would be able to climb out.

If either of their cell phones still worked after that, they might be able to warn Jonas. Not that it would matter.

Colt sped toward his house to get what he needed. This time he was taking weapons—and no prisoners.

FOR LOLA, WALKING into Jonas's cabin with the bundle in her arms felt a little like déjà vu. Only this time, there was a precious sleeping baby instead of rocks in her arms. As she entered, propelled by Brother Zack, she told herself that she would die protecting her daughter. Did Jonas know that, as well?

"Leave her," Jonas ordered. Zack started to argue, but one look at their leader and he left, saying he would be right outside the door if he was needed. The sisters scattered, and the door closed, leaving Lola and Grace alone with Jonas.

He still had a bandage on the side of his head, but she knew better than to think his injury might slow him down.

"You are a very difficult woman."

"Only when someone tries to force me into doing something I don't want to do or they take my child from me."

He glanced at the bundle in her arms. "May I see her?"

Lola didn't move. "What do you hope to get out of this?" she demanded.

"I thought I was clear from the beginning. I want you. It's what your parents wanted—"

"I don't believe that. I heard from my father before he…died. He wanted out of SLS. He was trying to convince my mother to leave. I believe that's why you killed them both."

Jonas shook his head. "Are we back to that?"

"You're a fraud. This is no church. And you are no god. All this is only about your ego. It's a bad joke."

"Are you purposely trying to rile me?"

"I thought maybe it was time you heard the truth from someone instead of Sister Rebecca telling you how wonderful you are."

"Sister Rebecca is no longer with us."

"So I heard. Did you kill her yourself or make one of your sheep do it?" She knew he could not let Rebecca simply walk away. She'd been with him from the beginning. She'd done things for him, knew things.

"Why do you torment me? I cared about Rebecca."

"And yet you had her killed. I don't like the way you care about people."

At the sound of vehicles and activity on the mountain below them, Lola moved cautiously to the window, careful not to turn her back on Jonas.

She frowned as she saw everyone appearing to be packing up and moving. Fear coursed through her. "What's going on? I thought they weren't leaving until tomorrow?"

"Our time in Montana has come to an end. We are abandoning our church here."

What Amelia had told her was true. "So they're scurrying away like rats fleeing a sinking ship. You're really going to let them go?"

"All good things must end."

She thought of Colt as she had on the ride to the compound. Something told her that he hadn't been brought here. "Where is Colt?"

Jonas shook his head. "As I said, all good things must end."

Tears burned her eyes. "If you hurt him—"

'What will you do? Kill me? They will put you in prison, take away your baby. No, it is time you realized that you have never been in control. You are mine. You will always be mine. I will go to any lengths, including having Grace taken away so you never see her again if that's what it takes to keep you with me."

Fear turned her blood to ice as she looked into his eyes and understood he wasn't bluffing.

"You have only one choice. Come with me willingly and Grace will join us once we are settled."

No, she screamed silently. She didn't trust this man. But she also knew she couldn't keep someone like Zack from ripping Grace from her arms. Just as she knew that Jonas wasn't making an empty threat. She'd known this man was dangerous, but she hadn't realized how much he was willing to give up to have her—and Grace.

"You have only a few minutes to make up your mind, Lola." He had his phone in his hand. "Once I push this button, Zack will take Grace. If you ever want to see her again, you will agree to go with me."

"Where?" She knew she was stalling, fighting to find a way out of this. Colt. If he was dead, did she care what happened to her as long as she had his baby with her?

"Europe, South America. I haven't decided yet. Somewhere far away from all this. I have money. We will live well. We will be a family."

She thought of the family Colt had promised her and felt the ring on her finger.

Jonas's gaze went to her left hand. His face contorted in anger. "Take that off. Take that off now!"

Chapter Eighteen

Colt dialed the number quickly, knowing he had no choice even if he ended up behind bars. It would be worth it as long as Lola and Grace were safe from Jonas Emanuel once and for all.

"I need to borrow a helicopter," he said, the moment his friend answered.

"Mind if I ask what for?" Tommy Garrett asked, sounding like a man dragged from sleep in the wee hours of the morning. Tommy worked as a helicopter mechanic outside of Great Falls. Colt had served with him in Afghanistan and trusted the man with his life— and Lola's and Grace's.

"A madman has the woman I love and my baby daughter."

There was a beat of silence before Tommy said, "You planning to do this alone?"

"Better that way. I'll leave you out of it."

"Like hell. Tell me where you are. Outside my shop I have a Bell UH-1 Huey that needs its shakedown. The old workhorse is being used to fight forest fires. I'm on my way."

Colt knew the Huey could do up to 120 mph. But a safe cruising speed for helicopters was around a hundred. Without having to deal with traffic, road speeds or winding highways, the response time in a helicopter was considerably faster than anything on the ground. It was one reason Colt loved flying them.

So he wasn't surprised when Tommy landed in the pasture next to Colt's house thirty minutes later. The sun was coming up, chasing away the last of the dark. He could make out the mountains in the distance. Within a matter of minutes, they would be at the compound. He tried not think about what they would find.

"How much trouble is this going to get you in?" Colt asked his friend as he loaded the weapons in the back and climbed into the left seat, the crew chief seat.

"You just worry about what happens when we put this bird down," Tommy said in the adjacent seat at the controls.

As they headed for the mountaintop in the distance, Colt told him everything that had happened from that moment in the hotel in Billings to earlier that night.

When he finished, Tommy said, "So this woman is the one?"

For a moment, Colt could only nod around the lump in this throat. "I've never met anyone like her."

"Apparently this cult leader hasn't, either. Tell me you have a plan." He swore when Colt didn't answer right away.

"There will be armed guards who are under the control of the cult leader, Jonas Emanuel. But we don't have time to sneak up on them. You don't have to land. Just get close enough to the ground that I can jump," Colt said as he began to strap on one of the weapons he'd brought. "Did I mention that these people are like zombies?"

"Great, you know how I love zombies. Except you can't kill zombies."

"These are religious zealots. I suspect they will be as hard to kill as zombies."

"This just keeps getting better and better," Tommy joked.

Colt looked over at him. "Thank you."

"Thank me after we get out with this woman you've fallen in love with and your daughter." He shook his head. "You never did anything like normal people."

"No, I never did. There's the road that goes up to the compound."

Tommy swooped down, skimming just over the tops of the pines, and Colt saw something he hadn't expected.

"What the hell?" As they got closer to the mountain, Colt spotted the line of vans coming off the mountain. He felt a chill. "Something's going on. Fly closer to those vehicles," he said to Tommy, who immediately dipped down.

Inside the vans, he saw the faces of Jonas followers. There were a dozen vans. As each passed, he saw the pale faces, the fear in their eyes.

"Where do you think they're going?" Tommy asked.

"I have no idea. Leaving for good, from the looks of it. What is Jonas up to? Are these people decoys or are they really clearing out?" He thought of Lola and the baby. How crazy was Jonas? Would he kill them and then kill himself, determined that Colt would never have either of them?

"Up there," Colt said, pointing to the mountaintop. Tommy swung the helicopter in the direction he pointed. Within a few minutes, the buildings came into sight. Colt didn't see any guards. He didn't see anyone. The place looked deserted. Had everyone left?

Not everyone, he noticed. There was a large black SUV sitting in front of Jonas's cabin.

"Think you can put her into that clearing in front of the cabin?"

"Seriously?" Tommy said. "You forget who you're talking to. Give me a dime and I can set her down on it." Colt chuckled because he knew it was true.

LOLA LOOKED DOWN at the antique ring that Colt had put on her finger. She swore she would never take it off. It felt so right on her finger. Colt felt so right.

Jonas moved faster than she thought he could after his injury. He grabbed the baby from her arms and shoved her. She fell back, coming down hard on the floor. "I told you to take it off. Now!"

"Give me Grace."

"Her name is Angel, and if you don't do what I say this moment…"

Lola pulled off the ring. She knew it was silly. Colt was probably dead. She'd lost so much. What did a ring matter at this point? The one thing she couldn't lose was Grace, and yet she felt as if she already had in more ways than one. Jonas had them captive. He could do whatever he wanted with Grace. Just as he could do whatever he wanted with her now.

"Happy?" she asked, still clutching the ring in her fist.

"Throw it away." He pointed toward the fireplace and the cold ashes filling it.

She hesitated again.

"Do as I say!" Jonas bellowed at her, waking up Grace. The baby began to cry.

Lola tossed the ring toward the fireplace. It was a lazy, bad throw, one that made Jonas's already furious face cloud over even more. The ring missed the fireplace opening, pinged off the rock and rolled under the couch. She looked at Jonas. If he really did have a bad heart, she realized his agitation right now could kill him. She doubted she would get that lucky, though.

He seemed to be trying to calm down. Grace kept crying and she could tell it was getting on his nerves.

She got to her feet. "Let me have her. She'll quit crying for me."

He shook his head. "I'm not sure I can trust you," he said slowly.

Colt was gone. The ring was gone. But Jonas had something much more precious. He had Grace. But Lola wasn't giving up.

"How do I know I can trust *you*?" she said.

The question surprised him. He'd expected her to cower, to promise him anything. She knew better than to do that. Jonas was surrounded by people who bowed down to him. Lola never had and maybe that's why he was so determined to have her.

She approached him. "You hurt my baby and I will kill you. I'll cut your throat in your sleep. Or push you down a flight of stairs. Or poison your food. It might take me a while to get the opportunity, but believe me, I will do it."

He chuckled as his gaze met hers. "I do believe you. I've always loved your spirit. Your mother told me what a headstrong young woman you were. She wasn't wrong."

It hurt to have him mention her mother. Was it possible that Jonas could get away with the murders he'd committed? She feared it was. She thought of Colt and felt a sob rise in her throat. She forced it back down.

She couldn't show weakness, not now, especially not for Colt. She had to think about Grace.

"We seem to be at an impasse," Jonas said. "What do you suggest we do?"

"I suggest you give me my baby and let me leave here."

He shook his head. "Not happening. Neither you or your baby will be leaving here—except with me."

"So what are you waiting for?" she demanded.

Jonas chuckled as he tilted his head as if to listen. "We're waiting for Colt. I just have a feeling he will somehow manage to try to save you one more time."

Lola listened as her heart thumped against her rib cage. Colt? He was alive? She thought she heard what sounded like a helicopter headed this way.

"I believe that's him now."

COLT FOUGHT THE bad feeling that had settled in the pit of his stomach. Jonas was playing hardball this time. He wasn't going to let Lola and Grace go—not without a fight to the death. That's if they were still alive.

"Change of plans," he said to Tommy. He felt as if time was running out for Lola and Grace. "Put us down and wait for me," he said, fear making his voice sound strained as he passed Tommy a handgun. "I hope you won't have to use this. It appears that the guards have left, but I've already underestimated Jonas once and I don't want to do it again. I'm hoping this won't take long."

As Colt started to jump out, Tommy grabbed his sleeve. "Be careful."

Colt nodded. "You, too."

"I'll be here. Good luck."

Colt knew that if there was anyone he wanted on his

side in a war it was Tommy Garrett—and this was war. These soldiers would die for their leader. They were just as devoted to dying for their cause as the ones he'd fought in Afghanistan.

The moment the chopper touched the ground, he leaped out and ran up the mountainside to where a large black SUV sat, the engine running and Brother Zack behind the wheel. Behind him, he heard Tommy shut down the engine. The rotors began to slow.

Colt looked around. The only person he'd seen so far was Zack, but that didn't mean that another of the guards hadn't stayed behind.

As he approached the SUV, he could hear the bass coming from the stereo. Closer, he saw that Zack had on headphones and was rockin' out. He must have had the stereo cranked, which explained why he hadn't heard the helicopter land. Nor had he heard him approach.

Colt yanked open the door. A surprised Zack turned. Colt grabbed him by his shirt and hauled him out. Unfortunately, Zack was carrying and he went for his gun. Zack was strong and combat trained. But Colt was fighting for Lola's and Grace's lives.

Colt managed to get hold of the man's arm, twisting it to the point of snapping as they struggled for the weapon. When the shot went off, it was muffled—just like Zack's grunt. Blood blossomed on the front of Zack's white shirt. The gun dropped, falling under the SUV.

As the man slumped, Colt shoved him back inside the vehicle, shut off the stereo and slammed the door before turning to Jonas's cabin. He'd seen suitcases in the back of the SUV and suspected the sheep weren't the only ones fleeing.

Colt pulled his holstered gun and climbed the steps. He had another gun stuck in the back of his jeans under his jacket. He always liked to be prepared—especially against someone like Jonas Emanuel.

He could still hear the sweep of the helicopter's rotors as they continued to slow. The wooden porch floor creaked under his boots. He braced himself and reached for the doorknob.

Before he could turn it, Lola opened the door. Her face had lost all its color. Her violet eyes appeared huge. He could see that she'd been crying. The sight froze him in place for moment. What had Jonas done to her? To Grace?

"Where is Jonas?" Colt asked quietly. Suddenly there wasn't a sound, not even a meadowlark from the grass or a breeze moaning in the pines. The eerie quiet sent a chill up his spine. "Lola?" The word came in a whisper.

"I'm leaving with Jonas," she said.

"Like hell." He could see that Jonas had put the fear into her and used Grace to do it. He'd never wanted to strangle anyone with his bare hands more than he did the cult leader at this moment.

"Please, it's what I want." Her words said one thing; her blue eyes pleaded with him to save Grace.

He pushed past her to find Jonas sitting in a chair just yards away. He was holding Grace in such a way that it stopped Colt cold.

JONAS RELISHED THE expression on Colt's handsome face. It almost made everything worth what he was going to have to give up. The cowboy thought he could just bust in here and take Lola and the baby? Not this time.

"Lola is going with me and so is her baby," he said as he turned the baby so she was facing her biological father and dangling from his fingers. He wanted Colt to see the baby's face and realize what he would be risking if he didn't back off.

"I don't think so," Colt said, but without much conviction. Jonas was ready to throw the baby against the rock fireplace if Colt took another step. The cowboy wasn't stupid. He'd figured that out right away. But he'd been stupid enough to come up here again. The man should have been dead.

Idly, Jonas wondered what had gone wrong at the gravel pit. He'd known he couldn't depend on Elmer, but he was disposable. Brother Carl had inspired more faith that he would get the job done. Jonas had assumed that Carl would have to kill both Elmer and Colt. Clearly, the job had been too much for him.

"Has he hurt you?" Colt asked Lola.

She shook her head.

Jonas was touched by the cowboy's concern, but quickly getting bored with all this. "Elmer and Carl?" he asked, curious.

"Swimming, that is, if either of them knows how," Colt answered.

"And Brother Zack?"

"No longer listening to music in your big SUV."

So he couldn't depend on Zack to come to his rescue. Another surprise. Everyone was letting him down. Just as well that he was packing it all in. He'd grown tired of the squabbling among the sisters and the backbiting of the brothers. Human nature really was malicious.

Still, he would miss Zack. And now who would lead his people to the promised land of Arizona? He chuckled to himself since he didn't own any land in Arizona. But they wouldn't know that until they got there, would they?

He saw the cowboy shoot a look at Lola. She was standing off to Colt's left as if she didn't know what to do. He could see the tension in her face. She wasn't being so smart-mouthed now, was she? As much as he was enjoying this, he didn't have to ask what she was hoping would happen here.

But, this time, she'd been outplayed. The cowboy was going to lose. It was simply a matter of how much he would have to lose before this was over. Did he realize that he wasn't getting out of here alive? At this point, Jonas wasn't sure he cared if Lola and the baby survived either, though he still wanted the woman, and damned if he wouldn't have her—dead or alive. The thought didn't even surprise him. His father used to say that one day he would reach rock bottom. Was this it?

"Why would you want a woman who doesn't love you?" Colt asked conversationally, as if they were old friends discussing the weather—and took a step closer.

"Because I can have her. I can have anything I want, and I want her. The baby is optional. I guess that's up to you."

"How's that?"

"You can't reach me before I hurl your baby into the rock fireplace. But if you try, I will, and then we will only be talking about Lola. The thing is, I don't think she will love you anymore, not after you got her baby killed," Jonas said. "Want to take a chance on that? Take another step…"

COLT COULD SEE that Jonas's arms were tiring from holding Grace up the way he was. He was using the baby like a shield. There was no way Colt could get a shot off with Jonas sitting and the baby out in front of him. Nor could he chance that, as he fired, Jonas wouldn't throw Grace into the rocks.

One glance at Lola and he knew that what they both feared was a real possibility—Jonas could drop the baby at any moment. Or, worse, throw Grace against the rock fireplace as he was threatening.

"Colt, I'll go with him. It's the only way," Lola pleaded as she stepped to him, grabbing his arm.

It was a strange thing for her to do and for a moment he didn't understand. Then he felt her reach behind him to the pistol he had at his back. She must have seen the bulk of it under his shirt. She freed the gun and dropped her hands to her sides, keeping turned so Jonas couldn't see what she held. Then she began to cry.

"You heard her," Jonas said. "Leave before someone gets hurt. Before you get hurt." His arms were shaking visibly. "If you care anything about this child…"

Jonas knew Colt wasn't leaving without Lola and Grace. Saying he could walk away was all bluff. Did he have a weapon handy? Colt suspected so.

Lola was still halfway facing him so she could keep the gun in her hand hidden. Colt feared what she planned to do, but he could feel time running out. Jonas was losing patience. Worse, his arms were shaking now. He couldn't hold the baby much longer—and he couldn't back down. Wouldn't.

"Tell him, Jonas," she cried, suddenly running toward the cult leader and dropping to her knees only feet from him after sticking the gun in the waist of her jeans. "Tell him I'm going with you, and that it's true and to leave."

The cult leader hadn't expected her to do that. For a moment, it looked as if he was going to throw the baby. Before he could, Lola grabbed for Grace with her left hand. At the same time, she pulled the pistol from behind her with her right. She had hold of Grace's chubby little leg and wasn't letting go.

Everything happened fast after that. Colt, seeing

what Lola had planned, took the shot the moment Lola managed to pull the baby down and away from Jonas's smug face. Colt had always been an expert shot. Even during the most stressful situations.

He missed. Jonas had fallen forward just enough that the shot went over his head and lodged in the back of the chair. Before he could fire again, he heard Lola fire. She'd taken the shot from the floor, shooting under Grace to hit the man low in the stomach. He saw Jonas release Grace as he grabbed for his bleeding belly.

Lola dropped the gun and pulled Grace into her arms. They were both crying. As Colt rushed to the cult leader, his gun leveled at the man's head, Lola scrambled away from Jonas with Grace tucked in her arms.

Jonas was holding his stomach with one hand and fumbling for something in the chair with the other. Colt was aiming to shoot, to finish Jonas, when he saw that it wasn't a gun the cult leader was going for. It was the man's phone.

He watched Jonas punch at the screen, his bloody fingers slippery, his hands shaking. It took a moment for the alert to sound. Jonas seemed to wait, one bloody hand on his stomach, the other on his phone. He stared at the front door, expecting it to come flying open as one of the guards burst in.

Seconds passed, then several minutes. Nothing happened. Jonas looked wild-eyed at the door as if he couldn't believe it.

"They've all left," Colt said. "There is no one to help you."

Jonas looked down at his phone. With trembling fingers he made several attempts to key in 9-1-1 and finally gave up. "You have to call an ambulance. It's the humane thing to do."

"This from the man who was about to kill my baby daughter?"

"You would let me bleed to death?"

Colt looked over at Lola, huddled in the corner with Grace. Their gazes met. He pulled out his own phone and keyed in 9-1-1. He asked to speak to the sheriff.

When he was connected with Flint, he said, "You were right. Jonas hit us in the middle of the night. He sent two men to kill me. I left them in the old gravel pits. He took Lola and Grace, but they are both safe now. Unfortunately, one of his guards tried to shoot me. He's dead outside here on the compound and Jonas is wounded, so you'll need an ambulance and a—" He was going to say *coroner*, but before he could get the word out, the front door of the cabin banged open.

He spun around in time to see Zack bleeding and barely able to stand, but the man could still shoot. He fired the weapon in his hand in a barrage of bullets before Colt could pull the trigger.

LOLA SCREAMED. GRACE WAILED. It happened so fast. She'd thought it was all over. Finally. She'd thought they were finally safe. And so had Colt. He hadn't expected Zack to be alive—let alone come in shooting—any more than she had.

Colt threw himself in Grace's and her direction. As he did, he brought up the weapon he'd been holding on Jonas. The air filled with the loud reports of gunfire.

Lola laid her body over Grace's to protect her, knowing that Colt had thrown himself toward them to do the same. It took her a few moments to realize that the firing had stopped. She peeked out, terrified that she would find Colt lying dead at her feet.

Colt lay on his side, his back to her. She put Grace

down long enough to reach for him. He was holding
his leg, blood oozing out from between his fingers. He
looked up at her.

"Are you and Grace—"

"We're fine. But you're bleeding," Lola cried.

"It's just a flesh wound," Colt said. "Don't worry
about me. As long as you and Grace are all right..." He
grimaced as he tried to get to his feet.

In the doorway, Zack lay crumpled on the floor. Lola
couldn't tell if he was breathing or not. Her gaze swung
to Jonas. He had tumbled out of his chair. He wasn't
breathing, given that the top of his head was missing.
She looked away quickly.

Grace's wailing was the only sound in the room. She
rushed to her. As she did, she saw Colt's cell phone on
the floor and picked it up. The sheriff was still there.

"We need an ambulance. Colt is wounded. Zack and
Jonas are dead."

"Tommy," Colt said, trying to get to his feet. "He
would have seen Zack heading for the cabin..." He
limped to the door and pushed it open. Beyond it, he
saw Tommy slumped over the controls of the helicopter. "There isn't time to wait for an ambulance. Tell the
sheriff we'll be at the hospital."

As she related to the sheriff what Colt had said, she
hurried to the couch. Squatting down, she fished her ring
from under it. Her gentle toss of it hadn't hurt the ring
or the diamonds. She slipped it on her finger, feeling
as if now she could face anything again. Then, holding
Grace in her arms, she ran after Colt to the helicopter sitting like a big dark bird in the middle of the compound.

COLT IGNORED THE pain as he ran to the helicopter. When
he reached Tommy, he hurriedly felt for a pulse. For a

moment, he thought his friend was dead, and yet he didn't see any blood. He found a pulse and felt a wave of relief. He'd dragged his friend into this. The last thing he wanted to do was get him killed.

On closer inspection, he could see a bump the size of a goose egg on Tommy's head. He figured Zack must have ambushed him before coming up to the cabin to finish things.

"Is he...?" Lola asked from behind him. She held a crying Grace in her arms and was trying to soothe her.

"He's alive, but we need to get him to the hospital. Come around the other side and climb in the back with Grace." Colt helped them in and then slid into the seat and took over the controls. He started up the motor. The rotors began to turn and then spin. A few minutes later, he lifted off and headed for Gilt Edge.

The helicopter swept over the tops of the pines and out of the mountains. Colt glanced over at Tommy. He seemed to be coming around. In the back, Lola had calmed Grace down and she now slept in her mother's arms.

He told himself that all was right with the world. Lola and Grace were safe. Tommy was going to make it. But he was feeling the effects of his blood loss as he saw the hospital's helipad in the distance. He'd never lost a bird. He told himself he wasn't going to lose this one—especially with the precious cargo he was carrying.

Colt set the chopper down and turned off the engine. After that, everything became a blur. He knew he'd lost a lot of blood and was light-headed, but it wasn't until he'd shut down the chopper and tried to get out that he realized how weak he was.

The last thing he remembered was seeing hospital staff rushing toward the helicopter pushing two gurneys.

Chapter Nineteen

Colt woke to find Lola and Grace beside his bed. He tried to sit up, but Lola gently pushed him back down.

"Tommy is fine," she told him as if knowing exactly what he needed to hear. "A mild concussion. The doctor is having a terrible time keeping him in bed. We're all fine now."

Colt relaxed back on the pillows and smiled. "I was so worried. But everyone's all right?"

She nodded. "I was worried about you." She pushed a lock of hair back from his forehead and looked into his eyes. "You lost so much blood, but the doctor says you're going to be fine."

He glanced over at the IV attached to his arm. "I remember flying the chopper to the hospital but not much after that." He took her hand and squeezed it. "How is Grace?"

"Sleeping." Lola pointed to the bassinet the nurses had brought in for her. "I refused to leave until I knew you were all right." They'd also brought in a cot for Lola, he saw. "I've just been going back and forth from your room to Tommy's."

Colt smiled, took her hand and squeezed it. "I almost lost you. Again."

"But you saved me. Again. Aren't you getting tired of it?"

He shook his head. "Never." He glanced down at the ring on her finger. When he'd come into the cabin, he'd seen her rubbing the spot on her left hand where it had been. He hadn't been surprised Jonas hadn't liked seeing the ring on her finger. "When are you going to marry me?"

"You name the day. But right now you're in the middle of selling your ranch and holding an auction, and the doctor isn't going to let you out of here for a while. The bullet missed bone, but your leg is going to take some time to heal. Also, I believe you missed your appointment with your Realtor."

Colt grimaced. "Margaret. She is going to be furious."

"I called her. Apparently, ending up in the hospital bought you some time."

"I need to talk to Tommy, but I want to talk to him about my plan for the future, for *our* future."

The hospital-room door opened and Sheriff Flint Cahill stuck his head in. "Our patient awake? I hate to interrupt, but I need to talk to Colt if he's up to it."

Colt pulled Lola down for a kiss. "I'll talk to the sheriff. You can leave Grace. If she wakes up, I'll take care of her."

She nodded. "I know you will." She said hello to the sheriff. "I'll just be down the hall."

Flint took off his Stetson and pulled up a chair. "I've already spoken with Tom Garrett and Lola. I have their statements, but I need yours. I have two dead men up on the mountain, two suffering from dehydration and two more in the hospital. Elmer and Carl have been picked up. They both said they were the ones who almost got killed, not you." He pulled out his notebook and pen. "Said you knocked them into the gravel pit."

Colt nodded. "After they took me from my house in the middle of the night, tied me up and planned to kill me and dump me in the pit. They probably didn't mention that."

"Actually, Elmer confessed this morning. They're both behind bars." The sheriff sighed. "Just give me the basics. You'll have to come down to the office when you're released."

Colt related everything from the time he was awakened by the cult members breaking into the house until he landed the helicopter at the hospital.

"It would have been nice if you'd given me a call," Flint said.

"Jonas would have killed them. He was so close to hurting Grace…" His voice broke. "If Lola hadn't acted when she did…"

"Jonas had one bullet in him from a gun registered to you, but all the others were from a gun registered to Jonas himself. We found it next to Zack's body. Why would Zack kill his own leader?"

Colt shook his head. "He came in firing. When I jumped out of the way, he kept firing…"

"He's the one who wounded you?"

"Yes. And the one who knocked out Tommy, but he might have already told you that."

"Actually," the sheriff said. "He didn't see who or what hit him."

"Zack was the only guard left. Everyone else vacated the property."

"Lola said that most of them were headed to Arizona, where Jonas had promised them a place to live, but we can't find any property owned by him or SLS," Flint said. "We did, though, find a variety of places where he has stashed their money, a lot of it. I would imagine there'll be lawsuits against his estate."

"Lola thinks he murdered her parents. They're buried on the compound."

The sheriff raked a hand through his hair. "We saw that there is a new grave in the woods. We were able to contact a couple of SLS followers who didn't make it any farther than town. They said they think he killed Sister Rebecca and that she is buried in the new grave." He shook his head. "He had me fooled."

"Me, too. For a while," Colt admitted.

Grace began to whimper next to his bed.

The sheriff put away his notebook and pen as he rose. "I'll let you see to your daughter." He tipped his Stetson as he left.

THE STORY HIT the local paper the next day. SLS members were spilling their guts about what had gone on up at the compound. A half dozen had already filed lawsuits against the fortune Jonas had amassed.

The article made Colt and Tommy sound like heroes. Colt figured that was Lola's doing since she'd told him she'd been interviewed by a reporter. She'd said she was anxious for her story—and that of her parents— to get out.

"Maybe it will keep other people from getting taken in by men like Jonas," she'd said. "He caught my parents at a vulnerable time in their lives. But if they could be fooled, then anyone can."

Lola picked him up after the doctor released him from the hospital.

He sat in the passenger seat of the SUV she'd had delivered to his house. The woman was damned independent, but he liked that about her. Grace grinned at him from the car seat as they drove out to the ranch. Drove home. Well, home for a while anyway. All he'd been able to think about was getting back to that old ranch house that had felt like a prison before Lola. Now it felt like home.

Not that he was going to get sentimental and hang on to the house. Or the ranch. He wanted a new start for his little family.

They'd been home for a while when Tommy stopped by the house to see how he was doing before taking his helicopter home.

"You've met Lola," Colt said.

Tommy nodded.

"We got to know each other while we were waiting on you to get well. I had to thank him for all he did in helping us." She turned to the man from where she was making cookies in the kitchen. "We owe you. If you can stick around for twelve minutes, I will have a batch of chocolate chip cookies coming out of the oven. It's not much, given what you did for us."

"I'm just glad you're all right," Tommy said, looking bashful. "Anyway, I owe your husband. He saved my life. I'd do anything for him. I got to tell you, I think our boy Colt has done good this time," his friend said, grinning at Lola, then Colt. "You got yourself a good one," he said with a wink. "So what's this plan you wanted to talk to me about?"

"You're not mad at me for almost getting you killed?" Colt asked.

Tommy looked embarrassed. "I let some cult member sneak up on me."

"Zack was ex-military."

"That makes me feel a little better, but let's keep it to

ourselves, okay? So what's up?" he asked as he took the chair he was offered at the kitchen table. Lola checked the cookies. Grace was watching her from her carrier on the counter. Colt liked watching Lola cook. He just liked watching her and marveling at how lucky he'd gotten.

"Colt?" Tommy said, grinning as he drew his attention again.

He laughed, then got serious. "Remember all the times we talked about starting our own helicopter service?" Colt and Tommy had spent hours at night in Afghanistan planning what they would do when they got out of the Army. Only Colt had stayed in, so their dream of owning their own flight company had been put off indefinitely.

"You still thinking about it?" Tommy asked.

"I know you're doing great with your repair business. I know you might not be interested in starting a company with me, but I've sold the ranch. I have money to invest. You don't have to answer right now. Take a few days to—"

"I don't need a few days. Absolutely," his friend said. "Where were you thinking of headquartering it?"

"There's a piece of land close by I'd like to build a house on. Right down the road from it would be the ideal place for the office, with lots of room for the shops and landing any number of birds."

Tommy laughed. "You really have been thinking about this." He glanced past Colt to Lola, who was busy taking the cookies out of the oven. "What about the military?" he asked, his gaze shifting back to Colt.

"I've decided not to take the upcoming assignment and resign my commission. I'm getting married. I have a family now. I don't want to be away from them."

"I get it," Tommy said as he took the warm cookie Lola offered him. "How soon?"

"I can make an offer on the land and we can get construction going on the shops and hangers—"

"How long before you get married?" Tommy asked with a laugh and took a bite of the cookie, before complimenting Lola.

"In three weeks. That was something else I needed to talk to you about," Colt said. "I need a best man."

LOLA WANTED TO pinch herself. She couldn't believe she was getting married. She'd never been so happy. She was glad they'd put off the wedding for a few weeks. There'd been a lot of questions about everything that had happened up on the mountain. The investigation, though, had finally ended.

It had taken a while for the bodies of her parents and Sister Rebecca to be exhumed. Just as she'd suspected, autopsies revealed that both of her parents had been poisoned. So had Rebecca. Lola made arrangements to have their remains flown to California and reinterred in the plots next to her sister's.

"You have nothing to feel guilty about," Colt had assured her.

"But if I'd come straight home after university and tried to get them out of that place—"

"You know it wouldn't have done any good. They were determined that you join them, right?"

She'd nodded. "But if I'd come right home when I got my father's letter, maybe I could have—"

"You know how Jonas operated. It wouldn't have made a difference. You said yourself that your mother adored Jonas. You couldn't have gotten her to leave and your father wouldn't have left without her, right?"

She'd known he was right. Still, she hated that she hadn't been able to save them. She was just grateful to Colt. If it hadn't been for him...

Lola looked down at her sleeping daughter. Yes, if it hadn't been for him there would have been no Grace.

COLT WANDERED THROUGH the days afterward, more content than he had ever been. He and Lola went horseback riding. She took to it so well that she made him promise he would teach Grace when she was old enough.

"I'll teach all of the kids."

"All of the kids?" she'd asked with one raised eyebrow.

He'd smiled as he'd pulled her to him. "Tell me you wouldn't mind having a couple more."

"You want a son."

"I want whatever you give me," he'd said, nuzzling her neck and making her laugh. "I'll be taking all girls if that's what you've got for me."

Lola had kissed him, promising to give him as many children as he wanted.

"And I'll teach them all to fly. Which reminds me, anytime you want to go for a ride... The helicopters will be coming in right after the wedding."

The new owners of the ranch had allowed Colt to stay on with his family until he was able to get a mobile home put on the land he'd bought back from them. "We'll live in it until the house is finished, then maybe use it for the office until the office building is done."

Lola seemed as excited as he was about the business they were starting with Tommy. She kept busy with her new friends Lillie and Mariah. They were actually talking playdates for the kids.

He ran into Wyatt a couple more times in town. He

hadn't wanted to slug him. Actually, he'd wanted to thank him. The thought had made him laugh.

Also, Colt hadn't been that surprised when Julia called. He almost hadn't answered. "Hello?"

"Colt, it's Julia. I saw your engagement announcement in the newspaper not long after that story came out. What a story."

He didn't know what to say.

"Wyatt and I are over. I know you don't care, but I wanted you to hear it from me first."

"I'm sorry." He really was. He no longer had any ill will toward either of them and said as much.

"I won't bother you again. I'm actually leaving town. But I had to ask you something…" She seemed to hesitate. "It's amazing what you did for this Lola woman. You really put up a fight to save her and the baby."

He waited, wondering where she was going with this.

"Why…" Her voice broke. "Why didn't you put up a fight for me?"

It had never crossed his mind to try to keep Julia from marrying Wyatt. She was right. He hadn't put up a fight. He'd been hurt, he'd been angry, but he hadn't made some grandiose effort like riding a horse into the church to stop the wedding—if it had ever gone that far.

"I hope you find what you're looking for," he said, because there wasn't anything else he could say.

"And I hope you're unhappy as hell." She disconnected.

He looked over at Lola and laughed.

"Julia," she said.

"Yep, she called to say she liked the article."

Lola smiled. "You're a terrible liar."

"She's leaving town."

"Really?" She didn't seem unhappy to hear that.

"She wished us well."

"Now I know you're lying," she said as he pulled her close.

THE WEDDING TOOK PLACE in a field of flowers surrounded by the four mountain ranges. Colt had purchased the property just days before. He'd had to scramble to get everything moved in for the ceremony.

What had started as a small wedding had grown, as old and new friends wanted to be a part of it.

"Lola, I know this isn't what we planned," Colt had apologized. They'd agreed to a small wedding, and somehow it had gone awry.

She had laughed. "I love that all these people care about you and want to be there. They're becoming my friends, as well." Lillie and Mariah had given her a baby shower, the three becoming instant friends.

He kissed her. "I just want it to be the best day of your life."

"That day was when I met you."

Colt couldn't believe how many people had helped to make the day special. Calls came in from around the world from men he'd served with. A dozen of them flew in for the ceremony. The guest list had continued to grow right up until the wedding.

"Let us cater it for you," Lillie and Mariah had suggested. "Darby insists. And the Stagecoach Saloon is all yours for the reception, if it rains."

Lola had hugged her new friends, eyes glistening and Colt thought he couldn't be more blessed. Lola had accepted their kind offer and added, "Only if the two of you will agree to be my matrons of honor."

So much had been going on that the weeks leading up to the wedding had flown by. Colt wished his father was alive to see this—his only son changing diapers, getting up for middle-of-the-night feedings, bathing the baby in the kitchen sink, and all the while loving every minute of it.

Tommy always chuckled when he came by and caught Colt being a father. "If the guys could see you now," he'd joked. But Colt had seen his friend's wistful looks. He hoped Tommy found someone he could love as much as Colt loved Lola.

She'd continued to amaze him, taking everything in her stride as the ranch auction was held and the sale of the ranch continued. She'd had her things shipped from where they'd been in storage and helped him start packing up what he planned to keep at the house.

He'd felt overwhelmed sometimes, but Lola was always cool and calm. He often thought of that woman he'd met in Billings—and the one he'd found on his doorstep in the middle of the night. Often he didn't feel he was good enough for her. But then she would find him, put her arms around him and rest her head on his shoulder, and he would breathe in the scent of her and know that this was meant to be.

Like standing here now in a field of flowers next to Lola with all their friends and the preacher ready to marry them. If this was a dream, he didn't want to wake up.

LOLA COULDN'T BELIEVE all the people who had come into her life because of Colt. She looked over at him. He was so handsome in his Western suit and boots. He was looking at her, his blue eyes shining. He smiled as the preacher said, "Do you take this woman—"

"I sure do," he said, and everyone laughed.

Lola hardly remembered the rest of the ceremony.

She felt so blissfully happy that she wasn't even sure her feet had touched the ground all day.

But she remembered the kiss. Colt had pulled her to him, taking his time as he looked into her eyes. "I love you, Lola," he'd whispered.

She'd nodded through her tears and then he'd kissed her. The crowd had broken into applause. Cowboy hats and Army caps had been thrown into the air. Somewhere beyond the crowd, a band began to play.

Lillie hugged her before handing her Grace. Lola looked up from the infant she held in her arms, her eyes full of tears. Colt put his arm around both of them as they took their first steps as Mr. and Mrs. Colt Mc-Cloud.

* * * * *

Can't wait for the next
CAHILL RANCH NOVEL?

Read on for a sneak preview of
RANCHER'S DREAM,
from New York Times *bestselling author*
B.J. Daniels!

You will die in this house.

The thought seemed to fly out of the darkness as the house came into view. The premonition turned her skin clammy. Drey gripped a handful of her wedding dress, her fingers aching but unable to release the expensive fabric as she stared at her new home. A wedding gift, Ethan had said. A surprise, dropped on her at the reception.

The premonition still had a death grip on her. She could see herself lying facedown in a pool of water, her auburn hair fanned out around her head, her body so pale it appeared to have been drained of all blood.

"Are you all right?" her husband asked now as he reached over to take her hand. "Dierdre?" Unlike everyone else she knew, Ethan refused to call her by her nickname.

"I'm still a little woozy from the reception," she said, desperately needing fresh air right now as she put down her window to let in the cool Montana summer night.

"I warned you about drinking too much champagne."

He'd warned her about a lot of things. But it wasn't the champagne, which she'd hardly touched during the reception. Her stomach had begun roiling the moment Ethan told her where they would be living. She'd assumed they would live in his New York penthouse since that was where he spent most of his time. She'd actually been looking forward to it for several reasons. She'd never lived in a large city. Also it would be miles from Gilt Edge—and Hawk Cahill.

She'd never dreamed that Ethan meant for them to live here, at the place he'd named Mountain Crest. All during construction, she'd thought that the place was to be used as a business retreat only. Ethan had been so proud of the structure, she'd never let on that she knew the locals made fun of the house, its name on the iron gate blocking entry—and its builder.

When Ethan had pulled her aside at the reception and told her where they would be living, Dierdre hadn't been able to hide her shock. She'd never dreamed... But then she'd never dreamed she would be married to Ethan Baxter.

"Is there a problem?" he'd asked when he'd told her the news.

She'd tried to cover her discomfort. "I just assumed we would be living in New York, closer to your business."

"I've given up the penthouse. When I have to go to the city on business, I'll be staying in a hotel." He'd sounded a bit indignant as if she should have been more excited. "Mountain Crest will have to do."

"I didn't mean…" She had seen that there was nothing she could say that wouldn't make it worse.

Now as she found her breath, the premonition receding, she had another paralyzing thought. *You've made a mistake.*

Don't miss
RANCHER'S DREAM,
available August 2018 wherever
HQN Books and ebooks are sold.

www.Harlequin.com

PREMEDITATED MARRIAGE

This book is dedicated to my aunt Susie in Houston,
Texas, in memory of the love of her life,
her hero and husband, T. O. Gressett.

Prologue

Late September

The warm harvest moon cast a silver sheen over the lake and the naked young lovers standing waist deep in the still summer-warm water. Just yards away, crouched in the darkness of the pines, a lone figure watched, trying to decide whether to kill them both now—or wait.

They shouldn't have been here.

No one came up the weed-choked road to Freeze Out Lake anymore. Not after all the tragedies. No one was fool enough to come near the place late at night—let alone swim in the eerie dark waters.

Except for these two.

They began to stroke each other, their mouths hungry as their hands caressed wet bodies shimmering in the moonlight, the boy's shoulders muscled, the girl's breasts large and white, bobbing in the water.

The boy lured her out deeper into the lake in a sort of sex-driven tag where he dived beneath the water, making the girl giggle and pretend to fight him off, daring her to swim farther and farther from the shore.

The lake was low, lower than it had been in years

because of the recent drought, making it dangerously shallow.

The boy swam away from her, calling for her to follow him as he dived and splashed. But a few dozen yards from the shore, the boy disappeared under the water and the girl slowed as if sensing the danger.

Suddenly the boy surfaced like a porpoise. "Hey!" he called, his voice a little unsteady. "There's something out here!"

"What is it?" The girl stopped swimming.

Letting them live was no longer an option.

"What is it?" the girl called again, alarm in her voice.

"I don't know." He sounded scared now, his voice rising, echoing off the bank of trees that surrounded the small, remote lake. "Whatever it is, I'm standing on part of it." Sealing his fate, he disappeared beneath the surface.

The girl continued to tread water, her attention on the spot where the boy had vanished, seemingly unaware of the movement in the trees behind her. A branch cracked in the underbrush.

She jerked her head around, her gaze riveting on a spot in the trees, a look of alarm skewing her expression as if she'd seen something moving through the darkness toward her and the boy.

The rumble of a vehicle off in the distance distracted her for just an instant—just long enough that when she focused again on the spot in the trees, it was clear she no longer saw movement. But it was also clear from the look on her face that she saw *something*. Maybe the shape of the person standing in the shadows of the pines at the edge of the moon-drenched shore. Or maybe just the glint of the filet knife's long, sharp blade.

Abruptly the boy's head broke the surface in a spray

of silver droplets. He began to swim in wild, frantic strokes toward the shore and the pile of clothing so carelessly discarded earlier.

"What's wrong?" the girl cried. "What is it?"

"Get out of the water!" the boy screamed, his moon-lit face twisted in horror as he beat the water with his arms and legs, swimming madly for the shore and what he foolishly thought would be safety.

The sound of an engine grew louder. Someone was coming up the lake road. Lights flickered erratically through the dark branches just before a pickup burst out into the open, stopping at the edge of the water.

"Oh God, it's my dad!" the girl gulped. She was still yards from shore and her clothing—trapped and naked as sin.

The unforgiving moon illuminated her as she sunk, neck deep in the water, neck deep in trouble. But she would never know just how much trouble she'd really been in—before her father had showed up.

He slammed out of his pickup, a shotgun in his beefy hands and guttural curses spewing from his wide mouth like bullets.

But the boy didn't seem to notice the gun or his own nakedness as he lurched from the water, choking out something about a car in the middle of the lake—and a body.

In the dark shadows of the pines, the knife blade glittered for only an instant before disappearing back into its sheath. By morning the sheriff's department would have dragged the car from the lake and found what was left of the body strapped behind the wheel. Nothing to be done about that now.

Chapter One

The headlights drilled a hole through the dark, exposing what finally looked like a place to pull over.

Augustus T. Riley braked and swung the rental car into the narrow patch of dirt on the right side of the highway. He hadn't seen a car in hours—just miles of nothing but old two-lane blacktop banked by towering pines now etched ebony against the moonless sky.

Once stopped, he sat for a moment, the dark night closing in around him, the headlights doing little to ward it off. He'd never known such darkness, certainly not where he was from. And certainly not this early— just a little after seven. Over the murmur of the car engine, he heard the *whoop whoop* of wings an instant before something flew through the pale path of the headlamps and disappeared into the woods.

Damn, this country was desolate.

Turning on the dome light, he checked the map. He couldn't be more than a few miles from the town. The drive had been long and gruelling, and not surprisingly, he was hungry and tired.

Once he got there, he'd have little to go on. Little

more than a name and a phone number. But he'd gotten by with far less in the past.

Refolding the map, he shoved it into his briefcase out of sight and, leaving the engine running, climbed out. The night air was colder than he'd anticipated and cut through his lightweight jacket, sending a chill skittering across his skin. He caught the rank smell of something dead and decomposing. Roadkill. Fortunately, he couldn't see what was lying in the tall weeds where the putrid odor emanated. Didn't want to. Probably a wild animal. A coyote. Or a deer.

Whatever it was, it had been dead for some time.

He shivered as he went to the front of the car, popped the hood and leaned in.

From the darkness came a hushed moan that made him jerk up in surprise, banging his head on the sharp metal edge of the hood. He swore, then fell silent, listening for it over the thud of his heart.

There it was again. He looked up to see the wind move through the tops of the pines in a low, sensual moan, not unlike a woman's.

He almost laughed. He hadn't realized how nervous he was. How anxious. Still, it was a damn eerie sound, and as foreign to him as this landscape.

All those miles without seeing another living soul— He felt as disconnected from civilization as if deployed into space. What he wouldn't give right now to see the golden arches of a McDonald's restaurant. Or an interstate. Even a 7-Eleven gas station would perk him up.

He ducked under the car's hood again and quickly made a few adjustments until the engine ran so rough it barely ran at all. Satisfied, he slammed the hood.

Just a few more miles.

As he moved back along the side of the car, he became painfully aware of the darkness just beyond the glow of his headlights. This far north it got dark early and with no lights anywhere other than his headlamps… His step quickened only slightly, just enough to amuse him as he opened the car door and slid in, closing it firmly behind him. He actually thought about locking his door. This made him laugh.

But it was a short laugh; an oddly sad sound inside the rental car on this lonely stretch of highway just short of hell.

He started to pull back onto the highway. Something caught in his headlights, no bird this time. He threw the car into Reverse, the lights arcing back across the pines, coming to rest on a weathered-white sign standing at a skewed angle in the weeds just yards from where he'd pulled off. Freeze Out Lake. Five miles.

His breath caught as his startled gaze followed the partially obscured dirt tracks in his headlights to the point where the lake road disappeared into the black forest of pines. Not far up there was where the bodies had been found. The gruesome grizzly-bear attack years ago that had made all of the papers. He would never forget the photo of the tent where the grizzly had gone through to drag out the campers inside.

And just last week, Josh Whitaker's car and body had been dragged from the same lake.

His hand actually shook as he shifted into first gear again. If a place could be cursed, it would be this one. The car engine tried to die. His pulse took off like a shot. For a moment he thought he'd overdone it under the hood, but the car moved forward, the engine still running. Just barely.

Once back on the pavement, he turned on the heater, as if mere heat could chase away the chill. Not a half mile up the highway, it began to rain. Giant, wet drops fell like buckshot, ricocheting off the hood, splattering against the windshield, making the already dark night even blacker.

The next sign he caught in his headlights was: Utopia, Montana.

Home of Charlie Larkin.

He'd expected the town to be small, but not just a few run-down buildings out in the middle of nowhere. If this was their idea of Utopia—

Through the curtain of rain, he spotted the garage first. Could hardly miss anything that big. Or that ugly. Plus, it sat right on the edge of town. And town, what there was of it, was perched on the edge of the highway as if pushed out there by the pines.

The once-red words Larkin & Sons Gas and Garage had faded on the side of the gray metal building. Not exactly an imaginative name, but definitely descriptive. Two ancient-looking gas pumps sat under an overhanging roof next to the gunmetal-gray garage. Several jalopies, stripped clean of parts, rusted under the encroaching trees.

He pulled in under the roof next to a pump. The rain pelted the metal roof loud as a drum. The hand-printed notice on the closest pump read Last Gas for Thirty Miles. He turned off the engine and looked expectantly toward the gas station office, wondering which of the Larkins were working tonight.

Unlike the lamps glowing over the pumps, no light shone in the office. It was empty—and dark—except for the round golden glow of a clock on the wall. Seven-thirty-six.

He hadn't even considered the place might be closed.

Not on a Friday night. Especially if it was the last gas for thirty miles.

He looked down the main drag through the rain. A few splashes of neon blurred in the wet darkness. Past that, he could see nothing but more highway and trees.

Swearing under his breath, he turned the key to start the car again, not sure what to do and certainly not where to go. The engine clattered to an uncertain life, ran just long enough to rattle his teeth, then quit. He tried it a couple more times without any luck before he turned off the key and slammed his palm against the steering wheel with an oath. Him and his great plan.

Rain beat on the metal roof and the night felt colder than his last stop beside the highway as he opened his door. He drew up the hood on his jacket, zipping the front closed, as he hustled to the front of the car. He'd just started to pop the hood when he heard music and the clank of tools over the sound of the rain on the roof. Glancing toward the garage, he noticed a sliver of light coming from under the second bay door.

He jogged to the office and found it unlocked. Moving toward the music, he stepped through a side door into a large empty bay. Past it, he could see the source of the light in the second bay.

A single bare bulb glowed under an old beat-up Chevy sedan in the second bay. Country music blasted from a cheap radio on the floor nearby. A pair of western boots were sticking out from under the Chevy.

"Hello!" he called over the radio to the soles of the boots.

From under the Chevy came a grunt and what could have been the word "closed."

He'd come too far to be put off. Not only that, he couldn't very well go out and fix his own car and risk the chance the mechanic would see him. Nor was he willing to give up his plan that easily.

"I need to talk to you about my car!" he called down at the boots, wondering if the small work-boot soles belonged to one of the Larkins. With a whole lot of luck, the feet in them would be Charlie's.

This time he thought he heard the word "Monday" over the racket coming out of the radio and something about "gas" and "cash."

He definitely had no intention of waiting a whole weekend without his car if he could help it. Nor was he about to wait that long to make contact with Charlie. He reached over and turned off the radio. "Hello!"

A loud painful thump was followed by the clatter of a wrench and an oath.

"If you wouldn't mind giving me just a minute of your valuable time," Augustus said sarcastically. This wasn't going anything as he'd planned. But the loud country music had given him a headache and he'd had all he could take of being ignored.

An instant later, the mechanic rolled out from the underbelly of the car on the dolly, forcing Augustus to step back or be run down.

Silhouetted by only the lamp still under the Chevy, the short, slightly built mechanic got to his feet without a word and methodically began wiping his hands on a rag.

Augustus was determined to wait him out. He could feel the grease monkey giving him the once-over and was surprised that someone so insignificantly built could look so arrogant standing there in dirty, baggy overalls and a baseball cap. At six-two and a hundred and eighty pounds, Augustus knew he normally intimidated men twice this one's size.

But if this was Charlie Larkin—

"Look," Augustus said, trying to keep his cool. He'd been jumpy ever since the turnoff at Freeze Out Lake. Now he told himself that he was just tired and impatient. That was true. But he was also a little spooked, which, under most circumstances, was good. It gave him an edge.

"My car isn't running," he continued, "it's raining like hell outside and I've been driving all day and I'm tired and hungry. If you could just take a quick look at the engine so I can go find a motel for the night."

The mechanic let out a long-suffering sigh and slowly reached for the light switch on the pillar next to him with one hand and the brim of his baseball cap with the other.

"I'm sure it wouldn't take you any—"

The cap came off in the mechanic's hand as an overhead fluorescent flickered on, stilling anything else Augustus was going to say. A ponytail of fiery auburn hair tumbled out of the cap and a distinctly female voice said, "You just don't take no for an answer, do you?"

Seldom at a loss for words, Augustus simply stared at her for a beat. In the light, it was obvious she was just a snip of a girl, eighteen tops, the cute little smudge of grease on her chin making her look even more childlike. The baggy overalls she wore seemed to swallow her. "*You're* the mechanic?"

She looked down at the overalls that completely disguised anything feminine about her. "Don't I look like a mechanic?"

Truthfully? No. She looked like a girl wearing her boyfriend's overalls, just fooling around under his car while he went out to get burgers and fries.

She stepped past him and headed for the office, but

not before he felt a small rush of excitement. The name stitched in red on the soiled breast pocket of the too-large blue overalls read: Charlie.

He hurriedly trailed after her, not sure where she was going or what she planned to do. "It says Larkin & Sons on the sign," he noted. "I was hoping maybe one of the *Larkins* could look at my car. Maybe you could call one of them? Maybe this… Charlie, whose overalls you're wearing?"

She stopped just inside the office and turned to look at him. "Is that your car parked next to the pump?"

Did she see any other cars out there? He nodded and she pushed open the front door and headed for his car. He followed.

She popped open the hood and, without looking at him, hollered for him to get in and try to start the engine.

Wondering what this would possibly accomplish, he slid behind the wheel, rolled down his window so he could hear her and turned the key.

The poor engine actually started, running noisily and jerkily, shaking the entire car—until she stuck her head around the open hood and motioned for him to turn it off.

"You drove all the way from—" she leaned over the front of the car to glance at the license plate "—Missoula with the car running like this?" she asked. She had a serious, concentrated expression on her face that made her look a little older.

"It just kept getting worse," he lied, leaning out the window a little so she could hear him over the rain.

Her gaze came back to meet his. He hadn't noticed the color of her eyes until then. They were a rich brown, the same color as the string of freckles that trailed across the bridge of her nose. He couldn't help but wonder exactly what her relationship was with Charlie Larkin.

She continued looking at him as if waiting for him to say something more.

Under other circumstances he might have felt guilty about what he was doing. But he'd made a rule years ago: the end would always justify the means. No exceptions. And in this case, it was personal, so God help Charlie Larkin.

"Won't be able to get it fixed tonight," she said at last, then slammed the hood and turned away from him.

What? He knew it was just a simple matter of adjusting the carburetor. Any mechanic could do it. Obviously she was no more a mechanic than he was and knew a damn sight less about car engines than even he did.

"Leave the key in the office and check back in the morning." She started for the office.

He stared at her back for a moment as she headed for the gas-station office door. "Wait a minute!" He scrambled out of the car and after her. She was already through the office headed for the bay and the vehicle she'd been under when he'd found her. Along the way, she'd put her baseball cap back on, the ponytail tucked up inside it again.

"And what do you expect me to do tonight without a car?" he called to her retreating back. "It's raining! Couldn't you call Charlie to fix my car tonight?"

His words seemed to stop her. She turned around slowly to look at him, tilting her head as if she hadn't quite heard what he'd said.

He rephrased his question, reminding himself this was his own fault. He should never have fiddled with the engine until he was sure Larkin was around to repair it. Now, more than ever, he couldn't go out there, adjust the carburetor and drive off.

"You're sure there's no chance of getting it fixed tonight?" he asked.

"No chance."

He swore silently. Okay. "Is there anywhere in town I could rent a car until mine is repaired?"

She shook her head, giving him a look that said he should have known that after one glance at the town.

"Well, is there somewhere I can stay for the night, a hotel or bed-and-break—"

"Murphy's, about a quarter mile up the road, only place in town."

"Fine," he said, resigned to the quarter-mile walk in the rain. He wasn't about to ask her for a ride and there was no telling when the man who belonged in those overalls would be back. "You're sure Charlie or one of the Larkins will be able to work on my car in the morning?"

"You can count on it."

He was.

She turned her back on him again and headed for the old Chevy.

He bit back a curse. "Don't you at least want me to leave my *name?* It's Augustus T.—"

"Gus," she said, cutting him off. "Got it. Just leave your key on the counter in the office." She snapped on the radio as she went by it. A country-western song echoed loudly through the garage.

He could hear her putting away tools as he left and wondered if Charlie Larkin worked tomorrow. Or if it would be one of the other sons or the father who'd be working on his car.

Leaving his key on the counter, he went out to pull

his briefcase and bag from the car, glad he traveled light. Then he started down the highway toward the far neon, the rain quickly drenching him to the skin.

He hadn't gone but a few yards when he felt the glare of headlights on his back and the sound of a car braking. It stopped next to him. He bent down in the rain to look in as the driver leaned over to roll down the passenger-side window a crack.

"Need a ride?" asked an elderly man.

The rain alone would have made him accept. "As a matter of fact—"

"Get in. I would imagine you're headed for May-belle Murphy's, right?" the gray-haired, wizened man asked as Augustus shoved his bag into the back seat and climbed into the front. "Not a night for man nor beast," the driver said as he started back down the highway. "Car trouble, huh?"

It was warm in the car and smelled of pipe tobacco, the kind his father used to use. The man didn't give him a chance to answer.

"Name's Emmett Graham, I run the only mercantile here in town. If you haven't eaten yet, the special at the Pinecone Café tonight is chicken-fried steak. Stays open till ten."

His stomach growled, reminding he hadn't eaten since morning. Emmett didn't seem to notice when he didn't reciprocate and introduce himself. "Sounds like you know the town and probably everyone in it."

"Hell, you've already met half the people here."

Augustus knew the man was exaggerating, but not by much. He was curious about the girl he'd met—and the man whose overalls she'd had on. "Well, you're definitely the friendliest half I've met so far."

The old man nodded with a smile. "Charlie ain't too hospitable at times." He pulled up in front of Murphy's.

Through the rain Augustus could see a short row of small log cabins set in the pines. "I haven't met Charlie yet. I assume he's one of the sons, but if he's anything like the girl I just saw at his garage—"

"Girl?" The old man let out a laugh. "Just goes to show that you shouldn't believe everything you read. There is no Larkin & *Sons*. Burt and Vera never had any sons. Burt just got all fired up when Vera finally got pregnant. He had a fancy-pants sign painter from Missoula come in and change the name to Larkin & Sons." The old man was shaking his head as if this wasn't the first time he'd told this particular story. "But after Charlotte was born, Vera couldn't have any more kids. Not that a half-dozen sons would have made Burt more proud than his Charlie. He died a happy man, knowing that Charlie would always keep the garage going. She quit college after his heart attack—he just fell over dead one day while working on a car—and Charlie took over running the garage."

Augustus stared at Emmett, telling himself the old man must be mistaken. That couldn't have been the Charlie Larkin he'd come two thousand miles to find. "She's just a *girl*."

The old man smiled. "Only looks young. She must be twenty-five by now—no, more like twenty-six." He looked up at Murphy's blinking neon. "Shouldn't be a problem getting a bed." There were no cars parked in front of any of the cabins. "Maybelle will see you're taken care of tonight and then Charlie will get your car running in the morning." Emmett glanced over at him and must have misread his expression. "Don't worry, Gus. Charlie is one hell of a mechanic."

Augustus wouldn't put money on *that*. But he nodded, thanked Emmett and, taking his bag from the back, climbed out. He stood in the rain, hardly feeling it, watching the old man drive away as he realized that Emmett had called him Gus. Only one person in this town even knew his name and she called him Gus.

He felt a chill quake through him that had nothing to do with the rain or the cold as he glanced back down the highway toward Larkin & Sons Gas and Garage.

Charlotte "Charlie" Larkin.

His killer was a woman.

Chapter Two

Charlie Larkin stood in the dark of the office watching the stranger through the rain and night, wondering who he was and why he'd come here. Especially now. More to the point, she wondered why he'd pretended he'd driven the rental car all the way from Missoula with the engine running that badly.

He'd lied about it getting worse. But why? A carburetor just didn't get that out of adjustment. Any decent mechanic would know at once that the engine had been fooled with.

She glanced out at the car. A tan sedan with a Missoula, Montana, license-plate number and a car-rental sticker on the back bumper.

A set of headlights blurred past, the rainy glow changing from a wash of pale yellow to blurred bright red as the car braked. She watched Emmett Graham offer the stranger a ride down to Murphy's, wishing perversely that she hadn't called Emmett and asked him to give the guy a lift. Maybe a walk in the rain would do the man some good. But she knew Emmett would be headed home and that he wouldn't mind and she didn't have the patience to wait for the man to walk that far.

She waited until she saw Emmett's car turn off the highway into Murphy's before she slipped the heavy wrench into the pocket of her overalls, then picked up the key from the counter and headed for the rental car.

No reason to look under the hood again. She didn't expect any more surprises with the engine, nothing more to learn there about the man than she already had.

She opened the driver's-side door and slid in, closing it firmly behind her, feeling vulnerable for those precious seconds when the dome light illuminated her through the rain. Now in the dark again, she saw Emmett back out of Murphy's, the right side of his car empty. The stranger would be checking in. She had time.

"How long will you be staying?" the elderly desk clerk inquired as she peered at Augustus through the lines of her trifocals with obvious curiosity. The air around her reeked of cheap perfume. Gardenia, maybe. Whatever it was, it made his eyes water.

It seemed Maybelle Murphy had been in a hurry. Tendrils of bottle-red hair poked out from under a hastily tied bright floral scarf. Her freshly applied red lipstick was smeared into the wrinkle lines above her lips and her cheeks flamed at two high points along her jawline where she'd slapped on color. She seemed a little breathless.

He could only assume guests at the motel were so infrequent they'd become an occasion. He couldn't imagine that her getting all dolled up had anything to do with him since she'd been behind the desk when he'd entered the office and she couldn't have known he was headed this way since he hadn't known himself until fifteen minutes ago.

She cocked her head at him, making the tarnished

brass earrings dangling from her sagging lobes jingle, as she waited for his answer.

How long would he be staying? He'd planned to stay in different hotels as he always did, having found that was the safest—and the most private. But it obviously wasn't going to be an option in Utopia.

"I'm not sure," he admitted, just anxious to get a room, a hot shower, dry clothes, food. Mostly, he needed time to think. About Charlie. He was still shocked she was the one he'd come so far to find.

"It's cheaper by the week," the woman offered sweetly.

It was cheap enough by the day and he doubted this would take a week. "Let's just start with one night."

She nodded. "Car's broke down, huh."

Either news traveled fast or car trouble was the only reason anyone slowed down, let alone stopped, in Utopia.

"Yes, car trouble," he said, sliding his credit card across the worn counter toward her, hoping to hurry her up.

She pushed his card back without even bothering to look at it. "Sorry, we don't do credit."

Of course not. He opened his wallet, took out three tens and handed them to her, putting his credit card away. "I'll need a receipt."

"Oh, so you're here on business, Gus?" the woman said as she counted out his change.

"No, I just like to keep track of my expenses," he snapped, annoyed that, like Charlie and Emmett, she'd called him Gus. Then remembering she hadn't even bothered to glance at his credit card, figured Charlie must have called Maybelle just as she had Emmett.

"Well, you're obviously not a hunter and it's the wrong time of year for a vacation up here, so…" She eyed him closely. "That doesn't leave a whole lot."

Nosy little busybody, wasn't she? "Just passing through," he said coldly and scooped up the room key, catching sight of a newspaper out of the corner of his eye, the headline bannered across the top: Missing Missoula Man Found At Bottom Of Freeze Out Lake. Foul Play Suspected In Doctor's Death.

"If you give me just a minute, I'll have that receipt you asked—"

He tuned Maybelle out as he snatched up the newspaper and quickly skimmed the story. Maybelle put the receipt and room key on the counter. He grabbed up both.

"Now let me show you how to find number five. It's—"

"I can find it," he said, tossing two quarters on the counter for the newspaper and drawing up the hood on his jacket as he pushed his way back out into the rain.

CHARLIE SAT PERFECTLY still in the darkness of the rental car, listening to the rain hammer the metal roof over the pumps, wishing she could get a sense of the man. A different impression of him than the one she'd picked up earlier in the garage.

The car smelled of his aftershave. A scent as masculine and confident as the man himself. She took hold of the wheel and closed her eyes for a moment, searching, as if he'd left something behind she could sense, something that would reassure her.

After a moment, she opened her eyes to the rain and the night, feeling empty and cold inside as she let go of the wheel. She'd been spending a lot of time alone in the dark lately.

Turning on the dome light, she quickly glanced around the car, not surprised to find it immaculate. No personal possessions of any kind. No beverage containers, spilled chips or empty fast-food bags with cold French fries in the bottom. The car looked as clean as when he'd rented it. Too clean for a drive halfway across Montana. He was a man who didn't like leaving anything of himself, she thought as she snapped off the light.

But as she opened the glove compartment, the bulb inside shone on the small fresh smudge of grease on the palm of her right hand. She looked from it to the steering wheel. He'd left more of himself here than he'd thought.

The rental agreement was right where she'd figured he would have forgotten it: folded neatly inside the glove compartment. Augustus T. Riley. He really called himself that? No street address. Instead, a post-office box in Los Angeles. A phone number.

She memorized the numbers, praying she would never need them, then carefully folded the form and put it back exactly as she'd found it. She'd learned that from her father the first time she'd taken an engine apart under his watchful eye. Remembering how you found it, how you took it apart was the key to putting each piece precisely back where it had been.

She closed the glove compartment and sat for a moment, expecting to feel guilty for this invasion of another person's privacy. *Wanting* to feel guilty. She felt nothing. Augustus T. Riley had given up his rights to privacy when he'd brought her his tampered engine to repair. When he'd come looking for Charlie Larkin.

She opened the car door, hit the lock and, pocketing the key, started back toward the office. The rain had slacked off a little and the temperature had dropped. There would be snow on the ground by morning. She glanced up the highway toward Murphy's, wondering where the stranger was now, concerned he was someone she had reason to fear but not knowing why.

She sensed, rather than saw, the furtive movement off to her left. A hooded figure came out of the darkness and the rain, barreling down on her. She half turned, her hand going to the wrench she'd slipped into the pocket of her overalls, stopping just short of the cold steel.

"Wayne," she let out on a relieved breath.

He didn't seem to notice. "Hey, Charlie." As always, he looked embarrassed and apologetic at the same time. "I didn't see you." He took a swipe at his wet face with his sleeve. "Raining pretty hard." He seemed to focus on her, his eyes always a little too bright. "I hope I didn't keep you past your dinner."

She shook her head and smiled her half smile. Friendly, but not too. "You know I stay open until nine on Friday nights."

He nodded vigorously, obviously not knowing anything of the kind. She'd always closed early this time of year, and with everything that had been going on lately, she'd shortened the gas station hours even more.

"I got your car running," she said as she led the way inside.

He pulled back his hood, throwing off a spray of rainwater as he trotted to keep up. "It's a good old car."

He always said that. She'd given up telling him he should look for something with a few less miles on it. She understood the sentimental value of a car, even one as bad-looking as this old Chevy. Wayne's dad, Ted, had given him the Chevy when Wayne was seventeen—just before Ted had died. That had been five years ago, five years of trying to keep the old car running.

Water dripped from the dingy cap Wayne wore under the hood as he dug deep into his worn jeans and pulled out two crumpled bills. Charlie watched him smooth one of them across his thigh, his curly blond head bent with such concentration it hurt to watch him.

"I get paid next Friday if this isn't enough," Wayne said, working the wrinkles out of the second twenty. He sacked and stocked groceries and supplies at Emmett Graham's small market.

"Actually, you could do me a favor," Charlie said, looking at the old Chevy rather than at Wayne. "I heard your mother raised more winter squash than she could use this year. You could save me a trip and get me some in payment. Otherwise, I'm just going to have to drive over and buy them from her."

Wayne looked up, both the surprise and confusion only momentary since this was how their conversations over the bill went every time. "Squash?"

"Aunt Selma has her heart set on winter squash for Sunday dinner."

Wayne nodded vigorously. "Mom's got lotsa squash."

"Great." She handed him the keys to the Chevy and touched the garage-door opener. The overhead rose slowly with a groan, letting in the wet and cold and dark. Just beyond the door, she could see puddles, night slick, but no rain dimpling the surface. Snow fell silent as death.

"I'll get the squash and bring them right away," Wayne said excitedly as he opened his car door.

Charlie started to tell him to wait till morning, but caught herself. Wayne would be back in a few minutes and she didn't want him worrying himself all night about paying his bill. "That would be great."

He drove off, hitting all of the puddles, reminding her he was part kid, part man, caught for this lifetime somewhere in between.

She started to close the bay door, then remembered the rental car. She still had the key in her pocket.

The interior smelled of Gus, even over all the others who had rented the car. Odd, she thought. A man who gave little away about himself and yet invaded whatever space he occupied—and didn't give it up easily. A dangerous man.

She coaxed the engine to run long enough to get the car into the bay, hurriedly closing the overhead door behind it, feeling vulnerable again, as if she'd let in more than she knew, more than she could handle.

At the sound of Wayne's old Chevy, she turned out the lights, left the rental car key on the counter in the office and stepped outside to find that he'd brought her two large boxes of produce, including apples and pumpkins. She helped him load the boxes into her van parked on the side of the building. Then watched him drive off before she went back in to lock up for the night.

Just inside the office, she stopped, chilled at the sight of the rental car in the second far bay—a small faint light glowing inside it.

The chill deepened as a knife of fear cut up her spine. She hadn't left a light on inside the car. That she was sure of. She stood in the doorway, heart pounding so loudly she couldn't hear over it. She breathed deeply, trying to still the cold dread as she caught the scent of Augustus T. Riley's aftershave over the deep-seated smell of motor oil and cleaner. *He was here.*

Blindly, she reached for the overhead light switch, her free hand going to the wrench in her overalls even as common sense told her it wasn't much of a weapon.

The fluorescents came on, illuminating both bays. He wasn't here.

But he had *been.*

She turned to look back at the counter. The key to the rental car was gone.

She moved slowly across the cold concrete to the car. Even from a distance she could see that the glove compartment was open, the small bulb illuminating one dark corner of the car—and the garage.

Walking around to the passenger side, she opened the door, not surprised he'd left the key in the ignition. He'd wanted her to know that he'd been here. *Because he'd left her something.*

The clipping had been torn from the newspaper, the edges ragged, the paper still damp from the storm. He'd left it where she couldn't miss the headline: Missing Missoula Man Found At Bottom Of Freeze Out Lake. Foul Play Suspected In Doctor's Death.

Chapter Three

Augustus brushed fresh snow from his jacket as he stepped through the door into the Pinecone Café. He should have been freezing cold. He definitely was wet, first from the rain, then the snow. Obviously, he wasn't prepared for this kind of weather, but he didn't care. He was on the chase—and he loved nothing better.

A hush fell over the café as everyone turned to look at who'd come through the door. He shrugged out of his lightweight jacket, realizing his dress shirt and slacks made him conspicuous enough, but now they were wet. He could feel all eyes on him. Forget anonymity in Utopia, he thought as he hung the jacket next to five tan canvas coats in various sizes, styles and stages of decline.

Feeling as if he was on center stage, he turned slowly to take in the café—and its customers. The Pinecone was just a hole-in-the-wall with three booths and a half-dozen stools along a worn counter that faced the grill. A middle-aged couple sat in the first booth, two men in the next, the third empty.

At the counter, an elderly woman knitted, her large bag on the stool next to her. A middle-aged woman in a waitress uniform and nurse's shoes stood across the counter from her smoking a cigarette, looking as if she owned the place. At the far end of the counter, a lone man sat bent over his coffee. He didn't look up.

"Good evening," Augustus said to the curious faces.

"Evenin'," the woman behind the counter replied. All except the guy at the counter gave him a nod, the women a polite smile as he worked his way past them to the empty booth. Friendly little place, wasn't it?

He slid in, his back to the wall so he could watch the door, an old habit.

Conversations resumed. The two men in the next booth talking about a tractor that the one named Leroy couldn't get to run. The middle-aged couple eating in silence, a sure sign they were married, and at the counter, the older waitress chatting with the knitter about a sweater she'd started for her granddaughter. The lone twenty-something man seemingly in his own world.

"Hi!" A perky young bottled blonde in a too-tight uniform came out of the kitchen to slide a plastic-covered menu across the table at him. "Our special is chicken-fried steak. Comes with soup, salad, mashed potatoes, gravy, peas, a roll and dessert for six-fifty."

Amazing. "Sold," he said, smiling as he slid the menu back at her without opening it. She looked to be in her late twenties, about Charlotte "Charlie" Larkin's age, if Emmett was to be believed, and she was a hell of a lot friendlier, both things Augustus hoped to use to his advantage.

She gave him the full effect of her smile. "Can I get you some coffee?"

"I'd love a cup. It's a little damp out there."

She laughed at that, considering he was soaked to the skin and wearing the least appropriate clothing possible. Everyone else in the place had on jeans or those tan canvas pants that seemed to be so popular in this town along with flannel shirts and winter boots.

"It's going to get a whole lot damper," she said, coming back with the coffeepot and a cup. She poured him some and said, "Supposed to drop a good eight inches of snow before morning."

Just what he needed. He'd have to buy a coat and boots. Fortunately he'd had the sense to bring a pair of jeans. "Isn't it too early in the year?"

She laughed. "This is Montana. It can snow any month—and has." She left and came back with a bowl of steaming vegetable soup. It smelled wonderful and tasted even better.

He ate his soup quickly, needing the warmth and hungrier than he'd been for a while. His clothes were starting to dry out, and while he was more comfortable, some of his earlier elation was starting to wear off and he wasn't sure why. He suspected it was because Charlie Larkin wasn't at all what he'd expected—and not just because she was female. He'd known his share of female killers and knew that they came in all sizes and shapes. Some were even as cute and innocent-looking as Charlie.

No, something else about her bothered him and he couldn't put his finger on it.

He blamed his sudden uneasiness on the fact that, while what evidence there was pointed to Charlie Larkin—it was only circumstantial. Nor was this the way he normally operated. All the other times, he'd come in after the arrest had been made, after the killer was behind bars—or out on bail. This time he was going after the murderer himself. This time, it was personal.

Taking a sip of his coffee, he reassured himself that he was dead-on with this case. What evidence there was had led him straight to Charlie Larkin—and his gut instincts hardly ever let him down. Except for that one time, which he tried not to dwell on.

But that one mistake had taught him well. He'd trusted one of his subjects and it had almost cost him his life—and his career. That's why he would never let himself get emotionally involved with a suspect, again.

Not that there was any chance of that with this case, he thought, remembering the churlish young woman in the baggy overalls he'd met at the garage. So at odds with her angel-cute face, the freckles, the big brown eyes, framed by all that dark-flame hair. Oh, yeah, he could see how a woman with her looks and spunk would be like honey to bears to most men.

But he wasn't most men. So what was it about Charlie Larkin that had him worried? Something about her reminded him of Natalie. The thought shook him to his core. He glanced out the window, feeling too isolated, too ill-prepared for the weather—and this dinky little town. How was he going to be able to accomplish anything without even rudimentary services? He'd tried to make a call from his motel room, which—big surprise—had no phone and he got no service on his cell phone.

He'd seen two pay phones so far, one tacked on the wall a few feet inside the café door and a primitive-looking one outside Larkin's. Neither exactly private. And the one was out in the weather and way too close to Charlie Larkin.

The conversation at the all-male booth had changed to the price of lumber and those damn tree huggers who were ruining the logging industry.

The woman in the waitress uniform put out her cigarette. "So, Leroy, did I hear you're still trying to get that old tractor running?" she inquired of the suspender-wearing man in the booth. She had a face with a lot of miles on it and a voice gravelly from smoking.

"Got to, Helen. Can't afford a new one. Goin' to have to plow snow with it pretty darned soon. Maybe Charlie'll have a look at it when she gets the time," he said, wagging his head.

Helen, who no doubt was the café's owner, looked over in Augustus's direction. "Get settled in at Murphy's, Gus?"

Gus. It wasn't bad enough that Charlie Larkin had told everyone in town about him, she hadn't even gotten his name right. "It's Augustus," he said and gave Helen a smile to soften it. "Augustus T. Riley."

She chuckled as if he'd said something funny, obviously not recognizing the name. "Well, welcome to Utopia. You're the big news of the day."

"Slow news day, huh," he said, seeing an opening. "I would think that fellow who got pulled out of the lake would still be news."

"Shoot, that was over a week ago. Old news now and not the kind we like to be known for." She stepped back into the kitchen and proceeded to finish up some cooking she had going on. "Trudi, your orders are up."

He wondered what kind of news Utopia liked being known for.

"Here ya go, T.J.," Trudi said cheerfully as she slid a plateful of food across the counter to the guy sitting alone. She wasted a big smile on him. He didn't even bother to look up at her, just grunted something Augustus couldn't hear.

Trudi stood there for a moment, then went to deliver a couple of burgers to Leroy's table and brought Augustus his salad. "Was creepy though, you know, if you think that his body was in the lake all this time," she said, picking up the thread of the earlier conversation.

"Since last fall," he agreed, trying not to think about it. "So, did you know him?"

She shook her head. "He wasn't from around here."

Augustus knew that. Josh Whitaker had been an emergency-room doctor in Missoula at the hospital. He was thirty-four, two years younger than Augustus, single and lived with two other residents in a large house near the hospital. His death was being investigated as possible foul play after the coroner reported Josh had been hit in the back of the head with a blunt object, his car then pushed into the lake where it sank from view.

No one knew what Josh Whitaker was doing in Utopia, thirty miles from the nearest real town. In this part of Montana, that thirty miles felt like three hundred. Augustus had never felt such isolation and couldn't imagine why Josh had come up here all the way from Missoula. Josh had been missing for almost a year, his body finally discovered in late September by two local teenagers, just before the cold spell.

But what Augustus knew that the press didn't, according to phone company records, was that Josh had received two phones calls from Utopia just before he disappeared. Both from the pay phone outside Larkin & Sons Gas and Garage. He'd almost placed several phone calls to that pay phone, along with another to a C. Larkin that same day, the call to C. Larkin less than a minute in length, making Augustus wonder if Josh had reached Charlie. Her name had also showed up in an old date book of Josh's with a notation beside it: help line.

What Augustus needed was to find out what Charlotte "Charlie" Larkin's relationship had been with Josh Whitaker, how they'd met no doubt through Josh's statewide help line program, why Josh might have come to Utopia to see her and why she might want him dead. No small task.

But hadn't Emmett mentioned that Charlie Larkin had to quit college when her father had his heart attack? Was it possible she and Josh had met while she was attending the University of Montana in Missoula? That was where Josh had started his first help line.

"What a terrible way to die," Trudi was saying. "Drowning." She shivered.

"I heard it's not that bad, like going to sleep," the knitting woman said.

"Marcella, I think you're confusing drowning with hypothermia," Helen said.

"Starvation," Leroy said. "I guess that or a quick heart attack is the way to go."

"Beats putting a gun to your head," Helen agreed.

An argument ensued over what caliber gun worked best. Augustus tried to steer the conversation back to the body in the lake. "Do they know what the drowned guy was doing here?"

The customers looked to Helen as if anyone in town would know, it would be her. She shrugged.

"Isn't this lake off the beaten path?" Augustus asked.

"Yeah, but maybe he'd heard about those campers that were eaten by that grizzly and wanted to see the place," Trudi said, all big-eyed.

Helen grimaced. "That's pretty morbid and it was years ago. I can't imagine he would have even heard about it."

Augustus remembered from the national news stories when he was a senior in high school and working on the school newspaper. Mostly he remembered because there were only a few things that ate you. Sharks. Gators. Grizzlies. "Didn't I read in the paper that he was seeing a local woman?" he lied, drawing the conversation back to Josh Whitaker.

"Wouldn't know anything about that," Helen said, going back to the kitchen to check on his chicken-fried steak. A few minutes later she handed Trudi a huge plate overflowing with meat, gravy and mashed potatoes and a side of canned peas through the pass-through.

"Charlie fixing your car, huh?" Helen asked him, returning to her spot at the counter across from Marcella.

"In the morning," he said, taking the opening. "I heard she's a pretty good mechanic."

"Best in five counties," Helen boasted as she lit another cigarette, definitely at home with the place, with herself.

Best in thirty miles, he could buy. Five counties though? That he seriously doubted.

"If anyone can get your car running, it's Charlie," Leroy agreed.

Anyone with even a little mechanical training could get his car running, if they wanted to. And if Charlie Larkin was as good as everyone in this town claimed, she would know that. The thought disturbed him.

"Yep, they don't come any better than Charlie," Helen agreed. "I wouldn't be surprised if she was over there right now working on your car."

He wouldn't put money on that.

"Like that time she found that family broke down outside of town," Marcella said, knitting as she talked. "Remember that bunch? Must have had a dozen kids in that old motor home. Charlie took them food and got the rig running, though heaven only knows how."

Helen was nodding, obviously savoring the story. "They didn't have two nickels to rub together, had spent all their money on gas trying to get to the coast—and a job the father said he had waiting for him. Sounded like a story to me, but you know Charlie."

He didn't. But he sure wanted to. He took a bite of the steak. It was delicious.

"Charlie told him he could pay his bill after he got settled." Helen shook her head. "I would have sworn she'd never see a dime of that money, but a year later she gets a check—with interest. Don't that beat all?"

"That's one hell of a story," Augustus agreed, wondering how much of it was now Utopia legend and how much of it was true.

"Oh, we could go on all night about Charlie," Helen said.

"Like the way she's helped Earlene with that baby," Marcella said. She glanced back at Augustus. "Earlene's a single mother. The baby's father's dead."

Charlie Larkin sounded like a saint. He'd found out a long time ago, though, that the nicest, most charitable person in the world was still capable of committing murder. But it certainly made him all the more curious about Charlie. And all the more determined to get her.

The twenty-something man at the counter Trudi had called T.J. suddenly pushed his half-full plate back, slapped down some bills on the counter and stalked out, grabbing his coat before disappearing through the door without a word.

"Who was that?" Augustus asked Trudi quietly when she came over to his table to refill his coffee cup.

She glanced toward the closing door. "Oh, that's just T. J. Blue."

"He seemed upset."

"He's always upset when Charlie Larkin's name

comes up," she whispered and then went off with the coffeepot to refill cups.

Upset when Charlie Larkin's name came up, was he? Augustus made a point of reminding himself to have a talk with this T. J. Blue who hadn't said a word when Helen and everyone else were going on about the virtues of Charlie Larkin. Interesting.

"Emmett told me that Charlie had to come home from college early and take over the garage after her father's heart attack," Augustus said to Helen who was clearing away T. J. Blue's dishes after his abrupt departure.

Helen nodded, but said nothing, as if he was on the verge of asking too many questions.

"She worked in the garage alongside her father every summer," Leroy said. "Burt insisted she get an education although everyone in town knew he hoped she'd come home and work with him after she graduated."

"What was she majoring in at Missoula before she had to quit?" he asked casually, taking a bite of his steak. It could have been cardboard for all the attention he paid it as he waited for someone to confirm his theory that Charlie Larkin had gone to college in the same town Josh Whitaker was a doctor.

Helen frowned, looking suspicious.

"Business, wasn't it, Helen?" Marcella asked, looking up from her knitting. "But she didn't go to school in Missoula. She went to Bozeman." Miles apart.

"I thought Emmett told me—never mind," Augustus said. "I must have heard wrong." So how had they met?

Charlie had to be the reason Josh Whitaker had come to Utopia and ended up in Freeze Out Lake last fall. Augustus would stake his reputation on it. But what was their connection? The obvious female-male one? Or something else?

A thought struck him like a brick. The use of the pay phone at the garage—rather than her home phone. "Charlie isn't married, is she?"

Helen studied him for a long moment. "No." Her gaze said he'd just asked too many questions.

"She sounds like someone I'd like to get to know better." He shrugged and grinned his you-know-us-guys grin.

Helen seemed to relax a little. She obviously knew how men could be. She went around the counter to sit next to Marcella and proceeded to tell her about some yarn she'd found on sale in Missoula.

"Got all that firewood split and stacked yet for winter?" Leroy asked the man across from him.

"See ya, Helen," the woman in the first booth said as she and her husband left, leaving money on the table.

"Take care, Kate. You, too, Bud."

Augustus concentrated on his food, listening to the conversations move from one mundane topic to the next. No one paid him any attention. He must be old news.

But he saw Trudi watching him when she thought he wasn't looking and he knew, the way he always knew, that here was someone who had something she was dying to tell him.

The chase always made him ravenous and this one was no exception. It wouldn't be easy with most of the town trying to convince him Charlie Larkin was a saint. But at least one person in town wasn't wild about Charlie: T. J. Blue. And Augustus had a feeling he'd find more. He smiled and dug into his dinner.

HE'D EATEN ALL he could and shoved his plate away when Trudi came over to his booth. She was all business, making a project out of writing up his bill, then taking his napkin to write something on it before sliding it and the bill under the edge of his saucer. She refilled his cup with coffee he'd just said he didn't want. She seemed nervous.

He could feel Helen's gaze on them, watching eagle-eyed, and Trudi must have felt it, too. She huriedly cleared up his dishes, everything but his coffee, and disappeared back into the kitchen again.

He stared after her for a moment, then plucked the bill and napkin from under the edge of the saucer. Along with the six dollars and fifty cents he owed for dinner, she'd written on his napkin: "I get off at ten."

He glanced at his watch. That would give him time to get ready for her. He pulled out his pen and wrote, Murphy's, No. 5 on the napkin, then dropped a ten on top of the bill. With luck Trudi had something good to offer him.

As he left the café, Helen called after him, "See ya, Gus." He could feel her watching as he walked past the front window of the café. He wondered how long it would take her to call Charlie Larkin and tell her he'd been asking personal questions about her. The thought pleased him, since he'd only just begun.

I'm coming for you, Charlie.

Chapter Four

Charlie pushed through the kitchen door of the old farmhouse she shared with her mother and aunt, a huge box of produce in her arms.

"Let me guess. Wayne Dreyer's old Chevy broke down again." Aunt Selma shook her freshly-permed, gray head as she walked over to the table to peer inside the box Charlie set down. Her aunt looked small and frail next to the huge box, older somehow.

"I've got another one in the van," Charlie said and went back out to get it through the falling snow, thick as cotton ticking, the old farmhouse and the surrounding trees a blur of white.

Her aunt was giving her that look when she came back in.

"Winter squash, apples and pumpkins," Charlie said, sliding the second huge box onto the table next to the first.

"I can see that," Selma said. "There's enough squash alone to last three winters. And pumpkins—Landsakes, what will we do with all of them? You'd better hope that boy's car doesn't break down again until berry season."

"He got the idea that we eat a lot of pumpkin pie," she said, shrugging out of her coat. This time last year the water pump had gone on Wayne's Chevy and she'd taken pumpkins as payment, going on about her Aunt Selma's need for fresh pumpkin for her pies.

Her aunt shook her head. "You remind me of your father."

"Thank you," Charlie said, going to hang her coat on the hook by the back door.

"That wasn't a compliment."

Charlie turned to smile at her.

Her aunt's gaze softened. "Is anything wrong?"

"No."

Selma waved that off. "I know you, girl," she said, frowning. "Something's happened."

Some people in town said Selma had The Gift, that she could practically look into your head and see things that no one else could—including the future.

There had been times when Charlie wasn't so sure they weren't right. But mostly she believed her aunt just paid more attention to the little things, things other people maybe didn't take the time to notice. Not that it wasn't damn eerie on occasion. And a real pain if you preferred to keep your problems to yourself.

The phone rang. Charlie tried to hide her relief as she gave her aunt a shrug and picked up the receiver from the wall phone.

"That guy whose car broke down—Gus—he just left," Helen whispered. "I thought you'd want to know."

"Really?" she said and smiled at her aunt, knowing there was more.

"He was asking a lot of questions."

"About what?" she asked, trying to keep her voice light.

"About that man who drowned in the lake and about you."

Charlie let out a little laugh and turned away from her aunt. "Well, you know what they say about curiosity."

"That's not the worst part," Helen said. "Trudi warmed right up to him. You know how she is."

Everyone knew how Trudi Murphy was. The stranger probably would know soon enough.

"I think you should try to find out something about him," Helen said. "I don't like the looks of him." She didn't like the looks of most men. Blame it on four bad marriages and a weakness for losers. "What's he wanting to know about you for anyway?"

"I don't know, but I'm sure it's nothing." She wished that were true.

"I hope you're right," Helen said. "Once his car is fixed, maybe he'll leave. Maybelle said he only paid for one night."

"That's good." But she had a feeling it didn't mean a thing. "Thanks for letting me know." She hung up and turned, feeling her aunt's intent gaze.

"Charlotte—" Selma began.

"What in the world?" her mother said from the doorway. Vera's eyes widened with wonder, as if the boxes on the table were brightly wrapped presents instead of vegetables from the gourd family and the fruit that destroyed Eden.

Her mother was smaller than Selma and lacked her sister's strength. Vera had always been the fragile one, her pale skin almost translucent, her hair now downy feather white.

Aunt Selma gave Charlie a warning look, one she knew only too well. *Don't upset your mother.* The words should have been stitched on their living-room pillows.

"I've been wanting to make some pumpkin pies," Selma said.

Vera Larkin smiled dreamily. Her cardigan sweater had fallen off one shoulder. "I do love pumpkin pie. With ice cream." She frowned. "Or is it whipped cream?"

"Either sounds good," Selma told her as she pulled her sister's sweater around her thin shoulders.

Charlie noticed that her mother's slippers were on the wrong feet as she watched the two leave the room. She closed her eyes, the pain too intense. It broke her heart to see her mother like this and growing worse each day.

If it wasn't for Aunt Selma... It was hard to believe that Selma was almost seventy, the older of the sisters. She'd never married. When Charlie was a child, she'd found a yellowed wedding dress in the attic. Her mother had told her a romantic story about Selma falling wildly in love with a soldier. They were to be married, but just days before he was coming home, his plane was shot down. Devastated, Selma had sworn never to love another man.

Of course, there were people in Utopia who swore the story was as phony as Trudi Murphy's bust. But then how did Charlie explain the wedding dress still in the attic? If Selma's "sight" was to be believed, maybe Selma had known long ago that Vera was going to need her and that's why she'd never married. Maybe Selma had called off the wedding after another one of Vera's miscarriages had laid her up. It would be like Selma.

Vera had never been strong, according to Selma. She'd married Burt at eighteen full of hope, but quickly became weakened both physically and spiritually by miscarriages and disappointments, until finally Charlie was born. Vera was almost forty by then.

Just twenty-one years later, she lost Burt to a heart attack. It had been a blow that had left her mother crippled emotionally and brought Charlie racing back from college to take over the garage. That had been four years ago. Aunt Selma had been there, though, each time Vera needed her. It wasn't surprising that Selma had been the one to notice Vera's Alzheimer's first.

"Are you warm enough?" Selma was asking Vera in the living room. "It's snowing out. Maybe I should throw more logs on the fire. Would you like that?" Selma glanced over her shoulder as she helped Vera into a wingback chair in front of the fireplace, her look clear: *We will talk later.*

Charlie had no doubt of that. Selma and Vera had already eaten dinner. Charlie could smell the chicken and dumplings Selma had saved her. There was a warm apple pie, too.

Charlie had tried to get Selma to slow down.

"Cooking and caring for my sister is what I've always done," Selma had snapped. "Let me enjoy myself and don't get in my way." She'd softened the words with a smile. "You know how much I love doing this."

Charlie had nodded and stayed out of her way, helping out as much as she could behind the scenes.

While Charlie ate, Vera chattered away about things that had happened forty years ago. Selma was too quiet, as if she could read Charlie's thoughts, which kept returning to the stranger in town.

After dinner and dishes, Charlie got her coat from the peg and went out on the porch, hoping the cold night air would clear her head. It wasn't long before she heard the soft creak of slipper steps on the floorboards behind her.

"Well?" Selma's voice sounded hoarse with worry.

She didn't turn around. "It's nothing." She tried to sound unconcerned.

"Then why do you seem…scared?"

Scared? Is that what this was? This quaking inside

her. This high-frequency jitter, like being connected to a high-voltage battery all the time. She wouldn't have been surprised if she started throwing off sparks. At first it had been a low buzz. Almost a nervous energy. Anxiety. Worry. But now she vibrated with what had to be more than fear. She hugged herself as if that would still her terror. At least long enough to reassure her aunt.

"There's something I need to ask you." Selma seemed to hesitate. "Does this have anything to do with that young man they pulled from the lake?"

Charlie turned slowly to look at her aunt. Selma stood in a pool of light from the kitchen window wearing a thick wool sweater over her polyester pantsuit. Charlie remembered her mother secretly knitting the sweater several years ago. A Christmas present in Selma's favorite colors, browns, golds and reds.

Even from here Charlie could see the mistakes in the pattern. The signs had been there that long ago, only Charlie hadn't recognized them. But then, it was so hard to admit that someone you loved was losing her mind.

"Yes," Charlie said. It had everything to do with Josh Whitaker.

Selma reached for the porch railing and closed her eyes, her bare hand pale and bony, veins blue against the white skin, frail.

Charlie started to reach for her, afraid her aunt was going to collapse. But she drew back her hand at the last minute as Selma's eyes snapped open.

Before she saw the tears, Charlie was going to tell her aunt everything. The weight of holding something like this inside just seemed too much to bear alone any longer. But the tears stopped her. Selma had always been strong, but this was too much of a burden for anyone, especially someone you loved.

"I'm just upset because the death reminds me of when Quinn was killed," Charlie said quickly.

The relief in Selma's expression was worth the half lie Charlie had had to tell.

"You still think about Quinn Simonson?" her aunt asked, sounding surprised but stronger. "That was so long ago and I didn't think your relationship with him was that serious."

Charlie shook her head. "No, but he was my *first* boy-friend."

"The Simonsons aren't giving you a hard time again, are they?" Selma demanded fiercely, reminding Charlie of a bantam rooster. "Those people. They just want to blame someone for their golden boy's death and you're an easy target."

Golden boy only fit Quinn because of his blond good looks and because Phil and Norma Simonson had put him on a pedestal above even their oldest son, Forest. To them, Quinn could do no wrong. Unfortunately, Charlie knew better.

"It's not the Simonsons," Charlie said. "This latest accident at the lake just brings back all the awful memories from before." Not that the Simonsons had let her forget for a moment over the past seven years what they believed she'd done—killed their son.

"I'm so sorry this had to happen now," Selma said. "You have enough to concern yourself with."

"I'm fine." She hugged Selma, tears springing to her eyes at the frailty she felt in her aunt's wiry-thin frame.

"Oh, Charlie." Her aunt brushed a dry kiss across her cheek. "You have taken on so much with your mother and me."

"That's not true," she said. "You and Mom have always taken care of me and now you have Mom to take care of as well."

Her aunt pulled her sweater around herself, her expression unconvinced. How much did she know? Or did she just *suspect* the truth?

"It's cold out here," Charlie said. "You should get back in before Mom misses you." She knew that, more than the cold, would get her aunt back inside, keep her aunt from asking any more questions.

With obvious reluctance, Selma scuffled back into the house without another word.

Charlie turned to look out at the snow, filled with relief—and regret. The snow had begun to stick and pile up. The way a lot of things in life tended to pile up. When Josh's body was pulled from the lake, she'd felt paralyzed with fear. She hadn't known he was in town. Still didn't understand what could have brought him up here considering that she hadn't seen or spoken to him in four years.

She shook her head, the horror of his murder almost more than she could bear. She closed her eyes. She had just let things happen and now she'd have to pay the price. But she wouldn't make that mistake again. She had to protect her family, no matter what it took.

From somewhere out in the snowy darkness came a low growl. Charlie moved down the porch toward the sound, trying to see the dog through the falling snow. Spark Plug, the name her father had given the puppy just before his death, growled again, this time the growl lower, more serious.

Something was out there. Someone. Charlie felt the soft hair on her neck stand up. Moving silently, she retraced her footsteps and opened the back door. The shotgun was high up on the top shelf, out of her mother's reach—even with a chair. Charlie pulled it down and dug out two buckshot shells from the kitchen drawer. She loaded the gun and stepped back out onto the porch.

By now, snow blanketed the yard and fell in a wall of white. She stood in the dark under the porch roof, staring out into the snowfall. Who was it she had to fear? Augustus T. Riley. What was he anyway? A cop? A private investigator hired by Josh's family? Did it matter?

Spark Plug growled again, only this time farther away, then began to bark. Past the barking, Charlie heard an engine turn deep in the pines somewhere on the county road. It sounded like a pickup with a bad muffler, one of a half dozen around town.

Spark Plug quit barking and after a few minutes wandered out of the snowstorm. He was a true mutt, shortlegged, with a spotted white, brown and black short-haired coat and big floppy ears. When he saw her, he wagged his stubby tail and climbed up the steps to the porch.

Charlie put the shotgun aside to brush snow from the dog's back. She waited until the sound of the truck died away, then she took him inside where Aunt Selma pretended to scold him softly for not coming home sooner for dinner.

"Spark Plug barking at another coyote?" Selma asked as Charlie returned the shotgun to the top shelf and the shells to the kitchen drawer.

"Sure seems that way." Charlie took her time cutting three pieces of apple pie, thinking about the truck she'd heard leaving and Spark Plug's worried growl.

Then she took the plates of pie into the living room where her mother was surprised all over again to see her.

Chapter Five

Augustus heard the tap at his door just after ten. He'd give Trudi one thing, she hadn't wasted any time.

He took one quick glance around the cabin to make sure he hadn't left anything important lying around—like his notebook. The cabin was straight out of an old Western. Knotty-pine walls, horse-motif bedspread, antler lamp and lonesome-cowboy painting on the wall. Hee-haw!

No one back in L.A. would believe a town like this still existed. He hardly believed it himself.

She knocked again, this time more insistent. Anxious, wasn't she? He doubted it was his charm. Some people took a malicious delight in dishing dirt about other people. As ugly as that trait was, it sure made his job a lot easier.

He swung the door open.

She stood on the tiny porch in an unbuttoned long camel-colored wool coat over a short, low-cut dress and black boots. She bit nervously at her lower lip as she shot periodic glances behind her.

"Hey," he said, a little surprised by the way she was dressed. Even more so by the suspicious way she was acting. Did she think she'd been followed? Or was she just afraid someone would see her coming here? Why was that? "Jealous boyfriend?"

She swung around, obviously startled, and quickly smiled. "I don't have a boyfriend. I mean not a steady one. I like my freedom," she said all coy.

He wished there was another way to get what he needed from her. Obviously she had something different in mind than he did. He leaned against the doorjamb, not wanting to ask her in but knowing that if he didn't he might never know what she was dying to tell him. But at what price?

The snow had stopped falling, the ground glittering cold and white behind her. And just when he thought Utopia couldn't be any more alien to him.

Reluctantly, he stepped aside. "Come on in." As he started to close the door, he looked out in the snowy darkness to see a pickup slow as it passed on the highway. The truck was a dark color, loud—and while he couldn't see more than a silhouette behind the wheel, it was obvious the driver had been looking this way. Looking for Trudi? Or him? The pickup sped up and on past, kicking up snow.

He closed the door and turned to find Trudi sitting on the end of his bed, her coat off, legs crossed, exposing a lot of skin. The little flowered dress was even skimpier than he'd thought.

Sometimes he hated the things he had to do to get what he wanted. But all that mattered was the end result, right? Right. "Can I offer you something to drink?" he asked. "I'm afraid all I have are plastic glasses and tap water."

She smiled and reached into the pocket of her coat, pulling out a bottle of beer. She handed it to him and dug out another from the other pocket. "I hope you like Moose Drool."

He glanced at the beer. "Who could pass up a beer with such an appealing name."

She laughed at that. In fact, she laughed at everything he said. It made this a whole lot harder.

He pulled out the straight-back chair from the small oak desk. "Are you old enough to drink alcohol?" he asked, straddling the chair to rest his arms on the back.

She gave him an "oh-you-tease" look and took a sip of her beer. "I'm twenty-six."

Charlie's age? "So you must have gone to school with Charlie Larkin."

She nodded and glanced around the cabin. It wasn't that interesting. Then her gaze settled on him. She wet her lips and gave him a come-hither smile. "Is that the only reason you asked me here? To talk about Charlie?"

He must be getting old, because he just wasn't up to this game tonight. He cut to the chase, unable to bear dragging it out any longer. "I got the impression at the café that there was something you wanted to tell me about her."

She seemed startled and suddenly ill at ease. "I can't imagine what it could have been."

He watched her dig at the beer label with her thumbnail. "Give it a little thought, I'll bet it will come to you."

Her eyes narrowed. "Are you a cop or something?"

"Something." Giving her his backup story would be a waste of a good lie. And there seemed little reason to tell her the truth since it would be out soon enough.

She took a drink of her beer, eyeing him over the bottle. "What's in it for me?"

Finally, solid ground. "Depends on if I find the information of value." When she didn't bother to nail him down on a price, it became apparent she wasn't in it for the money—just as he'd originally suspected.

She sat up straighter on the bed. "You were asking about the guy they found in the lake."

He said nothing.

"He wasn't the first, you know."

His heart kicked up a beat. "First to what?"

"End up dead at the lake. Quinn Simonson was killed leaving Freeze Out Lake right after high-school graduation. His car went off the road."

Augustus shook his head. "What does that have to do with—"

"Quinn was Charlie Larkin's high-school boyfriend. She was there that night. They had a big fight and—"

"What about?"

"Earlene Kurtz. Charlie found out that Earlene was four months pregnant with Quinn's baby." Augustus wondered if Trudi hadn't helped Charlie find out about the pregnancy. He let out a low whistle. "Charlie was mad?"

Trudi snorted. "She was furious. She refused to get back in the car with Quinn even though he promised to take her straight home. He was pretty upset about everyone knowing about Earlene and the pregnancy. He left and crashed his car on a curve coming off the mountain."

"Right, so I don't see—"

"Charlie did something to the car."

He took a breath. "Like what?"

She shrugged. "Something to make it crash. She'd just worked on his car the day before the accident—and that night at the lake, she was over by it just before he left."

He shook his head. "If she'd done something to the car, the cops would have found it and she'd have been arrested."

"No one suspected her at the time, everyone just thought it was an accident because Quinn had been drinking. By the time Phil Simonson—"

"Who's he?"

"Quinn's father. By the time he asked the sheriff to check the car, someone had stripped it for parts."

"So you have nothing."

She took another drink of her beer, tore at the label some more, finally looking at him again just as coy as before, only this time it was information she was teasing him with. "She knew Josh Whitaker, the guy they found in the lake."

He stared at her. Maybe this was the solid connection he needed. "What makes you think that?" he asked, trying to keep the excitement from his voice.

"I saw him at the gas station just before he left town and disappeared."

"He could have just stopped for gas," Augustus said.

"Gas and a *kiss?* I saw him kiss her and her push him off. I couldn't hear what they were saying, but it was obvious they were arguing. He left in a huff, but not before I saw Charlie reach under his car."

He stared at her, wishing he didn't suspect she was lying through her teeth. "And do what? Where was Josh? Where were you?"

She rolled her eyes impatiently. "I don't know what she did. I was across the street, at the general store, and I just happened to look out the window and see them. I guess Josh had gone around the side to the bathroom. I don't know."

Augustus held her gaze. "If what you're saying is true, why didn't you tell the cops?"

"I have my reasons." She got to her feet.

"Not good enough."

She glared down at him. "How do you know I *didn't* tell the sheriff and he didn't believe me?"

So that's the way it was.

"You don't live here," she snapped. "You don't know what it's like. Charlie Larkin can do no wrong but I tell the truth and everyone thinks I'm lying."

He could hear the bitterness in her voice. "Why is that?"

"See," she snapped. "You even think I'm only telling you this because I have something against Charlie."

"Don't you?"

Some of the heat went out of her gaze. "If you're asking if I'm a member of the Charlie Larkin Fan Club, I'm not. But everything I've told you is true."

He couldn't help but be skeptical, given that the sheriff, who must know her, hadn't believed her. "The thing is, all I have is your word. Quinn and Josh are dead." Suspicion was one thing. He needed evidence and it was obvious she didn't have any. "Why don't you tell me what you have against Charlie."

She drained her beer. "You wouldn't be here asking all these questions about Charlie and the body in the lake unless you were suspicious of her. Want to tell *me* why?"

"Not really."

"I didn't think so." She set her empty beer bottle on the desk near his chair and slipped into her coat, crossing it over her breasts as she met his gaze. "You sure information is the only thing you're interested in?"

He nodded, softening the rejection with a smile, and

withdrew the bills he'd put in his hip pocket earlier. It was too much for what little information she'd provided, but he had the feeling she had more to offer.

"Where does T. J. Blue fit into all this?" he asked.

She pocketed the bills without counting them. Maybe she had more class than he'd first thought. "He was Quinn Simonson's best friend." She walked to the door, stopped and turned to look at him. "If I were you, I'd be real careful. Any man who gets too close to Charlie regrets it." She smiled. "Ask Rickie Moss, if you don't believe me. He's one of the lucky ones."

CHARLIE SAW HER mother to bed, waited until her aunt turned out her light for the night and then, pulling on boots and coat, decided to take a walk. At least that's the story she told herself.

The night air was crisp and cold. It had stopped snowing although ice crystals danced in the air. The sky had turned an incredible midnight blue, almost black. White clouds moved across the moon and stars sparkling like snowflakes over her head.

She kicked up the light powdery snowfall as she took the shortcut. Getting from town to the old farmhouse where she lived required driving north, then taking the county road and circling back on a narrow private road. But she could walk a few blocks and reach town if she cut through the pines and crossed the creek, a trail she had used since she was a kid, only tonight it seemed more dark and isolated than she remembered.

As she passed Murphy's she spotted Trudi's car parked near one of the cabins, steam rising off the hood, tracks cutting through the snow to cabin number five, the only one with a light on.

Charlie kept walking, telling herself there was no

cause for concern, and yet she couldn't help but wonder what Augustus T. Riley would want with Trudi beyond the obvious. Maybe that's all there was to it. Just a little female company for the night.

The outside neon was turned off, the café closed for the night, but an interior light still burned and she could see someone moving around inside. She tapped at the door and Helen came to answer.

"I thought you might be by," Helen said, holding the door open. Charlie stepped in and she locked the door behind her.

"I had a craving for your coffee," she said.

Helen laughed. "I just happen to have the dregs of a pot waiting just for you. How about a piece of pie with it?"

Charlie shook her head as she slid onto the second stool from the end. "Selma made Dutch apple for dessert."

"Damn, that sounds good." She put two cups of coffee on the counter and took the empty stool next to her. "You can't get that woman to slow down, can you?"

Charlie shook her head. "I think if she stopped fussing over me and Mom she would wither and die."

Helen cradled her coffee cup in her hands. "I talked to Maybelle," she said, staring into the black liquid. "She said he was real unfriendly and acted suspicious."

They both knew who she was talking about. "You know how nosy Maybelle is," Charlie said. Augustus T. Riley didn't seem like a man who would take well to being questioned.

"He tried to use a credit card," Helen continued. "Had a whole lot of money in his wallet. You don't think he robbed a bank or something, do you?"

Charlie smiled to herself, knowing how this town

loved to talk. It seemed to thrive on stories and never got tired of repeating favorites, embellishing when necessary. As Helen always said, "No reason to tell a story if you aren't going to make it good."

"He's probably passing through just like he said," Charlie told her now.

Helen harrumphed. "You know better than that. No one just passes through Utopia. It's not like we're on the interstate or even on the road to anywhere." She said it with a kind of local pride that Charlie understood only too well. There wasn't anyplace like Utopia, locals always said. And it was so true.

"Maybe he got lost," Charlie suggested and took a sip of coffee.

"Maybe." Helen didn't sound convinced. She filled Charlie in on everything that was said at the café. "What's wrong with his car?"

"I haven't had a chance to look at it," Charlie told her. Pretty much true.

"Well, it just seems odd. Especially now."

Yes, especially now. "He asked if I was *married?*" Charlie smiled, trying to make light of it.

Helen pulled a face. "I think he might be interested in you."

Now, *that* Charlie believed, but not in the way Helen was thinking.

"There's something else," Helen said. "Trudi hightailed it out of here before we closed."

Charlie nodded and told her that she'd seen Trudi's car parked at Murphy's.

"That girl is such a tramp," Helen said. "Although, even I have to admit, he's damn good-looking."

Yes, wasn't he though? Charlie thought about Augustus T. Riley and Trudi. Maybe she'd overestimated him. If he could be distracted by someone like Trudi, maybe he wasn't as dangerous as she'd suspected. The thought made her feel a little better.

She finished her coffee. "I better get home." She started to take her cup to the back, but Helen shooed her out.

"You just fix that ol' boy's car in the morning and get him on the road," she said. "Mark my words, he's trouble."

Trouble, yes. But fixing his car wasn't going to solve the problem. She would bet on that.

As she walked back home, a snowy darkness had settled over the town, bringing with it a modicum of peace. The heavens twinkled, bright with stars, the moon setting the fallen snow aglitter.

On the edge of town, she glanced across the highway toward Murphy's. With a sinking feeling she saw that Trudi's car was already gone. So was her moment of peace.

Chapter Six

After a sleepless night, Charlie picked up the phone and dialed the number she'd memorized from Augustus T. Riley's car rental agreement. It was time to find out exactly who Augustus T. Riley was and what he wanted.

A woman answered. It took Charlie a few seconds to realize what she'd said.

A book publisher? "I must have dialed the wrong number," Charlie managed to say. "I was calling for Augustus T. Riley."

"Yes, Mr. Riley is one of our authors. I'm his publicist. What can I do for you?"

An author? She'd expected him to be a private detective. Or maybe an insurance investigator. But an author?

"What does he write?" she asked, feeling confused and wondering if she could have been wrong about Gus.

But then the publicist said, "True-crime books."

True crime?

"I'd be happy to send you a list of his books or an autographed bookmark," the woman offered. "Just give me your address—"

Charlie hung up. She stood for a moment looking at the phone. After a few moments, she walked over to her computer in the corner of the bedroom and booted it up. Within a few minutes she was typing in Augustus T. Riley under "author" at one of the major online bookstores. All of the Rileys came up and she scrolled down, stopping on the first Augustus T. Riley title.

Her heart begun to pound, her fingers on the mouse shaking. As she went from title to title, blurb to blurb, she saw a clear pattern in his subject matter.

Augustus T. Riley, it seemed, liked to write about women who killed their lovers or husbands.

AUGUSTUS WOKE TO the sun and snow. He opened his eyes amazed at how bright the day was outside the cowboy curtains. When he'd pushed them aside, he'd been blinded by the sun glistening on the new-fallen snow—and awed by the beauty. He'd never seen anything like it. Not the depth of the blue overhead or the extremes of contrast between sky and snow and sun.

But as beautiful as it was, it was also damn cold when he'd opened the door and he was ill prepared for it. His first stop was Emmett's general store, then he walked down to Larkin & Sons Gas and Garage to the pay phone, hoping to beat Charlie there.

He'd done a lot of thinking about Charlie last night after talking to Trudi. In fact he'd been able to think of nothing else. But he still had no evidence against her. Just rumor and innuendo. Nothing concrete. But today was a new day and at least now he had someplace to start, thanks to Trudi.

He dialed Miles Baker's number. With the time difference, it was two hours later in Texas but he knew Miles would be waiting for his call no matter what the time. He and Miles had been fraternity brothers at college and as different as day and night, but had formed a friendship that had survived their major differences.

Augustus had grown up in Laguna Beach, California, spending most of his life on a skateboard or a surf-board. Miles Baker had come from serious Texas oil wealth and a family deep in politics. From birth, Miles had been groomed to be the governor of Texas. His father was a state senator and there was talk of a chance at the presidency.

"Charlie Larkin is a woman," Augustus said with little preamble. "About twenty-six, cute as hell and adored by most everyone in this Podunk town. She's a car mechanic, owns a little garage she took over from her father."

"A woman?" Miles said. "That makes more sense, doesn't it, since we know Josh had gotten involved with some woman he met through the help line. So there could have been a romantic relationship. And we know that Larkin was possibly either a help-line volunteer or a client. You still think she's responsible for his death?"

"It's too early to say," Augustus hedged. "Anything new at your end?" Miles had always had a way of getting information either through connections—or with cash.

"A gold locket was found in Josh's pocket," Miles said. "The locket had a photo inside. But it had deteriorated. There was something engraved on the back though. The words 'Love, Quinn.' Who's this Quinn?"

"Maybe her first victim," Augustus told him and repeated what he'd gotten from Trudi. "I'll talk to the Simonson family today."

"If she's the killer, you'll see that she's caught," Miles said with confidence.

"I'll get her." He thought of the woman he'd met last night inside the garage, how she'd let him go on thinking she wasn't Charlie Larkin, how she'd kept his car when it was obvious she could have fixed it. Oh, yeah, he'd get her.

He hung up the phone. Josh had called this same pay phone before his death. Augustus closed his eyes, the pain blinding. He'd always been able to lose himself in the investigations, distance himself from the crimes as just the person who was writing it all down, trying to get to the truth.

Right now, he was fighting like hell to find some distance, needing it desperately. He was too close, too involved.

He opened his eyes, took a deep breath, the cold air filling his lungs as he tried to settle down. All he had to do was get to the truth and he'd done that dozens of other times. He was good at this. And he already had Charlie Larkin in his sights and was closing in.

WHEN CHARLIE DROVE up to the garage she spotted Augustus standing out front, obviously waiting for her. She thought about confronting him, demanding to know why he'd been asking questions about her and what he hoped to accomplish in Utopia.

But she feared the answer. Was it possible he'd come here because he thought she'd murdered Josh Whitaker? Surely he couldn't be thinking of writing a book about her. She told herself she was just being paranoid. Augustus T. Riley knew nothing that could harm her. At least not yet.

And there was always the chance that once she fixed his car he would be gone.

She parked alongside the garage and walked around to the front where he stood. He radiated an energy that wasn't all impatience. Her heart kicked up a beat, her traitorous body responding instinctively, nipples hardening as if the temperature had suddenly dropped.

"Morning, Gus," she said, trying to sound casual as she walked past him to the front door of the gas station.

He seemed to bristle at either her calling him Gus or just the sight of her. He'd obviously been pacing. She could see his tracks in the snow by the front door. And by the pay phone. He'd made one long call or several short ones—from the number of steps he'd taken the length of the cord.

"Good *morning*," he said and glanced pointedly at his watch, giving her a glimpse of his wrist, the skin tanned.

The watch was expensive. Like the shirt. The coat new, something he'd obviously just purchased that morning at Emmett's store. It looked odd on him, maybe because she couldn't imagine him wearing it anywhere but in Utopia.

That thought was like a weight crushing her chest, making it hard to breathe. He planned to stay around a while.

"I hope I didn't keep you waiting." She caught his reflection in the glass as she unlocked the door and felt strangely pleased that he'd recognized her comment for what it was: sarcasm. So many men didn't get sarcasm.

"It's off-season," she said, just in case he hadn't figured that out yet.

"What if someone needs gas to get out of here?" he asked, sounding irritable as he followed her inside.

She went around behind the counter and busied herself, her back to him. "The pumps are always open. Customers just leave their money in that can on top of the second pump. We work with an honor system."

"You have to be kidding."

She turned, his shocked expression making her smile. "Welcome to Utopia." She'd meant it as a joke.

"Thanks." His eyes narrowed, his gaze suddenly much more personal. "You could have told me last night you were Charlie Larkin," he said, voice low and soft as a caress.

"I thought it was obvious." She pointed to the stitching on her clean baggy overalls.

"In some places Charlie is considered a man's name."

"Is it? I'll bet in those places being a mechanic is still male territory as well."

He didn't respond.

She realized that something had changed since last night. The way he was looking at her. It was subtle at first, then more direct. He was looking at her as if trying to see inside her.

She felt her skin burn under all the clothing she'd put on this morning. She'd purposely dressed in long underwear, an old flannel shirt of her dad's, her baggiest overalls, boots and an old canvas jacket. And yet she felt naked under his gaze.

"About your car—"

"Yes, my car." A muscle jerked in his jaw. "You think you can fix it?"

He definitely understood sarcasm. Obviously he knew how easy it would be to get the engine running properly again. He could probably fix it himself in a matter of minutes. After all, he'd been the one to foul it up to start with. So, he either thought she wasn't much of a mechanic. Or that she was playing him for a fool.

Who was the fool here? she wondered as she stepped past him toward the first bay, feeling the need for more distance between them. "I took a look at your car last night and I've got some bad news." She could hear him behind her, his steps echoing solidly on the concrete floor. She could almost feel his disbelief. She smiled to herself in spite of the voice in her head that was screaming: What in the devil are you doing?

"It looks like I'm going to have to order in some parts." She stopped and turned to look at him, daring him to show his hand.

He looked flabbergasted. "You aren't serious?"

She raised an eyebrow. "You know how bad it was running when you brought it in. What did you think? That it would take just a few minor adjustments to get it going again?" Which was exactly what it *would* take.

She waited, giving him a chance to confess and offer up a good excuse for why he'd screwed up his carburetor, why he'd pretended to need a mechanic, why he'd been looking for Charlie Larkin in the first place.

She could see the battle going on in his eyes. Deep dark blue eyes like the lightless bottom of the ocean. Or Freeze Out Lake. It was clear he wanted to call her bluff and wanted to badly.

"Parts, huh?" His jaw was rigid as he turned away from her. "And what exactly is wrong with the car?"

"If you want, I can write up an estimate later but I really don't have time to go into it now." She watched him clench his hands into fists, his broad, muscular back to her, suddenly making her take notice of his size. Six-two or -three. Strong-looking, as if he lifted weights regularly.

Her gaze dropped to the jeans he wore and the muscled legs she could make out through the denim. A flicker of heat a lot like desire found flame inside her. She quickly doused the fire as she noticed the new winter boots. Why would a man from L.A. who was just passing through town buy snowpacks?

He turned so swiftly, startling her how fast he could move. She wouldn't stand a chance against him physically, she thought. Not without the benefit of surprise. And a weapon.

But she knew that wasn't what she had to fear from Augustus T. Riley. It was the way he made her feel. Vulnerable, the way an animal can sense weakness in his prey. It was as if Gus could see beneath the baggy clothing to that unfulfilled ache deep within her like an Achilles' heel he could use to destroy her. He couldn't have been more dangerous.

He stepped toward her, his gaze so intense she almost recoiled. The air seemed to crackle with tension. In the time and space it took for him to close the space between them, the tension changed to purely chemical. Helen was right; the man was incredibly good-looking. But that wasn't the half of it.

"How long do you think it will take?" he asked, his voice silky, the air alive with more electricity than her heavy-duty battery charger in the corner.

She shrugged, trying hard to hide the effect he was having on her. Her face seemed flushed although it was still cold in the garage and her eyes felt too bright, as if she'd had too much coffee.

Her voice sounded strange to her as she said, "I'll see if I can get parts from Missoula sent overnight, then do a complete inventory of what I'll need and check to see if the parts store there has them in stock."

"It's not like the car is some odd import."

"No," she agreed. "You might want to call your rental car agency. Maybe they can bring you another car and get you on your way. Or I can do it for you. We'll need their okay before I can work on the car anyway."

He didn't even blink. "I've already called. I'm picking up the expense for the repairs and they're going to reimburse me later. But there's no hurry."

She didn't think so. "I'll give you a call at Murphy's when I have the estimate written up." He hadn't taken the bait. She started toward the office again, wishing now that she'd just adjusted his carburetor. But she knew that wouldn't have gotten rid of him. At least this way he didn't have a car. The closest car rental was thirty miles away. He'd have to call—have a car delivered and that would take time. How much trouble could he get into on foot?

He grabbed her arm, the heat of his fingers seeming to cut right through all the fabrics to her naked skin.

She froze in midstep, her breath catching in her throat. She didn't dare look at him. Didn't dare move.

"I'm sorry if you and I got off on the wrong foot," he said quietly. His voice sounded strained. He let go of her as if suddenly feeling the charged air. Or maybe just recognizing it for what it was. "I could buy you a cup of coffee or a beer or something since I'm going to be around for a while."

"That's not necessary," she said and continued to the office and around behind the counter. She picked up the phone and began to dial. "The sooner I see what it will take to get parts shipped…"

He stood for a moment, silhouetted against the window and the blinding sunny snowy day beyond it. She couldn't see his expression, but she didn't need to. He was studying her again, looking for something. She could only guess what, given his occupation.

Her pulse throbbed in her temple, her body aquiver as if the room had been electrified. He might have come here to see her put behind bars, but if she let down her defenses, if she let him get too close, he could destroy her like no other man was capable of and she knew it.

Her hand trembled as she hit the last number and waited for the line to ring.

She didn't even know what number she'd dialed until she heard Jenny's voice. It was a number she thought she'd forgotten, it had been so long since she'd called it.

"Hello," she said much more cheerfully than she felt.

Gus gave her a nod, his large hand pushing the door open, the cold rushing in, and finally the door closed behind him. She slumped against the counter, weak with relief.

"Charlie?" Jenny Simonson sounded surprised. Almost suspicious.

She let out a sigh, fighting tears. "I don't know why I called you. Yes, I do. I've missed you. Could we get together?"

A slight hesitation on Jenny's end. Maybe still surprised. "Sure."

"Great." She felt relieved, glad she'd called, guilty that she hadn't tried to keep their friendship even after Jenny had married Forest Simonson. "How about today at the Pinecone. Say one?"

"Okay." Jenny didn't sound thrilled about the prospect.

She hung up, her hands shaking. Why had she called Jenny? Because they'd once been best friends? Or because she was looking for some sort of absolution? Maybe she just needed her friend back.

AUGUSTUS COULDN'T BELIEVE it as he started hiking down the middle of the icy highway. He couldn't believe it. Not the fact that when he'd touched her it had been like grabbing a live wire. Or the fact that she'd called his bluff. Why had he touched her? That shock of heat and electricity through all those layers of her clothing should have jolted him to his senses. Instead, he felt dazed and aroused. He hadn't felt anything like that since... He stumbled. Since Natalie.

He shook off the thought, telling himself Charlie and Natalie were nothing alike. Unless, of course, Charlie tried to kill him.

He swore, furious with his traitorous body. Hadn't he learned his lesson with Natalie? Obviously not.

And to add insult to injury, Charlie had called his damn bluff! The woman had called his bluff. She knew the engine didn't need parts. She also knew that he must have tampered with it—and had known since last night. So why had she kept the car overnight? So she could search it? Had she been onto him from the start?

But there hadn't been anything to find. Except for the rental agreement. He'd forgotten about that. Fortunately when he'd gone back last night to leave the newspaper clipping, he'd found the rental agreement right where he'd left it. But that didn't mean she hadn't seen it and didn't now know who he was—and suspected why he'd come here.

Not that he was so famous she'd recognize the name—unless she read true-crime stories. But it would be easy to find out who he was—if she wanted to or needed to.

If she knew who he was and had figured out why he'd come to Utopia, then why lie about his car needing parts?

Why keep him in town? Especially if she knew and was guilty of murder?

Maybe she ripped off every out-of-towner whose car

broke down. Except if what he'd heard about her charitable acts was true...

He stopped walking, oblivious to the fact that he was
standing in the middle of the icy highway, as a thought
hit him. She'd kept his car to keep him on foot! Maybe
she believed it would discourage him. He smiled at the
thought. She'd find out that he wouldn't be discour-
aged that easily.

He started walking again, finding himself shaking
his head in admiration. Charlie Larkin was something!
He let out a frosty breath and tried to calm down. The
woman had a way of setting him on edge whenever
he was around her. He blamed it on being that close
to a killer. But he'd been close to a lot of killers and
couldn't remember any of them making him feel so...
jittery when he was around any one of them. Except
for Natalie.

He was reminded again of that moment in the garage when he'd touched Charlie. He frowned as he recalled the sense of heat the woman had about her, a...
sexual temperature that would send mercury rocket-
ing. Was that how she lured men into her trap? A nice
guy like Josh Whitaker must have been child's play
for her. It made her even more intriguing—and dangerous. He wanted to nail this woman if it was the last
thing he ever did.

He heard the sound of a vehicle coming up behind
him and moved over to the edge of the highway as the
car slowed, then stopped. He turned, already knowing
who it was.

"Need a ride, Gus?" Emmett Graham asked as he
rolled down the passenger-side window. What a coincidence that Emmett had come along at just the right moment *again*.

Augustus glanced back at Larkin & Sons Gas and Garage, thought he glimpsed Charlie's small form just beyond the sun-glazed glass of the office window, thought he felt her gaze on him.

It seemed the woman wanted him on foot—and under the watchful eye of Emmett Graham. He just didn't know why she was trying to keep him in town. It was almost as if she was daring him to catch her.

"As a matter of fact, I could use a ride," he said, climbing into Emmett's car, no longer sure who was the hunter—and who was the prey.

Chapter Seven

Augustus found Rickie Moss working at the local saw-mill just north of town. Emmett had been more than happy to drive him, just as Augustus had suspected he would be. And Augustus liked the idea that Charlie would know what he'd been doing. She'd know he was after her. Let her run scared. For a while.

Huge piles of tree-length logs were stacked like straws in piles around a small shack and lean-to. Augustus walked toward the buzz of a saw under the lean-to. Snow melted, dripping from the roof into several large puddles around the edifice. The air smelled of fresh-cut wood.

Two men were running long boards through the blade, cutting the wood into two-by-fours. Another two were stacking them onto the back of a flatbed.

"Rickie Moss?" Augustus yelled over the ripping whine of the blade.

One of the men on the saw motioned to a stacker to take his place. The man jumped down from the raised floor of the lean-to and walked toward him.

Rickie Moss had once been a good-looking man, the kind of man Charlie Larkin might have been attracted to. But now a hideous scar carved across one cheek from the corner of his left eye to below his chin ravaged his face.

"I'm Rickie," the man said sourly. "What do you want?"

"I want to talk to you about Charlie Larkin," Augustus said.

Rickie Moss jerked back as if he'd been smacked. His eyes narrowed. "What about Charlie?"

"Any chance we could get away from that saw?" he asked as the blade ripped through another long board. "I'll make it worth your while." He flashed the sawmill worker a fifty.

Rickie glanced to the crew for a moment, then nodded and headed for the small shack. He shoved open the door and entered. Augustus followed.

There was just enough room inside for a man to turn around but not much more. Papers were strewn across a desk made from a broken sheet of plywood. A stool, the black vinyl cushion cracked, stuffing leaking out, was pulled up to the high desk, which also held a coffeemaker and a miniature microwave. The place smelled of stale coffee and nuked cabbage. But it was quieter.

"Yeah?" Rickie said impatiently.

"I understand you used to be Charlie's boyfriend," he said, leaping right in.

Rickie just stared at him, waiting.

"Is she the reason you have that scar?"

The question got a response out of him.

"What the hell is this about?" Rickie demanded.

"Information. I'm investigating that drowning up at Freeze Out Lake."

Ricky didn't seem surprised to hear this. Augustus was pretty sure that was the kind of story Trudi would have told anyone who would listen to her.

Augustus laid the fifty on top of the papers on the

desk. "Why do bad things happen to men who're interested in Charlie Larkin?"

Rickie looked from him to the fifty and back up. "I don't know."

"What happened to you?" He dropped another fifty on top of the first.

Rickie shook his head. "Didn't Trudi tell you?"

"No. She just told me to talk to you." Augustus figured Trudi had broken the ice for him. Rickie didn't seem like the type who would have given him the time of day otherwise.

"I only went out with Charlie once. It was years ago. It wasn't even much of a date. I bought her a burger at the Pinecone, then we went for a ride." He met Augustus's gaze. "Up to Freeze Out Lake."

Augustus tried not to show his surprise.

"We drank a couple of beers, necked a little." He shrugged. "I got out of the car to take a leak and something attacked me."

"Something or *someone?*"

Rickie shook his head. "I was hit from behind and I woke up with this." He ran a finger down the length of the scar.

"Where was Charlie during all this?"

Rickie picked up a pencil from the desk and turned it in his fingers. "In the car. She said she got worried and came looking for me. She's the one who found me and got me to the doctor."

"You believe her?"

He dropped the pencil and picked up the fifties, taking his time to fold them and put them into his flannel shirt pocket. "What do you think?"

"I think you're scared of her."

Rickie smiled. "A little thing like her? Now what kind of man would that make me?"

"Possibly a smart one?"

"I have to get back to work," Rickie said but didn't move.

"Are you trying to tell me that every man she's dated met with an accident?" Augustus asked. "Like maybe there's a curse on her?" He realized he was only half joking.

Rickie shrugged and looked a little embarrassed. "I just know what happened to T.J. when he tried to date her. And then to me. Maybe she dated at college and didn't have any problems."

"T. J. Blue?" Augustus asked.

Rickie nodded.

"I thought he was Quinn's best friend?"

"Quinn was dead and Charlie—well, Charlie is a fine-looking woman," Rickie said.

She was a lot more than that, Augustus thought. "What happened to T.J.?"

"One date and his trailer burned down. He barely got out with his life." Rickie shook his head. "All I know is that no one around here is fool enough to get within twenty feet of her." He raised an eyebrow.

Augustus shook his head. "Don't look at me."

Rickie laughed. "Smart man."

T. J. BLUE worked at a small wild-game processing plant north of town during hunting season, according to Emmett, who offered to drive Gus.

Augustus realized he was even starting to think of himself as "Gus" now, and he had Charlie to blame for that.

T.J. was standing on the frosty concrete floor beside a carcass-covered metal table, feeding strips of moose meat into a commercial-size meat grinder when Gus walked in. The freezer-cold air smelled of suet and sweat, the sound of the grinder echoing in the refrigerator-like room.

Blond with blue eyes, T. J. Blue wore a white butcher's smock splattered with blood and bits of dried red meat over winter clothes, his massive hands clad in gloves that had probably once been white.

Next to him, a dark-haired young woman sliced pieces of meat from a carcass with a knife. She glanced at Gus, her gaze hanging on him just long enough to make him pretty sure she knew who he was. T.J. gave him only a passing glance and kept dropping meat and chunks of suet into the grinder.

"Got a minute?" Gus yelled over the growl of the grinder.

T. J. Blue shot him a look that said Gus would be damn lucky to get a second out of him.

To Gus's surprise, the woman reached over and shut off the grinder. "Why don't you take a break," she said to T.J.

He gave her a dirty look. "If I need a break, I'll let you know, Earlene," he growled, but jerked off his gloves, threw them down, then turned and headed toward a door at the back.

"Break room's back there," Earlene said and flopped the carcass over and picked up her knife.

Gus watched her trim meat from the carcass with obvious skill, before he followed T.J. through the door into the break room at the back of the plant. The room was warmer than the meat shop, but not by much.

T.J. poured himself a cup of coffee, then turned to

look at Gus with obvious irritation. "I know who you are, but I don't have anything to say to you."

So much of getting people to talk to you was making them think you had the right to know what they had to tell you. "Then you don't think Charlie murdered Quinn," Gus said.

T.J. jerked back in surprise. "I don't think about Charlie Larkin at all."

Gus didn't believe that for a minute. "You don't seem to like her."

"What makes you think that?"

"The way you left the café last night. Tell me about Charlie Larkin," Gus pushed. "Tell me why you and every other male in this town with any sense is afraid of her."

A muscle jumped in T. J. Blue's jaw. "I have nothing to say to you." He threw the coffee into the sink, slammed down the cup and left Gus standing alone in the break room wondering for the first time about Charlie's motive.

All of this seemed to have started with Quinn Simonson. Was it possible she felt guilty about Quinn's death and hurt men who wanted to date her as some sort of warped penance? Or was it payback? Trudi said the night Quinn died Charlie had just found out that Earlene was carrying Quinn's baby. That would tick off most any woman. Gus wondered if Charlie had been mad enough to kill? And if she had, had she just gone on hurting men, killing the less fortunate ones?

"Get what you needed, Gus?" Emmett asked as he drove back to town.

Augustus watched the dense dark pines flicker past. "How long have you lived here?"

"All my life," the old man said proudly. "Born and raised. Can't find a nicer little town to settle down in.

Graham's General Store has been in that very spot for almost a hundred years. My father opened it back when this part of the country was nothing but wilderness."

As far as Gus was concerned it was still wilderness.

"At one time in its history, this town was booming," Emmett was saying. "But the mines closed, the logging industry went to pot, people moved on. Times change."

Gus couldn't imagine a lifetime here.

"It's busier in the summers," Emmett continued. "Fly fishermen, tourists up here for Glacier and Yellowstone Parks, people looking for back roads, looking for another, more simple time and place. That's Utopia."

Emmett stopped in front of Murphy's. "Is there anywhere else I can give you a ride to, Gus?"

"No thanks," he said as he got out of the car. "Don't you have a store to run?"

Emmett laughed. "This time of year it's a little slow, so my wife would just as soon I wasn't underfoot." He winked at Gus. "Truth is, she's really the boss. Just let me know if I can be of any help, Gus," he said, then glanced at his watch. "The lunch special at the café is tuna melt. You might want to beat the rush."

"Thanks." He smiled to himself as he watched Emmett drive off. Beat the rush. But his smile faded as he saw Emmett pull into one of the gas pumps at Larkin's. Charlie came out. Emmett didn't need gas. Gus had seen the gauge. It was on Full.

After a moment of obvious discussion, he saw Charlie glance down the highway in his direction. He waved and walked toward the café. He'd pass on the tuna melt, but he could use a cheeseburger and fries. At the very least, maybe Trudi would be working. He'd just bet she'd know where he could find Phil Simonson this time of the day.

THE PINECONE CAFÉ was nearly empty when Charlie came in a few minutes after one. Jenny Simonson was sitting alone in the back booth. She looked nervous as she glanced out at the street and Charlie wondered if she'd told Forest they were having lunch together.

"Hi," Charlie said, more glad to see her than Jenny could ever know. She slid into the booth across from her once–best friend, wanting desperately to feel that old connection, needing it now more than ever.

"Hi." Jenny's smile didn't quite reach her eyes.

"You look great!" It wasn't quite true. Jenny had changed over the years. She was thinner, her face drawn, making her dark eyes seem too large. Her once long, beautiful dark hair had been cut to her chin. It hung straight, all the shine gone from it—just like her eyes. Either marriage to Forest Simonson had aged her or motherhood had.

"So do you," Jenny said, a clear lie. Charlie had been having trouble sleeping since Josh's body was found. Actually long before that.

"So how is Skye?" Charlie asked. "Shoot, she must be how old by now?"

Jenny flushed and Charlie could have kicked herself for bringing up Skye's age although everyone in the county knew Jenny and Forest had had to get married right out of high school. Right after Quinn's death. "She's almost seven."

In the silence that hung between them, Trudi bopped up to give them menus. Helen was busy in the back washing the lunch dishes, but had waved as Charlie came in.

"I've missed you," Charlie said, hoping to find even a little of what she and Jenny had once shared in this almost stranger sitting across from her now.

Jenny nodded, looking uncomfortable, and glanced again to the street. "I've missed you, too."

"Forest doesn't know you're here, does he?" Charlie said, feeling sick at the realization.

Jenny's gaze jerked back to her in surprise, the first honest reaction Charlie had gotten out of her.

"It's okay. I understand." Jenny had made her choice when she'd married Forest, married into a family that had made hating Charlie Larkin into a religion because of Quinn's death. Fortunately, few people listened to the Simonsons' rantings and ravings or Charlie would be behind bars by now.

Jenny shook her head, tears in her eyes. "He's my husband."

Charlie nodded and reached across the table to squeeze her hand, realizing the courage it had taken Jenny to come here. "I know. This must be very hard for you. I shouldn't have asked you to do this."

"What? Have lunch?" Jenny said, pulling back her hand as she busied herself looking for a tissue in her purse. She sounded angry and upset. "I should be able to have lunch with anyone I want to. It's just that Forest—" She looked up, fresh tears flooded her eyes.

Charlie nodded. "Lunch was a bad idea. I'm sorry."

Jenny seemed to be fighting tears and losing the battle. She stumbled to her feet. "I'm the one who's sorry," she said and rushed out of the café.

Charlie sat staring down at the menus, shaking inside, wanting to go after Jenny, wanting to confront Forest and the rest of the Simonsons, wanting to just sit in the booth and cry.

"She coming back?" Trudi asked, standing over Charlie, her obvious curiosity about killing her.

"She just remembered that she left her oven on," Charlie said dispassionately.

Trudi smirked. "That's too bad."

Charlie reined in her emotions and looked at Trudi, wondering what had happened last night in Augustus T. Riley's cabin at Murphy's. It was better than thinking about Jenny and everything that had been lost between them.

"So what are you going to have?" Trudi asked.

"Get us both a bowl of the soup," Helen said, slipping into the booth across from Charlie. Charlie started to tell her the last thing she wanted right now was food, but Helen cut her off. "You have to eat and you know my seafood bisque is to die for."

Poor choice of words. But Charlie appreciated the sentiment. She smiled at Helen, grateful for friends like her.

"Don't let those Simonsons get to you," Helen said. "They're all a spineless bunch. If Jenny hadn't gotten pregnant, she'd never have married the likes of Forest Simonson and everyone in town knows it."

Trudi slid a couple of bowls of seafood bisque onto the table and a handful of crackers in plastic sleeves. "You want anything else?"

Helen waved her away. "I swear, sometimes I wonder why I keep that girl on."

They both knew why. Finding anyone who'd stay in Utopia and work was getting harder and harder as the older residents moved to Arizona and the younger ones moved to someplace that had a real video store.

"Are you okay?" Helen asked after she'd insisted Charlie eat some of her soup.

Charlie nodded, although she was far from okay. The soup could have been water for her ability to taste it.

"He was in for lunch," Helen said after a moment as if wanting to get all the bad news over with. "He got directions to Phil Simonson's place from Trudi."

Charlie nodded again, wondering if anything would surprise her at this point. Outside, the snow had melted off the black pavement. The gutters ran full with the runoff. Only a few patches of snow remained in the shade of the buildings and in the trees as the day warmed back to normal temperatures.

"What does he want?" Helen asked quietly.

Charlie shook her head, afraid she knew exactly what he wanted.

"I can give you the name of a private investigator I hired once out of Missoula. He got the goods on Frank." Frank was one of Helen's husbands. Charlie couldn't remember which.

But the last thing she wanted to do was involve a private investigator. "Let me do some digging on my own first."

Helen wrote down the investigator's name on her napkin. "Don't wait too long."

She took the napkin, her gaze locking with Helen's for a long moment. How much did Helen suspect? "Thanks."

Chapter Eight

Phil Simonson lived a short walk back in the pines in an A-frame cabin. He'd been a logger, Trudi had said, until he'd gotten hurt four years ago. Now he lived on disability and what he could make as a chain-saw artist.

Gus followed the buzz of a saw around to the back of the house.

Standing in a pile of wood chips and sawdust was a short, stocky man, bucking a chain saw. Before him, a large piece of log was being chewed into the shape of a bear.

"Hello!" Gus called out, but the saw was too loud for Phil to have heard. He moved closer and waited.

Phil finally glanced up, not looking surprised to see him. He shut off the saw and dropped it to the sawdust. It took a moment for the silence to settle in as Phil dusted off his hands on his dirty wool pants.

"I was just getting ready to take a break," the ex-logger said, turning to head for the house. He walked with an exaggerated limp as if his right leg was a good six inches shorter than his left. "Coffee's on. Wanna cup?"

"Sure." Gus followed him inside the house to the kitchen where Phil motioned for him to take a seat at the breakfast bar. The house was cluttered like a man's who lived alone. Trudi hadn't mentioned Phil's marital status, but Gus would bet divorced. There were enough cute things on the walls to suggest a woman's hand. And enough dust on them to suggest she'd been gone for some time.

Phil set a mug of steaming black coffee before him. "I've got some milk. No cream." He shoved a sugar bowl in his direction.

"Black is fine," Gus said. He didn't plan to drink much of it anyway. It looked like liquid sludge.

"So what do you want to know?" Phil asked, leaning into the counter across from him. "I heard you were investigating the latest murder."

Good ol' Trudi. But Gus knew the easy ones wanted to talk, to get their side out, to point fingers. They didn't care who they told. Or what that person wanted with the information. Getting them to talk wasn't the problem. Getting them to tell the truth was. "Tell me about Charlie Larkin."

Phil took a sip of his coffee. "She killed my boy."

Without any coaxing, Phil told him about how his son had fallen for Charlie Larkin at a young tender age. "There'd never been another girl for Quinn," Phil said. "All he talked about was how smart she was, how pretty, how someday he was going to marry her. But Charlie had other ideas."

Charlie and Quinn had graduated from high school a few days before the accident. Schools were in Libby, thirty miles away. Utopia students had to be bused there each school day. Gus couldn't imagine going so far to school and on such treacherous roads.

"Charlie didn't want to get married," Phil was saying. "It seemed she wanted to go to college, and since Quinn was planning to stay here to log with me, he was history." Phil sounded as bitter as his coffee tasted.

"I heard Quinn had gotten another girl pregnant," Gus said, trying to get a little truth out of the man.

Phil made a face. "Earlene. I'm not saying my boy was perfect. He made a mistake with Earlene, but that doesn't mean he had to lose Charlie. Quinn was trying his damnedest to keep from losing her the night he died. That's what makes it all so unfair."

"How did they end up at the lake then?" Gus asked, not wanting to talk about fair.

Phil shrugged. "A bunch of Quinn's friends were at a party up there. I knew he wanted to go. I heard him and Charlie arguing on the phone. I know Charlie didn't want to go but maybe he talked her into it."

Or maybe Quinn had just driven up there anyway, Gus thought, once he had her in the car.

"They got in a huge fight at the party," Phil said as he went over to a shelf in the dining room and took down a photograph framed in silver plastic. "Everyone saw it. Quinn had had a few beers with his friends. He left, driving fast. The sheriff thought that's what caused the accident. It wasn't until later that anyone remembered Charlie had worked on Quinn's car the day before and she'd been over by the car just before he left." Phil nodded as if that pretty much said it all and handed Gus the framed photo.

It was of a young man, blond and blue-eyed, handsome as Adonis. Quinn Simonson had looked nothing like his father and Gus wondered if he'd taken after his mother.

"But no one saw Charlie do anything to the car that night?" he asked.

"She's a damn mechanic," Phil snapped. "How long would it take her to cut a brake line or do something to the steering?"

He didn't know. He set the photo on the breakfast bar. Unlike everything else that was on the shelf, the frame was dustless as if it had been taken down so many times it had been wiped clean.

"What do you think her intent was?" Gus asked. "I mean, why kill him? What did she have to gain?"

Phil studied the coffee scum at the bottom of his cup. "Who knows what she was thinking?—she's a woman."

She couldn't have known the crash would kill him— or even if he would crash, Gus thought. It seemed a damn inefficient way to try to murder someone. But maybe Phil was right. Maybe, since Quinn was allegedly her first victim, maybe her actions had been just hotheaded.

Except for one thing. Charlie Larkin didn't strike him as a hothead.

"She killed him," Phil said and took his coffee cup over to the sink.

Gus heard a pickup in need of a muffler come roaring up outside the A-frame.

Phil didn't seem to hear it. A few moments later a young man who resembled Phil came through the door. He had the same stocky build, the same intense dark eyes, the same unruly dark hair and beard. He wasn't bad-looking, he just did nothing to improve his appearance.

"This that Gus guy who's asking around about Charlie?" the young man demanded, never taking those eyes off Gus.

"My son, Forest," Phil said as if Forest's manners were of no concern to him.

Gus held out his hand. "Augustus T. Riley."

Forest smirked. "That's a pretty highfalutin name. What is it you do that calls for a name like that?"

"It's just the name my parents gave me," Gus said, getting his back up. "I'm a crime writer," he said, deciding it was time to lay his cards on the table.

Phil let out a curse. "A writer? I thought he was a private detective." The older man mumbled to himself. "What's a writer going to do about my son's murder?"

Gus noticed the young woman and child who'd come in behind Forest Simonson. The dark-haired woman stood by the door, her hands on the little girl's shoulders, a wary look in the woman's eyes. "Hello," he said, looking past Forest to her.

The woman gave him a nod and said nothing. Her hair was chin length and straight, framing a pale face and large dark eyes. She looked to be about Charlie Larkin's age.

Phil glanced toward the door, his gaze immediately dismissing the two as he said, "My daughter-in-law, Jenny, and Skye," adding almost like an afterthought, "my granddaughter." The way he said "granddaughter" it was clear he would have much preferred a grandson.

Forest poured himself a mug of coffee, then opened the refrigerator door to scrounge around inside. He came out with a piece of cold grocery-store pizza. "So you going to write about Charlie and what she done, Gus?" he asked, taking a huge bite of the pizza.

"Maybe. If she's done anything."

Forest made an ugly face. "She killed my brother." He turned to his father. "Didn't you tell him that?"

"I told him," Phil said.

"But you have no proof of that," Gus pointed out.

Jenny hadn't moved from the doorway. Nor had Skye. And Phil hadn't offered either of them anything to eat or drink or even a chair.

Gus could see why the sheriff hadn't taken the male

Simonsons' accusations seriously. They were way too bitter over Quinn's death, bloodthirsty for vengeance, and right or wrong, had found someone to blame— Charlie.

"Charlie wouldn't—" Jenny's words were cut short by her husband's.

"I don't want to hear a word out of you," Forest bellowed, jabbing a warning finger at his wife. "I won't have you defending that woman in my house."

It was the man's father's house, but that didn't seem to make any difference.

"Did any of you know Josh Whitaker?" Gus asked into the tense silence.

Phil and Forest shared a puzzled look.

"The man whose body was recently pulled out of Freeze Out Lake," Gus prompted. "He was a doctor in the emergency room at the hospital in Missoula."

"Oh, yeah, I heard about that," Forest said. "Why would we know him?" He sounded suspicious.

Gus shrugged. "Just wondering since the sheriff's department found a gold locket on Josh that according to my sources might have belonged to Charlie Larkin." He saw Phil's eyes widen. The older man let out a curse.

"That's the locket Quinn gave Charlie," Phil said. "It was engraved on the back: Love, Quinn. What was this man doing with it?"

Gus shook his head. "I thought you might know."

"Where do you *think* he got it?" Forest demanded. "From Charlie Larkin, that's where."

"Why would Charlie give him a locket that Quinn had given her?" Gus asked.

"How the hell do I know?" Forest snapped. "Why don't you ask the lying bitch? Maybe she killed this Josh guy, too. Hell, I wouldn't put it past her." He glanced toward Jenny.

She was staring at the floor, her husband watching her as if he expected her to say something. Gus could feel the tension between them tight as piano wire. He wondered if Charlie was the only thing causing it.

Jenny ran a hand over her daughter's long blond hair, and when she finally looked at her husband there was a chilling hatred in her gaze.

Gus pushed his almost-full mug of coffee away and got up. "Thanks for the coffee," he said to Phil. He nodded to Forest and started toward the door.

"Wait a minute," Forest said. "What are you going to do about my brother's murder?"

Gus stopped and turned to look at the man. He didn't like him, couldn't imagine why Jenny had married him, but suspected it had something to do with the child. "It isn't my job to do anything about your brother's death. I'm not even sure he was murdered."

Phil jumped in. "Well, this other guy, Josh…"

"Whitaker," Gus provided.

"He was murdered," Phil noted.

"Yes," Gus agreed. "But there's no proof Charlie Larkin did it."

Forest slammed down his coffee cup, spilling coffee all over the kitchen counter. "You sound just like that damn sheriff of ours. Everyone knows Charlie's a killer, but no one has the guts to do anything about it." He glared at Gus.

"Thanks again for the coffee," Gus said to Phil. "It was nice meeting you," he said to Jenny and Skye on his way out. To his surprise, Jenny followed him out the door, closing it behind her.

"Charlie didn't kill Quinn," Jenny said in a burst

of emotion. "It was just an accident. Just an awful accident."

He studied her, thinking at one time she might have been quite pretty. "How do you know that?"

"I know… Charlie."

Gus glanced toward the house. He could see Phil and Forest Simonson watching out the window. He had a bad feeling that Jenny shouldn't have come after him, that it would get her into more trouble and she was already in enough. "What about Josh Whitaker?"

"Charlie wouldn't hurt anyone. Look how Charlie's helped Earlene and her baby when the Simonsons' wouldn't even give her the time of day." Jenny shook her head, tears rushing her eyes. She stepped back, then turned and ran to the house, no doubt realizing that she shouldn't have come out here.

Gus felt cold inside as he walked back toward the main drag. All he wanted to do at the moment was put some distance between himself and the Simonsons and the bad feeling they gave him.

Chapter Nine

When Gus got back to the motel, he had a FedEx package waiting for him in the office from Miles. He could see that Maybelle Murphy was just dying to know what was inside it and hoping he'd open it in front of her. Fat chance.

"Oh," she said with obvious disappointment as he started to leave. "You also have a message from Charlie Larkin about your car."

"What about my car?" he asked, turning to look back at the woman. She was all duded out again today and smelled to high heaven.

Maybelle shrugged. "She wouldn't say. Just that you are to see her about your car." It sounded as if it just hadn't been Maybelle's day when it came to finding out anything interesting. But life was full of disappointments.

He left the office, wondering what Charlie planned to tell him about the car now. Maybe that he needed a new transmission? Or maybe a complete overhaul?

He went to his cabin and opened the FedEx envelope from Miles. As promised, Miles had used his influence to get as much information as possible on any contacts Josh might have made with other residents of Utopia—besides Charlie Larkin.

Being an emergency room doctor, Josh could have treated someone from Utopia. It was a long shot, since the hospital in Libby was closer, but Gus had asked him to try to get that information any way he could. Wealthy and in line to be the next governor of Texas, Miles had his ways.

Gus was surprised to see that Josh had been working in the emergency room on two different occasions when residents of Utopia had been brought in. The first was when Phil Simonson had his logging accident and was taken to Missoula. That meant Josh might have met the whole family, including Forest. The second was when Earlene Kurtz had taken her son, Arnie, in for an asthma attack while shopping in Missoula.

Gus took the time to type up his notes from the morning on his laptop, then decided he'd better find out what Charlie wanted. He thought about walking over to the Pinecone and calling her from there, but decided he preferred to see her face when she lied to him again, and the walk would do him good. He didn't feel any closer to catching Josh's killer than when he'd hit town.

With the sun lower in the sky, the air was colder, the fallen snow a light silken gray. He wrapped his coat around him and started walking down the highway toward Larkin & Sons Gas and Garage, thinking about what the Simonsons had told him. The bad part was he'd *wanted* to believe them about Charlie's guilt—and couldn't. So far, all he'd heard was accusations and insinuations with nothing to back them up.

He looked up, surprised at how quickly he'd made the walk and relieved to see that Charlie's van was parked along the side. He pushed open the door to the gas station.

She wasn't in the office, but then he hadn't expected

her to be. The air felt cool and smelled of grease and oil as he stopped in the doorway to the garage. He could see his rental car in the second bay.

Charlie was bent over the fender of an older-model black pickup in the first bay. A slow country song played on the radio, the volume much lower than it had been the night before.

He stood there in the doorway just studying her backside wondering about her. Also wondering if he'd only imagined the electricity he thought he'd felt earlier when he'd touched her. It was clear to him that he was going to have to get a whole lot closer to her if he hoped to find out the truth—and he feared just how dangerous that could be.

Resigned, he moved toward her, surprised when he picked up the faint scent of flowers as he neared her. Was it possible Charlie was wearing perfume? The thought more than surprised him, it intrigued him, given the way she dressed. He followed the enticing fragrance as he quietly moved closer and closer until he was just inches from her.

Was this how she spun her deadly web? With something as innocuous as a sweet scent emanating from beneath layers of baggy clothing? What was she hiding under all those clothes? He could imagine a man being captivated by such a mystery. It was enough to make any man want to peel away the layers, one after another, leisurely, watchfully, until there was nothing Charlie Larkin could keep secret from him.

He leaned over her, breathing her in. It wasn't perfume. Too light. Had to be soap. She smelled fresh from a shower as if she was still damp and radiated a humid kind of succulence, her skin burning hot under all the clothes she wore.

The beguiling scents mingled around her, so at odds with the smells of the garage, reminding him Charlie Larkin was definitely feminine beneath those overalls—though it was obvious she tried damn hard to hide it.

Or maybe that was her allure—the way she hid her femininity, her sexuality...her duplicity.

He breathed her in, needing to capture her scent the same way he needed to ensnare her.

She jumped, springing back from him, a screwdriver clutched in her hand, fear making her eyes wide, her face taut.

He hadn't made a sound, so he knew she must have merely sensed his presence. "Sorry, I didn't mean to scare you."

She looked as if she might argue that and he noticed the signs of fatigue about her eyes. Amazing, it looked good on her, made her seem fragile and might make a man feel protective toward her.

"You could have said something sooner," she snapped.

He shrugged. "I didn't think you'd hear me over the radio."

Her look said she wasn't buying it. She seemed to be waiting for him to say something more.

She looked so innocent and sweet standing there in those awful baggy overalls, tendrils of her hair escaping her ponytail and cap to curl around that angel face. He could still smell her scent and didn't like the effect it had on him. The effect she had on him.

"I got a message. Something about my car?" he finally said.

Except for the fatigue and the obvious fact that he made her jumpy, she exhibited few signs she was under the kind of strain murderers often experienced. Or maybe she just hid it well.

"I took another look at your car," she said, avoiding his gaze as she hit a button on the pillar near her. The large overhead door on the second bay began to yawn open. "I was wrong about it needing parts." She bent back over the fender of the pickup. The tool clinked under the hood as she went back to work. "Your car's fixed," she said over the radio and the clanking of the garage door. "No charge. The key's in it."

"What?" He couldn't believe this. "Wait! One minute you need to order parts and the next you just fixed it?"

She continued working under the hood as if she hadn't heard him, but he wasn't leaving until he got an explanation. Not that he needed one. It was perfectly obvious, given what he'd done to the engine to start with. The car had never needed parts. She'd just said that to what? Keep him on foot? Keep an eye on him by having Emmett Graham chauffer him and report to her? Or call his bluff?

He stared at her behind. What he wouldn't give to see her without those baggy overalls. To see just how potent her powers over men really were. "Excuse *me!*"

She came out from under the hood slowly and turned to look at him, her eyes narrowing. "I fixed your car. There is no charge. What about that don't you understand?"

"Why you thought you had to order parts in the first place," he snapped.

For a moment, he thought she'd confront him about what he'd done to the engine. He welcomed it. It was time he turned up his investigation a notch anyway.

She locked eyes with him for several heartbeats. "I guess I made a mistake."

Like hell.

She gave him a well-what's-your-problem-now look, then turned back to her work.

What *was* his problem? *Her.* She'd erected a shell around her as cold and hard as this damn desolate countryside and he wanted to be the man to tear it down. He wanted to see some honest emotion in those brown eyes. It was high time this town knew the real Charlie she kept hidden the way she did her body beneath all those layers of baggy clothes. It was time to expose her to the world.

He grabbed her and spun her around. All he wanted was her undivided attention, to force her to look him in the eye, to see a glimmer of a crack in that shell. All he wanted was an honest reaction out of her.

He'd never planned to kiss her. Not even when his lips dropped to hers. But then it was too late. Her fragrance filled his senses as his mouth covered hers in a hard, demanding kiss. Her pupils widened only slightly as if the kiss hadn't been as much of a surprise to her as it was to him. Then his senses were filled with the tactile pleasures of her full, lush mouth, the warmth of her breath as she let out a whisper of a sigh and he felt her body tremble at his touch, her heart a hammer next to his.

"Charlie?" a male voice echoed through the garage.

Gus jerked back from the kiss, back from the madness. He stepped away, pleased to see emotion like golden sparks in the depths of Charlie's brown eyes.

Unfortunately, that emotion turned out to be anger.

"Don't ever do that again," she whispered hotly, sounding at least a little breathless. "Kissing me will get you killed." She stepped back over to the pickup as if nothing had happened. "Hey, Wayne! How ya doin'?"

Gus turned in the direction the voice had come from—the gaping open garage door—his heart still pounding from the impact of the kiss. Or maybe it was just from the stupidity of it. He'd only kissed one other woman he'd strongly suspected of murder—Natalie— and that had nearly gotten him killed. He hoped to hell kissing Charlie hadn't been the kiss of death.

A man with curly blond hair stood silhouetted in the garage doorway nervously fidgeting with his coat sleeve.

"I need to talk to you, Charlie," Wayne said, sounding upset as he looked from Charlie to Gus. "It's real, real important."

Charlie shot Gus a pointed look as she wiped her hands on a rag. "Well, come on in, Wayne, and tell me about it."

Gus felt as if he should say something to Charlie, the kiss still coursing through his veins like a powerful drug. But what was there to say? How could he have forgotten that kissing her could get him killed—just as she'd warned him? Just as it had Josh?

That thought sobered him.

He stepped around her and the pickup, headed for the rental car, wanting to tell her that they weren't finished. But he figured she already knew that.

"What's up, Wayne?" Charlie asked. "You having car trouble again?"

Gus had just reached for the handle on his rental car's door when the sheriff's car pulled up outside, blocking his exit. A uniformed man got out and started toward them, shielding his eyes as he tried to see into the darkness of the garage.

Gus heard a sound behind him and turned to see

Wayne disappearing through the back door, making a hasty exit.

"Bryan," Charlie said, nodding to the sheriff as he stepped into the garage. "What can I do for you?"

"Heard a knock in the engine on the way down from Libby. Thought you might take a look." The sheriff was gray-haired, probably in his sixties, possibly a contemporary of her father's. It was obvious he and Charlie knew each other and well. Another cause for concern.

"Sure," she said, sounding calm as hell. "Would you mind moving your car though so this fella can get out? He's anxious to be on his way."

Gus smiled at that as the sheriff went to move his car.

"Goodbye, Gus," Charlie said, turning her back on him.

He stared at her backside for a moment, disturbed that the sheriff's visit didn't appear to be causing her any concern at all. Was it possible, Gus wondered, that he could be wrong about her? Or was she just one cool cookie?

One thing was for sure, he thought, remembering the kiss. There was a hell of lot more to Charlie Larkin than he'd first thought.

"Charlie?" he said, realizing it was the first time he'd said her name.

She turned, seeming a little surprised herself.

Earlier when he'd grabbed her and kissed her, he'd just wanted to get a reaction out of her. Now all he wanted was to wipe out that unnerving calm composure of hers. He wanted her as off balance as he felt.

"That's something about Josh Whitaker having your locket on him," he said as he opened his car door and slid in. He smiled at her through the windshield as he closed the door and started the engine, her surprised expression what he'd hoped for.

He was betting few people knew about the locket being found on Josh. Gus couldn't imagine how Josh had come by it. But he'd lay odds Charlie knew.

As he backed out, she gave him a look that held a warning. Or was it a threat? Either way, he had her attention. And she looked anything but calm.

CHARLIE WATCHED GUS drive away, still fighting the disturbing effect of his kiss. She wanted desperately to blame it on the fact that it had been so long since she'd kissed anyone. Rather, since anyone had kissed her, she amended, afraid to think she might have kissed him back—even for an instant. She stood in the garage feeling weak and shaky, her heart still hammering, her lips branded with Augustus T. Riley's kiss. And now he knew about the locket.

Sheriff Bryan Olsen cleared his throat.

She looked up to find him standing with his hat in his hand, looking contrite, looking worried.

"That knock I said I heard in my engine," he said softly. "It was just pretense."

She nodded, having suspected as much. Bryan Olsen and her father had been best friends and she knew he thought it was his job to protect her. She wanted to unburden him of that task and had tried over the years, but she knew that Bryan would have walked through fire for her father—and now found himself in the middle of a firestorm because of her.

"There's been a leak about the locket," he said miserably. "I got a call from Phil Simonson not thirty minutes ago." He didn't need to tell her how incriminating it was to have her locket found on Josh Whitaker's body.

She could think of nothing to say.

"It's a murder investigation, Charlie, and I don't

think I need to tell you that the fact that you knew him doesn't help matters."

She shook her head.

"It sure would help though if we knew how Josh Whitaker had gotten that locket," the sheriff said.

Her heart thudded like a death march in her chest as she looked at him. He was trying to warn her. Had he found more incriminating evidence in Josh's car that would link his death to her? Or was he just worried, as she was, that it was only a matter of time before he did?

"I suppose Whitaker could have been poking around at the lake and just found the locket," he said.

They both knew what the odds of that were.

"But it doesn't explain what he was doing up here to start with," the sheriff ruminated. "It doesn't help either having Trudi going around telling everyone she saw you with Josh the day he disappeared." Bryan flicked his gaze at her. "She swears she saw you kiss him."

"I never saw Josh that day, so I couldn't have kissed him," Charlie said, reminded again of her most recent kiss.

"Well, I think we all know how Trudi is," he said.

Trudi had lied either for attention—or for Forest. Trudi and Forest had a history and might have been together today if it hadn't been for Jenny.

"Bryan, I told you that Josh and I didn't have that kind of relationship." They'd already been over this. She'd told the sheriff how she had met Josh when she'd volunteered on the help line in Bozeman. Josh had been starting a statewide help line and teaching volunteers.

Josh had been incredibly easy to talk to and she'd ended up pouring out her whole life history over coffee one night. They'd been friends. But that had been it. "I haven't seen him or talked to him in years."

The sheriff nodded. "Is there any chance he might

have forgotten you and that's why he didn't stop in when he came up here?"

She wanted to say yes, but she shook her head. She and Josh had been close. He was like the older brother she'd always wanted. "We were friends. I don't think he would have forgotten. I think that's why he had the locket."

The sheriff nodded. "Yeah, the locket. So if he'd somehow come in possession of the locket, he would have tried to see you to give it back?"

"I guess so." Josh had known how she felt about Quinn, so she found that hard to believe. But since she'd told Josh everything, he might have thought the locket would give her some kind of closure. She couldn't imagine him driving all this way and not coming by. "Maybe he never got as far as town. Maybe he went straight to the lake," she said more to herself than to the sheriff.

"To meet someone, you think?" he said as he turned the brim of his hat in his fingers for a moment. He stopped as if an idea had just come to him. "He didn't call you by any chance? Or you call him, say, from the pay phone outside?"

She stared at him, realizing this wasn't an idle question. "He tried to call me at the pay phone?" she asked in shock.

Sheriff Bryan Olsen looked down at his boots in answer. "And someone called him from the same number."

She had to fight to squeeze a breath out. "It wasn't me, Bryan. I swear to you, I haven't spoken with Josh in years. I told you some man called the house, but I can't be sure it was even Josh."

"Well…" He put his hat back on his head and stood looking down at her, worry in his gaze. Worry that he couldn't keep her safe? Or worry that she wasn't telling him the whole story?

"Why would I lie about him calling me?" she asked. "It doesn't make any sense."

The sheriff nodded. "Unless there was some reason you didn't want anyone to know you were talking to him."

Yes, that was exactly what it looked like. She felt sick.

"I'm just afraid all hell is going to break loose now that the Simonsons know about the locket," he said, obviously hesitant to leave her alone.

All hell had already broken out when Augustus T. Riley had come to town gunning for her.

"I'd just stay clear of the Simonsons if I were you," the sheriff said. "If there's any trouble, you call me."

She nodded, her heart a sledgehammer in her chest. The next time she saw Bryan it was more than likely he'd be stopping by to arrest her for the murder of Josh Whitaker and they both knew it.

He reached out to pat her shoulder, then put his hat on, turned and walked to his car.

She watched him leave. The moment he disappeared from view, she grabbed the top of the pickup's tailgate for support, her stomach roiling so badly she thought she might throw up. Someone was trying to frame her for murder. There was no doubt in her mind about that now. The locket had been planted on Josh to make her look guilty. The calls made from the pay phone outside the garage. But how had they even known about Josh? And where did the locket fit into all this?

At least she knew who had told the Simonsons about the locket, she thought, recalling Gus's parting words. Bryan said someone had leaked the information about the locket and Helen said Gus had asked Trudi directions to Phil Simonson's house after lunch—not long before the sheriff got the call about the locket.

Chapter Ten

Earlene Kurtz lived in a trailer on the north end of town. She opened the door in jeans and a large T-shirt, a spatula in one hand, her expression only mildly surprised to find Gus standing on her doorstep.

He recognized her from yesterday when she was at the wild-game processing plant working with T. J. Blue.

"My name is—"

"Gus," she said. "I know."

"Then you probably know why I'm here."

"You want to know about Charlie." She smiled and motioned him inside.

He stepped through the door, closing it behind him as she went into the kitchen where she was scooping dough onto a baking sheet. The trailer smelled of chocolate chip cookies.

"My son will be home soon. I always try to have a treat for him," she said, her back to him. "That's why I work the early shift."

He studied her. She was one of those women who carried her weight around the middle, giving her a square shape set on two legs. Her face was tight with the extra weight she carried. Her brown hair, long and dull, making her look older than he knew she was—a few years younger than Charlie.

"Would you care for a warm cookie?" she asked as she slid the new batch into the oven.

He shook his head and looked around. The trailer was an older model, but clean and neat inside. She seemed to do all right for a single mother. "I need to know about you and Charlie Larkin."

She turned to look at him. "We're friends." She shrugged as if that was the whole story. "Which most people don't understand, given the circumstances and who fathered my son."

"I heard Quinn Simonson fathered your son."

She nodded. "I was pregnant with Arnie when Quinn died."

"How pregnant?"

"Four months." She wiped her hands on a towel and glanced toward the living room. "You want to sit down?"

He pulled out a chair at the kitchen table and sat, trying to make sense out of this. Earlene was the reason Charlie and Quinn had gotten into a huge fight at Freeze Out Lake, the reason Charlie had refused to get back into the car that night and the reason Quinn had roared off—if not the reason he'd gotten killed.

"I guess I find it hard to believe you and Charlie are friends," he said at last. "I mean, I would think Charlie might be resentful toward you and vice versa."

"You don't know Charlie, do you," she said, making it sound as if he was missing something in his life because of that. "She hates it that Arnie doesn't have a father because hers meant so much to her. She's promised to teach him how to work on cars."

"Do you see much of her?" he asked.

"She takes Arnie for me when I have to go to Libby or Missoula for something," Earlene said. "And we get together for lunch. She really loves Arnie. I think she's afraid that because he resembles Quinn he might grow up to be like him." She continued to stand, leaning against the kitchen counter, watching him.

"How did Quinn take it when he heard you were pregnant with his child?" Gus asked, wondering if she would have been showing at four months. Possibly not, given her size.

"He wasn't interested in being a father—let alone a husband," she said and smiled sadly.

"Maybe he would have changed his mind after you had the baby," Gus suggested.

"I like to think so. I loved Quinn. He was charming and cute and I'd always had a secret crush on him," Earlene said. "He told me he wasn't seeing Charlie anymore. I believed him. But it turned out that was a lie. Quinn lied about a lot of things."

Something in the way she'd said that… "You think there were other women?"

She smiled. "I'd bet on it."

"Did Charlie know about them, too?" he asked.

Earlene shrugged. "Maybe. But Quinn was pretty persuasive. I mean, he got Charlie up to the lake that night for the party, didn't he? He might have been able to talk her into coming back to him if Trudi hadn't announced to the world that her sister who worked at the clinic had told her that I was pregnant with Quinn's baby. Of course Quinn denied he was the father, but I think it was the last straw as far as Charlie was concerned."

"Do you think she loved him?" Gus asked.

The timer went off. She picked up a hot pad and opened the oven. "You mean enough to kill him?" She shook her head as she pulled out the cookies, filling the room with the wonderful smell. "Charlie was going off to college that fall. She and Quinn had been *the* couple in high school but she'd broken up with him before the party. I think she knew he wasn't the guy for her. Not long-term. Quinn wanted his freedom, but he wanted Charlie, too, although looking back, I think it was Phil who wanted Quinn and Charlie together. Maybe he thought there was money to be had with the garage." She began to slip the cookies from the sheet to a wire rack with a pancake turner.

"So you don't think Charlie was serious about Quinn?" Gus asked, wondering why that pleased him when it took away her motivation for killing Quinn—if indeed he had been murdered.

"So why the big fight the night at the lake then?" he asked. Finding out Quinn had been cheating on her had to have made her angry. But angry enough to kill him if she didn't care that much about him?

"She was furious with him for bringing her up to the lake. I suppose she told you about the time Jenny almost drowned?"

Charlie hadn't told him anything.

"Charlie hates that lake and Quinn knew it but he still drove her up there against her protests," Earlene said.

If Charlie were that afraid of the lake, then would she lure Josh up there to kill him? "I'm sure you've heard about Charlie's bad luck with men," Gus said. "Any thoughts on that?"

She scooped the last of the cookie dough onto the baking sheet, her back to him. "Isn't it obvious? Someone in this town wants to hurt Charlie."

"Like who?"

She finished, slid the cookie sheet into the oven and set the timer before she turned around. "Trudi has always been jealous of Charlie. The Simonsons blame Charlie for Quinn's death." She shrugged.

"What about T. J. Blue and Rickie Moss?" he asked.

"I think they like perpetuating the idea that Charlie is cursed when it comes to men."

"There is no doubt that Rickie got cut that night on his date with Charlie, and T.J.'s trailer did burn down, right?"

She nodded. "But Rickie had tried to rip off some dope dealers a month before that. After his accident in the woods, he paid them the money he owed them. And T.J.? There are people in town who would tell you he set that fire to collect the insurance and started the rumor about the curse to shift the blame. It was arson but no one was ever arrested. T.J. collected the insurance and bought himself a cabin." She shrugged again. "So it all depends on who you talk to."

He could see that. "What about the Simonsons?" he asked. "Are they part of Arnie's life?"

She met his gaze. "What do you think?"

He thought Phil Simonson wouldn't acknowledge his own grandson if it meant he might be expected to help with support. "Did you know Josh Whitaker?"

"No."

"He was the emergency room doctor on call the day you took Arnie to the hospital in Missoula for his asthma attack."

Earlene looked surprised. "Really? I don't remember him. I can't say I paid much attention to anyone but my son." She frowned. "I do remember the doctor being very kind and caring, though. I'm sorry I didn't remember his name."

Gus studied her for a moment, convinced she was telling the truth.

"Do you think Charlie had anything to do with Quinn's death?" he had to ask.

"If she did, I wouldn't blame her," Earlene said.

"But your son doesn't have a father."

She nodded and looked away. "No, he doesn't."

On his way out, Gus passed Arnie Kurtz, a tow-headed seven-year-old with blue eyes. He looked enough like Jenny and Forest's little girl that they could be brother and sister. But he doubted Phil or Forest would ever let the two kids, so close in age, ever be friends. Some lines just weren't crossed.

As Gus neared his car, he wasn't surprised to see that he had company. "Hello, Sheriff. I was planning on paying you a visit."

Sheriff Bryan Olsen pushed himself off the patrol car he'd been leaning against. "Then my timing is perfect. Want to tell me what brings you to Utopia?"

Gus figured the sheriff already had a pretty good idea. "I'm just looking into Josh Whitaker's death for the family."

"Oh, really? I thought Josh Whitaker didn't have any family," the sheriff said. "Both parents deceased."

"I believe he has a half brother," Gus said.

"You know I don't think you're here on behalf of Josh Whitaker's half brother or any other member of the family," the sheriff said. "Your reputation precedes you, Mr. Riley."

Gus couldn't tell if that was good or bad.

"Word around town is that you've been asking a lot of questions about Charlie Larkin," the sheriff said, eyeing him. "Why is that?"

"She knew Josh Whitaker."

The older man nodded. "She told me all about that, but that doesn't mean she killed him."

Charlie had told the sheriff about her relationship with Josh Whitaker? "Then you know about the calls made to and from the pay phone outside the garage?"

"I received all of that information from the Missoula police," the sheriff said. "I'd like to know how you got the information, though."

Gus ignored that. "All the evidence in this case points to Charlie Larkin." He ticked off on his fingers. "She knew Josh, the calls were made from her pay phone, her locket was found on his body."

The sheriff's jaw muscle jumped. "All circumstantial." He pulled off his hat and seemed to study the brim for a few moments. "I've known Charlie Larkin all her life," he said slowly. "Her father was my friend. I'd stake my life on her being innocent of any wrongdoing, but I'm also a law enforcement officer, responsible for the lives of the people in this county. That's why I'm asking you not to get involved in my ongoing investigation. All things considered, it would be safer for everyone involved if you were to return to Los Angeles."

Was there a reason the sheriff wanted him out of the way? "Are you trying to run me out of town?"

"Just making a suggestion, Mr. Riley. You're smart enough to have noticed that any man who gets around Charlie Larkin seems to have bad luck. I don't think that's a coincidence. If I were you, I'd put a few thousand miles' distance between the woman and yourself. For your own good."

"If you're so convinced Charlie is innocent, then who *is* killing and maiming these guys?" Gus demanded.

"That's what we're trying to find out," the older man said.

"Not fast enough," Gus snapped. "Thanks for the

advice, Sheriff." He got into his car. In his rearview mirror, Gus watched the sheriff watch him drive away.

When he looked up, Gus realized he'd taken the wrong turn. The road wound around through the pines, passed some old logging equipment and a gravel pit. He was just getting ready to turn around and backtrack when he spotted two pickups parked on the far side of the gravel pit. Did everyone in this county drive trucks? It appeared so.

He recognized one of the trucks as Forest Simonson's about the same time he saw Jenny standing next to it talking to a man Gus didn't recognize until he had driven past. Both Jenny and the man had seemed startled to see a car as Gus passed. Startled and guilty-appearing. As the road curved, just before he lost sight of them, Gus glanced in his side mirror. Jenny Simonson was in T. J. Blue's arms. What the hell?

As Gus drove through town, he felt anxious. He'd spent the morning and part of the afternoon going over everything he'd learned from the time Josh Whitaker's body had been found. There was always a point in a case when he felt jumpy. When he'd found out enough that he wished he hadn't known the truth. He'd found out a lot about Charlie Larkin and yet he still had no proof that she was a killer. What evidence there was pointed straight to her, and all the good deeds she'd done couldn't change that.

So why was he having doubts? Because of some kiss? Or because of all her many loyal supporters and all her good deeds? Or because the people who professed her guilt all had an ax to grind?

He shook his head, realizing he wasn't basing those doubts on fact, but feelings. He'd been down that road before on the Natalie Burns case. Come hell or high water he wasn't going down that road again. The last thing he'd let himself do was get emotionally involved with Charlie Larkin and make the lethal mistake of trusting a killer again.

But he had to admit, he'd turned over a lot of stones and wasn't happy about most of what he'd found underneath. Like Jenny and T.J. He didn't even want to think about what Forest would do if he found out. *When* he found out.

Gus told himself it wasn't his problem. This wasn't his town. All he cared about was finding Josh's killer and then going home. Home. Los Angeles seemed like light-years away.

There had to be a way to flush out the killer—no matter who it turned out to be.

The problem was: Charlie had gotten to him. He didn't want her to be the killer.

He'd just found the road back into town, when an idea hit him like a two-by-four upside the head. It was crazy and way too dangerous for a sane man to even consider. But right now he was desperate and his sanity was in question because he was starting to doubt that Charlie Larkin had killed anyone—based on little more than a few nice stories about her and a damn kiss—and that was even more dangerous to his well-being than what he had planned.

CHARLIE WAS SITTING in the Pinecone, having a cup of tea with Helen when Gus walked in. She suddenly felt trapped, the air around her too dense to breathe.

His gaze fell on her and he moved quickly toward her as if he'd been looking for her. She felt her stomach lurch. What did he want *now*?

He slid into the booth across from her, smiling. "I've been looking for you."

That she'd gathered. "Are you having car trouble *again?*" She hadn't meant to sound so sarcastic.

His smile deepened. "We both know any trouble I've had has nothing to do with my car."

She stared at him, wide-eyed amazed that he would finally admit it—and here. Suddenly she was aware that, besides Helen, everyone in the café was watching them. And since it was coffee-break time in Utopia, quite a few locals were in the café, plus several of the worst gossips in town.

Gus reached across the table and took her hand in his before she could draw it back. "I've missed you," he said loud enough that everyone had to have heard him. He turned her hand palm up and began to caress the sensitive skin with the pad of his thumb. "After that kiss earlier—"

His touch set off tiny jolts across her palm. She jerked her hand free. "I know what you're doing," she whispered hoarsely, trying to keep her voice down so the others couldn't hear.

He smiled, flirting, as he leaned over to brush a lock of hair back from her temple, his touch making her shiver. "I'm doing what any man would do under the circumstances."

"You're going to get yourself killed," she whispered fiercely.

"You don't have much faith in me," he whispered back. "If getting close to you will lure out Josh Whitaker's killer, then that is exactly what I'm going to do. Unless you know something I don't?" He grinned, his face just inches from hers.

From a distance it would appear they were locked

in an intimate conversation—instead of an adversarial one. "I think it's high time someone tried to break that curse."

"This isn't about any curse," she hissed back. "This is about a book, the one you're planning to write about me."

He lifted an eyebrow. "Only if you turn out to be the killer."

"Please, Gus, don't do this," she pleaded, panicked. "You don't realize how dangerous it is."

"Oh, I think I do," he said, capturing her hand again in his. "You're trembling. What is it you're so afraid of, Charlie? That something might happen to me? Or that I might learn the truth?"

She stared at him, wanting to deny that she was responsible for any of this. But she couldn't. Because she had a terrible feeling that somehow she was responsible for all of it. As crazy as it sounded, there *was* a curse on her.

"I don't want to see you get hurt," she said, realizing that was true. He was the enemy. He'd come here to destroy her. But just the thought of the danger he was putting himself in—

"Do you have a better idea?" He cocked his head at her. "That's what I thought." With her hand still in his, he slid out of the booth and moved to her in a blink.

It was obvious he planned to kiss her again. She turned her head as he bent toward her. A soft chuckle emanated from deep with in him as he nuzzled her neck, brushing her hair back with his free hand.

"Mmm," he breathed against her bare skin. "I love the way you smell."

She felt goose bumps ripple across her skin as he trailed kisses down the column of her neck, finding a sweet spot between her neck and shoulder. A shaft of heat arced to her center, a sigh escaping her lips.

His chuckle this time was hoarse and she felt his breath quicken against her neck.

"Everyone in here is going to think we're lovers," she whispered breathlessly.

"Yes," he said softly into the hollow of her throat.

"We *aren't* lovers."

"No," he said, letting go of her hair and drawing back. "Not yet." He smiled as he cupped her chin in his warm palm and turned her to face him so quickly, too quickly to stop him. His mouth dropped to hers, stealing her breath, sealing the trap he'd just set for himself.

Then he was gone, whistling as he left, stopping at the door to grin back at her, aware everyone had seen. "See you later."

She watched him walk to his car. He turned as he reached it and grinned at her as if he'd known she'd be watching him. Damn him. She could feel his gaze, as hot on her skin as his kisses had been. Damn fool.

"What was that about?" Helen demanded as she slid into the booth Gus had just unoccupied.

"I wish I knew," Charlie said, surprised how breathless she was. Still. He made her feel things she'd never felt before. Damn him. Worse, it was just a game to him. All he cared about was catching a killer—and it was clear when the dust settled, he believed she'd be the one caught in his snare.

"Wow, he certainly has some effect on you," Helen said. "You should see yourself."

Charlie looked into the reflection in the café window. Her face was flushed, her eyes shiny bright. She looked like a woman who'd just made love with an exciting man. She touched her palm to her heated cheek and looked past her own reflection to see Gus back out and head south.

She watched him until the car disappeared down the highway. What did he plan to do now? And where was he going? There was nothing that way except— Her heart quickened as she realized where he was headed. Freeze Out Lake.

Chapter Eleven

Gus headed toward the lake. He'd set the stage and now had to play out his hand, no matter how it turned out. He reached into the bag on the seat beside him and pulled out the .38 special. He didn't have to check to see if it was loaded. He always kept it loaded on a case. He slipped it into the shoulder harness he'd pulled on before going looking for Charlie.

He told himself there was no reason to start looking over his shoulder just yet. Even with the small-town grapevine, it would take time for everyone to hear about him and Charlie. Not only that, no one knew he was going to the lake. He hadn't even known himself until he left the Pinecone and realized it was time he finally checked out the place that Josh had died.

He'd been putting it off. But knew he couldn't anymore.

He believed that Charlie was innocent. She couldn't have killed Josh. But someone had. Someone who wanted him to believe Charlie was a killer.

That's why Charlie's locket from Quinn had been found on Josh's body.

Someone else in this town had to have known Josh.

Gus couldn't be wrong. Not this time. What other answer was there? A curse? Or someone who didn't want

Charlie to find happiness as Earlene had suggested?
Neither wanted to fly, not when faced with the facts.
Fact: Someone had murdered Josh. Fact: Josh had Char-
lie Larkin's locket on him.

He shook his head and concentrated on his driving,
reminding himself of one of his first books. Her name
was Natalie Burns and she was out on bond after being
arrested for allegedly killing her lover. She was young
and beautiful and Gus had been green and stupid. He'd
bought into her innocence. And she'd tried to kill him.

He swore he'd never make that mistake again.

He hadn't gone far down the highway when he saw
the sign to Freeze Out Lake. Slowly, he turned off, remembering how eerie it had been in the dark less than
forty-eight hours ago. He had at least an hour before it
got dark again.

The turnoff spot didn't look all that much better in
the daylight. The snow had melted back where the weed-
grown road disappeared into the trees. Even though it
wasn't quite late afternoon, shadows hung heavy in the
pines, making it hard to see very far up the road.

He didn't relish the idea of driving up there now. But
he'd also never been one to back down from something
just because it was hard—or unnerving.

Shifting the rental car into a lower gear, he started
up the road to the lake, the tall weeds slapping the front
fender and hood as he wound his way through the dark
of the pines and up the mountainside.

He thought about the other men who had come up
this road and never lived to come back down it. The
tracks through the weeds were still visible where the
wrecker had brought out Josh Whitaker's body and car.
He tried not to think about that.

The road was narrow and snowy in some places,

muddy in others. He took it slow as he climbed higher and higher up the mountain, until at what seemed like the last moment, the trees opened and there was the lake.

He hit the brakes. For just a split second, he feared Charlie had done something to his car. Relief swept through him, making him almost giddy, when his brakes worked and he brought the car to a stop at the edge of the mountain lake.

The scene was beautiful in a creepy sort of way he couldn't explain. A perfect mountain lake surrounded by tall dark-green pines. Josh had died in this desolate place. The thought sent a chill through him hardening his resolve to see justice done—and at any cost.

He got out, surprised how cold it was. The water was clear, an icy-looking dark green. He stepped to the edge, knelt down and felt it. The water was warmer than he'd expected, as if it hadn't caught up with the change in weather yet.

Where had Josh's car gone under? he wondered angrily. Had Charlie been here? Had she watched it? Had she lured him up here? Someone had. It didn't make much sense for Josh to drive up here otherwise, not with the lake so far off the beaten path. Josh had been killed with a single blow to the back of the head with a blunt instrument. Had the killer been in the back of the car? Or had Josh been killed out here and then put back into the car before it was rolled into the lake?

Gus's blood ran cold when he thought that Charlie could have stood in this very spot and watched the car sink with Josh Whitaker in it. Another one down.

What had made Josh come up here? Who?

Too many questions and no answers. And so far, Gus reminded himself, he hadn't been able to find one piece of solid evidence that Charlie Larkin was responsible nor any solid proof that she was innocent either.

Suddenly he sensed rather than heard someone behind him. He whirled around going for his gun. Charlie stood directly behind him. A wrench gripped in her right hand.

"What the hell?" It came out on a breath, his heart lunging as he stumbled back into the water, almost falling on the slick rocks as he pulled the .38 from the shoulder holster and leveled it at her.

She stood with her arms at her sides, the wrench gripped so tightly in her fingers that her knuckles were white. She didn't move, didn't even seem aware of him as she stared out at the lake, her eyes glassy.

"What are you doing here?" he demanded and realized he was standing in six inches of water. He sidestepped her, getting back on dry land, putting a little distance between them. The damn woman had scared the hell out of him.

Why hadn't he heard her approach? His gaze flicked past her. Where was her van? He would have heard the van. Unless she hadn't wanted him to. Because she'd followed him here, her intention pretty obvious.

"What the hell were you doing sneaking up on me like that with a wrench in your hand?" His voice came out a rasp. The look on her face was freaking him out. "Answer me, dammit."

She seemed to shake herself out of a fog. Her eyes moved from the water to his face. She blinked, almost as if surprised to see him. But not nearly as surprised as she was when she looked down to see the wrench in her hand.

"Oh," she said and stuck the wrench back into a pocket of her overalls. "I didn't mean to scare you."

"Right." The same words he'd said to her earlier. What was this, payback? At least she wasn't still doing her zombie thing. Nor was he now floating facedown in the lake. Though that possibility didn't seem that far off.

"This place scares me more than it does you," she said, glancing at the gun in his hand and dismissing it.

He doubted this place scared her more right now. She could have killed him!

Her gaze went to the lake again. Her eyes widened as if—He swung around expecting to see—Hell, that was just it, he didn't know what he expected. Maybe some waterlogged, weed-covered dead body emerging from the deep.

But there was nothing. Just the last of the sunlight leaving a gold film on the surface. Not a whisper of a breeze in the pines. No sound at all. Except for the pounding of his pulse like surf in his ears.

He swung back around to face her again, feeling like a fool for turning his back on her. But she hadn't moved, hadn't gone for the wrench, hadn't taken her eyes off the lake, as far as he could tell. Her skin looked chalky and her eyes—those dark-brown mesmerizing eyes—seemed to be seeing something horrible that only she could see.

He recoiled at the thought, drawing back from her, realizing what she might be envisioning. Josh's car sinking into the eerie dark water.

He stared at her, not sure what frightened him the most. That he didn't want to believe she was a killer. Or that he couldn't get a bead on her, couldn't be sure of anything about her. Except for the fact that she scared him. Hell, he was still shaking from finding her standing behind him with that damn wrench in her hand. But when he'd set up this trap at the Pinecone, he'd known she might come after him and try to kill him. Just not this soon. He reminded himself that she hadn't tried to kill him. Yet.

"Charlie?"

Her pupils were dilated. Sweat had broken out on her upper lip. Her freckles practically jumped off her face. She began to sway.

He swore under his breath as he holstered the gun and caught her.

The moment he touched her, she blinked, then seemed startled to see him again. She righted herself, drawing back, as if afraid of him. What a joke that was. With relief, he watched her color come back, afraid of what he'd just witnessed, realizing just how much he didn't want her to be the killer.

"What was *that* about?" he asked. This lake was freaking her, that much was for sure.

A tremor seemed to quake through her. "I've only been up here one other time since—"

He thought she was going to say "The night I killed Josh Whitaker."

"—the day my friend Jenny almost drowned."

He stared at her, remembering what Earlene had told him about Jenny almost drowning and Charlie's fear of the lake.

She shifted her gaze to him. "Jenny Lee Simonson, now. We were swimming and she must have gotten a cramp—" She looked back out at the lake. "I swam to her and grabbed her arm—" Another tremor rattled through her. She hugged herself and looked over at him again, seeming a little embarrassed, definitely shaken. "I know it's crazy, but it almost felt as if someone, something, was trying to pull her under."

"You saved her life," he said, more to himself than to

her. Another heroic deed. Or had she tried to kill Jenny as well? He felt as if he kept peeling away layers and still couldn't get to the real Charlie Larkin.

"How long ago was that?" he asked. "Before or after Quinn died?"

She looked at him, as if surprised he'd bring up Quinn. For a moment, he didn't think she'd answer. "Before. I didn't want to come up here that night with Quinn, but he—" She shook her head and looked away again.

"I heard he brought you up here to a kegger and the two of you had a huge fight that night."

"Is that what you heard?" She sounded tired and didn't even bother to look at him.

"Actually, I heard that you found out that he'd fathered Earlene's baby and you were angry. Angry enough to kill him?"

She said nothing and he wondered how far he should try to push her, given where they were and the fact that she might have more than a wrench in the pockets of her baggy overalls.

"So what made you come up here today if you hate this lake so much?" he asked, figuring he probably wouldn't get an answer to this either.

"You." Her gaze swung to his, her eyes suddenly as dark and cold as the lake and just as hostile.

He felt a tremor of his own. "You followed me?"

She seemed to find amusement in that. "Haven't you been tracking me?"

He didn't answer. It surprised him now that she'd ever reminded him of Natalie. Charlie was much more complex, much more intriguing, much more dangerous. He'd never known a woman like her. And doubted he ever would again.

"After what you did back at the café, I couldn't let you come up here alone," she said.

"Oh, so you planned to *protect* me with that wrench, not knock me in the head and leave me floating face-down for dead."

She glared at him. "You really believe that I'm a killer? Did you know that Josh was deathly afraid of water? He almost drowned when he was young and he'd never been able to get over his fear."

Yes, he knew that. He thought of Jenny and her near drowning. He wondered if she'd gotten over it, wondering if anyone ever really did get over it. "So he'd have to trust someone implicitly to meet them here."

"I can't imagine any reason Josh would let himself be talked into coming up here. It had to be a matter of life or death."

"Seems it was. His death," Gus said.

She met his gaze. "You aren't taking this seriously."

"Oh, but I am."

"Not if you don't realize how dangerous it is for any man who gets too close to me," she said, her voice low.

"Right, the curse," he said. "How close did Josh get to you?" Silence. "Talk to me. What do you have to lose?"

"I could end up the subject of your next book."

"Only if you're the killer," he said and smiled. She would make one hell of a book.

"So tell me about you and Josh. I know he tried to call you before he disappeared last fall. Your name was also in an old address book of his."

"I'm impressed," she said.

"Don't be. I didn't even know you were a woman until the night before last at the garage."

She nodded and gave him a small smile.

He realized he'd never seen her really smile, but he would like to. "Then when Josh's body was found in Freeze Out Lake with your locket in his pocket..."

She blew out a breath. "All the so-called evidence led right to me."

"There's more. A doctor at the hospital overheard a phone conversation of Josh's just before he disappeared. The woman doctor said Josh was agitated and upset. When she asked him if anything was wrong, he said it had something to do with a friend. She got the impression it was a woman, a woman he was obviously worried about." He took a breath. "So you and Josh were...lovers?" he asked, knowing he was going to hate her answer.

She cocked her head at him. "Sorry to disappoint you, Josh and I were just friends, but maybe the person who killed him didn't know that," she said. "Or maybe it was enough."

He hoped his relief didn't show. She hadn't seduced Josh. Or at least that was her story. "So how did you meet?"

"We were both working on a help line and got to talking one night."

"When was this?"

"Not long before I returned to Utopia." She made a face. "Don't look at me like I'm some sort of saint. I was volunteering for class credit in college. Josh, well, Josh had started the help line and was training volunteers. He really was something special."

"This was in Bozeman then. I heard he was a hell of a nice guy," Gus said, trying not to let praise of Josh affect him the way it had for most of his life—negatively. "So you were *good* friends?"

She nodded. "What are you getting at?"

"Was he easy to talk to?"

"Yes. He liked helping people," she said. "It wasn't just me."

Had Josh thought he was helping someone when he'd driven up to this lake a year ago?

"Did you tell him about Utopia and the people who live here?" Gus asked.

She stared at him. "What does this have to do with—"

"Did you tell him about Quinn?"

"Yes, but—"

"Let me guess," he said. "You told him you felt responsible for Quinn's death."

"I *do* feel responsible for Quinn's death," she snapped. "After all, if he hadn't taken off from the party the way he did maybe he wouldn't have wrecked on the way down the mountain."

"You can't hold yourself responsible for his temper," Gus said. "Is that the only reason you feel responsible?"

"Isn't that enough? He died so young and he was about to be a father. He'll never know Arnie."

Nor would Arnie ever know his father.

She bit at her lip. "Have you seen Arnie? He looks exactly like Quinn did at that age."

Gus nodded. "That's why you help Earlene out with him? You realize, Charlie, you're almost too good."

"Don't make more out of it than it is," she said. "I like kids. Earlene's a friend."

"After she slept with your boyfriend?" He shook his head. She wasn't just too good, she was too naive.

"What's wrong?" she asked, eyeing him.

"Nothing."

She let out a sigh. "You're afraid I'm another Natalie Burns."

He blinked in surprise. Both that she knew about Natalie…and that she'd hit so close to the truth.

"It made national news, I read all the newspaper articles when I looked you up on the Internet," she said by way of explanation. "She almost killed you."

"You checked up on me?" If she knew about Natalie, then she'd done a lot of checking. Why? Because he scared her? Because she was guilty? Or because she really was innocent?

"You're surprised by that?" she asked, studying him.

"Everything about you surprises me," he said.

She looked past him, the last of the day's sunlight on her face, dusk settling in the pines.

He followed her gaze. "What is that?" he asked, seeing something in the darkness of the pines. A structure.

"The old Simonson lodge," she said, her voice a whisper, as if she was afraid someone would hear her.

"I want to take a look inside," he said. He saw her recoil at the idea of going up to the lodge.

"It's been boarded up for years," she said quickly. "I'm sure there's nothing in there. Just dust and spiderwebs and…"

"And memories?" he guessed.

Her expression gave her away. He glimpsed a vulnerability that under other circumstances would have made him soften toward her. "If you're afraid, I can go by myself," he said and walked over to his rental car to get his flashlight. He knew she'd come with him. But why? Because she worried that something would happen to him? Or worried about something he might find? "Coming?" One thing was for certain. He wasn't letting her out of his sight until they left the lake.

She fell into step beside him as he walked toward

the woods, the beam of the flashlight trailing over the rocky shore as they neared the old lodge.

He stopped a few yards out to admire it, the walls constructed of hand-hewn logs, the foundation of rocks taken from the shoreline. She was right. It had been boarded up, but some of the boards were missing, others broken.

He climbed the steps to the porch, not surprised to find that someone had been here recently. The rusted padlock on the door had been busted. The door stood ajar.

He shone his light into the crack between door and jamb. There were dusty footprints on the old wooden floor. He pushed with one hand and the door creaked open.

A rustling sound came from deep within the lodge.

"It isn't safe," Charlie said and grabbed his arm. "Please."

He turned to look at her, her face pale in the glow of the flashlight, her eyes wide and frightened, and he remembered kissing her earlier, remembered the feel of her against him and was shot with an arrow of desire so strong he almost took her in his arms again.

He heard another noise, this time it sounded as if it was behind the lodge. Another limb cracked. He stepped around the edge of the porch to shine the light into the pines behind the lodge. It was getting darker, pockets of blackness had settled under the trees. The air seemed colder. His light picked up movement in the pines, something shapeless, the crack of dry, dead twigs as it moved away.

"Please," Charlie said behind him.

He turned to look at her again, the beam of the flashlight pointed at her feet. She looked scared and cold. He decided he'd seen enough. He could always come back up here and look around the lodge in the daylight. The thought had little appeal right now though. And what was the point? The tracks were probably the sheriff's when he'd searched the area for evidence.

"Okay, let's go," Gus said and shone the flashlight ahead of them as they left the lodge and walked up the shoreline to his car.

The surface of the lake mirrored the night sky. A cold silence seemed to hang over the place like an icy cloak and he was glad she'd talked him into leaving. He didn't like it here, didn't like thinking about the tragic things that had happened here. Josh had died here. That reminder hit him harder than he wanted to admit. Hurt him more. Normally, it took a lot to scare him. But he felt anxious and would have sworn they were being followed.

He saw Charlie glance back, pretty sure she sensed the same thing. He turned and shone the flashlight back along the shoreline. The light skittered over the rocky shore, across the silky green of the dense pines, glowing for a moment on the weathered boards of the Simonsons' old lodge, but found nothing else in the darkness.

Was it the lake? Or was it knowing Josh died here? Or was it being with Charlie that had him jumping at his own shadow? he wondered as they reached his car.

He looked over at her, half expecting her to pull a real weapon from those baggy overalls and kill him. He wondered how long it would take someone to find his body. Especially if she weighted it down with rocks.

The problem was, she looked a hell of lot more frightened than he felt. Could he be wrong about her? She scared him. But was it because she was a killer?

Or because he was afraid of falling for a woman who could break his heart? Or worse?

He glanced toward the rental car, suddenly worried she might have done something to it before he'd found her standing behind him. "You need a ride back to town?"

She shook her head and looked at him as if there was something more she wanted to say. Or do. "I have my van up the road."

"Any reason you didn't drive it down here?"

"I was afraid I'd get stuck."

He hadn't thought about getting stuck when he'd pulled up so close to the water.

"At least let me give you a lift to your van," he insisted, thinking about what Phil Simonson had said about her refusing to get into Quinn's car that night, the night the car crashed and Quinn was killed. "It's getting too dark to walk."

She glanced toward the deep pines back by the lodge as if she'd heard the sound again. Something was definitely out there. An animal? Or the real killer? Then she looked at the rental car. "All right."

Relieved they were both leaving, he opened the passenger-side door for her. She seemed nervous, he thought when he got in. She kept looking out into the trees as if afraid of what was out there. He kept thinking about the grizzly that had killed those campers. About the person who'd murdered Josh.

He couldn't see anything in the dense pines as he drove back up the road, the headlights illuminating only a narrow swath of overgrown-weed road in front of him.

Her van was right where she said it was. He pulled up next to it, and for a moment he thought she wasn't going to get out and he knew if she didn't pretty soon, he might be tempted to touch her—worse, to take her in his arms and kiss her.

"I wish you hadn't done what you did back at the Pinecone," she said, not looking at him. "I'm afraid for you."

"Just worry about yourself, Charlie," he warned her.

She shook her head, her eyes suddenly gleaming with unshed tears as she looked at him. "You're still convinced I'm a killer. Funny, but when I get around you, I *do* have the urge." She climbed out without another word, slamming the door behind her.

He watched her walk around the front of the car to her van, then reached over and notched up the heat. Sometimes he acted like a jackass, he thought as he waited until she got into her van. She motioned for him to go first. He shook his head and motioned that he would follow her. She didn't seem happy about that, but took off down the mountain ahead of him, her tail-lights glowing bright red.

He lost her partway down. Probably because she was driving so much faster than he was. Also because he was busy concocting a second assault as part of his original plan as he drove.

Sometimes he had to be as cold-blooded as the killers.

Chapter Twelve

The moment Charlie lost sight of Gus's headlights behind her, she pulled off onto a logging road and cut her lights to wait for him to pass.

Then she doubled back up to the lake. She'd heard the movement in the pines near the lodge and suspected it wasn't a wild animal. The only predator around here that stalked human prey was human.

She could see part of the lake, the surface glassy. Knowing someone had been out there watching her and Gus, was probably still watching her now, turned her blood to slush. Where was the person now? *Why not finish what you started?*

She knew the answer, just as she knew that the person in the woods had killed Josh and would kill Gus if he didn't get out of town and soon. What she didn't know was why. Or who hated her enough to do this to her.

Angrily, she pulled out her flashlight from the glove compartment and got out. "Come and get me, you coward, you crazy bastard," she said to the thick darkness of the trees. Silence answered.

She listened, hearing nothing but the thudding of her pulse in her ears. Whoever was after her wasn't through making her suffer. She avoided the lake, cutting through the pines to the lodge, just wanting this finished now, before Gus could be hurt. She didn't want his death on her conscience, too. But she knew her feelings when it came to Gus were much more complicated than that.

The lodge stood silhouetted against the night sky. She shone the light on the weathered siding, finding the door. It stood open, just as Gus had left it. Again, she listened, but heard nothing except her own heart now a steady drum in her chest.

Slowly, she climbed the porch steps, her courage faltering at the thought of going inside. She wondered how many girls had lost their virginity in this musty old lodge. How many in particular lost it to Quinn Simonson.

She shoved the door open a little farther and shone the flashlight inside. The beam trailed over the worn wooden floor to the fireplace, following a set of footprints in the dust. Someone had definitely been here—and recently. There was burned wood in the old fireplace and a spot that looked as if someone had lain down a blanket in front of the fire.

She'd caught a glimpse of something on the lodge floor earlier with Gus. Now she found it in the beam of her light. Cautiously, she stepped inside the room, the smells taking her back to a time she didn't want to remember. Her light picked up the object again. She moved to it and reached down to pick up the toy from the floor where it had been dropped. It was a small yellow metal pickup truck.

She turned it in her fingers, shining the light on it, trying to remember where she'd seen it before. Earlene's little boy, Arnie. He'd been playing with it the last time she'd seen him a couple of weeks ago. She was sure it was the same toy truck because it had looked old—just like this one.

She put the toy in her pocket and turned with the flashlight, suddenly wanting out of here, wanting to be far from this lake, far from this place where two men she'd known had died. She didn't want to think about how the toy had gotten here. Or why she'd felt such a need to come back for it.

A movement in the doorway caused her to swing around, her heart lunging and a scream catching in her throat as the beam of the flashlight fell on the dark shape of a man.

"Oh, you scared me half to death," she cried, the flashlight beam wavering in her hand as the light fell on Wayne.

He stood in the doorway, both hands buried deep in the pockets of his coat, his expression sullen. "I saw you with him," he said, sounding funny.

She didn't need to ask what he'd seen or with whom. It was clear he was upset about seeing Gus kiss her earlier in the garage. "What are you doing here?" she asked, trying to keep her voice light.

He didn't answer, just stood glowering at her, and she realized with a jolt that he was angry.

"You shouldn't be here," he said morosely. "It isn't safe."

She told herself she had no reason to fear Wayne. But before this moment, she hadn't realized he could be jealous of her. She tried to hide her anxiety. "I was just leaving. Do you want to walk me to my van?"

He didn't answer. Didn't move.

"I better get home," she said too brightly. "Aunt Selma will be waiting for me." She stepped toward him, afraid he'd block her way. Her hand dropped to the pocket of her overalls. She felt the cold steel of the wrench and prayed she'd never have to use it against Wayne. "Did I tell you Selma loved the apples and pumpkins? She's making a pie for dinner tonight."

He blinked, his expression a little less hostile. "What about the squash?"

As she neared the door, he moved aside to let her pass. Relief swept through her, making her weak. She stepped out into the night, her flashlight beam bobbing ahead of her across the porch. She wanted to run, but didn't dare. What was Wayne doing here?

"Selma baked one of the big squash last night," she said as she walked down the shoreline, even though it was the longer route back to the van. But she felt safer out in the open than in the woods, and knew it was nothing more than an illusion.

Had it been Wayne she'd heard earlier when she was with Gus here at the lodge? She told herself Wayne wouldn't hurt anyone, that Wayne couldn't have found out about her friendship with Josh or been able to lure Josh to the lake—let alone kill him.

But right now, she couldn't be sure of anything. Right now, all she hoped to do was reach the van safely.

Wayne trailed along beside her, still obviously angry, judging from his brooding expression. She knew he must have a flashlight, but he didn't use it, just kept his hands buried in his coat pockets. What else might he have in there besides a flashlight? she wondered. A weapon?

As they neared her van, she saw his car parked just up the road. It couldn't have been him earlier. Unless he'd moved his car after Gus left, after she headed back to the lodge.

"Why don't I follow you," she suggested. "In case you have any trouble."

He looked over at her. "You are awful nice to me."

"You and I are friends," she said.

He nodded, biting at his lower lip, his gaze dropping to his boots. "I don't like him."

Gus. "He's leaving town soon," she said, hoping it was true.

Wayne certainly didn't look convinced.

She glanced pointedly at his car. "I'll follow you." Then she opened the van door, almost expecting him to stop her. Out of the corner of her eye, she saw Wayne move toward the old Chevy.

Her heart was hammering against her ribs as she climbed into the van and watched through the windshield as he walked to his car and got in. A moment later the lights flashed on and the Chevy began to pull away. She let out the breath she'd been holding.

Tears rushed to her eyes. Until that moment, she had refused to admit how frightened she'd been. Now she shook from the fear and relief. She'd known Wayne her whole life. Did she believe he was capable of murder?

As the Chevy disappeared down the road, she leaned over the steering wheel and tried to stop shaking, no longer sure what she believed.

After a while she became aware of the cold. She lifted her head and looked around, surprised how dark it was, and reached for the key. She couldn't wait to get out of here, suddenly desperate to get home, needing the warmth of the old farmhouse, the familiar smells, the comforting sounds of her mother's and aunt's voices, the feeling of being safe, even if it was a lie.

As she drove down the winding mountain road, the pines thick and black on each side, the sky starless, she kept expecting to come around a corner and find a dark figure standing in the middle of the road.

When she finally hit the highway, she turned toward Utopia, with panicked relief. Only a few more miles.

But as she came around a corner in the highway, she spotted a vehicle pulled off on the edge of the pavement and recognized it as Wayne's Chevy. She slowed, letting her headlights illuminate the vehicle. The right rear tire was flat, the car at an angle as it leaned toward the ditch.

For a moment she thought about not stopping. But as she stared at the car, she remembered what Wayne had said earlier in the garage about needing to talk to her. She'd completely forgotten about that and obviously so had Wayne. Why had he hightailed it out of the garage when the sheriff had arrived? Was he in some kind of trouble?

She realized he could have followed her to the lake to talk to her. To tell her whatever it was that had been so important. But when he'd seen her with Gus at the lodge, he'd probably completely forgotten about it. That would be like Wayne. Better than believing he'd had anything to do with the "accidents" involving the men around her.

She flipped on her brights as she pulled closer, expecting to see Wayne hunkered down beside the car in the weeds trying to change the tire in the dark.

An uneasy feeling came over her as she stared at the empty space beside the flat tire. Rolling down her window, she called out, "Wayne?", thinking he might have gone into the trees for some reason.

No answer.

Maybe he didn't have a spare and had walked into town. It wasn't that far, especially if he cut through to his mother's place.

A limb cracked in the trees off to the left. "Wayne?" She felt the hair stand up on the back of her neck as she stared blindly into the darkness. But why wouldn't he have waited, knowing she was behind him?

Earlier she'd been ready to face whatever was after her, just wanting it to be over. But now she wanted out of here. She didn't want to think about the toy she'd found or what it meant, any more than she wanted to think about Wayne and what he'd been doing at the lake.

She rolled up the window and locked the doors, all the time telling herself she was acting ridiculous. Probably just a wild animal this time.

She stopped at the garage to call the sheriff on the pay phone and told him about seeing Wayne's car. Bryan promised to check on him. As she started back toward the van, she stuffed her cold hands into her pockets, felt the toy truck. Her thumb ran along the side of the metal. It was old. Had it been Forest's or Quinn's? Is that why it was in the Simonsons' lodge? But she was sure she'd seen Arnie with the toy.

The county road was coming up in her headlights. Just a half mile on up the road was Earlene's trailer. It wouldn't take but a minute to stop by her place.

EARLENE WAS SURPRISED to see her. "You're just in time for dinner."

"Thanks, but I'm headed home. You know Selma, dinner will be ready and waiting." Charlie picked Arnie up as he came running out from the rear of the trailer. "You get bigger every time I see you. I have something of yours," she said, putting him down. It always jolted her, the fact that he was the spitting image of Quinn at that age.

She pulled the tiny yellow toy truck from her coat

pocket and held it out to him. The boy frowned and looked to his mother.

"That isn't his," Earlene said, her voice tight.

"Are you sure? I thought I saw him playing with it the last time I was over," Charlie said, feeling the tension, but unable to understand what was wrong here.

"It's Skye's," Earlene said.

Skye Simonson? "Jenny's daughter's?"

Earlene nodded. "It belonged to Quinn." She looked over at her son. His eyes welled with tears, his lower lip quivering. "Arnie took it from Skye at school when he heard it was Quinn's. I made him return it."

Arnie had taken the toy that had belonged to his father. "When was that?" Charlie asked, still worried why it had ended up at the boarded-up Simonson lodge.

"A couple of weeks ago right after that day you were here," Earlene said, drawing her son to her, her hands on his narrow shoulders. "Where did you get it?"

"I found it at the old lodge at the lake," Charlie said.

Earlene nodded and looked away. Charlie guessed that was where she'd lost her virginity to Quinn Simonson as well. The man was anything but imaginative.

"I wonder how it could have gotten there," Charlie said, putting the toy back into her pocket. "I'm sorry I thought it was Arnie's."

"No problem." Earlene smiled. "Sure you don't want dinner?"

Charlie felt better by the time she turned onto the county road. A mile and a half later, she pulled up in the front yard of her family's farmhouse, not bothering to put the van in the garage out back by the barn, just glad to see the lights on inside the house, warm, welcoming. Safe.

As she got out, she smelled snow in the air and knew

it would be falling again within hours. It made the evening seem colder, definitely darker, and she remembered that Selma was making pot roast for dinner. Her favorite. Suddenly she felt as starved as if this might be her last meal.

As she opened the back door, she wondered where Spark Plug was. He usually met her at the door. She stepped into the kitchen and was hit with the wonderful aroma of pot roast and garden vegetables and pumpkin pie. She shrugged out of her coat and started to hang it on a hook by the back door. Her hand froze, all her fears coming back in a sickening rush.

Mingling with the wonderful smells of supper was another familiar fragrance—one that balled her stomach in a knot. The distinct aroma of Augustus T. Riley's aftershave.

The realization had only just hit her when she heard the unlikely sound of his laughter. The aftershave she could easily have conjured from memory since she'd smelled it on her skin ever since their last kiss. The scent was haunting.

But not the laugh. It was rich and deep, lyrical and not at all what she would have expected from him.

Then she heard her mother's high voice and the spell was broken. She rushed into the living room to find Gus sitting in her father's chair, Spark Plug lying at his feet. That dog had never liked any man other than her father.

And Spark Plug wasn't the only one who Augustus T. Riley had charmed, it seemed. Vera's cheeks were flushed with excitement, her eyes brittle bright. She laughed at something Gus said, her laugh painfully pure and sweet. Even Selma, it appeared, wasn't immune. She sat next to Vera on the love seat, also smiling at Gus.

He looked up, the first to see Charlie. Something in his gaze changed in a blink. It became cold and calculating, the humor leaving his face. And yet he smiled. "Why, here she is now," he said and got to his feet. Spark Plug lifted his head, but didn't bother to get up.

"Isn't she just lovely?" her mother said.

"What are you doing here?" Charlie demanded without thinking.

Her mother looked startled then disapproving. "Why, he came by to see you, dear," she said. "I've invited him to join us for dinner since it sounds as if he'll be staying in town for a while."

Selma looked surprised by her niece's behavior as well as she got to her feet. "Speaking of dinner—" She moved to Charlie, touched her arm as she headed toward the kitchen. "Help me, will you, dear?"

"Is there anything I can do?" Gus asked from behind them.

"No," Charlie said without turning to look at him. "You've already done enough."

Once in the kitchen, Selma turned to stare at her. "What in heaven's name—"

"I don't like that man," Charlie whispered angrily. That was putting it mildly. "He has no business here."

Selma's eyes widened. If her aunt had The Gift, then why hadn't she recognized this man for what he was: a wolf in sheep's clothing. "For heaven's sake, why not? He seems perfectly charming and quite taken with your mother."

Charlie groaned inwardly. "Believe me, it's all an act. The only thing he cares about is getting me."

Her aunt raised an eyebrow. "*Getting* you?"

She shook her head. Now wasn't the time and what was she going to say anyway? She took a breath. "I was just surprised to see him here, that's all." The last thing she'd expected was for Gus to show up at the house. But she guessed she should have known that trying to warn him off wasn't going to work. How far did he plan to take this?

She shot a glance toward the living room where he was visiting with her mother and suddenly felt afraid of what her mother might say and Gus might believe.

When she looked back, she found Selma eyeing her intently. "He is a very attractive man."

Charlie looked at her askance. "You aren't trying to fix me up, please."

"Maybe I still notice a good-looking man when I see one," Selma said, getting her back up. "Can you say the same? When was the last time you spent some time with an attractive man? Maybe tonight will do you good."

Charlie wasn't about to get into this now. "What can I do to help with dinner?" She just wanted this over with as quickly as possible.

"Go change into something more…appropriate. I think we'll eat in the dining room. Your mother would like that."

"Why don't we break out the best china?" Charlie said sarcastically. "Or have you already put that in my hope chest?"

Selma made a face. "I don't see why you're so upset. He said his business was going to keep him in town for a while and he'd forgotten something he wanted to ask you, so he stopped by. It seemed like the polite thing to do, asking him to dinner."

His business was keeping him in town, was it? *She* was his business. And who knew what he planned to ask her now.

"He's just having dinner with us, Charlotte," Selma

chastised. "I can't see what that could hurt. You know how your mother loves company."

Charlie nodded, feeling trapped.

"Unless there is something I don't know." Her aunt left the statement hanging.

"I thought you knew everything?" Charlie said, only half-joking. How could she tell Selma that this man had come to Utopia to destroy her without telling her everything else? Worse, he'd just invaded her last stronghold: her home. And now he'd discovered her Achilles' heel: the two people she loved most in the world, Selma and her mother.

"I'm not young enough to know everything," her aunt said, stealing a line from Oscar Wilde. "But I do know he's interested in you. He could be just what you need."

Right. "It's only dinner," Charlie said to herself, wondering how she'd get through it. She could hear her mother's laughter. She didn't want to leave Gus alone with Vera a minute longer. "I'd better get changed."

When she came back down in a loose-fitting, long-sleeved forest-green corduroy jumper, her aunt gave her a disapproving look. It was the least formfitting clothing she owned—other than the overalls she worked in.

"Isn't she just lovely," her mother said. But her mother always said that when she saw her.

Charlie could feel Gus's eyes on her and finally looked directly at him. He smiled as if amused that she would try to hide her body from him any more than she would try to hide any other truths about herself.

Dinner was a nightmare. Her mother told embarrassing stories about Charlie's childhood. Gus urged her on, no doubt taking it all in to use against her. Selma, thankfully, tried to steer the conversation to other topics—such as Augustus T. Riley himself—and it would work for a few minutes before Vera would remember something else funny to tell about Charlie.

Gus laughed at all the stories, along with her mother. He would glance over at Charlie occasionally, his gaze always calculating, as if trying to see under her skin.

"So what brought you to Utopia?" Selma asked him between her mother's stories.

He smiled and chewed a bite of roast beef as he studied Charlie. "I suppose I can tell your aunt the truth." He took his time, chewing, swallowing, all the while watching her. "I'm a writer," he said as if confessing something Charlie didn't know, his gaze shifting to Selma. "I travel around looking for interesting stories, something out of the way, unusual." Sounded innocent enough. Unless you knew the truth about Augustus T. Riley's books.

"Utopia is out of the way," her mother said gaily. "And unusual, I suppose. Isn't it, dear?"

"I'm sure there are a lot of other places that are more out of the way and unusual than Utopia," Charlie said, pretending more interest in her pot roast than him.

"I can't imagine that anyplace could rival Utopia for its uniqueness," he said, a smile in his voice. "I'm fascinated. In fact, so much so that I'm considering doing a story on Utopia's female mechanic. I want to know everything about her, as long as it takes."

"Oh, isn't that wonderful!" her mother cheered. "We must show him all the photo albums."

Charlie choked on the bite she'd taken.

Gus quickly poured her more water. "Are you all right?" he asked, sounding concerned.

He wouldn't want her to die, she thought angrily. Not until he got his book—and saw her behind bars.

"Fine," she managed to say. "And what if I don't want

a book written about me?" she whispered fiercely so her aunt and mother couldn't hear.

He smiled. "I think we both know the answer to that one," he whispered back. Raising his voice, he said, "I'd love to see your photo albums of Charlie."

"Maybe some other time," Charlie said, looking pointedly at her aunt.

Selma got to her feet. "Your mother would like ice cream with the pumpkin pie I made for dessert—"

"I'll get it," Charlie said and got up so abruptly she almost spilled her freshly refilled water glass. But she had to get out of the room, and the freezer was out in the shed behind the house. The cold snowy night was just what she needed.

She didn't even take her coat, just rushed out the kitchen door and across the yard, bucking snowdrifts, to the shed. Spark Plug trailed behind her, obviously trying to make up for being a Judas.

Charlie noticed that Gus had parked beside the barn, his car hidden from view of the road. Had he purposely wanted to surprise her when she came home by hiding the car? She wouldn't put anything past him.

Once inside the shed, she leaned against the closed door and took long breaths, trying to calm herself. Her body vibrated with the familiar fear. He'd as much as told her she was his next book. His next female murderer.

But hadn't she known when he'd come into the garage two nights ago that he was after her? She closed her eyes, feeling the tears, warm on her cheeks. She didn't want to see anyone else get hurt. Especially Gus. But how could she stop him?

Something bumped against the outside of the shed. Her eyes flew open but she didn't move, didn't even breathe. Spark Plug began to growl low in his throat.

Chapter Thirteen

Gus wondered if she was going to come back. He listened, half expecting to hear her van engine as she left. But she lived here. Where could she go?

He glanced across the table at her mother. No, Charlie couldn't leave her mother. Nor her aunt. They obviously depended on her. And if Charlie had ever planned to run, he suspected she would have done it a long time ago.

But she was gone long enough that he was beginning to have doubts.

"I think I'd better see if I can help, Charlie," he said, excusing himself. He walked to the back door and opened it, expecting to find her on the porch, avoiding him.

The sky had turned to a satin gray, the fallen snow reflecting upward to make the night not quite as dark as it had been. He could feel tiny snowflakes and see his breath coming out in white puffs.

He stepped to the edge of the porch. There were tracks in the snow leading to the shed and the stand of pines beyond. "Charlie?" That's when he heard the dog growling. He couldn't see Spark Plug, just hear him, a low rumble of a growl coming from the outbuilding. "Charlie?"

Just before he reached the shed, he saw something large move away from the dark side of the building. At the same time, the shed door flew open and Spark Plug came barreling out. The dog's growl turned into a bark as a shadow sprang into view and took off toward the pines.

Gus started to go after the dog and the retreating figure of a person, but Charlie came hauling out of the shed just then, brandishing a shovel, the blade catching the snowy light.

"It's me!" he called out before she could level him with it.

She stopped, silhouetted in the otherworldly gray light, the shovel raised above her head, then she stumbled toward him, dropping the tool in the snow.

He caught her, pulling her to him awkwardly. "Are you okay?" He could feel her trembling in his arms. Just the fact that she had seemed glad to see him was enough to make him wonder if she was all right.

She nodded against his chest and took a shuddering breath. Even in the dim light from the open door of the shed he could see her dark eyes and the fear lodged there.

Spark Plug ran back from the pines. From the distance came the groan of an engine, the sound dying off as the vehicle left. A pickup in need of a muffler. Much like the one that had driven by Murphy's last night when Trudi had come by.

"Who was that?" he asked.

She shook her head and stepped from his arms.

"Look, I can tell you're scared. Talk to me. Tell me what's going on."

She glanced toward the trees where the figure had disappeared. "I've been trying to tell you but you haven't believed me. Someone is trying to frame me for Josh's murder." Her gaze came up to meet his. The look in her eyes made him weak. Just like the sweet warm feminine scent of her.

He wanted to believe her. Oh, at this moment, with her so close, he definitely wanted to.

"That person will try to kill you next," she said.

"Not if I find him—or her—first."

She shook her head and smiled ruefully. "Is it really worth it? Risking your life for a stupid book?"

"It's more than a book," Gus said evenly.

"Bull," she snapped, the word sounding alien on her lips. "You're dead set on me being your killer so you can write another book about a woman who murdered her lover. That is what you do, isn't it? Go after women killers."

"I do find them the most…intriguing," he admitted.

"Except Josh wasn't my lover and I didn't murder him," she said angrily. "But what do you care about the truth or about Josh Whitaker." She started to turn back toward the shed, but he grabbed her and jerked her around to face him again.

"I care. And it's more than a book to me. A hell of a lot more. Josh was my brother."

She stared at him in surprise. "I'm sorry. I didn't know he had a brother."

Gus nodded and looked past her to the snowy darkness. "He was my half brother. Our mother remarried after my father died. Josh and I weren't—" he stumbled on the word "—close. I was the black sheep of the family and Josh was—" He glanced at her. "Well, Josh was like you. Damn near a saint."

She jerked free of his hold. "Josh was a good man who cared about other people," she said defensively.

"Yeah, and that's probably what got him killed."

"Too bad you're not out looking for the killer instead of trying so hard to pin this on me," she said. "Your mind is already made up about me, isn't it?"

Not hardly, he thought. In fact, the more he learned about her, the more confused and uncertain he became. And he hated it.

"Okay, let's say someone found out that you knew Josh and got him up here to frame you for his murder," he said, thinking what a long shot that would be. "How did that person get the locket Quinn gave you?"

Her eyes glistened. "I haven't seen that locket since the night I threw it at Quinn seven years ago at Freeze Out Lake."

"Could Quinn have picked it up?"

"I don't know. I threw my locket at him and went for a walk I was so angry with him. I suppose anyone could have picked it up."

He sighed. "What about Quinn's death? And Rickie Moss's accident and T.J.'s fire?"

"I didn't hurt anyone," she said, sounding tired, "but I don't expect you to believe that. You'd already made up your mind that I was guilty before you even hit town, didn't you?"

He flinched at the truth in her words. "You have to admit you were the likeliest suspect."

"Exactly. Doesn't that make you just a little suspicious?"

Admittedly, it did. But she was right. He'd made up his mind about her before he'd even known Charlie was a *her*. He had wanted to nail Charlie Larkin for Josh. For himself because he hated to be proven wrong. Because he owed his brother. But that was before he met her. Before he had kissed her.

He glanced toward the trees, wondering about the person he'd seen run off. He doubted Charlie went after just anyone with a shovel. Nor did he question the fear he'd seen on her face. He wanted more than anything to prove her innocent. And it scared him.

She looked past him, toward the house, as if she'd heard something, and immediately stepped away from him.

He followed her gaze and saw the small form of her aunt come out onto the porch.

"Charlie?" Selma called. "Is everything all right?"

"I just couldn't find the ice cream," she called back. "We're coming." She turned to get the ice cream from the freezer in the shed.

"Let me do that," he said quickly and stepped into the outbuilding. It was dark except for a small night-light on the far wall. Beside it was a large chest freezer. He opened it and spotted a carton of vanilla ice cream.

She still looked scared when he came back out and he felt a rush of doubt. What was she so afraid of? The truth coming out? Or was there really someone after her?

For just a moment he felt guilty for forcing his way into her life. For relentlessly going after her with one single-minded intent: proving she'd killed Josh.

"If you let me, I might be able to help you," he heard himself say.

"We both know you didn't come here to help me. Just the opposite." She turned and walked away from him. It was clear she was sorry she'd fallen into his arms.

The dog came up and touched his hand with a cold nose. He bent down to pet Spark Plug, watching Charlie follow the narrow snow trail back to the house and the light.

He felt conflicted, unsure of himself, something he hated. It scared him. He feared being suckered in by another femme fatale. And yet, he could never have imagined anyone like Charlie Larkin and just how tempting it would be to believe her.

He and the dog followed her back to the house. She was standing in the kitchen digging in the silverware drawer when he walked in. Her cheeks were flushed from the cold, her eyes bright. She was trying hard to pretend that nothing had happened out by the shed and he wondered what she'd feared most: whoever the dog had been growling at or those few moments when she'd dropped her defenses with him.

"Let me at least scoop the ice cream," he said, watching her, fascinated and feeling an even stronger compulsion not only to believe her, but also get closer to her, closer to the truth—not to nail her but to free her. She was even more appealing here in this house, in her home, with her aunt and mother, and this sudden urge to protect her made him weak with desires that scared him.

He could see her getting ready to argue. "You can dish up the pie," he told her, "while I do the ice cream." He looked up at Selma who stood watching them both from the doorway, suspicion and worry in her gaze. "We'll bring dessert right in."

Selma nodded and with obvious reluctance left them alone in the kitchen.

"I like your aunt and mother," he said to Charlie as he moved to her side and took the ice-cream scoop from her still-trembling fingers.

She dug in a silverware drawer again, this time coming out with a knife. "Only because you think you can use them," she said, brandishing the knife.

He smiled and stepped back, pretending she and the

knife frightened him. She frightened him all right, but not that way. "I'm not here to hurt anyone, just get to the truth."

"I wish I believed that," she said and glanced toward the other room where her aunt and mother were talking quietly, then at him again.

"Haven't you heard that the truth will set you free?" he asked, only half-joking.

"Then you should be out looking for a murderer," she said. "Not here scooping ice cream." She set about cutting the pie, lifting out portions onto plates as if at home in the kitchen as she was in a garage.

He scooped ice cream onto each of the plates with the warm pumpkin pie, wondering how he'd ever be able to eat pumpkin pie again without associating that cinnamony smell with Charlie Larkin.

She licked the side of her finger where she'd spilled a little of the pie filling.

He watched her tongue flick out and slide along her finger, her eyes coming up to meet his. Desire burned through his veins hot enough to burn down the house.

She dropped her gaze and turned away to wash her hands at the sink, her back to him.

He took a breath and let it out slowly, remembering her in his arms, wanting to kiss her again, only this time for an entirely different reason.

"You sure you don't need help in there?" Aunt Selma called.

"No, I think we've got it," he said. Charlie still had her back to him. She shut off the water and made a project out of drying her hands before she turned. Her cheeks were flushed, but the kitchen was hot.

He took two pieces of pie and ice cream into the dining room.

Vera brightened, clapping her hands lightly at the sight of the pie and ice cream. "I love pie."

He put one down in front of her, the other in front of Selma, who was eyeing him hard.

"What kind is it?" Vera asked, staring at the plate as if she'd never seen pie before.

"Pumpkin," he said, and heard the back door open and close. "Charlie, I can take the ice cream back out to the freez—"

"I just put it on the porch for now, it's plenty cold out," Charlie said behind him, surprising him. She hadn't wanted to go back out to the shed. Not that he could blame her. But it still surprised him. She really was afraid of whoever the dog had been growling at.

He tried to tell himself that she might have been meeting someone out by the shed, someone she hadn't wanted him to see and the whole shovel thing might have been a distraction to throw him off, but even he couldn't make himself buy that story.

She put one of the servings of pie and ice cream in his spot at the table and, with hers in her hand, sat down again, smiling at her mother. "I think Selma outdid herself this time, Mom."

"Selma, did you make this?" Vera asked incredulously. "I didn't know you could cook."

A strained silence fell over the table as Gus pulled out his chair and sat down again. "This is the best pumpkin pie I've ever had," he said after one bite. It was the truth. He looked up to see Charlie looking at him as if everything out of his mouth was a lie. "I mean it. This is…amazing." He took another bite, watching Charlie. "It's good with ice cream, too."

She took a bite as if she was also enjoying it. He liked watching her eat. Hell, he liked watching her do most anything. She couldn't have killed Josh or anyone else. But he knew what he based that on had nothing to do with facts or evidence.

"I can't eat any more," Vera said, sounding tired. She pushed her nearly untouched plate back.

He finished the last bite of his pie and ice cream and put down his napkin. "Thank you for a wonderful meal and delightful company." He let his gaze move from Vera to Selma to Charlie where it lingered. "Let me at least help with the dishes before I leave."

"That is very kind of you," Selma said. "But unnecessary."

"Yes," Charlie agreed. "It's getting late. I'm sure you'll want to get back before the roads get any icier." She pushed to her feet and looked pointedly at him. "Good night, Mr. Riley."

"Gus."

She raised an eyebrow. "I thought it was Augustus T.?"

He smiled. She's the one who had everyone in this town calling him Gus, as if she didn't know. "Gus to you." A look passed between them.

"I think I'm going to bed," Vera said, rising unsteadily to her feet. "I don't know why I'm so tired."

"It's the weather," Selma said, quickly getting up to assist her. "Winter always makes you a little tired."

"Does it?" Vera frowned, then smiled at him. "Thank you for the pie. It was delicious. Imagine a man baking pies." She chuckled as Selma took her arm and they started across the room. "Burt can't boil water. I hope you didn't let him help with dinner. Has he gone out to put away the ice cream?"

"Yes," Selma said. "That's where he's gone all right."

"He's so good about doing for me," Vera said, a smile in her voice. "I'm lucky to have a man like him, aren't I?"

"Yes, you are," Selma agreed as the two disappeared into a room that had obviously been converted into a bedroom off the living room. Gus could see two twin beds and knew that Selma slept in the same room as her sister. That meant Charlie's bedroom was upstairs. Obviously, Vera couldn't be left alone.

"You were leaving?" Charlie said behind him.

"Some type of dementia?" he asked quietly, turning to look at her.

She waved a hand through the air and looked away, biting her lower lip for a moment, her eyes suddenly brimming with tears. "Alzheimer's." She looked so vulnerable, so devastated by her mother's disease, he wanted to take her in his arms and try to soothe her pain. But he knew he would only add to it, because he couldn't stop trying to find Josh's killer. If she was guilty. That damn "if" had only become bigger.

She walked to the back door, opened it, holding it for him. "Good night, Mr. Riley."

He followed her. "Gus." He could smell the scent of her soap still on her skin. Her gaze locked with his for a few precious seconds, then she looked away.

"It's getting late."

He nodded, knowing that leaving might turn out to be the only smart thing he did all tonight.

She found his coat and handed it to him. "Be careful, Gus."

"You, too." He shrugged into the heavy coat, not wanting to leave her alone here, alone with her mother and aunt who would be of no help if that person out by the shed came back. But he couldn't stay, even if she would have wanted it. He felt off kilter, confused and aroused, scared for himself, scared for her. This book—and catching the killer—meant everything to him, didn't it? He owed it to Josh. He'd failed Josh in life. He couldn't in death.

He stepped through the open door into the cold darkness. "Good night, Charlie." He picked up the ice-cream container and took it out to the shed, then walked through the snow to his rental car.

The engine started with a few coughs and groans. He wondered what the temperature was outside. Colder than he had ever been. The seat under his butt felt like a block of ice. He let the car engine run for a few minutes, a cloud of white exhaust billowing up behind it as the defroster went to work, blowing cold air up through the vents.

He wiped the condensation from the windshield with one of the gloves he'd purchased along with the coat and saw Charlie watching from the kitchen window. He thought of her mother and aunt, and the way she was with them. Feeling himself weaken toward her, he swore. Forgetting for even a moment that Charlie was a murder suspect could prove fatal. Natalie Burns had taught him that in spades. Only, Charlie was nothing like Natalie.

The defroster cleared enough of the windshield that he could see to drive. He shifted the car into Reverse. Charlie was still watching from the window. Reluctantly, he backed out, a desire to prove Charlie Larkin innocent ringing like a liberty bell in his head.

CHARLIE WAITED UNTIL Gus finally left, driving off in a fog of cold air, taillights disappearing into the trees that lined the snow-covered narrow gravel road out to the county road and eventually the highway and town.

Then she grabbed her coat and headed for the trail she'd taken last night into town.

In her flashlight beam, she found the boot tracks in the snow. It was impossible to tell whether the person who'd been by the shed tonight had been a man or woman from the footprints. The ones heading toward the house were closer together; the ones leaving obviously someone running.

She walked to the nearest road, found the tracks where the person had parked. From the tire tracks, the vehicle had been a pickup. She looked down the road, seeing nothing but darkness and the deeper black of pines silhouetted against a starless sky. For two nights now, Spark Plug had chased someone away. Both had left in the same pickup, one with a loud muffler. Forest Simonson drove a pickup with a bad muffler. But most of the men she knew drove trucks that could use a new muffler. Blame Montana winters.

What had the person in the pickup wanted? Just to harass her? Or had they been looking for Gus? The thought gave her a twinge because tonight his car had been here.

She headed back toward the house before she was missed and had the dishes done by the time Selma came into the kitchen.

"I got Vera down," her aunt said, pulling out a chair at the table.

Charlie could hear the exhaustion in her voice. "You can't keep doing this."

Selma looked up, surprised.

"I've been thinking," Charlie said, softening her tone as she pulled up a chair across from her aunt. "We're going to need to get someone to come in and help with Mother soon, so why not do it now?"

Before Charlie could finish, Selma was already shaking her head. "We're doing just fine."

"I'm worried about you. I'm amazed how strong you are and how capable you are at your age—"

"Don't start with that age stuff."

Charlie reached across the table and placed a hand over her aunt's. "You know what I'm trying to say."

Selma looked up, her eyes bright with hurt. "That you don't think I can keep up my end."

"You know that's not what I'm saying. I'm worried about you. About…" She looked past her aunt to the window where she'd watched Augustus T. Riley drive away. "If something should happen and I wasn't here to help—"

"I don't want to hear that," Selma said, pulling her hand free.

"Maybe you'd better hear it," Charlie whispered, remembering this was the second time in two nights that someone had been outside the house. The evidence against her seemed too great. And she didn't believe for a moment that the person trying to frame her for Josh's murder was going to stop.

"Things have a way of working themselves out," Selma said, straightening her back before rising from the chair. "It's not like we could find someone to come in and help anyway. Not out here in the sticks."

Charlie started to argue, but Selma cut her off. "We're both tired. I'm sure we'll both feel better after a good night's sleep," her aunt said.

What Charlie wouldn't give for one.

Her aunt touched her shoulder as she went by on her way to bed. "No more talk about getting someone in. You know your mother wouldn't like that."

After she left, Charlie thought about Gus. She felt

torn between worrying about his safety—and worrying what he'd do next.

She stared out into the night, afraid.

GUS FOUND HIMSELF thinking about the stories he'd heard at dinner, especially those about Charlie and her dad. It was obvious Charlie had idolized her father and spent many hours with him at the garage. Gus could understand now why she'd become a mechanic and stayed in this town.

He couldn't help but admire her obvious loyalty to her family. It was clear she would do anything for them. That's why it was hard for him to imagine her doing anything that would jeopardize that close relationship. And that realization was playing havoc with his thoughts.

He tried to concentrate on the narrow snowy road as he left the farmhouse. He'd never driven in snow before.

Ahead, a sharp curve cut into the side of a hillside. The road rounded a corner above the creek. Of course there was no guardrail. Nothing between him and the snowy rocks in the creek but air. On top of that, the packed snow was shiny slick.

He took his foot off the gas, afraid he was going too fast for the corner, and touched his brakes.

The moment his foot hit the brake pedal, he knew. An image of Charlie Larkin flashed in his head. My God!

He pumped frantically at the brakes for a few heart-stopping moments, panic completely obliterating common sense. Too late, he thought, to downshift.

The road turned, dropping off to the left in a steep incline that ended in the rocky creek below. He turned the wheel and felt the back end of the car begin to come around. He overcorrected as the car began to slide toward the edge of the road. It veered the other way, toward the hillside. The back of the rental car slammed into the embankment. The car spun the other way, toward the drop-off and the creek.

The left back tire dropped over the side of the road first. Gus watched in disbelief as he and the car went over the edge.

Chapter Fourteen

Charlie heard the whine of the siren and bolted upright in bed. She couldn't be sure if she'd actually been asleep. Or if she'd been lying in bed awake, waiting.

She scrambled out of bed, following the faint shrill cry to the window on the north side of the room. Even from here she could see the flashing lights through the trees and knew whatever had happened, happened at the curve.

Hurriedly, she dressed, trying hard not to let her mind get too far ahead of her. But fear constricted her throat and the pounding of her pulse in her ears drowned out everything except the sound of the siren. Her heart hammered so hard she thought it might kill her. Actually welcomed such relief.

But as she started the van, she knew dying would be the easy way out—and there was no easy way out of this.

Long before she reached the curve, she saw the lights of the sheriff's car blocking the road. She pulled the van over as much as she could without getting off into the ditch and the deeper snow. Then she got out and walked toward the curve, trying to see past the flashing lights of the patrol car to the activity beyond.

"Hold up there," a uniformed officer said as she approached. She recognized him right away. It took him a moment. "Ms. Larkin," Fred Mitchell said and seemed to relax. She'd met him when he'd come in the gas station with the sheriff asking about Josh Whitaker a year ago.

"I saw the lights from my house." Did she just feel guilty or was he looking at her as if questioning her story? "The siren woke me. What's happened?" Her heart was lodged in her throat.

"There's been an accident," Fred said. "Car went off into the creek."

She nodded, having known that's what it had to be. "Anyone hurt?" Her voice sounded strained, hoarse, scared.

"Wasn't a fatal. I think the guy was just shaken up, but the ambulance is running him to the county hospital in Libby just to be safe."

The night air suddenly felt too rarefied. She hugged herself, sucking in large gulps.

"Are you all right?" he asked, reaching out to take her elbow.

She nodded, tears stinging her eyes as she fought hard not to cry. "I think it might have been someone I know. A man who had dinner at my house earlier tonight."

"According to his driver's license, his name is Augustus T. Riley," Fred said.

"Oh" was all that came out. Her body had begun to vibrate.

"Looks like he was going too fast and slid off the curve. Not the first time it's happened on this stretch of road. I'm sure it won't be the last. The guy probably wasn't familiar with winter driving, being from California and all."

She nodded, her teeth chattering.

"Nothing you can do here," Fred said as he let go of her elbow and eyed her closely. "You should get home before you freeze to death. I'm sure your friend will be just fine."

Gus wasn't her friend. Far from it. She nodded, and turning, started back toward her van.

"Oh, by the way," he called after her, "the wrecker is hauling the car to your garage for now until Mr. Riley can decide what he wants done with it. There wasn't much damage considering it slid down that embankment and landed in the creek."

"Thanks." She didn't turn around. She just kept walking, slogging through the snow, her body aquiver with the now too familiar terror. Gus had gone off the road not a mile from her house. What was the chance it was an accident?

She drove back to the house, knowing she wouldn't be able to sleep the rest of the night but having nowhere else to go.

She climbed the stairs silently, not wanting to wake her mother or aunt. All she could think about was Gus. Thank God he hadn't been killed. Not even hurt badly.

Why hadn't he listened to her? She'd tried to warn him. She was shaking from a mixture of fear and relief.

The worst part was, she feared this close call wasn't going to dissuade him. No, quite the opposite. If she knew Augustus T. Riley the way she was beginning to, this would only make him more determined. But what if it hadn't been an accident? Wasn't that what had her so frightened?

Before dawn, she dressed in her overalls and drove to the garage. The van's headlights shone on Gus's rental car where the wrecker had left it outside the garage.

Charlie parked and, taking the flashlight from her glove compartment, got out and walked toward the car. A steely-gray sky hung over her. Snow blanketed the town as deep and cold as the intense silence. No lights shone at any of the other businesses. No sound. No cars on the highway. She was completely alone, just as she knew she would be.

She slowed as she neared the car, her mind racing with possibilities. Something easy. Something obvious. Cutting the brake line. Or disabling the steering mechanism. Something that would survive the crash. Something that would come back to haunt her.

She shone the flashlight under the car. There was a long, wide scrape along the skid plate where the vehicle had slid over the rocks in the creek. She stepped closer, then knelt down to look under the engine to the brake line. Her heart began to pound. She gripped the flashlight, but her hand trembled so hard the light bobbed. She steadied it long enough to confirm her worst fears.

Her legs suddenly wouldn't hold her. She fell back in the snow, oblivious to the cold or wetness, and put her head down on her knees. Any investigator would see the cut brake line and know immediately Gus's crash wasn't an accident.

She could replace the brake line. It wouldn't take her any time. The sheriff wouldn't even question the tracks around the car. She could just tell him that she'd taken a look at the car. Even that wouldn't be unusual since it appeared she could get it running again and save the rental agency from having it hauled back to Missoula.

No one would have to know. Except her.

She could feel the sky lightening around her. If she was going to do it, she had to do it now. *Fix the line. Save yourself.*

GUS HAD BEEN waiting in the cold for so long, he'd convinced himself Charlie wasn't coming and was starting to feel guilty about hiding out here with a camera and binoculars. He hadn't realized how badly he didn't want her to show up until he'd spotted the van's headlights and was filled with an overwhelming sense of regret.

But there she was and too early to have come to open up the station. Charlie had gone right to the car and shone her light under it as if she'd known that the brake line had been cut, something Gus had discovered earlier.

He didn't want to believe she'd had anything to do with his accident. But then, what was she doing here before dawn? Had she expected the wreck to be more dramatic, any evidence against her destroyed? No one would have questioned the accident in that case. Just a California boy driving off a snowy county road.

And here he'd been waiting and hoping it had been the trespasser the dog had chased off who'd cut his brake line.

He feared the truth was staring him in the face. Charlie was here. Why? What was she going to do about the cut break line?

He felt sick. If she'd cut the line, the only way she could hope to get away with the act now would be to fix the brake line before anyone saw it.

He watched her through the binoculars from his hiding place, the camera with the telephoto lens next to him. Neither the binoculars nor the camera had been easy to come by in the town of Libby after he'd checked himself out of the hospital last night. But desperation often made things possible.

Charlie slowly got up from the snow. It would be light soon. Why didn't she get moving? If she was going to cover her tracks, she didn't have much time before this Podunk town woke up.

She turned off the flashlight and walked slowly through the semidarkness of predawn toward the garage.

Gus stomped his feet trying to warm them. Even with all the winter gear he'd had to purchase at Emmett's store, he was cold. And disappointed.

Why didn't she step it up a little? Was she so confident that no one would suspect her that she would tamper with evidence in broad daylight?

The thought gave him a twinge as he remembered what Trudi had said about no one believing anything bad about Charlie Larkin.

A light came on in the gas station office, then in the garage. Come on, Charlie. His feet were freezing. He didn't know how long he'd been watching his wrecked rental car, how long he'd been waiting for her. He was cold, and right now he just wanted it over.

When she came back out with her tools to cover up her crime, he'd get her photograph. Isn't that what he'd wanted? Some hard evidence against her. If she'd tried to kill him, then there was more than a good chance she'd killed Josh. Gus knew he should be elated. He'd been right about her from the first.

Hadn't he suspected she'd cut his brake line the moment he touched his brakes and the pedal went clear to the floorboard? And yet there still had been that instant of disbelief. Not Charlie. Not the Charlie he'd come to know.

He stared at the light burning in the gas station office, waiting for Charlie to come out with her tools to fix the brake line, wishing she would surprise him as she'd done so many times over the last couple of days.

So where the hell was she?

CHARLIE STOOD IN the doorway between the office and the garage bays, struck with the oddest sensation that if she looked, she would see her father standing by the tool bench, a cup of coffee in his hand, waiting for her to show up so he could talk about the latest job.

He loved being a mechanic, compared it to being a detective. Each car came in with a mystery, most too easy for his years of experience, but every once in a while he would get one that challenged him. Those he loved and he would talk about them for days after, the way cops talked about tough cases they'd solved.

She could almost feel his presence, the feeling so strong she would have sworn she smelled the strong coffee he loved to drink.

With great pain, she shifted her gaze to look toward the tool bench, afraid she'd find his ghost standing there, afraid she wouldn't.

The spot where her father stood was empty.

Tears sprang to her eyes, a combination of relief that she wasn't losing her mind and unbearable disappointment. Right now, there was no one she would have loved to have seen more than her father.

There'd been days when she'd felt his presence in the garage, that presence so strong she'd almost turned to him, to ask his advice, or to tell him about a recent job she knew he'd enjoy hearing about. But none of those times had been as strong as this morning and she knew why.

She closed her eyes, aware of the lightening sky outside, the passing of time. But she felt no urgency because she knew she wasn't going to fix the brake line. She had never planned to. Couldn't. And the reminder of her father only made her more aware of that.

She opened her eyes, the sky a light silver outside the windows. Another day. Gus would be getting out of the hospital. He'd be coming back to Utopia, back to destroy her with a vengeance.

She turned away from the empty bays and stepped back behind the counter in the office. Josh had been murdered and now the brake line had been cut on Gus's car. Since Quinn's death, any man who got close to her only got hurt—or killed.

Gus was still alive. Maybe if she acted quickly— She picked up the phone and dialed Sheriff Bryan Olsen's number.

"WHAT THE HELL?" Gus swore as he watched Charlie on the phone inside the garage office through his binoculars. Now didn't seem like the time to call anyone.

She hung up, but still didn't come through the door with her tools. Was it possible she wasn't going to fix the brake line? A surge of hope flooded him. Was it possible she hadn't cut his brake lines?

Ten minutes later, the sheriff's car pulled up in front of the garage. Charlie came out of the gas station office, locking the door behind her. The sheriff had gotten out of his vehicle and walked over to the wrecked rental car. He crouched down to inspect under the car. Charlie joined the officer.

It appeared she was pointing out the cut brake line. "What the hell?" Gus whispered, his breath frosty white, and found himself grinning.

He put the camera and binoculars in his bag and walked across the street to join them as the sun topped the pines.

"What's up?" he asked.

Charlie didn't seem all that surprised to see him. "You seem to be all right," she said, sounding anything but concerned about his welfare.

"Just a little banged up," he said. "Nothing to worry about."

She met his gaze, definitely not looking worried. Instead, she appeared angry with him—as if this were his fault.

The sheriff straightened to full height. "It appears your brake line was cut," he said to Gus with a sigh. "Charlie called to tell me a little while ago. Any idea who might have done it?"

Gus glanced over at Charlie. She was looking at him as if she expected him to denounce her. "No idea at all," he said, turning back to the sheriff. "I'm sure Charlie told you about the trespasser on her property last night."

The sheriff gave her a surprised look. "No, as a matter of fact."

She was shaking her head. "I checked out the tracks. Could have been just about anyone in town wearing snowpacks and driving a pickup with a bad muffler."

The sheriff wagged his head and looked at Gus again. "I'll get the forensics guys over here but I doubt we're going to find anything on the car that will help us. I can also send them over to the house."

"I wish you wouldn't do that," Charlie said. "It will only upset my mother and aunt, and I assure you there is nothing to find."

The sheriff didn't seem pleased. "Okay, Charlie, if that's agreeable with Mr. Riley. He's the one who ended up in the creek."

Gus shrugged. "I trust Charlie's instincts on this."

The sheriff looked at him as if he'd lost his mind. Or another valuable body part. "I've got some more bad news," he said to Charlie.

She didn't look as if she needed more bad news right now.

"It's Wayne Dreyer," the sheriff said kindly. "He was

killed last night. I'm sorry, Charlie, I know he was a friend of yours."

Charlie turned white as a sheet. Gus started to reach for her, sure she was going to collapse. But she seemed to find some inner strength and remained standing.

Gus remembered the young man who'd come into the garage yesterday and caught them kissing. "What happened to him?"

"He had an accident last night," the sheriff said. "After I got your call, Charlie, that you'd seen Wayne's car on the side of the road south of here with a flat, I rang his house. His mother said he was fine, heading back to change the tire. I got another call, a wreck between here and Libby so I didn't hear about Wayne until later. The jack must have slipped out while he was changing the tire. Happened about eight-thirty. A trucker found him pinned under the car just a little after that."

All Gus heard was the time of the accident. He'd been with Charlie at her house having dinner with her mother and aunt from eight-twenty-five. Charlie had a damn good alibi for this one—him. If it *was* an accident. It seemed too much of a coincidence that one minute Wayne was desperate to tell Charlie something and the next he was crushed under his car.

Gus looked over at her, anxious to get her alone. She'd told him last night that she thought someone was trying to frame her for Josh's murder. He had a bad feeling the murderer was getting tired of just trying to frame her. Gus was afraid Charlie would be the next victim.

Chapter Fifteen

Charlie just wanted to be alone. Wayne was dead. He'd said there was something important he needed to talk to her about. He'd been acting strangely at the lake last night and now he was dead. Another accident.

"We have to talk," Gus said the moment the sheriff left.

"Not now," she said, moving past him toward her van. The day had broken gray, no sun, the air heavy with the promise of snow, the trees stark against the silver sky. It matched her mood.

He grabbed her arm and spun her back around. "Yes, *now.* I'm worried about you."

She'd been angry with him from the moment she'd seen him come out of his hiding place earlier. "Do you think I don't know what you were doing across the street this morning?" she snapped, breaking free of him.

He held up his hands in surrender. "You had the chance to fix the brake line and save yourself and you didn't. I had to know."

She could only shake her head at him. "I didn't fix the brake line. What does that prove?"

"It just confirms what my instincts have been telling me."

She raised an eyebrow. "Your instincts?" She'd

thought they'd gotten a little farther than that last night, but obviously she'd been wrong. "And what are your instincts telling you now?"

"I was wrong about you originally," he said, the words seeming to come hard to him. "I'm sorry."

She eyed him suspiciously, knowing it must be hard for him to trust—given what had happened on the Natalie Burns case. Last night when his brakes had failed, he must have thought she and Natalie were a lot alike—both having tried to kill him.

But she couldn't help being angry. And hurt. "If you expect me to jump up and down with joy at that news, I'm sorry to disappoint you." Last night she'd let herself believe he really wanted to help her. More than that, she'd felt a connection between them. It had been so strong that—

She shook her head, wondering what she'd been thinking. She and Gus weren't just from different worlds, they were from different planets. Los Angeles, California, and Utopia, Montana. Light-years apart. Just like what she and Gus each did for a living.

"So what has changed?" she asked.

"You. That is, not you, but the way—What I'm trying to say is that you aren't what I expected." He reached out to cup her cheek with his gloved hand. "Charlie, I care about you. I want to help you."

She drew back, out of his reach. "I don't want to talk about this, not now." She felt too raw. Too much had happened. Josh's death. Now Wayne's. And worse, she felt responsible for both.

"You're not responsible for what happened to Wayne," Gus said as if reading her mind.

Her head snapped up as her gaze met his. "But you suspected I was, didn't you?"

"I suspect everyone," he said, sounding angry, but with himself, not her. "It's what I do. I can't let myself trust a suspect."

"And that's what I am, isn't it? A suspect."

"You were and maybe you still are to the sheriff, but I don't believe you killed Josh. I know you couldn't have killed Wayne because I was with you at the time of his death." His gaze softened. "I don't believe you could hurt anyone."

She looked into his handsome face, her heart a dull ache. She could see what it had cost him to say those words, to trust again. She didn't want him to trust her any more than she wanted him to kiss her again or take her in his arms and tell her everything was going to be all right. Because she knew it wasn't.

She closed her eyes, unable to look at him without weakening. "Gus, someone cut your brake line."

"And I'm going to find him."

Slowly she opened her eyes. "If he doesn't find you first."

Gus smiled. "You keep underestimating me."

No, she thought, not in the least. Maybe that's why her heart always beat a little faster around him, the air seeming to crackle with expectation, the world more intense when he was near her. She'd known right away that he was dangerous. But she hadn't known just how dangerous.

"I hate that you're risking your life to find the killer," she said angrily. "It's senseless. It won't bring Josh back. Nor will it clear your conscience."

"Don't you think I know that?" he asked through clenched teeth.

"Then why not walk away now while there's still time?" she pleaded. "The sheriff will catch the killer.

You'll get the justice you need. And you'll write other books."

He grabbed her upper arms and pulled her to him. "You think I could walk away now? Knowing someone is trying to frame you for murder? Knowing the way I feel—" His lips dropped to hers.

It was almost impossible not to lose herself in his warm mouth, in the full firmness of his lips, in the whisper of his breath.

She dragged herself away, heart pounding. "Please, Gus." She felt tears rush into her eyes. She couldn't even be sure what it was she was pleading for.

He shook his head. "Let me help you."

She stared at him, finally admitting to herself what she wanted—the very last thing she should want from a man like Augustus T. Riley.

"I don't want your help, Gus. I certainly don't want you risking your life on my account. Now, please, just leave me alone." She turned her back to him, felt the burn of tears. Damn him.

"Where are you going?" he asked behind her.

"Home."

She got into the van and drove down the street, refusing to look back at him. She hoped he would give this up, save himself. She couldn't bear the thought of him being hurt. Or worse, killed. And yet, the only way she could hope to stop him was to walk away from him.

Gus wanted to kick something. He watched Charlie leave and swore under his breath. At least she was headed home. Her aunt and mother were there. She'd be safe. He hoped. Last night, someone had come to Charlie's yard to cut his brake line. Would they dare come back in broad daylight?

The killer appeared to be after Charlie's boyfriends. Not her. Jealousy seemed the obvious answer. But, if Gus was right, it had all started with Quinn's death, so revenge could be the motivation as well. Between the two, he could come up with a handful of suspects including Trudi, T.J., Rickie, Forest, Phil and Earlene.

As he watched the van turn off on the county road and disappear, he couldn't shake off the feeling that time was running out. That he had reason to be fearful for Charlie.

He stood for a moment, unsure what to do next. Eventually, the killer would come after him again. Not Charlie.

As he started across the street, he heard the sound of a pickup with a worn-out muffler coming up the street. He turned, expecting to see Forest Simonson's pickup. It was a dark color, just not the same dark color as Forest's. The pickup pulled into a space in front of the Pinecone Café and T. J. Blue got out.

Gus decided it was time to have breakfast. He got the new four-wheel-drive rental car he'd picked up in Libby and drove down to the Pinecone, remembering that the pickup he'd heard last night leaving Charlie's had had a loud muffler. And so had the pickup he'd seen drive by Murphy's that night Trudi stopped by.

SPARK PLUG DIDN'T run out to meet her as Charlie pulled up in the yard. She parked and looked around for the dog, wondering if he was over in the woods giving the squirrels a hard time.

She found the note on the kitchen counter. Her heart sank.

Emmett and I have taken Vera to the hospital. She's all right, so don't fret. She had a little fall.

Her wrist might be broken. I didn't know where to find you. I'll call later, Selma.

Charlie fought tears. She should have been here. Now she had no idea what time they'd left. She picked up the phone and called Libby General Hospital and asked for the emergency room. It took only a few minutes before her aunt came on the line.

"Her wrist is broken," Selma said. "The doctor is going to put it in a cast and give her some medication to keep the pain down, but she's fine."

"I'll drive right up," Charlie said.

"No, there isn't any reason. Your mother is fine, really. But they've put her on pain pills and want to keep her overnight to see if there are any adverse reactions to the different drugs she's on. I was just getting ready to call you. I'm staying here with her."

"You're sure that's all there is to it?" Charlie asked. "I think I should be there."

"No. Your mother needs her rest and you would just excite her. Bryan's here. He's going to take me out for a bite to eat."

"The sheriff?"

"He heard Vera and I were in the hospital," Selma said. "He told me about Wayne. I'm so sorry, Charlie."

Charlie could do no more than nod at the phone. "I'm not going to open the garage today."

"Good. Make yourself a cup of tea and take a nice long hot bath," Selma said. "That always helps."

Charlie hung up, shaking her head. Her aunt thought a cup of tea could solve most any problem. But the hot bath did sound like a great idea.

The house seemed strange, alien to her, as if she hadn't spent the better part of the last twenty-six years here. As if she didn't know every creaking floorboard, every leaky faucet, every drafty corner.

It was the silence, she thought as she stopped in the living room. There'd seldom been silence in this house. Not with her mother and Selma chattering away as far back as Charlie could remember. There'd always been someone home when Charlie had returned from school, college, work. There'd always been something cooking on the stove and wonderful warm smells to come home to.

But standing in the large living room, the fireplace empty, only the soft tick of the old grandfather clock on the mantel, she got a sudden flash of the future without her mother, without her aunt, and the house felt as empty as she did. She couldn't bear it.

She moved through the house quickly, turning on lights and finally the water in the upstairs bathtub. She tried not to think. There was nothing she could do for Wayne. Her mother was fine. And Gus… The man was a fool, no wonder she couldn't get him out of her thoughts. She told herself he was doing this for a book. For his brother. Not her. No matter what he said.

Closing the bathroom door, she stripped off the overalls, the long underwear, the layers of clothing that she wore like a coat of armor to protect her from what? Men? Or from herself and a need to be held, to be loved and to love back?

As she stripped off the last layer of clothing, she realized there was only one man the armor hadn't protected her from. Gus.

Nothing could protect her from him because he'd seemed determined to tear down the wall she'd built around herself—even if it killed him, which she feared it would.

Where was he? Had he come to his senses and left

town? The thought made her ache inside, and yet the thought of him staying here and getting hurt, possibly killed, devastated her.

She wondered how long it would be before Bryan came to arrest her. Maybe that's all the killer wanted, to see her behind bars. Gus would be safe.

The steam assaulted her as she stepped into the tub filled with hot water and closed the shower door after her.

As she slid down into the wonderfully warm water scented with bath beads and frothy with bubbles, she hoped to wash thoughts of Gus away—at least for a few moments. But the warmth of the water on her skin reminded her of his touch.

She felt the ache deep within her becoming unbearable. What had made her think she could live without the touch of a man? It had seemed possible before she'd met Gus. But now she knew that staying away from men wasn't the answer. Look what had happened to Josh. Someone had killed him and for what reason? Josh had never been interested in her romantically nor she him.

She turned on the hot water and let it run for a few minutes, steam rising until she felt wrapped in a cocoon of wet cotton. Leaning back, she closed her eyes, but not even the hot water could burn away thoughts of Gus from her mind, from her body. The memory of his kisses was imprinted on her lips just like the feel of being in his strong arms. For the first time in her life she was falling for someone. Her timing couldn't be worse. Nor her choice in men. Gus was all wrong for her. She sunk deeper in the hot water, trying hard not to cry.

A floorboard creaked downstairs in the living room. She opened her eyes, sitting up as she held her breath and listened. Another creak of the floorboards. Someone was downstairs.

THE PINECONE WAS fairly empty this early in the morning. T. J. Blue had taken a stool at the counter and was now hunched over his coffee cup.

"Good morning, Gus," Helen said. She slid a cup across the counter to him as he took a stool next to T.J. and thought about yesterday when he'd seen T.J. with Jenny Simonson.

T.J. didn't acknowledge his presence, but Gus could feel the tension coming off the man like a bad odor.

"Morning, Helen," Gus said, feeling as if he'd been in this town for weeks rather than days.

"The special's blueberry hotcakes, two eggs, side of ham and coffee. Three forty-nine."

"Just coffee," he said, not in the least hungry.

She filled his cup, remembering that he took it black, and moved off.

At the other end of the counter, Marcella was sitting on the second to last stool as usual, knitting. He wondered if the woman pretty much lived on that stool.

He overheard Helen tell Marcella that Trudi hadn't shown for work this morning.

"I saw you talking to Jenny Simonson yesterday," Gus said to T.J., figuring whatever was bothering the man would quickly become apparent.

T.J. swung his head around, his nostrils flaring, ready for a fight. "It's none of your business who I talk to."

"I couldn't help but notice that she seemed to have a black eye," Gus said quietly.

T.J. turned back to his coffee. "Also none of your business."

"Or yours?"

T.J. let out a snort. "You're just asking for it this morning," he said, keeping his voice down. The women were talking at the end of the counter. Gus didn't think they were paying any attention, but he figured Helen could probably listen to a half-dozen different conversations at once, given all her years in the diner.

"Didn't I hear that your car went off the road last night?" T.J. asked. "Take a hint. Somebody in this town doesn't like you."

"Any idea who that somebody might be?" Gus asked.

T.J. gave him a look that insinuated there were too many people to number and that T.J. himself was at the top of the list.

Gus took a sip of his coffee. "How long has Forest been knocking her around?"

T.J. didn't answer but tightened his grip on the coffee cup until his knuckles where white.

"You have to know what Forest will do when he finds out about the two of you," Gus said, wondering how far to push T.J. Wondering just how dangerous he might be.

The cup shattered in T.J.'s hand, coffee and pieces of white china skittering across the counter.

"What in the world?" Helen demanded as she hustled back down to them, a dishrag in her hand.

T.J. was on his feet. He threw a five-dollar bill onto the counter. "Sorry about the cup, Helen." With that, he turned and stalked out.

Helen eyed Gus. "Want to tell me what that was about?"

"Too much caffeine, I guess," Gus said, turning to watch T.J. leave, pickup tires spraying ice and snow. T.J. and Jenny. Gus swore, afraid what Forest would do when he found out. And how could he not in a town this size?

Helen sighed and gave Gus an impatient look. She cocked a hip against the counter as if settling in to give him a piece of her mind, but before the door could close behind T.J., it flew open. They both turned to see Trudi come in looking harried and apologetic.

She raced to the kitchen to dump her coat and purse, then came back and hurriedly filled Marcella's coffee cup.

Helen just groaned and looked away.

"More coffee?" Trudi asked, holding the pot over Gus's almost empty cup. She'd been cool toward him ever since that first night. Which was fine with him.

He shook his head. "Gotta go."

Emmett Graham came through the door as Gus was getting up to leave.

"Coffee, Emmett?" Helen said.

He nodded and slid onto a stool. "I just got back from Libby. Vera took a fall this morning. I ran her and Selma up to the hospital."

"Is Vera all right?" Gus asked, heart pounding.

Everyone looked at him for a moment before Emmett said, "Broke her wrist, but she's fine. They're keeping her overnight, a little concerned how the painkillers will react with the Alzheimer's medication. Selma's staying with her."

Gus felt a surge of relief, but it was short-lived. He glanced down the highway. Charlie was home alone.

"Is there a faster way to get to Charlie's than the county road?" he asked Emmett.

"There's a trail that cuts through the trees, but you'll have to cross the creek," he said as Gus rushed for the door. "You'll find it right across the way. Just take it north."

"Thanks," he called over his shoulder as he grabbed his coat and rushed out, unable to keep from thinking about his cut brake line, the person Spark Plug had chased away from the farmhouse last night, Charlie alone in that big old house. What if he was wrong about her being safe?

Chapter Sixteen

The first thing Gus saw was two sets of fresh tracks leading up the steps and onto the porch. Past the tracks, the front door stood ajar.

He hit the steps at a run. "Charlie? Charlie!"

From inside he heard a scream, followed by the sound of glass shattering. He didn't even think about grabbing a weapon on his way through the kitchen he was moving so fast. Nor did he realize he was screaming her name. "Charlie! Charlie!"

He heard the hammer of footfalls on the stairs and a door banging open. Then the haunting howl of a dog in the distance. Spark Plug? He rounded the corner of the living room in time to see movement through the pines on the side of the house.

Gus knew he'd never be able to catch the person— and he had to see to Charlie. He raced up the stairs.

"Charlie!" There were snowy wet prints on the stairs. He followed the prints to the partially opened bathroom door, scared to death of what he was going to find.

He stopped and slowly pushed open the door, his heart in his throat. A sob came from inside the bathroom. "Charlie?"

"Gus!"

He rushed in to find the mirror over the sink shattered, shards of silver glittering on the tile floor. Charlie stood stark naked and dripping in the corner of the full tub, a bottle of shampoo clutched in her fist, half of the glass shower door gaping open, a look of pure terror on her face.

"Charlie," he said in a whisper and she leaped into his outstretched arms, dropping the shampoo to wrap her arms around his neck as he lifted her and carried her to the corner, away from the broken mirror. Grabbing a large, soft yellow towel from the rack, he pulled it around her, cradling her in his lap, in his arms. He held her to him as if that simple act could chase away all of their fears. "You're all right," he said against her wet hair, against the warmth of her cheek. "You're all right." He wasn't sure which one of them he was trying to convince.

After a few moments, he pulled back to look down into her face. The gold flecks in her brown eyes were electric, her color heightened by the heat of the shower and the fear. "You're all right," he whispered, desire making his voice hoarse and tight. "Can you stay here while I run downstairs and lock the doors?"

She nodded slowly.

When he returned just moments later with the robe he'd found in her bedroom, she was still huddled in the corner, the towel wrapped around her.

"I found Spark Plug closed up in the shed," he said. "He's downstairs now and the doors are locked. You're safe."

"Thank you," she whispered.

"Did you see who it was?" he asked gently.

She shook her head. "All I saw was a dark figure through the steamy glass, then a gloved hand opening the shower door." She shuddered. "I guess I screamed, grabbed the conditioner bottle and threw it."

He nodded, kneeling down beside her. "It appears it hit the mirror." He touched her face, brushing away a tear with the rough pad of his thumb. "I called the sheriff, Charlie. He just picked up Forest Simonson speeding on the county road about a half mile from here headed toward town."

"Forest." She looked up at him, tears welling in her eyes.

He reached for her, taking the towel as he slipped her into the robe.

Her fingers trembled as she tried to tie the sash. He took it from her. Her gaze came up to meet his. He tied the sash around her slim waist and brushed his fingertips across her cheek. Tears beaded on her lashes as she caught his fingers in her hand and brought them to her lips.

Her widened eyes locked with his, so filled with promise. He swept her up into his arms as if his whole life had been leading to this one moment in time.

She stretched up to kiss his cheek, then the corner of his mouth, then his lips, her breath warm and sweet. She pulled him down to her, her lips parting, clinging to him as if clinging to life. Her kiss a reaffirmation.

The need that had been smoldering between them for days burst into bright, flickering flame. She feathered light kisses across his face until her mouth lighted on his again, her taste sweet nectar. He wanted her like nothing he'd ever wanted before. He could feel the heat of her body, her skin hot against him even through all his clothing. He couldn't imagine his bare skin against hers. The thought made his knees weak.

Her fingers tugged at the buttons on his coat, burrowing under his shirt, her touch both pain and pleasure.

He carried her into her bedroom and set her on the bed. She pulled him down with her as her hands worked at his clothing. He brushed back a lock of her wet hair from her cheek with the pad of his thumb and cupped her jaw in his palm, drawing her face up, stilling her fingers.

"Charlie?" he said, his voice low and heavy with need.

She looked up into his eyes and slowly untied the sash of her robe. The fabric slipped from her slim shoulders. He watched her, desire molten inside him as he reveled in the body she'd kept hidden under all the clothing. How long had she been hiding that sexuality?

A lump rose in his throat, the ache in his chest making it hard to breathe. He didn't deserve this. Not after the way he'd treated her. "Charlie."

She touched her fingertips to his lips, her eyes lit with gold and unbridled desire. She smiled as she drew him closer. Her kiss was warm and demanding, her hands working again at his coat and shirt until she had both off of him. A sigh escaped her lips as she flattened her palms against his bare chest and looked up at him. "Gus." It was all she said.

CHARLIE HAD NEVER known anything like it. She'd had sex before, but she'd never been made love to. Slowly, achingly, luxuriously made love to. The rest of the day blurred with memories of his warm, strong body, wrapped up in his arms in sleep and lovemaking. Whispered words, satisfied sighs and wonderful restful sleep, free of fear as long as she was curled in Gus's arms.

She woke, knowing before she even opened her eyes

that he was gone. Abruptly, she sat up, feeling her heart lurch. Then she heard him downstairs and smiled.

"Hello," she said from the kitchen doorway.

He turned and smiled, his gaze giving her a lazy caress before he said, "I'm making hot chocolate and sandwiches. I thought you might be hungry."

She returned his smile. "Not anymore."

"For food," he said quietly as he moved to her, pulling her to him to give her a kiss.

"Actually hot chocolate and sandwiches sound wonderful." She moved to the table where he had one of the photo albums lying open.

"Just curious," he said to her inquiring look as he placed two cups of cocoa and two plates with sandwiches on the table. "You were one cute little kid. And one gorgeous woman," he said, nibbling at her neck before he sat down next to her at the table.

This close to him, her skin felt as if touched by flame. It was hard to breathe, hard not to just stare at him, remembering everything they'd shared. She felt bowled over. By him. By the lovemaking. By this odd turn in her life. Gus had come here because of Josh's death. It gave her a strange feeling that also left her scared. For years she hadn't felt she deserved to be happy. Every time she tried, it was snatched away from her.

Only this time, she couldn't bear the thought. This time, it mattered too much.

"Is this you and Jenny?" Gus asked, changing the subject as he pointed to one of the photos.

She nodded as she looked at the photograph of the two of them. They must have been about six.

He flipped through a few more pages, stopping to smile at ones of her. "I thought I had a perfect childhood growing up on the ocean in Laguna Beach, but from the looks of these photos, yours was idyllic."

"It was," she had to admit. "Parents who doted on me, Aunt Selma..." She let out a sigh. "Actually a whole town, as small as Utopia is. People looked out for each other here."

"So it was good until Quinn died?" he asked.

She could feel him watching her closely. She nodded. That was when it had changed.

"Do we have to talk about this now? I mean, Bryan has Forest in custody—"

He brushed his fingers across her cheek. "Yeah, baby, we do. The sheriff couldn't hold Forest. All he could do was give him a speeding ticket. Bryan suggested you get a restraining order against Forest in the morning."

"That's it?"

"Afraid so, Charlie. There's no proof that Forest's the one who was in the house earlier, you didn't get a good look at him and he was wearing gloves. Also he didn't do anything more than come into the house. The door wasn't locked. No breaking and entering. No assault."

She sighed.

"Also, we can't be sure he's the one who's trying to frame you for Josh's murder," Gus said quietly. "Forest is just the hothead among the suspects. I wouldn't rule out Phil Simonson or T. J. Blue at this point. Also Trudi Murphy seems to have an ax to grind. And there's Earlene, who was pregnant with his son. There were probably other women..."

She'd thought of that. "You're wrong about Earlene."

"I hope so. I like her."

Charlie reached over to flip through the pages of the photo album, her thigh brushing his as she leaned toward him. She stopped at one large color photograph of what appeared to be senior prom.

"You looked beautiful," Gus said, ignoring the boy in the prom photograph to stare at Charlie in a form-fitting emerald-green prom dress that accentuated everything about her.

"Thank you." She sounded shy, embarrassed.

He shifted his gaze to the man next to her in the photo and felt a jolt he couldn't explain. Was it just jealousy? "There's something I don't understand. You and Quinn had broken up, right? So why did you even get in the car with him that night, let alone let him take you to the lake?"

She let out a short, harsh laugh. "Let him? Quinn did pretty much what he wanted. But I wouldn't have gotten into the car at all if it hadn't been for Jenny."

Gus jerked back as if surprised. "Jenny?" He felt a sharp stab of recognition slice through him. Jenny and Quinn. Was it possible there was a reason her baby looked so much like Earlene's?

"Quinn had been flirting with Jenny, trying to make me jealous since our breakup. I was afraid he'd use her to get to me."

"How did Jenny feel about Quinn?" he asked, his heart pounding.

"I'm sure Jenny was flattered by the attention, but she was too smart to fall for it. Anyway, she must have been dating Forest." Charlie frowned. "I'm sure she never told me about her and Forest because she knew I never liked him. I wanted to, when Jenny married him, but he made it impossible."

"I've met Forest," Gus said. "I would imagine he has always been an ass and that his bitterness over his brother's death has only made him worse."

"I don't think Forest misses Quinn in the least. The two never got along. Forest was always horribly jealous of Quinn. Quinn was smart and popular and a good athlete and he was better-looking than Forest." She flipped back to a shot of Forest and Quinn when they were about five.

Gus felt his heart take off at a gallop. Skye Simonson and Arnie Kurtz couldn't have looked more like Quinn.

"Charlie." He pointed to the photograph. "Are you sure Jenny wasn't interested in Quinn? You have to have noticed how much Skye and Arnie resemble each other—and Quinn."

She stared at the photo of Quinn when he was about Skye's and Arnie's age. Tears welled in her eyes. "Oh, Gus, you don't think—"

"You said you weren't aware of her dating Forest," Gus said, ticking off the points. "Quinn was after Jenny to make you jealous. And given when Jenny and Earlene gave birth and how much their babies resemble Quinn…"

Charlie felt as if she'd been kicked by a mule. She leaned back, pushing the photo album away the same way she wanted to push away even the suggestion… "Oh, no," she whispered. Suddenly so many things made sense. Why she'd been so surprised when Jenny had married Forest. "I had no idea Jenny was even pregnant, but I wondered why she was in such a rush to marry Forest. Jenny said they'd been dating in secret. But why would they have done that?"

Jenny and Quinn. Of course. Charlie closed her eyes, the betrayal just as painful now as it would have been seven years ago. Hadn't she suspected Quinn was seeing someone else long before she'd heard about Earlene Kurtz's pregnancy?

She felt sick remembering. "If it's true—" She remembered how suddenly Jenny didn't call or stop by. The distance between them had started *before* Quinn's death, before Jenny's engagement and rushed marriage to Forest, before anyone suspected Charlie Larkin of murder.

She opened her eyes, brushed at the tears.

"I'm sorry," Gus said.

"It's not Quinn. I knew Quinn wasn't faithful, but I really didn't care. It's Jenny. She was my best friend. But if you're right, it explains a lot of things," Charlie said quietly.

"Like why Forest abuses her?" he asked.

She looked up, surprised. "Forest never seemed to care anything about Skye," she said, realizing it was true. "Or Jenny for that matter."

"I assume Jenny was at the party that night at the lake?"

She nodded, wondering where he was going with this.

"I was just thinking about two scared pregnant young women witnessing Quinn trying to get you back at the party and I can imagine how they must have felt," Gus said.

She stared at him for a moment, then got up and went to the window. "They must have hated Quinn. And me."

He came up behind her, his large hands touching her shoulders lightly. He began to rub away the tension knotted in her muscles. She let out a sigh and leaned into his strong hands, closing her eyes.

"You told Josh all of this," he said, working her shoulders, his hands heaven. "Did you mention names?"

She nodded.

"So he knew all the players," Gus said.

"What are you thinking?" she asked, not wanting

him to stop what he was doing to her, not wanting to open her eyes.

"Josh tried to contact you—he had the locket Quinn had given you, the one you threw at Quinn the night of his death," Gus said. "It's a leap, but in order for him to have the locket in his possession, it is reasonable that he had some contact with whoever has had the locket all these years. Whoever picked it up at the party. That person must have given Josh the locket or left it where he could find it."

Gus let go of her and moved back to the photo album. "All of our suspects were at the party that night, right? Any one of them could have picked up the locket. But what connection could they have had with an emergency room doctor in Missoula?"

She had opened her eyes and was watching him.

"Miles found out that Phil Simonson was taken to the Missoula hospital the day of his logging accident," Gus said. "Josh was on duty. That means Forest and Jenny were probably there. Earlene also took her son to the emergency room when Josh was on duty in another incident."

"I see where you're going with this," she said. "Josh might have gotten caught up in a single mother's life. Or an abused wife's."

Gus nodded.

Charlie felt sick. "There's something I need to tell you. I went back to the lodge last night after you left me at the lake. I'd noticed something on the floor by the fireplace. Someone has been hanging out up there. I found one of Quinn's toys on the floor. It was a toy that Arnie had taken from Skye Simonson at school and been forced to give back." She nodded, anticipating his next question. "Skye got the toy back right before Josh's death."

"Jenny," he said.

"I think she might go up there sometimes, maybe when Forest is being abusive," Charlie said, realizing what Gus suspected really could be true. No one had tried to help her. Except possibly Josh?

"I don't think she's been going up there alone," Gus said. "I saw her the other day with T. J. Blue behind the gravel pit off the main highway. She was in his arms."

Charlie stared at him, surprised. "T.J.? If Forest finds out—" Her heart dropped like a rock. "Oh, Gus, what if Forest suspected she was seeing someone and followed her to the lake. What if she was meeting Josh there?"

He swore. "This whole thing is starting to feel like a time bomb ready to go off and I'm afraid you're somehow at the center of it."

A cold chill stole up her spine. "You don't think Quinn's death was an accident, do you?"

"I don't know."

"I can't believe either Earlene or Jenny would do anything to hurt me," she said, praying that was true.

"What about Jenny's husband? Or father-in-law? Or Rickie Moss? If he thinks you're responsible for his scar…"

She covered her face with her hands. "I can't bear the thought that someone in this town hates me that much." She looked up at him, tears blurring her eyes. "These are people I've known all of my life. It is easier to believe it's some sort of curse or that—"

"That you might somehow be responsible?" he asked softly.

She nodded, tears stinging her eyes as they overflowed.

He pulled her to him, wrapping his arms around her. "You aren't responsible. Don't worry, we'll find out who is. I promise you."

Chapter Seventeen

Charlie woke to darkness. She blinked and felt the side of the bed where she last remembered Gus's warm body. He was gone. Again. Then she heard the clatter of dishes and water running down in the kitchen. Hot chocolate and sandwiches again?

She glanced at the clock: 5:00 a.m. Pulling on her robe over her flushed nakedness, she hurried down the stairs, not wanting to spend even a moment out of his arms.

"Sleep well?" Helen asked with a knowing grin as she continued washing up the dishes in the sink.

"Where's Gus?" Charlie asked, noticing with disappointment that he was nowhere in sight—and his coat was missing from the hook by the back door.

"He had to take off for a while," she said with a shrug. "He asked me to hang out here until he got back. He told me about Forest—or at least that's who he thought got into the house." She shook her head. "Talk about a nutcase." She paused, eyeing Charlie. "You all right?"

Charlie nodded sheepishly and pulled her robe around her.

"It's nice to see a little color in your cheeks for a change," Helen said and smiled.

"Did he tell you where he was going?"

Helen shook her head. "Hungry? I could make you something."

"No, thanks." She shivered, wondering where Gus would take off to this time of the morning. It had to have been something important or he wouldn't have left her. That she was sure of. So what could have made him leave? "Who's opening the café this morning?"

"Trudi," Helen said and grimaced. "But Emmett promised to stop by and make sure she doesn't burn down the place." She laughed, then narrowed her eyes. "Don't try to run me off. I'm staying right here with you. No arguments."

Charlie saw that arguing would indeed be a waste of time. Her mind was on Gus and where he'd gone anyway. "I'll get some clothes on."

"I'll make us some coffee," Helen said.

As she started for the stairs, Charlie thought she remembered something from her sleep. The sound of the phone ringing. Just once. Gus must have answered it before it could ring again.

She hurried up the stairs, even more worried. She'd felt so safe in Gus's arms, but neither of them was safe, especially Gus. Especially now that they were lovers. If the killer found out—

The moment the caller ID came up she recognized the number. Her heart slammed against her chest. It was Jenny's old number, the one Charlie had called recently to ask her former friend to lunch. Jenny and Forest's number. He'd called the house. Talked to Gus. And now Gus was gone. To meet Forest?

She dressed quickly in jeans and a sweater, unable to go back to wearing baggy clothing after a night with Gus, all the time, her mind racing. What could Forest have said that would convince Gus to go out at this hour?

Picking up the phone, she dialed the number, not sure what she planned to say when Jenny answered. All she could hope was that Jenny would know where Forest had gone.

"Hello."

Charlie was too startled to speak at first. "Forest?"

Silence, then, "What the hell do *you* want?" He sounded as if she'd awakened him. She didn't know what to say, afraid to ask for Jenny, afraid to ask why he'd called now that she was sure he wasn't with Gus.

She started to hang up when he swore, then demanded, "Where the hell is Jenny? Don't think I don't know that she's been meeting you behind my back." He let out a laugh that held no humor.

She could hear the rustle of clothing being hurriedly pulled on.

"She thinks I'm a fool, that I don't know where she goes and who she meets. She thinks I don't know about her little secret hiding place at the lake." It sounded as if he'd dropped the phone.

She could hear him banging around, then cursing something about "that cheating, lying bitch." But it was his last words before he hung up the phone that had her shaking. "I'm going to kill her. I'm going to kill them both."

Charlie stared at the phone for a heartbeat, then dropped the receiver back into the cradle. If Forest hadn't called Gus to meet him, then Jenny had. She tore down the stairs.

Helen looked up, eyes wide as Charlie jerked the shotgun down from the top shelf and hurriedly dug a half-dozen shells from the kitchen drawer.

"Charlie?" Helen asked, sounding scared.

"Call Sheriff Olsen. Tell him that Gus has gone to the lake to meet Jenny. Forest is on his way up there, threatening to kill her. Kill them both." Charlie pulled her coat from the hook by the back door and shrugged into it. She picked up the shotgun. "I'm going up there to warn Gus."

"With a shotgun?" Helen asked.

"How long has Gus been gone?"

Helen glanced at the clock. "About fifteen minutes. But he said not to let you leave until he got back."

Charlie raised an eyebrow. "You aren't going to try to stop me, are you?"

Helen smiled sadly and shook her head. "I've known you far too long to know not to even try. I'll call Bryan right now." She reached for the phone. "Just be careful. Forest is more dangerous than anyone knows. I've been trying to tell that dumb Trudi that. I swear she's been moon-eyed over that idiot since high school."

Charlie headed for her VW van, putting everything out of her mind except Gus. She had to get to the lake before Forest. Either way, the sheriff wouldn't be far behind her. With luck she could reach Gus in time.

As she passed the large old tree outside her bedroom window, she was reminded of the summer she and Jenny were twelve. Charlie used to climb down the tree late at night to meet Jenny. They'd formed their own club and met in the barn. It was their little secret.

Jenny. Charlie couldn't help but wonder what other secrets Jenny might have been keeping all these years. The photos in the album haunted Charlie as she drove out to the county road. How could she not have seen how much Arnie and Skye looked alike and what that had to mean? How could she not have known about Jenny and Quinn?

Because she hadn't wanted to, she realized. She hadn't wanted to see, just as she hadn't wanted to see why Jenny had married Forest, why she'd put up with his abuse all these years.

Is that why Jenny had called the house? Because she needed help? Or did Jenny know who had murdered Josh? Is that what she'd lured Gus up to the lake with?

Josh had been the kind of man who would have also agreed to meet Jenny at the lake, Charlie thought with a chill. Josh knew about Jenny almost drowning there. He knew about the Simonsons' old lodge. Jenny might have even lost her virginity there to Quinn—just as Charlie and Earlene had. And if it was Jenny who'd been going up to the lake, hiding out in the lodge with Skye, to get away from Forest—

But how could Jenny find solace in that lodge given that Quinn had taken advantage of her there? Unless Jenny really had been in love with Quinn. Was it possible that Jenny had good memories of the lodge—and Quinn? That thought startled Charlie. If Jenny had been in love with Quinn then it also made sense that she could harbor ill feelings toward Charlie.

She drove down the highway, the sky still dark, the pines etched black against it. It hurt to even think about Jenny. Sometimes the truth stared her in the face and she refused to see it. Like Skye's uncanny resemblance to Quinn. Like the town ignoring Forest's abuse of Jenny. And Jenny taking it.

Charlie felt guilty for not doing something to help her friend. But what could she have done that wouldn't have made matters worse? Forest hated Charlie, blamed her for Quinn's death. As long as Charlie had stayed away from Jenny—With a jolt Charlie realized she hadn't done that. She'd asked Jenny to lunch and Forest had known. Had she put her friend in worse danger?

And now Forest was headed for the lake. Just as he had the night Josh Whitaker died?

In her headlights, Charlie saw the turnoff to Freeze Out Lake ahead and slowed, anxious to get there, to get to Gus to warn him about Forest. She had the shotgun on the seat next to her. The thought frightened her. But not as much as Forest hurting Gus.

She turned onto the narrow dark road, the tall pines closing in around the van as she started up the mountain. The van's headlights shone into the darkness, reminding her of the night Quinn had brought her up here, the night he'd died. She'd been so angry with him, demanding he take her back to town, but him ignoring her. Then at the party, when she'd found out about Earlene being pregnant with his baby—

She shifted down as the road switchbacked up the mountain, higher and higher as it carved a narrow path through the dense trees. It was almost six. It would be getting light soon.

The darkness reminded her again of the night Quinn died. Who'd been standing on the edge of her vision when she'd thrown the locket at Quinn? She'd been so angry with him, she hadn't paid any attention. But someone had picked up the locket. Quinn? No, the locket would have been found on his body after the wreck.

Suddenly her headlights picked up a vehicle in the road ahead. Gus's rental car was stopped in the middle of the road, blocking it. Another vehicle had tried to go around it, but had gotten stuck in the trees.

She stopped as she recognized Forest's truck, snow

up to the wheel wells. Oh God, he was ahead of her. In the light of her headlamps, she could see from where she was that the cabs of both vehicles were empty. There were tracks in the snow near the pickup where Forest had taken off on foot up the mountain toward the lake.

There were several old logging roads that would get her to the lake, but she didn't want to take the time to backtrack. She pulled the van to the edge of the road behind Gus's rental car, careful not to get into the snow and get stuck like Forest had.

She could see now what had kept Gus from going any farther up the road. A large tree had fallen over. No, not fallen over, she thought as she stared out the windshield. She could see wood chips next to the base of the pine. Someone had cut down the tree—purposely blocking the road.

With trembling fingers, she hurriedly loaded the shotgun and put the rest of the shells in her coat pocket, then with her flashlight in hand, she climbed out of the van and started up the mountain.

The snow had melted back from the road, the cold night had made the ground hard. She'd left no tracks.

She hadn't gone far up the road when she spotted tracks cutting through the snow and trees on what appeared to be a path. Forest's tracks. Did he know a shortcut to the lodge?

She followed his tracks, praying she would reach the lodge in time.

As she walked, she forced herself to remember the night of Quinn's death. The locket. She tried to see herself throwing it at him, turning… She could recall images off to the side. Forest was there by his brother. T.J. off by the campfire. Earlene had gone to one of the cars, upset and crying. And Jenny—

Suddenly Charlie had a flash of memory so sharp it almost blinded her. She stumbled. Jenny had been standing beside her that night. As Charlie had turned away, she'd seen Jenny stoop down to pick up the locket from the dirt!

DARKNESS HAD DROPPED over the lake like a sack, clouds obscuring any stars or moon. But Gus knew daylight wasn't far off. He could make out the roofline on the lodge to the east of him as the sky began to lighten.

He sat on a large rock by the shore, the lodge nearby, waiting, wondering if his brother had waited in this same spot. Only Josh hadn't known he was waiting for a killer. Gus knew it was more than a good possibility.

When Jenny had called, she'd been crying. She'd wanted to talk to Charlie. Gus had calmed her down, offered to help. She'd said Forest was in the other room asleep, that he would kill her if he knew she had called Charlie, that she needed to get out of the house. She was going to the lake lodge. No, Skye was at a friend's house. Forest had been drinking and Jenny had wanted Skye out of the house.

She'd said she needed to tell someone the truth.

He'd agreed to meet her at the lake, knowing all the time that it was more than likely a trap.

He'd opted to wait out here in the open rather than in the lodge. When he'd found the tree across the road and realized it had been sawed down, he hadn't been surprised. Just a little more anxious. He was finally going to find out who'd killed his brother. Who was trying to frame Charlie.

On the way up the mountain, walking through the dark of the pines, he'd asked himself why he was doing this. Risking his life. It had started out as vengeance and repentance, finding Josh's killer, writing a book that would vindicate Augustus T. Riley of any guilt about his brother.

Then he'd met Charlie, fallen for her like a rock from a cliff. Now more than ever he wanted the killer. He never wanted to see fear on Charlie's face again—not like he'd seen last night.

He also wanted to make up for all those years he hadn't been close to Josh. Had resented his younger half brother.

He felt no small amount of guilt for being angry at his mother when she'd remarried so soon after his father's death. Then when she'd become pregnant right away with Josh—

Gus shook his head, thinking of all the years he'd wasted by being angry. Feeling left out. Not that it helped that Josh had been nothing short of a saint. So different from Gus.

He shook off the memories, letting his flashlight beam skitter across the road ahead of him. In the distance, he could smell the lake. Where was Jenny? Or had she never planned to come? Had she always planned to send Forest instead?

He ached to flick on the flashlight, even for an instant, and chase away the darkness. It closed in on him, so thick it seemed to have texture and substance. Just like the silence.

Then he heard it. The sound of a vehicle grew louder and louder, the rusted-out muffler making a throbbing sound that echoed through the trees. The same pickup he'd heard last night when his brake line was cut?

The truck stopped in the pines, the engine dying, pitching the lake back into that awful eerie silence.

Gus listened to the pickup's door creaking open, then clicking closed. He held his breath, his gun ready.

A flashlight beam cut through the pines toward the lodge. Whoever it was had known about another road to the lake.

Gus pushed himself up off the rock and headed toward the bobbing light, hanging back just enough he hoped he wouldn't be heard. The person with the flashlight headed for the lodge, straight as an arrow. Was it Jenny?

He thought he heard what sounded like another vehicle coming up the lake road as he walked, but when he stopped he heard only silence. He was almost to the lodge when a limb cracked like a gunshot somewhere behind him, making him jump. Closer, he heard the door to the lodge groan open.

He could see nothing in the darkness of the trees behind the lodge.

Through the broken slats of the shutters, a flashlight beamed flickered. If it was Jenny, wouldn't she call out for him?

Gus moved closer to the lodge, stumbling in the dark, but determined not to use his flashlight, not to give away his position. Another limb cracked off to his right, behind the lodge. He stopped to listen again, suddenly afraid there was more than one person out there. Worse, one was tracking the other.

He hoped to hell it was just some small rodent—and not a grizzly looking for a quick meal before hibernation.

Someone was moving around inside the lodge as if looking for something. The toy that Charlie had found? What other evidence could there be?

Cautiously, Gus moved closer, wondering if he dared

climb the creaky steps to the porch or if he should wait until his visitor came back out to confront whoever it was.

Forest's angry voice suddenly shattered the quiet night. "What the hell are *you* doing here?" Forest demanded. "What the hell—" Gus heard what sounded like scuffling. He rushed the steps, but as he reached the porch, from inside came the thump of something heavy hitting the floorboards. He edged toward the door, half expecting someone to come flying out any moment.

Silence. The occasional creak of a floorboard. The screech of an owl on the other side of the lake. Then that awful silence again.

He cautiously pushed open the door and, with the weapon in one hand and the flashlight in the other, he burst in, shining the light ahead of him into the room.

Forest Simonson was sprawled in a pool of blood on the floor in front of the fireplace. Gus swept the light around the room, his hand shaking. The room was empty. The attacker apparently gone.

Gus quickly knelt beside Forest, putting down the flashlight as he felt for a pulse. Blood gurgled up through a cut in Forest's coat at heart level. Forest struggled to speak, his lips moving, but nothing coming out. His fingers clutched at Gus's coat sleeve, pulling him closer.

As Gus bent over him, he caught Forest's whispered last word. "Jenny." Then the fingers gripping his coat sleeve released and Forest Simonson was gone.

Gus got to his feet, the hair on the back of his neck standing on end, the cold room suddenly short of oxygen. He shone the flashlight around the lodge again. Whoever had stabbed Forest had escaped.

But Gus didn't think the killer had left the lake. Just the lodge.

He turned off the flashlight and stood in the pitch blackness listening, expecting someone to jump him at any moment and bury the blade in his chest before he could get off a shot. Thank God Charlie was safe back at the house.

Hurriedly, he turned on his flashlight again. The beam fell on drops of blood a few feet from Forest's body on the dusty floor along with two sets of footprints. He followed the bloody trail and the tracks to a back entrance to the lodge. The door stood open. There was blood on the steps and drops on the dried pine needles at the head of what appeared to be a trail.

THE GROUND LEVELED off some and Charlie knew she had to be nearing the lodge. She scrambled through the pines along the narrow game trail, climbing over downed trees and around boulders, following the thin insignificant beam of the flashlight up the mountain, the shotgun cumbersome.

The darkness in the pines felt so close it was suffocating. At times, she stopped to listen, imagining that she was being followed. But those times, she could hear nothing over the pounding of her heart. Even if she hadn't been half running to reach Gus, her heart would have hammered with the fear and worry she felt. She had to get to him before the killer did. She had to warn him.

The trail swung off to the right. She knew she was close now. She and Jenny had spent many summers up here at the lake with their parents before that incident in high school, the almost drowning. Charlie had forgotten all the good times with Jenny. Now they came back in a rush and she felt sick with worry that she knew who the killer was.

She came around a large pine that encroached on the trail and for an instant thought she'd conjured up the image standing in the middle of the trail.

She stumbled to a stop, heart in her throat as the penlight beam illuminated Jenny's face.

"Charlie." Jenny's eyes seemed too bright, reminding Charlie of Wayne's when he was excited or upset. Jenny stood, one arm at her side, the other slightly behind her as if she was holding her side. She looked out of breath and Charlie realized that Jenny could have been running to get ahead of her and cut her off.

"Jenny, what are you doing here?" The words came out on a hoarse breath.

"I'm sorry," Jenny whispered and rubbed her lips with her visible hand as if agitated. She wore no gloves and in the light Charlie could see that her hand was bright red from the cold. "I never meant to hurt anyone."

Charlie's heart leaped to her throat. *Be cool.* "Who did you hurt, Jenny?" she asked softly.

Jenny looked dazed as she met Charlie's gaze. "Quinn."

"Quinn?" Charlie thought she must have heard wrong.

"I went after him that night, you know, on this trail until it came to the road. He stopped when he saw me standing in the middle of the road, waiting for him. He smiled and opened the door for me as if he'd known I'd come after him. As if it was always me he wanted. Not you."

Charlie felt her blood run cold. She'd forgotten about the shotgun, heavy in her left hand, and realized she would have to drop the flashlight to fire the weapon. The thought skittered past. She could never shoot Jenny and she knew it. Is that why Jenny hadn't even seemed to notice the shotgun Charlie carried? Jenny stood not six feet from her. On either side there was nothing but dense trees and underbrush. If Charlie made a run for it, she would have to just bust through the pines and hope for the best.

"He put his arm around me while he drove." Jenny smiled, as if lost in the past, but tears spilled down her cheeks and she never took her eyes off Charlie as she talked. "I was so sure everything was going to be all right. I told him about the baby we made that night at the lodge. I thought he'd forgive me for lying about being on the Pill. I loved him so much, I knew I could make him happy. Happier than you ever could."

"Oh, Jenny, I never knew," Charlie whispered, seeing the pain in her once–best friend's face.

"You never knew because you were so busy playing hard to get with Quinn," Jenny snapped. "It's the only reason he kept chasing you."

Charlie felt a chill as she realized the depth of Jenny's pain and anger.

Jenny's demeanor instantly changed. She cocked her head to one side as if she was listening to someone Charlie couldn't see. "Quinn said horrible things to me," Jenny said in a childlike voice. "Horrible things. I started hitting him, trying to make him stop. He was yelling at me and driving so fast. He hit me hard. Knocked me across the seat. I felt the car swerve and crash." Jenny's eyes were wide, dazed, her voice rising, her words coming faster. "I must have blacked out. Quinn was dead. I crawled out the car window. I walked back up the road to the party. No one even missed me."

"It wasn't your fault," Charlie tried to reassure her. "It was an accident."

"That's what Josh said and now he's dead, too," Jenny snapped.

Josh. Oh God, Josh. Charlie felt the air rush from her lungs as if Jenny had hit her. She began to shake, her teeth rattling from the cold, the horror. *Dead, too?* Who else was dead? Not Gus. Oh, please God, not Gus.

"Where is Gus?" Charlie asked, her voice cracking.

Jenny didn't seem to hear. "Josh thought I was staying with Forest as penance for what I'd done. He thought he could help me." Jenny leveled her gaze at Charlie. "He wanted me to tell you about Quinn. To free you from the curse of Quinn's death and free myself from Forest." She let out a harsh laugh. "Like Forest would ever let me be free. Once he found your locket in Quinn's car—" She glared at Charlie as if it had all been her fault. "Forest saw me pick it up from the ground where you'd thrown it. He knew."

Charlie stared at her, shocked. "Forest *blackmailed* you into marrying him?" Forest had used his brother's death to get Jenny and then abuse her, knowing she could never leave him with Quinn's death hanging over her head. And he'd blamed Charlie all this time when he'd *known* she hadn't killed his brother. She felt sick. If only Jenny had told the truth years ago.

"I begged Josh not to come up here," Jenny was saying. She was crying now. "Josh thought he could talk some sense into Forest, *reason* with him. He thought *talking* was the answer. Him and his stupid help lines. I should never have called. I should never have told him about Quinn, about Forest."

Over Jenny's crying, Charlie heard a car coming up the lake road. Sheriff Bryan Olsen.

"Listen, Jenny, I'm freezing. Let's walk on down to the lodge—" She had to find Gus.

"We can't go down there," Jenny said as she swiped at her tears with her free hand and slowly withdrew her other hand out from behind her.

The blade of the knife she had gripped in her fingers caught in the beam of Charlie's flashlight. Even from where she stood, Charlie could see the blood on the long slender filet blade. Her heart lunged. No!

"It's not safe down there," Jenny said, holding up the knife. "Ask Forest."

Charlie moved without thinking, without feeling. She dived into the pines off to her left, the boughs gouging at her face and clothing as she ran blindly in the direction of the road—and the lodge, the flashlight beam bobbing wildly as she ran. She thought she could hear Jenny behind her, almost feel the sharp blade cut through her coat as she barreled through the trees, jumping over fallen logs and off boulders. At some point, she threw the heavy, cumbersome shotgun off into a small ravine, thick with timber, and kept running.

She fell once and scrambled to her feet, but didn't look back for fear she would see Jenny. Not the Jenny who'd once been her best friend, but someone else in Jenny's body. Jenny had traded the truth and her freedom for her own private hell and now Charlie was at the center of it. Maybe always had been.

Through a break in the pines, Charlie spotted the road ahead. Just a few more yards.

She could hear a car, knew it had to be the patrol car. He must have come up one of the old logging roads. The sheriff would have a gun and could use it. Together they would find Gus. Everything was going to be all right now. She knew who the killer was.

Suddenly Charlie was jerked off her feet. A hand clamped down over her mouth before she could get a scream out and she was dragged back into the trees, struggling with her last breath. The flashlight fell from her fingers and then there was only darkness.

"Charlie, it's me—Gus. I've got you, baby. It's okay."

She closed her eyes and let the tears come as he released her and she turned to let him take her, never having been so happy in her life as to be in his arms again.

"Oh, Gus, it's Jenny," she cried against his shoulder.

"I know, I heard everything," he said, holding her as if he'd never let her go.

"Gus, I'm scared. She had a knife. It had blood on it."

"I know, baby. Forest is dead in the lodge. He was stabbed," Gus whispered back. "We have to get out of here."

Chapter Eighteen

Gus had followed the blood trail from the old lodge until the drops became fewer and fewer and finally ran out. The pines were dense and dark and he had started to turn back when he'd heard Charlie's voice. He'd started to call to her, but then he'd heard Jenny's strained words and had frozen in midstep. He'd listened to Jenny's confession and decided the only reason she was telling Charlie was that she didn't plan to let Charlie live long enough to tell anyone. Forest was already dead.

But he didn't dare try to get closer and he couldn't see Jenny from where he stood to get off a shot. He knew he couldn't get to Jenny before she got to Charlie. It was too dangerous to try. He also knew Charlie couldn't use the shotgun—not against Jenny. So he'd waited, praying Charlie would apply that smart mind of hers. And she had. She'd taken off and he'd come after her.

"Do you hear that?" he asked next to her ear as the sound of a vehicle grew louder and louder until it was almost to them.

"It's the sheriff. I had Helen call him to fol-low me."

Gus didn't even want to know how she'd gotten away from Helen. Nor was it a good time to lecture her, although he certainly wanted to. He was still shaking at how close she'd come to getting herself killed.

The lights of the car flickered in the trees as the vehicle drove slowly down to the edge of the lake near the lodge and stopped.

"How did he and Forest get up the road?" Gus whispered to Charlie. "It was blocked when I came up."

"There are some old logging roads, if you know where to find them."

"I assume you chucked the shotgun?" he asked, afraid Jenny might now have it.

"I threw it down a ravine," she admitted sheepishly. "I couldn't use it, Gus. And it was too heavy to carry and run…"

"It's okay, baby," he said and pulled her closer.

Gus hadn't heard anything in the woods behind him but he couldn't be sure that Jenny wasn't out there, waiting to jump them. He didn't like staying in one place long. It felt safer to keep moving. And once they reached the sheriff—

He picked up Charlie's flashlight from the dried pine needles, turned it back on and handed it to her. He could see the road from where they stood. But if they stayed in the pines they could reach the car without exposing themselves to the open road. "Let's go."

They moved through the pines, edging closer to the lake and the car. Off to his right, Gus could see the lodge roof against the lightening sky. The lake shimmering in the gray light of the coming dawn beyond the lodge.

As they drew closer to the vehicle, Gus hoped to hell it *was* the sheriff. He doubted Jenny had driven here with Forest, so she had to have her own vehicle.

In a break in the trees, Gus saw something that made

him stop. Charlie'd been right. It was Bryan's patrol car. The engine was running, the headlights shining out across the silver waters of the lake, the driver's-side door open, the interior light glowing. But there was no one behind the wheel.

Gus crouched down, pulling Charlie with him. He motioned for her to be quiet. Had Bryan gotten out? They waited for several long minutes, but there was no sound of someone moving around. It was still too dark to see in the pines.

Gus edged toward the patrol car with Charlie right behind him. As soon as he reached the side of the patrol car, he saw Sheriff Bryan Olsen sprawled across the seat.

"No," Charlie whispered as Gus moved to the cop and felt for a pulse.

"He's alive," Gus said. He turned off the headlights, but left the car running as he moved Bryan so the door would close. The interior light went off. Gray darkness fell over them like a thick blanket. The air was cold and damp.

Charlie crouched and stayed against the side of the patrol car, the shock starting to set in. Jenny. Tears burned her eyes again, but she refused to break down now. She swallowed back the pain, searching for the anger that would keep her strong.

Good ol' trusting Bryan. He would have opened his door to Jenny. Just as Josh must have. And Jenny was still out there.

"We need to get him to a doctor," Gus whispered. "Come around to the other side of the car with me. Once we're both in, lock the doors. We're going to take the patrol car and get out of here."

"Take me with you," said a voice out of the darkness.

Gus swung around, snapping on the flashlight, the gun in his other hand, as he moved to protect Charlie. The flashlight beam lighted on a dark figure just a few feet away in the pines.

"T.J.," Gus said, instantly on guard.

"Where's Jenny?" T.J. asked, glancing from the gun to Gus's face. He sounded scared.

"I don't know," Gus admitted.

"She'd dangerous," T.J. said. "Who knows what she'll do next."

"Did she ride up with you?" Gus guessed.

T.J. nodded and stepped a little closer, watching the gun in Gus's hand. He had both hands in his pockets, shoulders hunched as if he was cold. "She said she was worried about Forest. She talked me into following him up here. She was acting strange, saying she wasn't going to put up with his abuse anymore. When we got here, she jumped out of my truck and took off through the trees." T.J. glanced around behind him as if he feared she'd be coming after him next. "She had a knife."

"Forest is dead," Gus said. "He was stabbed."

"Oh, man," T.J. moaned, looking away. "I had no idea she was really going to hurt anyone." He met Gus's gaze. "I don't expect you to believe this, but I've been trying to help Jenny, that's all. She wanted to leave Forest, but she was afraid he'd kill her if she tried. He was mean to her, man."

A limb cracked in the pines nearby. Suddenly it seemed colder, as if an icy breeze had sneaked up off the lake. The sheriff groaned inside the patrol car.

"Where's your truck?" Gus asked.

"Back up the road," T.J. said. "She cut both my front tires."

Had Jenny planned to kill them all? Maybe she felt she had nothing to lose. A limb cracked, closer this time.

"We have to get the sheriff to a doctor," Gus said. They were all exposed standing out here with the flashlight on. Jenny could come out of the dark from any direction and kill one of them before they could react. "We'd better get going."

T.J. nodded and started toward them.

"Noooooooooo!" It came out of the forest, echoed across the lake, chilling Gus's blood.

Gus turned at the sound of Jenny's cry to open the patrol car door to get Charlie inside. T.J. hit him upside the head with something hard. Gus's legs buckled under him and he fell to his knees, dropping the flashlight. T.J. jerked the gun from his hand before Gus could get off a shot, slammed him against the side of the patrol car, shoving him down with a boot to his back—the icy barrel of the gun jabbing him in the back of the neck as stars glittered in his head and he fought not to pass out. He lay still, pretending he was out cold, waiting for the blackness to pass, waiting to make his move.

The flashlight had fallen to the cold ground, the beam shining toward the lodge, but Charlie could see T.J.'s face and the grin on it.

"You and your boyfriend think you're so damn smart," T.J. spat. He grabbed her arm and jerked her to him, encircling her neck with his arm in a headlock as he turned to face the pines and the lodge. "Come on out, Jenny, or I'll kill her!" he yelled. "You said you wanted to be free of Forest. Well, you're free. Thanks to me. So come on down here, Jenny. Don't I always take care of you? I'm going to take care of this, too. Just like I took care of that nosy doctor from Missoula. I'm the only one you can trust, Jenny."

Charlie let out a cry as T.J. tightened his hold on her. He still had the barrel of the gun pointed at Gus's back. "Pick up the flashlight," he ordered Charlie, forcing her to bend down with him.

She did as she was told, feeling light-headed. He was holding her so tightly around the neck, he was cutting off her oxygen.

"Shine it out in the trees," T.J. ordered. "No, over to the right by the lodge." The sky behind the trees had lightened to silver, making the darkness in the pines seem blacker.

She tried to pry his arm away with her free hand, but he only clamped down harder.

She had to do something and quick. She'd thought Gus was knocked out, but she saw him move his fingers like a signal. With the flashlight in her hand, she brought it down as hard as she could, connecting with T.J.'s knee. A loud crack filled the air, then T.J.'s furious curse.

He shoved her away as he grabbed for his knee. Charlie stumbled and fell, losing the flashlight. It hit the shore and tumbled into the water. Fighting for air, she groped on the ground for the next best thing: a rock.

She turned to see T.J. trying to get into the patrol car, but Gus's body was in the way.

She rushed T.J., hitting him in the back of the head with the rock clutched in her hand at the same moment Gus grabbed T.J.'s injured leg. T.J. slammed into the patrol car as Gus scrambled to his feet.

T.J. let out a howl and grabbed a handful of Charlie's hair, putting her between him and Gus. "You stupid bitch." He shoved the barrel of the gun against her temple. "Make another move and I kill her!" he yelled at Gus.

Gus froze.

All Charlie caught at first was movement, something dark coming out of the misty blackness of the pines near the edge of the lake. Jenny rushed in, the knife in her hand, her eyes looking glazed in the new light of day, her teeth bared in a grimace as she buried the knife blade in T.J.'s back.

He screamed, releasing his grip on Charlie's hair. Jenny stumbled back drawing the knife out as T.J. spun around, the gun still in his hand.

Gus dived for him, taking T.J. down, but not before he got off a shot. The report echoed across the lake, loud as a cannon. Gus wrestled the gun away from T.J.

Charlie watched Jenny, afraid of what she'd do next. But she stood, the knife in her hand still, her head cocked to one side, as if listening to a voice only she could hear. Then her gaze went to the lake where just a few feet offshore, the flashlight had landed, its beam now slicing through dark, gloomy waters like an elusive sea monster.

Jenny suddenly sat down hard on the rocky shore. Charlie reached for her and stopped when Jenny turned to look at her. The front of her coat was dark with blood where T.J. had shot her.

"I'm sorry," Jenny whispered, then looked past Charlie down the shore toward the old lake lodge. She smiled, looking young again. Her last word was "Quinn."

Epilogue

Charlie remembered little of the drive to Libby to the hospital—except for her last glimpse of the lake. The sun had climbed up, golden over the pines, setting the surface afire with color. Mist rose ghostlike from the water as the silken pines shimmered along the shore.

She had stared at it as Gus turned the patrol car around, wondering at how peaceful it looked, how beautiful—as if nothing horrible had happened here. Or ever would again.

Gus drew her close as they left. She didn't look back. She snuggled against him, but not even the warmth of his body could chase away the cold inside her.

At the hospital, she knew long before the doctor came out to tell them that Bryan had a concussion but would pull through, that Gus was leaving. She'd seen it in his eyes, felt it in the way he held her.

"I have to write this book," he said, his hands cupping her shoulders as his gaze held hers. "I need to do this for myself, for my brother."

She nodded, understanding what he was saying. He couldn't do it without leaving her. Hadn't she known that from the first?

"I do understand," she said and smiled as she reached

up to brush the tips of her fingers across his stubbled jawline.

He closed his eyes as if in pain. "Charlie, what happened between us—"

She silenced him, pressing her fingers to his lips.

He opened his eyes and pulled her into his arms, hugging her hard and long, her face pressed against his chest.

She listened to the beat of his heart, a sound she knew she would never forget.

The days that followed were little more than a painful blur. Jenny and Forest were buried in the small cemetery outside town. Jenny's parents didn't come back from Florida to attend. But the rest of the town was there as they hadn't been for Jenny during her life.

Forest was buried next to his brother, Quinn. Phil broke down over his sons' graves, alone as he'd never been before.

Gus stayed for the burials, then left. "I won't be calling for a while," he said. "I can't, not if I hope to get this story down."

She'd kissed him, her mother and aunt gazing from the kitchen window, and stood watching him drive away from the farmhouse until the rental car disappeared in the pines.

She threw herself back into her work, taking on Leroy's old snowplowing tractor even though she knew she couldn't get parts for it. So she made the parts she needed, determined to get it running as if making that ancient tractor run were a matter of life and death.

Earlene filed papers to adopt Jenny and Forest's little girl, Skye. Phil Simonson didn't even put up a fight. In fact, he started going over to spend time with his two grandchildren on Sunday afternoons. Earlene said the first time he held Arnie and Skye in his arms, Phil wept like a baby.

T.J. was in jail, denied bail, awaiting trial. From his cell, he told a classic tale of love and betrayal, sex and seduction, jealousy and murder that was repeated over the lunch special at the Pinecone, until it had taken on a life of its own.

To the end, T.J. saw himself as Jenny's hero. He'd tried to save her from Forest, a man who'd blackmailed Jenny into marrying him but soon realized that while he might be able to keep Jenny with the horrible truth he held over her, he couldn't make her love him. When Skye looked so much like his brother, Forest became even more bitter and had began to take it out on Jenny.

But T.J. had demanded almost as much as Forest had of Jenny. He would keep her secrets, but she must always turn to him. Jenny made the mistake of calling the help line one night and pouring out her soul to Josh Whitaker. Later she would meet Josh at the hospital when her father-in-law was injured in the logging accident. Josh would have recognized Jenny as an abused woman.

T.J. had found out about Josh's plan to meet Jenny at Freeze Out Lake and get her to tell the truth about Quinn and free herself from Forest—and free Charlie as well.

T.J. had gotten there first, killed Josh and disposed of the body and car, believing he was protecting Jenny. Jenny had thought Forest had killed Josh and taken on that guilt as well until it had become a tangled web of lies.

Bryan was released from the hospital after a few days. Selma insisted he come stay at the farmhouse until he had completely recuperated. By the end of the week,

Bryan had retired as sheriff and asked Selma to marry him to everyone's surprise. Finally, Charlie understood the never-worn wedding dress in the attic. Bryan had been her mystery beau all those years ago. Selma turned Bryan down, just as she had all those years ago, saying she had to take care of her sister. Bryan said he would wait for her. Just as he always had.

The day before Thanksgiving, Charlie was in the garage. She'd been working on Leroy's old tractor and had just started it up, more than pleased when it finally ran.

She was hoping it was an omen of good things to come, when she looked up to see Gus standing in the gas station office doorway.

At first she thought he was only a mirage, she'd imagined him standing there so many times. But then he walked toward her and she caught the scent of his aftershave.

She wiped her hands on a rag, watching him, wondering what he was doing here, her heart pumping so hard it hurt.

"Leroy's tractor?" Gus asked, glancing past her to the monstrous orange machine behind her.

She could do no more than nod as he closed the distance between them. The moment he touched her, her heart began to pound even harder. He was flesh and blood. No mirage.

He traced a finger along her lips, then down the slim column of her throat to the hollow between her breasts, his gaze locked with hers.

"God, I've missed you," he whispered. He pulled her to him and dropped his mouth to hers with a hunger than made her stagger. His kiss brought it all back, the wonder of their lovemaking, the pain of his leaving.

She pulled back, shaking inside with need for him—

and a fear that unlike the first time he walked in here, this time he really was just passing through. "What are you doing here?"

"Isn't it obvious?" he asked as he dropped to one knee on the cold concrete. "I'm asking you to marry me."

Her heart lodged in her throat, tears springing to her eyes. She was shaking her head, unable to find words, her disappointment was so great.

She couldn't possibly marry him. Didn't he realize that she couldn't leave Utopia? Couldn't leave her mother and aunt? Or the garage? Not even for him.

"Don't turn me down until you hear the proposal," he said, nonplussed. "I want to marry you, Charlie, but you have to know first that you'd be marrying an unemployed dreamer who has always dreamed of writing the great American novel in some small, out-of-the-way town in Montana."

She stared at him. "Since when?"

"Since I met you." He smiled, his eyes bright with love.

"Are you sure?" she had to ask.

He nodded. "When I finished the book about my brother and his death, I knew I was finished with that part of my life. I don't want to write about murder or the lives it devastates anymore, Charlie. I can't. It's not in me anymore, not since you."

He pulled a small velvet box from his pocket and held it out to her. "Say you'll marry me. You wouldn't want to destroy a man's dream, would you?"

She took the velvet box in her trembling fingers and opened it. A beautiful diamond ring winked up at her. "You really think you can live here and be happy?"

"What man wouldn't want to live in Utopia," he joked, then said, "Honey, this floor is very cold and hard. I'd live with you anywhere. I've never been more sure of anything in my life. Say yes so I can get up."

"Yes!" She threw herself into his arms as he straightened.

He kissed her slowly as if savoring the taste of her, then he drew back to take the ring from her and put it on her finger.

"You realize we will be living in the farmhouse with my aunt and mother," Charlie warned.

"I already talked to Selma," Gus said. "She says once we get the nursery added on there will be plenty of room for all of us. Emmett said he'd start working on it right away."

"Nursery?" Charlie asked.

He cupped her face in his hands. "When were you planning to tell *me?*"

"What?"

"About the baby," Gus said.

"What baby?"

"The one Selma says you're going to have." Gus grinned at her. "Don't worry, she didn't tell me until after I'd told her about the ring—and my plans. I assured her that I've saved enough money to support you until I sell my first work of fiction. I also have royalties coming in from the crime books, but that's not the kind of legacy I want to leave to our children."

"I'm going to have a baby?" Charlie asked, still in shock. She knew it was way too early to know if their lovemaking had made a baby.

"Just in time for the Fourth of July celebration here in Utopia, according to your aunt."

Charlie began to laugh. Her aunt the seer.

Gus swung her up into his arms. She caught a glimpse of the future in his eyes and could see their stories woven into the fabric of the town. Gus and Charlie and their children.

As Gus put her down, Charlie looked over by the workbench, wishing her father could have been here. He was standing in his spot, his coffee cup in his hand. He glanced at Leroy's tractor and gave her a thumbs-up. Then he looked at Gus and nodded his approval. Slowly he put down his coffee cup. She felt tears rush her eyes as her father started for the door. She heard his words in her head as he stopped and turned, "You're going to be just fine now." Then he was gone.

"Are you all right?" Gus asked, thumbing away the tears on her cheeks as he looked down into her face, worry in his eyes.

She nodded. "I'm going to be just fine now."

Gus kissed her again, then worked the top button of her shirt free.

She let out a sharp intake of breath as he freed the next button, then another one, his fingers brushing her warm skin.

"I couldn't bear to spend another day away from you," he said as he slipped a strap of her overalls off her shoulder. "I've been thinking about getting you out of these clothes for the last hundred miles." He slid the other strap from her shoulder. The baggy overalls dropped to the floor.

"What if someone comes by for gas?" she protested as he continued to undress her.

"There's a can out on the pump. They can just help themselves and leave the money." He grinned. "I also locked the front door and put up the Closed sign on my way in."

"How did you know I'd be here?"

"I know *you,* Charlie," he said, brushing his finger-tips across her cheek.

She caught his hand and brought it to her lips, closing her eyes as she kissed his palm. "Yes, you do, Augustus T. Riley."

"Gus," he said.

* * * * *

We hope you enjoyed reading

COWBOY'S REDEMPTION

and

PREMEDITATED MARRIAGE

by *New York Times* bestselling author

B.J. DANIELS

HARLEQUIN

INTRIGUE
Edge-of-your-seat intrigue, fearless romance

From passionate, suspenseful and dramatic
love stories to inspirational or historical,
Harlequin offers different lines to
satisfy every romance reader.

New books available every month.

HARLEQUIN

The Edge Emergency Department, Chicago
Monday, June 4, 5:30 p.m.

Dr. Devon Pierce listened as administrators from more than a dozen hospitals in metropolitan areas across the nation bemoaned the increasing difficulty of maintaining emergency departments. Once the opening discussion concluded, Devon was the featured speaker.

He rarely agreed to speak to committees and groups, even in a teleconference, which was the case today. His participation required only that he sit in his office and speak to the monitor on his desk. He much preferred to remain focused on his work at the Edge. There were times, however, when his participation in the world of research and development was required in order to push his lagging colleagues toward the most advanced medical technologies. Emergency treatment centers like the Edge were the future of emergency medicine. There was no better state-of-the-art facility.

Devon had set his career as a practicing physician aside and spent six years developing the concept for the center's prototype before opening it in his hometown of Chicago. The success of the past year provided significant evidence that his beliefs about the future of emergency rooms were correct. This would be his legacy to the work he loved.

The subject of cost reared its inevitable and unpleasant head in the ongoing discussion, as it always did. How could a person measure the worth of saving a human life? He said as much to those listening eagerly for a comment from him. All involved were aware, perhaps to varying degrees, just how much his dedication to his work had cost him. He'd long ago stopped keeping account. His work required what it required. There were no other factors or concerns to weigh.

Half an hour later, Devon had scarcely uttered his closing remarks when the door to his office opened. Patricia Ezell, his secretary, silently moved to his desk. She passed him a note, probably not containing the sort of news he wanted if her worried expression was any indicator, and it generally was.

You're needed in the OR stat.

"I'm afraid I won't be able to take any questions. Duty calls." Devon severed his connection to the conference and stood. "What's going on?" he asked as he closed a single button on his suit jacket.

Patricia shook her head. "Dr. Reagan rushed a patient into surgery in OR 1. He says he needs you there."

HIEXP0518

Ice hardened in Devon's veins. "Reagan is well aware that I don't—"

"He has the surgery under control, Dr. Pierce. It's..." Patricia took a deep breath. "The patient was unconscious when the paramedics brought her in. Her driver's license identifies her as Cara Pierce."

A spear of pain arrowed through Devon, making him hesitate. He closed his laptop. "Few of us have a name so unique that it's not shared with others." There were likely numerous Cara Pierces in the country. Chicago was a large city. Of course there would be other people with the same name as his late wife. This should be no surprise to the highly trained and, frankly, brilliant members of his staff.

"One of the registration specialists browsed the contacts list in her cell phone and called the number listed as her husband."

Devon hesitated once more, this time at the door. His secretary's reluctance to provide whatever other details she had at her disposal was growing increasingly tedious. "Is her husband en route?"

Patricia cleared her throat. "Based on the number in her contacts list, her husband is already here. The number is yours." She held out his cell phone. "I took the call."

Devon stared at the thin, sleek device in her hand. He'd left his cell with Patricia for the duration of the teleconference. He hated the distracting vibration of an incoming call when he was trying to run a meeting. Normally he would have turned it off and that would have been it, but he was expecting an important work call—one that he would pause his teleconference to take if necessary. So he'd assigned Patricia cell phone duty with instructions to interrupt him only if that call came in, or if there was a life-or-death situation.

He reached for it now.

"Thank you, Patricia. Ask the paramedic who brought her in to drop by my office when he has a break."

The walk from his office in the admin wing to the surgery unit took all of two minutes. One of the finely tuned features of the Edge design was ensuring that each wing of the emergency department was never more than two to three minutes away from anything else. A great deal of planning had gone into the round design of the building with the care initiation front and center and the less urgent care units spanning into different wings around the circle. Straight through the very center, the rear portion of the design contained the more urgent services, imaging and surgery. Every square foot of the facility was designed for optimum efficiency. Each member of staff was carefully chosen and represented the very best in their field.

As he neared the surgery suite, he considered what his secretary had told him about the patient. The mere idea was absurd. There'd been a mistake. A mix-up of some sort.

Cara.

His wife was dead. He'd buried her six years and five months ago.

SIN AND BONE by Debra Webb is available June 2018!

www.Harlequin.com